You Know It's Love

THE *Love in the City* SERIES
BOOK TWO

JEN MORRIS

You Know it's Love Copyright © 2021 by Jen Morris

First edition February 2021

Kindle ISBN: 978-0-473-56069-0

Epub ISBN: 978-0-473-56068-3

Paperback ISBN: 978-0-473-56067-6

Cover illustration by Elle Maxwell

www.ellemaxwelldesign.com

For the one man who truly knows me.

Have enough courage to trust love one more time, and always one more time.

— MAYA ANGELOU

AUTHOR'S NOTE

Please note that this book contains sensitive topics such as parental abandonment, attempted sexual assault, infidelity, and divorce. I hope I have treated these issues with the care they deserve.

1

This was the absolute worst choice in underwear. I don't know who invented the G-string, but he should be shot. And yes, I'm quite certain it was a guy.

I wiggle my butt on the bar stool, trying to reposition or somehow dislodge said undergarment, but with no luck. A quick glance around the bar and I can see it's quiet, so I twist in my seat, reaching back behind me. I tug at my dress, trying to get a hold of the flimsy lingerie through the fabric. Why is this so—

"You okay there?"

Shit.

I freeze, one hand grasping my underwear through my dress, the other on the bar giving me the leverage I need to reach back.

There's a chuckle from behind me, and I turn slowly to see a bartender leaning forward on his hands against the bar, the corners of his eyes creased in amusement.

Fuck it. I'm already halfway there now.

With one final yank I reposition my lingerie and

straighten up, giving the bartender an embarrassed smile. "Sorry. Underwear mishap."

"Ah." He grimaces on my behalf. "Drink?"

My gaze flicks to the door and back. I'm waiting for a date—someone I matched with on Tinder—and a drink would definitely take the edge off. But this isn't my usual bartender.

I've chosen this particular East Village bar, Bounce, because my brother Cory owns it. I always meet my dates here to keep things low-key. Exposed brick walls, red vinyl booths on one side, long bar stretching the other side, small dance floor near the back, low lighting. It's a bit of a dive, but it's fun and cozy, and most importantly it's familiar ground. It's always easier to meet someone new in a place where I already feel comfortable. If the wheels fall off and the guy turns out to be a psycho, I've got Cory—or the bouncer, Jimmy—to help me out.

And, you know, Cory gives me free drinks. What else are big brothers for?

"Where's Cory?" I ask, scanning the bar.

The bartender rolls his eyes, leaning back and folding his arms. "Of course, you're here for Cory. That's who the underwear is for."

I stifle a snort. *No, I'm not wearing a thong for my brother.* But I know he picks up his fair share of girls here, so I'm not surprised by this guy's response. "Uh, no. Who are you?"

He gives me a wide grin. "Myles."

"You're new."

"Yep." He raises a tattooed arm to drag a hand through his hair. "Started last week. So, what are you drinking?"

"Just a vodka soda, thanks."

He nods, reaching for a bottle of Absolut. Then he does that cheesy bartender thing that they all do when they think they're hot shit: he tosses the bottle up in the air so it spins, then catches it with a flourish.

I run my eyes over him as he pours my drink. He's about five-foot-eleven, early-thirties, lean and slightly muscular without being ripped. His eyes are gunmetal-blue, his nose strong with a little upturn at the end. It makes his face look almost boyish, despite the scruff along his jaw. He has a sleeve of tattoos covering his right arm; mountain ranges and trees on his bicep, which fade down his forearm into a map, with a compass that wraps around his wrist. My gaze lingers on it before moving to his hair—chestnut brown and shaved close on the sides, but longer in a mess of curls on top. Just the right length for tugging on, I register absently.

He slides my drink across the bar. "So you're not here for Cory. I'm guessing... date?"

I take a sip of vodka. "Yeah."

His eyes move to my bare shoulder and trail over my own tattoo—a bunch of wildflowers done in black outline— then back to my face. "Well, he's lucky."

"I'm sorry—" I set my glass down in disbelief. "Are you actually hitting on me, right before a date?"

"Maybe." He shrugs, flashing me a grin that's all teeth.

I stare at him, trying to suppress my smile. As much as I want to be irritated by his confidence it's quite disarming, and I just shake my head with a little laugh.

"First date?"

I nod, chewing on my straw as unease ripples through me. This is always the worst part, right before you meet. They seem okay on an app with a handful of photos and a funny bio—then you meet them in person and realize they've got a voice like Mickey Mouse or a penchant for threesomes and you wish you'd never left the house.

"How'd you meet?"

Jesus. I'm really getting the third degree from this guy.

I huff an uncomfortable laugh. "Don't you have other people to serve?" I say, glancing along the bar. But there are only a few others, all with drinks in their hands. When I look back at Myles he gives me a smug grin and I sigh. "We haven't met yet. Not in person." I pick up my drink and take a long sip. "I found him through a dating app."

"Right. Real long-term potential there, then."

I lift a shoulder. "You never know." But I kind of do know, really. Because I've been on a million of these things and I've yet to meet anyone halfway decent.

"Well," Myles says, taking a dishcloth and wiping down the bar, "I'll be here, when the date's over." He gives me another cocky grin and I arch an eyebrow. He's certainly sure of himself, this one.

"I'll keep that in mind," I respond wryly.

He pauses, and the smile fades from his face as he studies me. "Seriously, though, if the guy's a creep and you need rescuing, give me a wave."

"Uh... thanks." I'm taken aback by his sudden sincerity, then his lips tip back into a cheeky smile and I chuckle.

Pulling my compact from my purse, I do a final check of my reflection. My chin-length, ash-blond hair is straightened. Dark, winged liner accentuates my brown eyes, and my peaches and cream complexion is painstakingly perfected by foundation, contouring, blush, highlighter, and every other product under the sun—just so I look like I don't have makeup on at all.

Snapping the compact shut, I glance up to find Myles looking at me. His gaze flits to something over my shoulder.

"Hey. I'm Simon."

I turn to see a tall, lean guy with light brown hair leering at me, and my heart sinks. It's not that I have an issue with brown hair or lean builds—they really do it for me, actually —it's the leering. Gross.

No, I tell myself, straightening up in my seat. I'm too quick to jump to conclusions about these guys before I even say two words to them. You can't tell what a person is like by their first impression. Maybe he's got some kind of eye disorder or facial tic.

I force a smile and extend my hand. "I'm Cat."

He takes my hand, his gaze stuck fast to my breasts. That is some serious eye problem he's got there.

Myles is hovering behind the bar and I glance at him with uncertainty. He's regarding Simon through narrowed eyes, his arms crossed over his chest. Then his gaze swings to me and he raises his eyebrows.

I turn back to Simon, trying to push away the feeling of disappointment weaving through me.

"Let's get a booth," he says, finally looking at my face.

I hesitate, glancing back at Myles, wondering again where Cory is. I'm not sure I want to sit in a dark booth with this guy, and while Myles did offer to help me out, I don't actually know him. "Why don't we have a drink here first?" I gesture to the bar and Simon shrugs, sliding onto a barstool beside me.

"Jagerbomb," he says to Myles.

I can't stop the snort that comes from my nose. I mean, come on. Everyone knows only a douchebag orders a Jagerbomb. At seven o'clock. On a Tuesday.

But the snort comes out louder than I'd intended, and when Simon gives me a strange look I quickly cough, patting my chest for effect.

Myles bites back a smirk as he reaches for a glass, cracking open a can of Red Bull and upending it into a glass, then placing a shot of Jagermeister on the bar. We both watch in mild disgust as Simon drops the shot into the glass and throws it back, then wipes his mouth.

"So, it's really nice to meet you," he says, giving me a genuine smile. This time he's focused on my face, and I feel a little wave of relief. Maybe I did judge him too soon.

Myles is still right there, third-wheeling our date, so I shoot him a look. He frowns, throwing the dishcloth over his shoulder as he saunters off to serve another girl who's taken a seat along the bar. I hear him say something to her and while I don't catch the words, I catch the tone. It was the same one he was just using with me, and I resist the urge to roll my eyes as I turn back to Simon.

"It's nice to meet you, too." I shift on the stool. "It's always a bit awkward meeting someone new like this."

"I know, right?"

We sit in silence for a moment, and Simon picks up one of the cardboard coasters off the bar, fiddling with it. It occurs to me for the first time that he might be nervous.

"So, um, how was your day?" He asks, his gaze meeting mine again. "You work in a shop, right?"

"Yes." I smile. "Well, I own the shop. It's called Loved Again, a couple of blocks down from here. I sell vintage clothes along with some of my own designs."

"Right." Simon nods. "That sounds interesting."

He focuses back on the coaster and I take a second to size him up. Good height, not unattractive, full head of hair. Shame about his crap choice in drinks, but I'm sure we can work on that. There's a faint flicker of hope inside me, like there always is at this point in a date. Is there a chance this could be something?

He glances up at me, his eyes tracking over my face. "You know," he says thoughtfully, "you look a lot like my favorite porn star."

Right. Well. Maybe not then.

"Do you have a Porn Hub profile?"

I rub my temples, releasing a long, resigned breath. "No, Simon. I don't."

He leans forward, leering at me again. "We should set one up for you, make some videos together. I'd be happy to help."

Despite this undeniably generous offer, I shake my head, pressing my lips together to hold in a frustrated scream.

I always do this. I want to give guys the benefit of the doubt, and they turn out to be awful. I need to trust my gut response and stop being so damn nice.

I glance down the bar to where Myles is standing, watching us with interest. I might have only known him for five minutes longer than Simon, but suddenly his presence is making me feel safe. His eyebrows lift in question and I grimace in response. Then he gives me the tiniest nod, appearing in front of us again.

Thank fuck.

"Excuse me, miss?" Myles leans on the bar, giving me a meaningful look. "You have a phone call."

I muffle a laugh. Is that the best he could come up with? Honestly, who would be calling me *here*, rather than on my cell? What is this, 1995?

But it's the only exit strategy I have right now, so I play along, making my eyes wide. "Really? Who is it?"

"Uh..." His gaze slides left, then right. "It's your mom. She's in the hospital."

"Oh." I raise a hand to my chest, glancing at Simon. I'm expecting him to be a bit suspicious of this blatant charade, but he's staring at me with the most dim-witted expression that I almost burst out laughing. Somehow, I manage to contort my face to appear apologetic. "You don't mind, do you? I wouldn't normally do this, but..."

"It's quite urgent," Myles continues, his eyes dancing as he gets into character. "She fell down fifteen flights of stairs and broke eight bones. The doctors are saying that if they don't operate now—"

"Okay, thank you," I say hastily, glaring at Myles. "I'll take the call." I hop off the barstool, making another regretful face at Simon. "It was *great* to meet you. We can, uh, do this another time?"

He gives me a nod, his uncomprehending eyes following me as I snatch up my purse and hurry behind the bar and around the corner, out of sight.

I lean back against one of the refrigerators, chuckling to myself. Usually when I need Cory to help me out he just tells the guy to leave. That was quite creative.

Myles appears out back a moment later. "He's gone. You okay?"

"Yeah." I exhale with relief. "He asked me if I wanted to make porn with him."

"Shit."

"I know." I contemplate Myles for a second and a laugh bubbles up my throat. "Fifteen flights of stairs? Really?"

He spreads his hands, a sheepish grin on his face. "It was all I could think of."

"Well, it did the trick. Thanks." I poke my head around the corner, checking the coast is clear, then wander back out and hop up on my barstool again.

"Another drink?" Myles asks, reaching for the vodka.

"Yeah, thanks." I pull my phone out—the one that, let's face it, my mother *would* have called me on if she'd actually been at the hospital—and send a text to my friend Geoff. It's too early to go home and I'm all dressed up. We should at least have a drink, if he's free.

Cat: Disaster date. Where are you?

Geoff: Ugh, that sucks. Stuck at the shop but could meet you in the Village in an hour?

Cat: Okay, will head over soon.

I set my phone down with a weary smile, taking my drink from Myles. It's a shame Geoff is gay, because he's such a good guy. It would be so much easier if I could just shack up with him and call it a day.

Myles wanders down to serve a couple of guys and I lean on the bar, sipping my vodka, suddenly feeling tired. Not just normal, end-of-the-workday tired, but bone-deep, sick-of-dating tired. I've been on this treadmill ever since my divorce and it's exhausting.

Okay, I know. I could just stop dating and focus on my work. I do love my shop and creating my own designs. But all around me I've watched friends meet great guys and settle down. I'm thirty-five now, and as much as it pains me to admit it, I want that too. I want a great guy who knows how to treat me well, and that takes a little work to find. But I'm sure he's out there. Somewhere.

My phone buzzes on the bar in front of me and I reach for it, thinking it will be another text from Geoff. I unlock it and there, filling the screen, is a shot of someone's dick.

Oh, not just someone's—Simon's.

A shadow falls across me and I glance up to see Myles. "You recovering okay?"

Mouth hanging open, I turn my screen to show him and he recoils with visible horror.

"Jesus. I don't want to see that."

"Neither did I," I mutter, deleting the image. If only I could delete it from my brain.

I look at Myles again and he's rubbing his chin, brows pulled together. "Does that happen a lot?"

I shrug. "It's a good week if I don't get one."

Josie, another bartender here, wanders out from the back room. She gives me a little wave then turns to serve a group who've piled into a booth.

"Why do you do it?"

I look back to see Myles still studying me, and I give him a funny look. "Dating? Because I want to meet someone."

"Come for a drink with me then." That cocky grin is back on his face. "I have a break soon." He leans onto his elbows on the bar so we're at eye level, his gaze locked on mine. He might be cute, but he's so damn sure of himself that I can't help but want to take him down a peg.

"That's very... sweet. But I don't date bartenders." My ex-husband was a bartender when we met and I'm *not* doing that again.

At that moment a guy strides into the bar; six-foot-six, disheveled dirty-blond hair, mischievous brown eyes. To most girls who come here he's the hot bartender who will likely, at some point, bed them. To me, he's just Cory: the older brother who always looks out for me. His gaze swivels in my direction and he grins as he lopes across the bar.

I turn back to Myles, sucking down the rest of my drink and hopping up off the stool. "And I especially don't date guys who work for my brother," I add, giving Cory a squeeze as he sidles up to me.

Cory's eyes narrow as he catches the end of my sentence, his gaze darting between me and Myles. "New guy giving you a hard time?"

I glance at Myles and chuckle when his eyes widen and crimson streaks across his cheeks.

"Nah, he's alright," I say, offering him a smile. "He helped me out with a bad date earlier."

Myles lifts his chin, his self-assured grin gone, but a more sincere smile passes over his lips.

"Thanks for the drinks, Cors." I grab my purse, giving Cory a quick kiss before he ducks behind the bar. Myles waves as I head out, and I'm surprised to find myself smiling all the way across town.

2

By the time I get to the West Village I've almost forgotten my brief meet-up with Simon the would-be porn director. That's what happens when you have enough bad dates; you learn to let them roll off you so you can move onto the next. If I didn't do that, I'd never get anywhere.

I head into the bar where I'm meeting Geoff. We've known each other for over a decade now, and he's one of my best friends. He's the kindest, most selfless person I know, and he has a fantastic sense of humor. He loves hearing about my dating disasters, so he's going to enjoy this latest installment. I don't know what he's going to do for entertainment when I finally meet someone good and stop going on these random meet-ups.

Not that we're in danger of that happening anytime soon.

I stop at the bar and grab a Diet Coke, spotting Geoff at a table in the corner. His slightly-pudgy frame is dressed in a polo shirt and tan chinos, square-rimmed glasses on his nose.

"Hey," he says as I slide into a chair. "Another bad one? What was it this time?"

"He offered to help me get my porn career started." I take a sip of my drink, watching as Geoff screws up his face.

"Ugh."

"Yeah." I give a hollow laugh. "It was a generous offer, but still..."

He chuckles, his green eyes sparkling behind his glasses. "Did Cory help you escape?"

"Actually," I say, twirling my straw and picturing Myles's cocky face, "there was a new bartender there tonight. He helped me out."

"New?" Geoff regards me curiously over his glass of merlot. It's always merlot. "Cute?"

"He was alright, I guess. He actually reminded me a bit of Mark." My ex-husband's face flashes into my mind and I wrinkle my nose, quickly pushing the image away.

"Speaking of, how are things there?"

I suck in a breath and force it out through pursed lips. "Same. Still showing up at the shop whenever he feels like it. Still pretending it's his shop, too."

This has been an on-going issue with me and Mark. He was a bartender when we met, but shortly after he moved into real estate, gradually acquiring a bunch of run-down commercial spaces in random locations across Manhattan and Brooklyn. One of those was renovated and became my shop, in the heart of the East Village—a few streets over from Tompkins Square Park. He still owns the space to this day, so we have this dysfunctional dynamic where he is both my ex-husband and my shop landlord. It mostly works in my favor because he hasn't raised the rent in years, but it also means that he thinks he can drop by whenever he feels like it. I think he hangs around just to mess with me, because he's annoyed that I got the apartment—a rent-controlled, first floor place in the gorgeous West Village. I fought tooth and nail for that in our divorce, and he's pissed he lost it.

Perhaps he shouldn't have cheated on me multiple times, then. But I digress.

"Have you given any more thought to how you might get out of there?" Geoff asks. This is a conversation we have periodically, where Geoff insists it's not healthy for me to be under Mark's thumb, and I always give the same response.

"You know I can't, Geoff. I'll never get a deal that good again."

"But you know he's only keeping the rent at that rate to manipulate you."

I grind my molars. "Yes. I know. And you know I can't afford to move." I stir my drink aggressively. Talking—or thinking—about Mark always gets me worked up. I take a long sip of Diet Coke and, after a pause, I relax. "It's not that bad. I have to see him a few times a week but otherwise it's not really an issue."

Geoff nods, saying nothing more. His gaze catches on something by the door and a grin splits his face. "I hope you don't mind, I invited Alex too."

"Of course!" I smile as she waves to us then heads to the bar. "I would have texted her, I just assumed..."

"She'd be with Sexy Michael?"

I laugh at Geoff's nickname for the boyfriend of my ex-roommate, Alex. Michael is our upstairs neighbor and Alex developed a huge crush on him when she moved into the building after arriving from New Zealand, late last year.

She wasn't the only one who had a crush on him but, unfortunately for Geoff, he doesn't swing that way.

I elbow Geoff in the ribs. "You should probably stop calling him that."

"Yeah, you're right." He cringes, chuckling awkwardly. "I'd be horrified if he found out."

"I'm sure Alex has told him by now."

Glass of wine in hand, Alex settles in at our table. "Told who what?"

"That Geoff calls Michael *Sexy Michael*," I say, watching Geoff's face redden.

"Oh, totally." Alex waves a hand. "I told him ages ago. He thinks it's funny."

Geoff huffs in exasperation. "Nothing is sacred," he mutters.

She laughs, then turns her attention to me. "So, disaster date?" Her hazel eyes shimmer with compassion. "Geoff sent an SOS."

"Yeah. Total bottom of the barrel." I fill her in on Simon and she makes the appropriate disgusted face.

"I don't know how you keep going." She raises her wine glass to her lips with a shake of her head.

I shrug, finishing off my drink and glancing toward the bar. But Geoff—bless him—is already on his feet, going to order another round. See what I mean? So considerate. He'd be perfect to marry.

"So, what's living with Michael like?" Geoff asks Alex as he slides back into his chair.

She beams. "I love it."

"Great," I say faintly, ignoring the dart of jealousy that shoots through me. I hate to admit that, but it's true. She met Michael after what felt like five seconds of being in the country, without even trying. I, on the other hand, have been doing the rounds on the dating circuit for four years now—and nothing.

"This is the real deal, isn't it?" Geoff says. "You and Michael?"

Alex nods, her eyes misting over in the way they always do when she talks about Michael. "I'm so in love with him. I never thought I'd meet someone like him. Is it—" She pauses, glancing between Geoff and I, a smile creeping onto her lips. "Is it too soon to say that I think he's the one?"

I snort, ready to tell her to *slow down*. But Geoff kicks me under the table, so I swallow my words down with a gulp of Diet Coke.

"It's not too soon," Geoff assures her. "They always say that when you know, you know."

Alex sighs, her expression dreamy. She's a hopeless romantic, so it's hardly surprising that she's feeling this way.

"Maybe just don't tell *him* that yet," I say.

"Oh, no!" She laughs self-consciously. "I know I'm not supposed to do that."

"Don't listen to the cynic over here." Geoff jerks a thumb in my direction. "You do what's right for your relationship."

"Hey—" I protest but he silences me with a knowing look.

"Not everyone wants to play by *The Rules*, Cat."

I smirk. When I started dating in earnest a couple of years ago, Geoff gave me a copy of *The Rules* as a joke. He thought it was hilarious, but it made me think more about my dating life. It's been a bit of a rough road since my divorce, and while I did meet a few guys I liked, it took me some time to see they weren't the *right* type of guys. It's like I was innately drawn to assholes, like I had no inner compass to steer me away from them. And if I *did* meet a nice guy, I'd usually say something that just made him think I was cynical and angry at the world. Which I kind of am, especially after what Mark put me through. But I probably shouldn't broadcast that on a date. You catch more flies with honey than vinegar, right?

It all kind of came to a head after a particularly unpleasant incident in a bar in Brooklyn a year ago. I decided to create a few of my own rules when it comes to men, so I wouldn't keep making such stupid mistakes. There are only three, but each is important:

1. Always be my best self on dates

2. Don't put out too soon

3. Stay the hell away from anyone who reminds me of my ex-husband—including liars, cheaters, guys with more looks than substance and (especially important) bartenders

So far, these rules have served me very well.

"It's okay." Alex smiles, twirling her wine glass. "I get it. Meeting guys is difficult."

"Meeting a guy is *not* difficult," Geoff mutters. "It's meeting a *good* guy that's difficult."

"Exactly."

Alex gives me a sympathetic look. "You'll meet someone soon."

I send a brittle smile her way. I can't stand it when my friends say things like this to me. I know they mean well, but I hate the pity. "Yeah," I mumble. "Here's hoping."

A LITTLE WHILE LATER, Alex and I wander home together along Bleecker Street. It's beautiful in the Village; boutique shops and restaurants, row houses and brick apartments, tiny one-way streets lined with trees. And being mid-April, the streets are vibrant with flowers and greenery.

Alex and I live in a redbrick building—me on the first floor, her on the next floor up, with Michael and his son

Henry. We say goodnight and I push into my apartment, kicking off my shoes. I set my purse down on the counter and glance around. It's not very big, but it's enough: one bedroom with an open-plan living space; the kitchen separated from the living room by a breakfast bar. The whole place is simple, plain, mostly white. In the living room I have a couple of red sofas to brighten things up, but that's most of the color. Mark liked it pretty minimalist and I haven't made many changes since we split.

I look over at the nook in the corner of my living room, separated from the main space by a partition-wall. Alex lived there when she first came to the city, but she moved in with Michael a month ago. Now it's just an empty, abandoned space, gathering dust.

Kind of like my heart, I catch myself thinking. I have to roll my eyes.

I peel my jacket off and hang it on the back of the door with a sigh. I love living here, but sometimes it reminds me of the life I had before—the one with Mark. And while my feelings for him died a swift death long ago, the desire to meet someone to share my life with hasn't.

Anyway, enough. Just because tonight's date sucked, doesn't mean I need to be morose. The next one has to be better.

Right?

3

I hang the 1950s-inspired dress on the rack, stepping back to admire it. It's one of my best yet: low sweetheart neckline with a red halter strap, fitted red waistband and a big flared skirt—all done in a navy fabric printed with red cherries. I've always loved clothes from this era. They're just so pretty and fun and feminine.

With a smile, I turn the sign in the door around from "closed" to "open," and head back behind the counter, taking a long sip of black coffee.

This place has been my haven for eight years now and I can't imagine doing anything else. I got my first sewing machine at age ten, spending many late nights in the attic of my mom's Long Island house, one foot rhythmically tapping the pedal, my hands smoothly guiding fabric under the needle. Over the years, I made all my own prom dresses, as well as some for friends. They were always full of life and color.

When Mark and I got together, I was on the cusp of setting up my own store with all my own original designs. I didn't have a lot of money but I had a dream—and he wanted to support me. Except, he thought that maybe selling *just* my designs wasn't a good idea. He convinced me to turn it into a vintage store, with a few of my own designs thrown in. And I didn't mind too much, because I love vintage stuff almost as much as I love making clothes. That's why my store is called Loved Again; it's full of clothes and other items I think deserve a second chance to be loved.

The actual shop is not huge. I'm wedged between a cafe and a barbershop in the East Village, with a single front window and door. The store stretches back from the street, and there's a staircase that leads to a basement which doubles my shop space, as well as providing some storage. Each wall, both upstairs and down, is lined with racks of clothes, and upstairs a narrow table runs down the center with accessories and other interesting vintage bits and pieces like toys and homewares.

I glance around the store as I sip my coffee, soaking in the silence before the day begins. For the most part the store has done okay, but over the past three months, things have been tough. I made the mistake of trusting a friend to orga-nize a business deal and the shit hit the fan, leaving me in debt.

Anyway, no point dwelling on my stupid mistake. Time to put my game face on, seize the day and all that.

I plug my phone into the sound system, selecting a playlist. Marvin Gaye's *I Heard it Through the Grapevine* comes on and I hum along under my breath.

The door opens with a little ding of the bell and I smile as a couple of twenty-something women enter the store. They look through the racks, occasionally showing pieces to each other, then one of them turns to me, gesturing to the fifties cherry-print dress I just hung on display.

"Do you have any more like this?"

"Yes!" I lead her to a small rack of my dresses by the counter.

"These are so cool," she murmurs, fingering the fabric of another dress with black and white polka dots. "Who is the designer? Do you know if she does custom orders?"

"Oh," I say, unable to stop the smile tugging at my lips. "They're my designs. I could do a custom piece if you like?"

She gives an enthusiastic nod, and I take down her details so we can arrange a time to do her measurements and finalize everything. After she leaves, I lean against the counter, smiling to myself. I haven't done a custom dress for ages and I'm excited to explore some new ideas. I love making beautiful dresses like these, even if I don't wear them anymore.

I pull one of my dresses out and hold it up over my frame, turning to look at my reflection in a full-length mirror. At five-foot-three I'm short, but I'm not petite. I've got curves, though I do my best to stay in shape with the gym and yoga. I've been dying my naturally dirty-blond hair gray-blond for the past few years, keeping it cut to chin-length. I used to dye it funky colors—and wear more of my own designs—but that's just not practical anymore. Most of the time I wear a black tank top, black jeans, and combat boots—or if I'm going on a date, a sexy little black dress. I seem to only have two modes: work and date.

Etta James's *Something's Got a Hold on Me* comes on over the speakers and my mouth twitches into a smile as I place the dress back. This kind of music makes me happy.

"Morning," Hayley says, breezing into the store. She's my part-timer, and she's fantastic. She loves the store like it's her own, she's flexible with her hours, and she hates Mark almost as much as I do—a fact I'm reminded of later that day, when Mark shows up.

"Ugh, I didn't know *he* was dropping by," she mutters, peering out the front window along the street. She's spent most of the day creating a new window display, but now she's hurrying toward the stairs. "I'll be pricing stock in the basement if you need me."

I turn back to the front door just as Stevie comes trotting in, her leash trailing behind. It's silly, but Mark and I share custody of this little pug. We got her when we were married, and neither of us wanted to give her up.

Actually, I think, as I scoop to pick up her warm body and nuzzle her fur, she was the one good thing to come out of that marriage.

"Hey," Mark says, sidling over.

I glance at him over Stevie, holding her protectively against my chest. Mark is wearing his usual dark ripped jeans and tee, silver chain around his neck, mermaid tattoo on his forearm. He's tall and lean, with dark mussed hair and gray eyes, a stubbly jaw. Some days I look at him and remember the man I used to make love to, planning our future together. Other days I look at him and am filled with rage for all the hurt he's caused me.

"Hi." I place Stevie down on her little pillow behind the counter.

"Do you have a minute?" Mark scratches his chin. "I need to chat with you about something."

I frown. Mark hates to talk. This can't be good.

"I wanted to tell you... Well, I'm sure this won't come as a surprise, but I'm afraid I'm going to have to raise the rent here, Cat."

I'm quiet for a beat. He likes to say things like this sometimes to get a rise out of me, then he always takes it back. I'm used to his antics by now. "Okay, Mark," I mutter, turning to pat Stevie.

"I mean it."

My hand stills and I glance back at him, feeling a pinch of alarm. "What? Seriously?"

He nods.

"But... why now?"

"Come on, you know I'm making next to nothing on the current rate. I should have raised it years ago."

Shit. He *is* serious.

Dread creeps over me. "How much are you going to raise it?"

He reaches into his pocket, pulls out a slip of paper, and slides it face-down across the counter to me. It takes all my strength not to scream at him to stop with the theatrics and just tell me.

I lift the paper and examine the number, my eyes widening with shock. "This is ridiculous." It's significantly higher than what I'm paying now. Even without having to deal with my recent debt, it would be a stretch to get there.

"Sorry, but it's market rate." He shrugs. "It's what you should be paying for this place."

"And if I can't?"

He hesitates, then looks away. "Well, then... it might be time to move on."

Oh, no. Oh, fuck, fuck, fuck. I can't lose my store. This place is everything to me.

Okay, no. I know this man; I used to be married to him, for Christ's sake. I'm sure I can talk him around, get him to hold off for a while. I'll just negotiate with him until we can reach an agreement that works for both of us. I'm sure he can be reasonable.

Well, I'm not sure at all—but I have to try.

"Mark," I begin, attempting to keep the panic out of my

voice, "is there any chance this could wait a couple of months? I just have to—"

"Cat, I'm losing money here." He stuffs his hands into his pockets, not meeting my gaze. "I've been pretty generous, letting you have this place at such a low rate. But you couldn't have expected it to go on forever."

I narrow my eyes. "Did *she* put you up to this?"

The "she" I'm referring to is Mel—my ex-friend turned Mark's girlfriend. She knew me when Mark and I were married and she was married; we were neighbors and good friends for years. We both went through a divorce a year apart from each other, and that brought us closer together. For ages we did the whole dating thing side-by-side, sharing the ups and downs, drowning our sorrows in margaritas. We did all kinds of things, like group dates, set-ups, speed-dating—even registering with match-makers for a while. It was a lot more fun doing things like that with a friend going through it, too.

Until, suddenly, it wasn't. Because she met someone. Not just someone—*someone* I could handle. No, it turned out the guy Mel was seeing was none other than my ex-husband—after everything he'd done to me—and she was doing it behind my back. Needless to say, the friendship came to an abrupt end—especially when I found out she'd been lying about a bunch of other stuff, too.

But here's the kicker: right before I discovered she was sleeping with my ex-husband, she helped me make a business deal with a friend of hers who owned a string of boutiques in the city. We'd arranged for me to create a whole line of dresses and stock them in her friend's stores, which was a huge step up in my business—and would have given me the opportunity to move away from Mark. So I invested in a *lot* of new fabric—much more than I would ever need for my tiny store—along with a brand new, state-of-the-art sewing machine. Then when I confronted Mel about Mark, she sabotaged the deal. So I was left with too much stock, a sewing machine I didn't need—and thousands of dollars of debt.

But honestly? I blame myself. I didn't sign any contracts, or get anything in writing; I simply took Mel and her friend at their word. And that was plain foolish. Because I knew better, really. I knew better than to count on someone else, especially after how spectacularly my marriage failed. You sort of expect *men* to screw you over, but not your best friend.

Mark sighs. "Mel brought it up, yes."

Anger simmers in my gut. Of course she did.

"But she's right, Cat." His brow furrows. "I've been doing you a favor for years now, and it's time to put my needs first."

I snort. "Wasn't that the basis for our whole marriage?"

Shit, this is not going well.

"Don't be bitter." Mark gives me a bored look. "It doesn't suit you."

It does, actually. But anyway.

I inhale a slow, calming breath, trying to regain control of the situation. "Mark, please. After all we've been through, after everything that *happened*..." I pause, letting my words linger in the air. I don't need to say it because he knows what I mean. *You screwed me over. You owe me.*

He considers me for a moment and there's a flicker of uncertainty in his eyes. I feel a premature sense of triumph, but it's quickly shot down when he shakes his head, his jaw set.

"I'm sorry. This isn't personal, it's just business. It's long overdue."

Not personal, my ass. If Mel's behind this, she's trying to hurt me—and that doesn't surprise me in the slightest.

"So you've got one payment left on the old rate," Mark continues, "then it's going up. Look, I'm sure you'll figure it out." He pushes away from the counter, and I fight the urge to simultaneously cry, scream, and punch him in the throat. "I'll catch you later." And he turns and lopes out the door.

I stare after him, my mouth hanging open, frozen with shock.

Well.

Fuck.

4

"So, I think I owe you an apology."

I take the vodka soda from Myles's outstretched hand and throw half of it back in one gulp, hoping it will make me feel better. Wiping my mouth, I tilt my head at him. "For what?"

"Uh, you know..." He rubs the back of his neck, glancing up and down the bar, then back at me. "Hitting on you last time you were in here. I didn't know you were Cat *Porter*—as in, Cory's little sister."

I chuckle, reaching down to pat Stevie's head under my stool. She's used to being brought in here and doesn't have a problem with the people or the noise, but I still feel a bit anxious when I have her with me. "Did Cory say something?"

"Yeah, he's pretty protective of you. He didn't seem to want me to—well, I guess as my boss's sister, it wasn't exactly appropriate for me to ask you out."

Wow, who is this guy? Last time I was in here, he was all ego and brash self-confidence.

I reassure him with a smile. "Honestly, it's okay." I pick

up my drink and drain it, setting it down on the bar and gesturing for him to make me another.

"Cool." A relieved grin broadens his face as he reaches for the Absolut bottle. "I'd like it if we could be friends, though."

"Sure. It's always a good idea to be friends with the person who has access to the booze." I take my drink and knock it back in one go. Ah, sweet alcohol. I might be about to lose my shop and everything I care about, but as long as I've got vodka, I'll be fine. "Another." I slam my glass down on the bar and look up at Myles.

"Seriously?" His steel-blue eyes observe me with suspicion. "You've barely taken a breath. You got another date coming or something?"

I glance down at my black jeans and combat boots. As if I'd ever wear this on a date. "No, just..." I release a weighted sigh. "Bad day at work."

"You want to talk about it?"

I give him a faint smile. "Thanks, but I need to talk to Cory. It's an issue with my business."

Myles leans against the bar. "I might be able to help."

"I really don't think so," I mumble, trying not to be impolite. I mean, Cory runs this place and he does it well; he understands business. Myles just pours drinks. Speaking of... "Um, another vodka, please?" I shake my empty glass and the ice rattles against the side.

"Yeah... I'm going to wait for Cory, I think," he murmurs, not taking his eyes off me.

"What?"

"I'm not about to get you drunk. Cory will be here any moment. It won't kill you to wait."

I gaze longingly at the bottles of spirits lined up behind the bar. "It might."

A group of women hop onto stools down the other end and Myles gestures for me to stay put. I harrumph and peek under the stool to check on Stevie. She's curled up in a ball asleep, and I slump against the bar, watching Myles saunter toward the women.

"Ladies," he says in the same cocky voice he used on me last time. "What can I get the three most beautiful women in Manhattan to drink tonight?"

Barf. Thank God he didn't use that line on me. I would have socked him in his pretty mouth.

But it works like a charm on them. They coo and fall all over themselves as he makes them sugary cocktails, tossing the bottle up in the air and catching it with ease, performing to his adoring crowd. As he works, I study him. His smooth moves, his outgoing demeanor, that gleam in his eye that tells the world how sure he is of himself. He might have been apologetic and restrained with me just now, but that's only because he's afraid of Cory. I've already seen his true nature, and I'm not sure I like it.

The girls do, though. They can't tip him enough, and one even reaches out to touch his tattoos, asking him about them. As I watch him flirt, I get a flashback to when I met Mark in a bar downtown, all those years ago. He was a hotshot bartender too. He made me a margarita and I asked him about his tattoo, flirting with him until he asked for my phone number. We were married six months later, and while I didn't love watching him flirt with women as he worked, I knew it was part of the job and I figured it was harmless. Besides, I trusted him.

That was my first mistake.

I'll never forget the first time Mark cheated on me. I caught him kissing some girl in a booth at the bar one night when I surprised him with a visit. I guess I probably should have walked away then and there, but we were young and we hadn't been married long—and I sure as hell wasn't going to be another divorce statistic like my parents—so we talked it through and Mark promised it would never happen again. He quit bartending and moved into real estate shortly after and I was relieved, to say the least. I put it behind me and for years, things were good. No—they were great.

That's the thing about liars, though. They lull you into a false sense of security, then pull the rug out from under you when you least expect it. Suddenly you're lying face-down in the dirt, wondering why you didn't see this coming from a mile away, and swearing you'll never let it happen again.

I reach for my glass, crunching on an ice cube. It's been four years since our divorce and as much as I hate what Mark put me through in our marriage—and what he's put me through since—he helped me learn something fundamental about life: at the end of the day, you can't trust anyone but yourself.

Actually, that's not true. Because I'm the idiot who chose to stick around with him for all those years. So I can't even trust myself, either. This is why I need my dating rules, otherwise I'd keep making the same dumb mistakes.

Anyway, something good came out of it all, because without Mark I wouldn't have my store.

I laugh bitterly into my empty vodka glass, the events of the afternoon replaying in my mind. The truth is, I should have seen this coming. I always meant to move, one day, but I never did. And now that I'm in debt and can't afford to move, I'm screwed. In some ways it makes perfect sense that since Mark helped me get my store, he has the power to take it away from me, too. After all the years of hard work I put into building my little business, it feels like I never really had it—like all my work was for nothing. Maybe I've been kidding myself; maybe this whole time it was never really mine. And now that I could lose it, just like that, I've never felt more powerless.

I heave out a breath, crossing my arms on the bar in front of me and lowering my head. I've never been the type to feel sorry for myself, but right now I'm struggling to fight back the rising tide of self-pity. Because this sucks.

"Hey, sis."

A hand ruffles my hair and I lift my head, giving Cory a bleak smile. "Hey."

Concern etches into his brow when he sees my face. "You okay?"

I shake my head, holding my empty vodka glass out. "Another. Please."

He nods, quickly making me my usual. Then he crouches under my stool to pat Stevie, before hauling himself up onto the stool beside me.

I look at the bar around us with a frown. It's getting busy now. "Cors, it's okay. You should—"

"Hey," he says gently, reaching an arm around my shoulder and giving me a squeeze. "Myles can handle it, plus Eddy and Josie are here. Now, spill."

I reach for my drink with a grumble. "Mark's raising my rent. A lot."

"Oh. Shit." Cory wipes a hand down his face.

"I tried to talk to him, to see if he could wait for a bit until I can figure it all out, but he said it's time, and it's not personal, blah, blah, blah."

"Fucking jerk." A muscle ticks in Cory's jaw.

Despite everything, a small smile touches my lips. Ever since Dad left when we were kids, Cory's been the one to look out for me. He can't help it. He might go through women like I go through vodka, but when it comes to the people closest to him, he's the most fiercely loving guy I know. He understands better than anyone what Mark put me through, and after the nasty incident in Brooklyn last year, he's been more protective than ever.

"What are you going to do?"

I shrug, taking a deep swallow of vodka. "Drink."

"No." He reaches for the glass but I hold it behind my back. "Seriously, Cat. We can figure this out. I can loan you some money until—"

"No way." The last thing I'm going to do is take money from Cory. He built this place from the ground up without taking a dime from anyone, and while Mark might have helped me out in the past, I want to do this on my own now.

"It's no big deal. I'd be happy to loan you—"

"No," I repeat, setting my glass down. "No, I need to figure this out by myself. But I don't think there's anything to figure out. I can't afford what he's asking and I can't afford to move—at least not anytime soon. I'm screwed." My eyes land on Myles down the bar, twirling his bottle for another group of women. "You think I could pull off bartending?" I ask Cory, only half kidding.

A laugh chuffs out of him. "It won't come to that. Look, you need to meet with Derek and break the whole thing down. He can help you come up with a plan."

Derek, of course! He's been my accountant for years—he does Cory's books too, that's how I found him. It didn't occur to me to meet with him.

I feel a jolt of hope as I grab my phone and text Derek. Maybe he can find some kind of loophole or unnecessary expense I've completely overlooked. I should have met up with him months ago.

My phone buzzes with Derek's prompt reply, saying that he can meet me tomorrow afternoon. Fantastic.

I down the rest of my drink and pull Cory into a hug. "Thanks, Cors. I knew you'd be able to help me."

"Of course. And if you ever need a loan, you just have to say the word."

I offer him a grateful smile. "Thanks. Right, I'm off." I push to my feet. Time to go home, get a good night's rest, and prepare for a productive meeting with Derek.

5

I really don't feel like doing this.

Actually, what I feel like doing is going out dancing with Alex and Geoff and forgetting my problems. What I *should* be doing right now, instead of sipping a drink and waiting for a date, is brainstorming every possible way I can increase sales in my store. That's going to take a miracle.

I met with Derek at the store today, and something very odd happened; Mark showed up with the new lease agreement, at a lower rate than what he offered yesterday. He said he'd thought about it and while he still had to raise the rent, he was prepared to "meet me halfway." I'm not sure what kind of game he's playing, but this has not reassured me in the slightest—not even when Derek crunched the numbers and told me that if we can "just" increase sales by twenty percent we'll be "fine." I decided not to point out that if I knew how to increase sales, I'd already be doing it.

Instead, I accepted a Tinder date at Bounce with a guy named Shane. Well, we'd already arranged to meet, but with all the business panic I'd forgotten. When he texted to remind me, I thought it might be a nice distraction from everything.

There's no sign of Cory tonight, but Myles is in rare form. I've already seen him perform for two different groups of women and I've only been here ten minutes. Now he's languishing against the bar in front of me, his gaze wandering over my dress when he thinks I'm not looking. And every time I catch him and shoot him a look that says *really?* he just smiles sheepishly and shrugs. I knew he was only being reserved the other night because of Cory. Still, Myles's presence is oddly comforting, especially with Cory not around.

"Hey, Cat." Josie wanders over from where she's been mixing mojitos, and leans across the bar to peek under my stool. "Stevie with you?"

"Not tonight," I say with an apologetic smile. Josie's been bartending here for a few years and she's a real sweetheart —a total animal lover, volunteering a lot of her time at local shelters whenever she's not working. Cory talks about her a lot, and sometimes I catch him watching her work with this look in his eye. It's not surprising—she's beautiful: late twenties, slim, short dark hair, big green eyes and a wide smile. For a while I thought maybe she'd be the one to get Cory to give up his playboy ways and settle down, but they just seem to be friends.

She straightens up and leans against the bar beside us. "Another date?"

I nod, stirring my drink.

Myles glances from Josie to me. "You have a lot of dates here?"

"Yeah. Cory likes to keep an eye on things, in case it goes south."

"And that happens a lot?" he asks.

"What, does it turn to shit a lot?" I lift a shoulder, watching as Josie goes to clear some glasses from a booth. "More often than I'd like, yeah."

Myles's brow knits. "So why keep doing it? You don't really think you're going to meet someone this way, do you?"

"Well... I see it as a bit of a numbers game. Like, I know that a lot of the guys I meet on apps are not going to be great, or they're just going to be looking for something casual or whatever. But I figure that if I just meet enough of them, statistically, *one* has to be decent. And that's all I need: one decent guy."

Myles rubs his scruffy chin, contemplating me. "I guess," he says at last. "But... whatever happened to meeting people the old-fashioned way?"

I trail my eyes over him. With his hipster distressed-on-purpose fitted T-shirt, tattooed arm and nightly performances for the ladies, he hardly seems the type to be old-fashioned. "What, you mean like in bars?"

A little smile quirks the corner of his mouth. He turns to serve a couple seated a few stools away, then focuses his attention back on me. "You could meet someone at a coffee shop, or something."

"Have you ever met anyone at a coffee shop?"

"No." He chuckles, reaching for the vodka to top up my glass.

"That only happens in movies."

He nods, thinking. "Maybe at the gym?"

I wince, picturing my red, sweaty face. "Nobody is asking me out after a workout, trust me. Besides, lately I've only been managing to get to the gym like once a week, at most. Not good enough odds."

Myles laughs. "Well, you could meet someone through friends."

"True. That is a bit of an untapped resource. I guess I just feel a bit pathetic asking them to set me up."

"Yeah, I get that. What about through work?"

"Nope. I run a tiny store with one female employee, and the customers are mostly women."

"Oh, right. Yeah I heard you say something about your shop on your last date. What's it called?"

"Loved Again," I say with a proud smile. "I sell vintage clothes."

"Did you sort out the problems you were having?"

My smile slides away and I sigh, leaning my elbows on the bar. "No. Well, sort of. I know what I have to do, I just don't know how. I think I'm in for a bit of an uphill battle. All thanks to my stupid ex-husband. That guy is the bane of my life."

Someone climbs onto the stool beside me and I sneak a glance at him. He's tall, muscular, light-haired, handsome. And he looks *really* out of place in here—more like he should be in a fancy cocktail bar in the financial district. When he turns to look at me, I realize who he is.

"Shane?"

His face breaks into a grin. "Yeah."

"I'm Cat." I take in his expensive suit as I extend my hand. Poor guy, I don't know why he agreed to meet me here. Still, I'm not interested in a guy, no matter how rich or fancy, if he can't appreciate a funky place like this. "Thanks for meeting me."

"Sure." He turns to Myles, ordering a whiskey. Taking his drink, he fixes his attention back on me. "This place is... interesting."

"Yeah. It's my brother's bar, so I'm here a lot. I like it."

I do love this place. Not just because Cory owns it and I get free drinks, but because I love the funky vibe, the fact that it's a bit of a dive, that it's not taking itself too seriously. Most of the East Village is like that. The brick buildings and row houses, similar to the West Village, feel different over here. There's more street art, more cute and fun shops like mine, more low-key bars like this. Even though I love my apartment, I can't say I've always felt as though I belong in the West Village. It's so much more upmarket, with designer stores and fancy restaurants that aren't really my thing. But it was where Mark wanted to live, years ago, and I guess I've just never left.

Shane smiles over his whiskey. "You work around here, right?"

"Yeah. I have a shop a few blocks over, selling vintage clothes along with my own designs."

"How's business?"

"Great," I say without thinking. But I decide not to correct myself. It doesn't seem wise to tell this insanely handsome and obviously successful man that I'm on the brink of losing everything. From the corner of my eye, I see Myles watching with interest as he hands a Budweiser to a guy down the bar, and I give Shane a carefree laugh. "What do you do?"

"I'm in real estate."

Real estate? Wow. He looks like he's doing a *lot* better than Mark.

"That's cool," I say, twirling my straw.

Shane nods, letting his gaze dip down to my dress and back up to my face. But it's okay, because I'm sizing him up, too. Sandy blond hair, golden stubble lining his sharp jaw, hazel eyes, and a suit that I can tell is worth a few thousand, easy. This guy is hot—like, *seriously* hot. Why on earth is he on a dating app? I inhale to ask him, but he speaks first.

"So, what are you doing on Tinder anyway? You seem like a perfectly nice chick."

"Oh." I huff a laugh. "Yeah, well. It's hard to meet people, I guess."

"You're divorced, right?"

"Yep," I say, stirring my drink. The mention of Mark reminds me of my store. Somehow, speaking to this gorgeous man I'd let myself forget about it, but I feel a fresh wave of dread. I can't stop the thoughts that pile in on top of each other, reminding me I'm up shit creek.

Shane clears his throat and my focus snaps back to him.

"Sorry," I mumble, feeling heat creep up my neck. "Yes, I'm divorced. But... uh, my ex and I are on good terms." Well, we were... once.

"That's good." He smiles, raising his glass to his lips, and I see a flash of an expensive watch. Ooh, I do love a watch on a guy. The sight of it sends a little fizzle of heat along my limbs, and I straighten up, willing myself to concentrate on him. Because he is very nice, indeed.

"So, what do you do for fun?"

"All kinds of things." His lips tilt at the corner. "I love to get out on the water in summer, go hiking, just get outdoors. When I'm not working I spend a lot of time in the gym."

I bite my lip, trying extra hard to keep my eyes from wandering over his shoulders and chest. I can already tell he spends time in the gym, and... damn.

"What about you? Do you hit the gym?"

I nod vigorously. "Oh, yeah. I workout... often. Most days if I can." As I speak I can feel the weight of Myles's gaze, and I force myself to ignore him.

The truth is that I *used* to go to the gym most days, but it hasn't been that way for a while now. Between dating and running shop I don't always have the time, or the energy. But I'm sure I'll get back into it.

Thinking about the store again, I droop. Because pretty soon, if I lose my store, I'll have loads of free time. I just won't be able to *pay* for a gym membership, or food, or rent. In fact—

"Are you okay?" Shane cocks his head. "You seem a little distracted."

Shit.

I rub my forehead in agitation. I'm ruining what could be a good date, with a lovely, sexy guy. I'm supposed to be dazzling him, making him laugh and charming him with my bubbly personality and fascinating life. Instead, I'm letting myself be pulled into a whirlpool of self-pity.

"We can do this another time if you like," Shane says kindly. He surveys my face for a second. "Look, I'm just going to say it. You're better in person than I thought you'd be and I'd like to see you again. If tonight isn't good, then let's reschedule. I can take you out for dinner." He glances around us with a grimace, then looks back at me, adding, "Someplace nice."

A relieved laugh rises up my throat. I'm really off my game tonight, and I would like to see him again when I can make a better impression. "That would be great. I'm sorry, I actually forgot we were meeting tonight. And I'm just, uh, not feeling very well. But I would like to see you again, too."

He grins, finishing his whiskey and setting the glass down. "Great. Well, I hope you feel better. I'll text you tomorrow, okay?"

I nod, then before I can say anything, he leans across to kiss me on the cheek. He smells like delicious cologne, and my heart flutters when his lips brush my skin. I watch as he stands and pushes his way through the growing crowd, no doubt relieved to be getting out of here.

But I don't care. Because he's nice and he likes me. And don't get me started again on how attractive he is.

With a happy sigh, I turn to the bar. Now I can get back to the matter at hand: figuring out what to do about my business. I'll head home, get into my PJs, and start coming up with ideas. Worry knots my stomach as I think about the shop and I quickly try to push it away.

"You scared him off?" Myles slides another drink across the bar to me.

I hesitate. I was about to head home, but one more drink would take the edge off my nerves. "No, we just agreed to catch up another time." I reach for the glass and take a sip. "I've got too much on my mind with work."

"Yeah, that was interesting," Myles says, clearing Shane's glass from the bar. "What you said about how business is great? I thought you were having some issues?"

"Oh. Well, yeah, I am. But I'm not going to say that on a first date. You have to put your best foot forward, right?"

"Is that why you told him you go to the gym everyday, too? And that you're on great terms with your ex?"

Irritation trickles down my spine. "Did you listen to our entire conversation?"

"I caught parts of it, yeah. Do you always lie on dates?"

My jaw tenses. "I wasn't *lying*. I mean, I *used* to go to the gym every day, and I'd *like* to be on better terms with Mark, so it's not that far from the truth."

Myles lifts his eyebrows, folding his arms over his chest.

"But, you know, it's a first date," I continue. "I'm not going to sit there and tell him my ex is making my life awful and I haven't made time for the gym lately. It doesn't look good."

"And you don't feel like you're misleading him?"

"I'm not—"

"You never tell guys your full name, either. What's that about?"

I splutter in disbelief. "You're kidding. I'm meeting a guy from a *dating app*, Myles. What do you expect me to say? 'Hello, I'm Catherine Marie Porter. Here's a DNA sample and my current address'? You're acting as though I'm giving a fake name, or—"

"Hold on," he interrupts, glancing down the bar to a pair of young women. He gestures for me to stay put and sidles over to them. I roll my eyes, watching as he goes to perform —telling the women how beautiful they are and how lucky he is to be their bartender this evening—and try not to throw up in my mouth. It hardly seems fair that he's here judging me when he carries on like that. So I present the best version of myself on a date, who doesn't? At least I'm not like him; using my job to pick up women.

He returns with that cocky grin on his face again, as if he wasn't just here a moment ago implying I'm some sort of con artist. "I had a look at your website," he says, taking a dishcloth and wiping the bar beside me.

"My... website?"

"Yeah, for your store."

"Oh, right," I say, bemused. Mark made our website years ago, and it mostly just exists to give people information—all of which they can get from Google, anyway.

"How long have you had it?"

"A while," I admit.

"Yeah, it's quite outdated." He gestures to my glass, silently asking if I'd like a refill, and I shake my head. "And it's awful to navigate."

I frown. "Yeah, well, it's not exactly a priority right now."

"Have you considered getting it redone?"

I exhale, setting my empty glass down on the bar, the irritation I felt from before returning. This guy really can't read the room. "Not at the moment."

"Well, it's a little old, so—"

"Jesus, Myles." I push to my feet. "I have enough going on right now. I don't need this."

The pair of girls at the end of the bar erupt into giggles over something and we both turn to see. One of them waves to Myles, and I glance between them and him with a knowing look. I've spent enough time watching him hit on women here that I have a pretty good handle on his routine. Hell, he tried to hook up with me before he knew I was Cory's sister.

"Have fun with them tonight." I smirk, swiping my purse off the bar. "I'll see you later."

And with that, I turn on my heel and head through the crowd, out onto the sidewalk. I don't have time to stay here and argue with Myles. I need to go home and get to work, so I don't lose my business.

6

I kick at a clump of grass, the heat from the takeout coffee cups getting uncomfortable in my hands. Where the hell is Geoff? He said he'd be here by now.

"You're not supposed to do that," I hear from behind me. I turn to see Geoff gesturing to the grass.

I grunt and thrust one of the takeout cups into his hand. "Here," I mutter. I didn't want to waste what little money I have on coffee, but Geoff buys me drinks all the time. It's the least I can do.

"Thanks." He eyes me carefully. "Everything okay?"

"No," I snap. I look at Geoff's wary face and soften. "Sorry. Let's walk."

He falls into step beside me as we head north along The Highline—a public park created on an old elevated railway track, running through the Meatpacking District and Chelsea. Even though it's one of the nicest spots in the city, I don't often come up here. Today, it's beautiful; the sun is high and warm in the cobalt sky, and the raised garden beds along the track are filled with gray birch trees which throw dappled shade across the path. It was Geoff's idea to get out on our shared day off, and I'm already feeling better for the fresh air and sunshine.

He raises his coffee for a sip and glances at me as we stroll. "So, what's up?"

"Mark is increasing the rent and I'm not sure I'll be able to keep the store."

"Wait." He stops walking, placing a hand on my arm. "Really?"

I nod, shielding my eyes from the sun to look at him.

"When did you find out?"

"A couple of days ago."

"Why didn't you tell me?"

I shrug and turn to walk again, Geoff beside me. "I don't know. I felt stupid. This is my own fault, right? I'm the one who made a bad business decision and now I'm in debt. I'm the one who should have moved on from the store years ago, like you've been saying all along."

"This isn't all your fault. Okay, yes, you could have moved, but you had your reasons. And as for the other thing... you were let down by someone you trusted. You can't blame yourself for that." Geoff links his arm through mine and steers me toward a bench. We sit, overlooking Washington Street, and after a while he turns to gaze at me. "Are you still making your clothes, designing new things?"

"Not much. Running the store takes up most of my time. Well, that and going on Tinder dates." I think back to my date at Bounce the previous evening. "I met a nice guy last night, though. So that's something." Myles's face flashes into my mind and I scowl, remembering his words.

"If he was nice why are you making that face?"

"No—" I shake my head. "It was just... you know that new bartender I told you about? We had an argument. He said all this stuff about how I lie on dates, then he randomly started going off at me about how my website sucks."

Geoff watches me with interest, and I sag, forcing my breath out through my teeth.

"I do feel bad, though," I mumble. "I was kind of judgmental and then I stormed off."

Geoff gives me a kind smile. "It's probably just misdirected anger about everything with the store." He ponders me over his coffee cup for a moment. "You need to sew, Cat. You know that's what makes you feel better. If you don't do the thing you love, you'll go crazy. You know how uptight Alex gets if she doesn't write?"

I chuckle. Alex writes romance novels and if she goes more than a few days without writing she has to shut herself away to write or she gets stressed. She says it's the thing that keeps her sane.

Ugh, Geoff's probably right. Designing my dresses and sewing has always been the thing that makes me feel better. It was, after all, the reason I started my shop in the first place—even if the focus changed over the years.

"You might be right, but I can't think about that now," I mutter. "I need to work on getting more money into the business if I want to save it."

"Did you ever consider that your creations—your designs—could be the thing to do that?"

I gaze down at my lap, fiddling with the plastic lid of my coffee cup. There was that girl who wanted to order a custom dress, but she never got in touch with me. Other than that, well, my designs don't do brilliantly in store.

"Maybe," I mumble. I know Geoff is trying to cheer me up, trying to inject a little self-belief into me, but I'm not sure he's heading down the right path here. All the ideas I came up with last night to make more money involved the vintage goods: scouring eBay for more bargains and hitting up some flea markets, then marketing more around the East Village with fliers, holding a sale, having an in-store party... that sort of thing.

"Just think about it, okay?" Geoff says, leaning his head on my shoulder and looking up at me.

I laugh, reaching an arm around him and squeezing, angling my face up toward the sun. I really do love this guy.

"Creating something will make you feel better. Oh!" He sits back, a grin lighting his face. "You should meditate. That will help you to de-stress and deal with some of the anger."

I snort. I'm not the meditating type and he knows that. "Punching Mark in the face would help me deal with some of the anger, too."

"True," Geoff says with a chuckle. "But at least this is legal. I use a meditation app and it has changed my life." He takes a swig of his coffee. "Or you could go to a class. I know a great one in the Village."

"I don't need to meditate. I need to come up with a way to save my business."

"Sure. But you're stressed, Cat. It's not good for you."

I think again of how I snapped at Myles last night and sigh. As much as he was getting on my nerves, I think Geoff's right—it was misdirected anger. It wasn't fair to take it out on him. I am stressed, and I'm not feeling like myself.

"You won't come up with any good ideas while you're feeling so strung out," Geoff adds. "Meditation can help to clear your head so you can focus on what you need to do to save the store."

I look at Geoff, squinting against the sun. "You really think it could help?"

He shrugs. "It couldn't hurt, right?"

7

"Okay, everyone. Please find a seat."

I hover in the doorway, still undecided. I wasn't going to come but I spent most of the night tossing and turning, thinking about the shop, replaying the way I walked out on Myles, wondering why I haven't heard from Shane. As the night wore on, I found myself getting more and more wound into a tight coil, panicking about what I'd do if I lost my business, if I lost my apartment, if my friends decided they hate me and all my hair fell out...

By the time 5 a.m. rolled around I'd barely slept a wink and I decided I'd give this meditation thing a try. I found an early class in the East Village, figuring I could pop in for an hour to relax then head off to work clear-headed, ready to tackle the day.

But now, as I peek inside the packed studio, I feel very out of place. I mean, I do yoga, so I am familiar with the whole Eastern approach to things. But with yoga it's mostly about the body, which I can handle. I always steered away from the airy-fairy side of it.

"Come on in, don't be shy," the instructor calls from the front of the room.

I glance around and realize she's talking to me. A few heads turn and I slink into a row near the middle, flopping onto a spare cushion. I slide down to the floor, resting my head on the pillow. What I could *really* use, after the night I had, is a nap. I wonder if she would mind if I just laid my head down here while everyone else did the thing. Because this pillow is good...

"Right, okay. Sitting up with your back straight, cushion positioned under your buttocks."

I jerk up, wrinkling my nose in disgust. This pillow has had a million butts on it and I was just snuggling my cheek against it. Ugh.

I haul myself into a sitting position, crossing my legs in front of me like everyone else seems to be doing. Right, okay. I can do this. Time to meditate, take control of my mind and get some clarity with my business. Let's go!

"Begin by closing your eyes," the instructor says in a low, soothing voice. "We're going to start with a few deep breaths. In through the nose for a count of five seconds, hold for five, then out through the mouth for a count of eight seconds. Let's do it together. In; one, two..."

I breathe in through my nose, trying to follow her counts. But I get to the end of my breath long before she gets to five, so I have to hold my breath for nine seconds to catch up with her, and by the time we're supposed to breathe out I'm so dizzy that my breath rushes out and I gasp another in.

Not off to a great start.

Okay, no. Let's try again.

I tune her out for a moment and draw in a breath, counting to five in my own head. I hold it and release, then repeat it and, gradually, I feel my body begin to relax.

"You want to feel the breath expand in your belly," the instructor says.

What?

I breathe in again, feeling my chest expand. My stomach isn't expanding, because my lungs aren't down there. Because *nobody's* lungs are down there. What is she talking about?

"Clear your mind. Remove all thoughts and just focus on the breath."

I frown, opening one eye to glance around the room. Everyone is perfectly still, their eyes closed in blissful surrender, their minds all apparently wiped clear at the mere mention of it. The instructor is just sitting silently and my frown deepens. Is that it? Isn't she supposed to teach us *how* to clear the thoughts from our mind?

"Whenever you feel your mind wander," she adds, "just gently bring it back to the breath."

I close my eyes again, willing myself to focus. *Come on, Cat. You're not even trying.*

Right okay. Focus on the breath. *In, count; hold, count; out, count. In...*

What am I going to do about the store? Geoff suggested doing more with my own designs, but I don't see how that's going to help, because—

Whoops. *In, count; hold, count; out...*

I wonder why Shane hasn't texted me. He said he'd text me the next day. It's just that he was really cute, and we seemed to get along okay, despite what Myles said—

Goddammit, I'm hopeless. *In, count; hold, count...*

Myles was annoying the other night. What is it with that guy? I've never met a bartender who is so nosy, so involved in my business—

Arrrgh! *In, count; hold...*

But was he right? Do I mislead guys? It's not like I try to *deliberately* mislead them, but I do think it's a good idea to show your best self—like a job interview. But still, judging Myles for what he does at work is harsh. It's really not my business how he meets women, and I shouldn't have—

Oh for fuck's sake! *In, count...*

Why am I the only one here who can't do this? Why is no one else battling to keep their mind focused on their breath? What's wrong with my brain? Geoff said this would help me but I'm feeling more tense and aggravated than ever! It's absurd that we are expected to just know how to keep our mind focused without—

"You're doing great, everyone." The instructor's voice interrupts my spiraling thoughts and I dig my nails into my palms. "Remember to keep focusing on the breath, and if your mind wanders, just notice without judgment and gently bring it back."

I open my eyes, glancing around the room in frustration. I'm just about to tiptoe out when the instructor's gaze lands on me. I lift my chin, throwing her a defiant look. I don't give a shit what she says, this isn't working.

"Okay." She looks away from me and over the room again. "I'm now going to lead you through a guided visualization."

Oh, what fresh hell is this?

I twist around and spy the exit, four rows behind me. Maybe I can slip out?

"I want you to imagine you're walking along a beach."

Ooh, I love the beach.

I turn back to the front and, without even trying, a picture of the beach appears in my mind. My eyes flutter closed, my shoulders relax down from my ears, and I settle back into the cushion. Maybe I will stay for this.

"It's a beautiful sunny day, not a cloud in the sky," she continues. "See the golden sand stretching before you, feel the spray from the ocean on your skin, taste the salty air."

I let out a long, relieved sigh, feeling my limbs loosen. This is more like it. The beach I can do.

"The waves are lapping at the shore; cool and welcoming."

Ahhh, bliss. My head lolls to one side, my body swaying ever so gently as all the stress leaves me. My breathing has become rhythmic and gentle, my whole being turning to jelly.

"...go into the light..."

Wait, what? I straighten up, trying to bring my focus back to her words.

"You're enjoying the sunlight," the instructor says. "You're lying on the warm sand, enjoying the sun."

Oh, right. I smile to myself, realizing I was just on the brink of falling asleep, her words becoming distorted as my mind floated off. I'm so tired after last night. Must not fall asleep. Must not...

My head lolls forward again, my shoulders droop, and before I know what's happening my whole body collapses and I slide off my cushion, crashing into the back of the person in front of me.

"Shit," I mutter, trying to clear the fuzz that's gathered in my head as I scramble back onto my pillow. My face is hot as several people nearby turn to look, but that is nothing compared to the shock I feel when the person in front of me —a guy, I hadn't even noticed—turns around.

"Myles?" The word comes out at normal volume before I can stop it, piercing through the silence in the room as if I'd yelled it through a megaphone.

The instructor hisses a loud "Shhh!" and I shrivel,

clamping my lips together, trying to make sense of what's happening. One second I'm on a beach drifting off to sleep, the next Myles is in front of me, eyebrows raised in surprise.

He lifts a finger to his lips, amusement glittering in his eyes as he registers my shock. His gaze lingers on me for an extra second before he turns back around, placing his hands on his knees and straightening his spine.

But I'm too rattled to focus now. What is he doing *here*? He seems so out of place, like when you were a kid and you saw a teacher outside of school. I mean, seriously. Is he here to *meditate*?

I shake my head, baffled. That is... unexpected.

Finally, the instructor wraps up the session and I couldn't be more relieved. As soon as she gives the word, I spring to my feet and dash for the exit, breathing out when I'm finally back on the sidewalk in the real world.

That was surreal—and there's no way in hell I'm going back. I don't know what Geoff was thinking. I turn and trudge in the direction of my store, a few blocks away.

"Cat!" Myles appears beside me, that confident grin on his face as always. He's in a black T-shirt and faded jeans, hair styled deliberately messy, and I can't help but think again how odd it is that he was in there, *meditating*. Weird.

"Hey. Sorry about crashing into you. I fell asleep." I give an embarrassed laugh.

He laughs too, but not in an unkind way. "Yeah, I've done that a few times. I've never seen you in there before. Was that your first class?"

"First and last."

His smile drops. "Really? It's normal to fall asleep sometimes."

I shrug, unwilling to admit that's not the reason I'm not

going back; it's because my stupid brain wouldn't shut up for more than three seconds and it was excruciating.

"What are you up to now?" Myles asks. "Want to grab a coffee?"

I open my mouth, glancing down the street then back to him, laughing awkwardly. "Aren't you annoyed with... you know, at the bar, the way I acted..."

He slips his hands into his jeans pockets. "Yeah, well, we were both a little out of line. That's why I thought it might be good to talk."

"To *talk*?"

He chuckles. "Yeah. That's usually how people work things out."

"Er, okay. Sure. Coffee."

"Great." He leads the way toward a coffee shop further down the block and I trail after him, bewildered.

He gestures for me to find a table and goes to order for us both. A moment later he's pulling out a chair and sliding into it with an easy grin. But it's not his cocky, smug smile that I see at the bar; it's a genuine, almost boyish smile, that doesn't quite fit with the image I have of him in my head.

I feel a rush of guilt as I remember the way I stormed off. "Listen, I'm sorry about the other night. I'm just having a hard time with my store at the moment and you pressed my buttons with all that stuff about my dating, and you were kind of a dick..."

His mouth twitches. "Is this your first apology?"

A laugh escapes me. "Shit, you're right." I rub my forehead and inhale, meeting his gaze. "I'm sorry for snapping at you. And, you know... for judging you. What you choose to do on your own time is up to you, and it's not my place to comment."

Our coffees arrive but his gaze doesn't move from mine. "And you think what I do is take women home from work?"

"Well, yeah." I reach for the sugar. "You tried to take me home that first night we met, and I've seen you with the women at Bounce."

"No," he says, still not moving. His brows draw together in a frown. "I asked you to have a *drink* with me. That's not the same thing. And as for the women, I mostly just flirt to get tips. It helps a lot to give compliments and flirt. The extra cash is good."

I take a moment to process this, not entirely convinced. "Right. Well, anyway, I shouldn't have snapped at you. So, I'm sorry."

"Yeah, I should probably apologize too." He sighs, cradling his coffee. "I didn't mean to stick my nose in with the dating stuff. And as for your website... I don't think I went about this the right way, but I was trying to offer to redo it for you."

"What?"

"Like I said, it's pretty outdated. I'd be happy to redo it for you."

"Do you... know how to do that?"

His forehead wrinkles humorously. "Uh, yeah. I wouldn't offer if I didn't."

"Oh," I say, taken aback. I had wanted to redo the site, but after everything fell apart a few months ago, I'd been forced to put it out of my mind. Right now it's the last thing I need to spend money on. "That's really kind, thanks. But I'm sort of, well, a bit short on funds, and I don't think—"

"No, I wouldn't charge you for it."

"What? Why not?"

"Believe it or not, bartending is not my life's passion." Little creases form around his eyes. "I want to start my own web design business, but I need to put together a portfolio before I can charge clients. So if I create a site for you, it would help me out too."

Huh. A web design business. I didn't see that coming.

I stir some sugar into my coffee. "Well... I guess it would be good to have it updated. I'm not sure how comfortable I am having you do it for free, though." I raise my cup to my lips, savoring the malty taste on my tongue, thinking. "I can't afford to pay you right now, but... maybe we can barter? I make clothes. Is there anything I could make you?"

He smiles. "I don't know, maybe. You don't need to pay me, honestly."

I run my eyes over his sincere face. I'm not sure who this guy sitting in front of me is, but it's *not* the same guy from Bounce.

"I'm happy to help," he adds. "Cory said you were having some trouble with your landlord, and I thought—"

"Wait." I hold up a hand. "Cory told you that?"

He nods, his expression shifting at my tone.

"Fuck, Cory," I mutter to myself. I guess I kind of expected he wouldn't go around telling people I'm having business issues. No wonder Myles is offering to do the site for free—Cory probably asked him to. And now Myles feels like he has to help out the pathetic woman who can't get her life together. And I don't like that one bit.

I finish my coffee, rising to my feet. "Look, I appreciate the offer but I think I'll pass. I'm going to sort things out on my own, and I don't want any pity or charity." I turn to go, and pause. "Thanks for the coffee."

Then I head off to work, no more relaxed than I was this morning.

8

Geoff might have been way off with the meditation, but he was right about one thing: working on my own designs is definitely making me feel better. I've made two dresses and three skirts in two days. It's the most productive I've been in months.

Still nothing from Shane. It's a shame, because he was so cute and nice and, well, *normal*. I guess I put him off with that terrible date. That whole evening was a mess.

Actually, I've been avoiding Bounce the past couple of days. I'm still annoyed that Cory told Myles—and God knows who else—about my business. It's humiliating.

Hayley, however, has been spectacular. Take this, for example: while I've spent the past two days glued to my sewing machine at the back of the store, stress-sewing, she's been coming in early and making fliers to hand out around the East Village, reorganizing the store to give it a fresh look, creating a sale rack to put out the front, redoing the window display and coming up with all kinds of ideas. She's brilliant.

The truth is, though, I'm not sure we're going to be able

to do it. We have less than sixty days to increase sales by
twenty percent and it just feels impossible, even with
Hayley's enthusiasm and creativity. It doesn't matter how
many fliers we hand out, how many items we add to the sale
rack—some things are just meant to fail. I'm beginning to
wonder if my business is one of them.

Around lunchtime on Wednesday, I send Hayley home
for the day. She's doing so much extra work—work I can't
afford to pay her for—and I know she's got other things to
do. What, I'm not sure exactly, because she's a bit all over the
place (last month it was dog-walking, and a few months
before that she was painting portraits, plus I know she does
some temp work) but either way, I'm feeling super guilty at
all the time she's putting in here.

I smile gratefully as she heads out. "You know I appreciate everything you're doing, right?"

"I do," she says, pulling her long braid over her shoulder.
She's naturally pretty—curvy, with strawberry-blond hair
and blue-green eyes—and she has the dorkiest laugh, which
I love. Even though she's in her early thirties, she's got this
fun, happy-go-lucky nature that I envy. She moved here
from the UK a few years ago, and hasn't lost the accent
one bit.

She squeezes my shoulder. "I'm only a call away if you
need anything, remember that."

"Thanks, hon."

Once she's gone I return to the counter and sit down,
taking out my ham and cheese sandwich. It's not the most
appetizing lunch, but given I need to watch every penny, it's
all I have.

The bell at the door rings and I glance up, smiling, to
greet the customer. Maybe they'll come in and spend a
fortune and all will be saved.

But it's not a customer. It's Myles.

He pushes into my shop, wearing a white tee over ripped jeans and a black, flat-brimmed baseball cap on his head. He doesn't look over at the counter; instead, his eyes are drawn to the display table, currently boasting an assortment of vintage salt and pepper shakers. He steps up to it, a smile playing on his lips as he picks up a salt shaker. It's a tiny, yellow, ceramic owl. They're my favorites.

I set my sandwich down with a sigh. I bet Cory sent him. Cory has texted me several times over the past couple of days and I've ignored him, so he knows I'm pissed.

Myles returns the salt shaker to the table and his gaze slides to mine. "Hey."

"Hi."

He wanders toward me, shrugging a messenger bag off his shoulder and placing it on the counter, not saying anything.

"What are you doing here?"

Pulling his cap off, he places it beside his bag and rakes a hand through his messy curls. "I've come to work on the website."

I frown. "I said—"

"I know what you said." He opens his bag and slides out a Macbook. "And I'm going to do it anyway."

"I don't want any charity, Myles."

"God, you are so stubborn." He sets his laptop down on the counter and looks at me squarely. "This isn't charity. It's a friend helping another friend, because they can."

There's a pinch in my stomach at his words, because the last time I trusted a "friend" to help me, it landed me in shit.

"And don't forget that doing a website for you helps me, too," he adds.

I saw my teeth across my bottom lip. I guess there's no

harm in him making a site if it's going to help him out. But it's pretty damn arrogant of him to just sweep in here and expect me to fall on my knees in gratitude.

Myles pulls up a stool at the end of the counter, opening his laptop. And as he begins to type away, I feel myself start to soften. Even though I'm a little annoyed he's here when I told him I didn't want his help, I'm also kind of impressed.

And—okay, I'll admit—a *little* grateful.

"Fine," I say, picking up my sandwich again. "Just don't get in my way."

He gives me a look.

"And... thanks," I mumble.

He asks me to write down my login details so he can access the site. But once he loads the old site again, he grimaces. "I'm going to start from scratch. Is that okay?"

I nod, feeling a wry smile twist my mouth. Our old site is awful—I'm not surprised he wants nothing to do with it.

We sit in silence for a while, me eating and him banging away on his keyboard. A few customers come and go, but no one buys anything.

"You're not working today?" I ask.

He shakes his head without looking up.

"Why'd you come here to do this, anyway?"

"I don't know anything about you or your business. I don't know your branding, your message. I can't create a site if I don't know anything."

My branding, my message.

The words sift through to my brain and I sag. "Actually... there's a chance I might lose the store."

Myles stops typing and raises his gaze to mine. "Really? Why?"

"Because..." I hesitate. Why did I tell him that? Ah, what does it matter? He's probably already got the gossip from

Cory, anyway. "I can't afford the new rent, as I'm sure Cory told you."

He gives a little nod.

"I'm in a bit of debt," I admit with a cringe. "I made a bad business decision a few months back."

Myles spies the sewing machine over my shoulder. "You said you make clothes?"

"Yeah." I gesture to the rack behind him with my designs. "Those are mine."

He turns in his seat, taking a second to look at a couple. "They're awesome. Why don't you have more of those and less of the vintage stuff?"

"My own designs have always been more of a hobby. Mark—my ex—told me it didn't make financial sense to prioritize them, because there's more money in vintage stuff."

"And you believed him?"

"Well... he had experience in business." I look down at my hands. "I just loved to sew."

Myles glances at my dresses again, then lets his gaze wander out across the store, saying nothing.

The truth is, I'd love to do more with my designs—I was thrilled when Mel's friend agreed to stock them in her store a few months back. That's why I jumped at the chance without taking the proper precautions. That's why I'm in this mess.

"Anyway, my accountant told me I need to increase sales by twenty percent if I want to make the new rent while still paying off my debt. And that's just to scrape by. It's not exactly how I imagined my business—struggling to make ends meet."

"Yeah." His face creases with sympathy. "That's rough."

Unease scratches at my insides—like it usually does

when people pity me—and I force a bright smile. "Doesn't matter. Everything happens for a reason, right? I'll move onto other things."

He inhales to say something, then stops himself. His gaze drops back to his laptop, and there it stays for the next couple of hours. I almost tell him to stop working. I mean, if the shop is closing I'm hardly going to need a website. But he's doing it for his portfolio, so I guess it will be useful to him. Plus, as much as I hate to admit this, a tiny part of me is comforted by having him here.

Weird.

I spend the next few hours working on another design, helping customers, making a couple of sales but nothing big. I can feel Myles watching me when I talk with customers and show them clothes, when I joke with a couple about an outrageous eighties pantsuit. I know he's gathering information for the site, so I don't mind. And the truth is, I'm starting to realize that I like him. Not like *that*, obviously, but he's a much nicer guy than I originally thought. For the first time, my snap judgments about a person might have been wrong.

"You don't have to stay," I say after a while.

He looks up, blinking as his eyes adjust from staring at the screen. "Do you want me to go?"

I gaze at him for a moment and smile. "No. I'm just saying, if you want—"

"I'm happy working here." He shrugs, smiling too.

"Do you want a coffee, or something?"

"Sure, thanks."

I hover for a second, debating whether or not I should go and buy him something decent. I'm trying to save money, but he is here doing me a favor. "Is instant okay? Otherwise I could—"

"Instant is fine," he says, and I feel a little spasm of relief.

"Okay. Back in a sec." I wander down the steep steps to the basement, surprised to find myself feeling lighter. I don't know why; I mean, my business is probably about to fold. Maybe it's the whole problem shared thing. Or maybe it's because someone is here, helping me, even though I'm sinking.

Whatever it is, I can't stop the smile pushing at my lips as I make two cups of coffee.

9

My good mood doesn't last long. Because as I climb back up the stairs I discover Mark, lurking beside the counter.

Great. Just who I feel like seeing. Still, it's been a few days. I'm overdue for a visit.

"I asked if I could help him," Myles says, eyes glued to his laptop. "But he said he was here for you."

"Thanks." I set our coffees down on the counter and turn to Mark. "Hi," I say warily. "Why are you here? Raising the rent again?"

He draws in a breath with exaggerated patience. "I came to see if you'd signed the new lease agreement."

"I'm still thinking about it."

His eyebrows slant together. "Well, the rent is going up next month, either way."

"I understand," I say, gritting my teeth.

His gaze travels over Myles and he extends a hand. "I'm Mark."

Myles glances up, eying Mark's hand before reluctantly

offering his own. "Myles." Then his eyes fall straight back down to his screen.

Mark gives me a strange look, mouthing, "Who's he?"

"He's my web guy," I say casually. I can tell by the ticking muscle in Mark's jaw that he's irritated, and I feel a swell of satisfaction. "He's redoing the site. It's *really* awful."

Mark looks indignant. It didn't occur to me that redoing the website might annoy him—since he made the last one —but that is a fun little bonus.

I glance down at Mark's feet. "You didn't bring Stevie?"

He huffs, turning toward the door. "Mel has her. Hold on."

There's a chill down my spine. Mel's here? Fuck. I thought seeing Mark was bad, but *she's* the last person I want to see.

Myles looks up from his laptop, as if sensing my anxiety, and a line forms on his brow. "You okay?"

"No," I mutter, turning back as the little bell rings again and Mark and Mel enter the store. When I spot Stevie in Mel's arms my stomach lurches, and I quickly pry her away.

"Hi, Cat," she says, handing the leash over. "How are you?"

I hold Stevie against my chest and glower at Mel. "I'm just dandy. How are you?"

"I'm great, too." Her dark eyes spark. "*We're* great, aren't we, Mark?"

Mark stuffs his hands into the pockets of his black jeans. "Great," he mumbles.

Mel and I stare at each other for a moment, neither of us willing to back down, the air crackling with tension.

Myles stands from his stool beside me, extending a hand. "Hi, I'm Myles."

I glare at him. You see, the thing about Mel is, she's

beautiful. Like model, movie-star beautiful. Long, silky dark hair, full lips, perfect cheekbones. She's naturally slim and tall, always dressed immaculately. These things never bothered me when we were friends; I always admired her sense of style and how down-to-earth she was, despite her beauty.

Except she wasn't down-to-earth. I was just stupid.

And now, her beauty really bothers me. Not because I feel threatened—because I don't—but because she doesn't deserve to be so beautiful on the outside when she's so hideous on the inside.

This is all lost on Myles, though, who apparently can't help but introduce himself.

"Mel," she coos in response, taking his hand.

I narrow my eyes as she gives him a simpering smile. It takes all my strength not to thump her. When her gaze swivels back to me, her smile turns plain malicious and my eyes become slits.

Myles clears his throat. Mark shifts his weight. I look at the two of them, standing side-by-side. God, they're so similar. Everything from their hairstyle, to their ripped jeans, to their armful of tattoos. And the bartending thing. Hell— even their names are similar.

"Well, anyway," I say at last, setting Stevie down. I watch as Myles crouches down to pet her, then sits back on his stool, returning to his laptop. I turn back to the others. "It was just *lovely* to see you two, but I've got work to do."

"Of course," Mark says.

Mel slides her hand into his, not taking her eyes off me. "We'll see you soon," she says, then pauses. "That is, if you're still in business."

And before I can say anything in response, she pulls Mark toward the door. I clench my jaw so hard I nearly break a tooth. I *knew* Mel was behind the rent hike; I knew she was trying to hurt me.

I wheel back toward the counter and raise my eyes to the ceiling. "*Hi, I'm Myles,*" I say in a mocking tone. "Very subtle, Myles. Trust me, you do *not* want to get involved with her."

"That's not why I introduced myself." Amusement crinkles his forehead. "It was super awkward and I was trying to break the tension."

"Oh."

"What was that all about?"

"She used to be one of my best friends. Before... Mark."

"Is Mel the reason you got divorced?"

"No. We got divorced for many other reasons. I don't know all their names." I smirk bitterly. "But... she knew me when Mark cheated, when I went through the divorce. Then a few years later, she started seeing him behind my back. What kind of friend does that?"

Myles grimaces.

"And she also... She's the reason I'm in debt. She said she'd help me out with some business and totally screwed me." Oof. I don't know *why* I'm telling him all this.

"Shit." He frowns and begins to say something more, but cuts himself off with a shake of his head, looking back down at his laptop.

I sigh. "What?"

"Nothing."

"Myles, you obviously have something to say, so just say it."

"It's not my place."

I snort. "Since when has that stopped you? Come on, out with it."

He pauses his typing. Releasing a long breath, he brings his gaze back to mine. "It's just... that is seriously fucked up, right? That your ex-husband is your landlord, then on top of that he's dating your friend?"

"Ex-friend."

"Yeah. That's fucked up."

I give a slow nod of agreement as I put some music on. Ella Fitzgerald comes on over the speakers and it makes me smile.

"Have you ever thought about moving somewhere else?"

A humorless laugh shoots from my mouth, and I lean back on my elbows against the counter, looking around the store. "Of course I have. I think about it all the time. But I can't afford the cost of moving, not to mention the rent. Even with the rent increase here, this place is still cheaper than most of the places out there."

He drags his lower lip through his teeth, thinking. "I don't want to overstep here, so if you want me to shut up, then just say."

I twist around to face him properly. "Okay... What?"

"Have you considered setting up an online store? Selling your things online?"

"Yeah. It's hard to compete with eBay and places like that, though, when it comes to vintage goods."

"No." He sets his laptop down on the counter and stands, pulling out my cherry-print dress. "I mean, selling your *own* designs online—building a brand around your original creations, offering limited runs of designs, doing custom orders, charging a higher price point. That sort of thing."

I hesitate, examining the dress. "Not really, no. I love making these clothes but they don't sell that well."

Myles laughs, cocking his head as if he doesn't under-stand me. "They're hidden down here on a rack behind the counter. No one can see them!"

"No—" I step back, looking between the rack and the rest of the store. "They're not hidden."

"Yes, they are. I've been watching you with customers all afternoon and most people don't even notice they're there." He softens. "Look. There are a million vintage clothing stores in the East Village alone. I know, because I checked. That's tough competition. But these"—he gestures to my clothes—"are unique. I don't know anything about fashion, but these are your own designs, right?"

I nod.

"So they're different from everything else. They're your thing, your niche. You're trying to appeal to everyone by selling vintage clothes and other things, and it's watering your brand down. If you focused on your own designs—the thing you love and are clearly good at—you'd be able to set yourself apart."

I gaze at my rack of clothing, seeing it through new eyes. I'd always listened to Mark's advice in the past, but what Myles says makes sense. No one has ever explained it like that—that I'm watering my brand down with the vintage stuff—but now that he has, it seems so obvious.

Still, my whole business is built around selling vintage clothes, in a physical store. I don't have the first clue how to overhaul it into an online store, focusing solely on my own designs. And to make a living doing that? It seems like a long-shot.

"It's a cool idea, but I wouldn't know where to start. I don't know the first thing about rebranding and setting up an online store, or marketing online. I don't have the time to even *think* about it, let alone actually do it."

He places the dress back. "But if you did do it, I'm sure you could make more than you're making now. At the moment, your entire client base is the East Village, maybe a little broader. If you go online, you literally have the whole world at your fingertips. You could afford to move, if you wanted to. To get away from"—he gestures to the door after Mark and Mel, screwing up his face—"that."

"But I don't know *how* to do it," I repeat, failing to keep the frustration out of my voice. "Sure, it's great in theory. But it's not doable."

"It is." He folds his arms across his chest and regards me carefully. "If you let others help you."

"*Who*?"

"Me." His cocky grin slides back onto his face. "Let me help."

"Myles—" I rub my forehead. "That's sweet. But it's a bit of a jump from building me a simple website to launching and running an online business, isn't it? You're talking about changing the entire structure of my business, creating a whole new brand, finding new clients, marketing..."

"Yes." He nods, his face serious. "But I know what I'm doing."

"Really? How?"

He sits down and picks up his laptop again. "Business school."

"*You* went to business school?"

Mirth lights his eyes. "You don't have to sound so shocked."

"I'm not—I mean, well..." I pause, studying him, picturing him behind the bar twirling bottles and flirting with anything with breasts. "Sorry. I guess you just don't seem the type."

"And you don't seem the type to put on an act to get guys to like you, yet here we are." He levels his gaze at me, daring me to disagree with him.

"Myles—"

"I'm just saying, people aren't always as they seem."

I open my mouth to argue again, but he's right. Ever since that meditation class, I've realized some of my judgments about him missed the mark.

The bell on the door trills and a middle-aged woman wearing a polka-dot blouse comes in. I give her a friendly smile then turn back to Myles. "You really went to business school?"

"I did. It was a few years ago now, but yes." His eyes move over my face and he sighs. "Look, I know you want to do all this on your own, but very few people succeed in business without some form of help or support. You have an accountant, right? You outsource the numbers stuff, because it's not in your skill set. This is no different."

"But... why would you help me? I can't afford to pay you."

"I know. I want to help. Besides, one day you'll be earning good money and you can pay me back then."

"That's putting a lot of pressure on me. I can't guarantee I'll be a success."

"I think you will. But in the meantime, you could always pay me in... other ways."

I give him a withering look. "Really?" One minute he's playing Mr. Nice Guy, offering to help simply from the goodness of his heart, the next he's suggesting I should sleep with him. I mean, he's not unattractive, but he's so similar to Mark that it's uncanny. He's exactly the type of guy I would have been interested in years ago—and that's how I know I'm *not* interested in him now. "I'm not going to sleep with you."

"*No*, not that." A laugh rumbles from his chest, then he pretends to look thoughtful. "Although, come to think of it—"

I whack him on the arm. "Seriously, Myles."

He shakes his head, laughing again. "No. I was just thinking..." He places his laptop down again and pushes to his feet, pulling a unicorn-print dress off the rack of my designs. "These are really cool. Do you make them in kids' sizes?"

"No. Why?"

"Just... this print. Is it something a seven year old might like?"

"I have no idea. I don't know any seven year olds, do you?"

He nods, saying nothing.

"Who?"

He scrubs a hand over his chin, still inspecting the dress. "My daughter."

My lips part in shock. "You have a *daughter*?"

He nods again, not looking at me, then places the dress back with a heavy exhalation. "I don't see her as much as I'd like. Her mother and I aren't together."

A thousand questions flood into my head at once, but I force myself to keep quiet. There's something about the look in his eye that's telling me not to ask more. Not now.

"Excuse me." I almost jump out of my skin as a customer appears beside me.

I turn and give her a bright smile. "Yes! Sorry, how can I help?" It's the lady in the polka-dot blouse.

"Did I hear you say you make these dresses for children?" She gestures to the rack beside Myles, reaching for the unicorn-print dress. "My niece would love a dress like that. She's all about unicorns."

"Well, no, but—"

"She does, yes," Myles interrupts. He reaches behind the

counter for a scrap of paper and a pen. "Why don't you give us your email address and Cat can contact you?"

"Oh, great!" The woman takes the paper, scribbles, then hands it over.

Once she's gone I turn back to Myles, stunned. "What was that?"

He flashes me a grin—the confident, self-assured one that's all white teeth, the one I always associate with him. "See? People love them."

I glance down at the paper in my hand, thinking. Is this really possible, building an online business based entirely on my own designs? Geoff suggested the same thing—and if it's so obvious to both of them, why am I resisting this idea so much? Is it because Mark made me feel like my own designs aren't enough?

No, that's not the only thing holding me back. The truth is, I'm not sure if I'm really prepared to take another risk with my business—to trust someone to help me out again. I'm sick of being let down by people, time and time again. And let's face it, I hardly know Myles.

But what choice do I have? My business is slipping through my fingers and I don't have any other ideas to save it. They say desperate times call for desperate measures— and I'm feeling desperate.

Besides, a tiny voice inside me asks, what if it actually *worked*? How cool would that be? I could run my own business on my own terms and Mark would have nothing to do with any of it. If that means I have to get a little help from Myles to make it a reality, that would be worth it.

"Do you really think this could work, this online business idea?"

"Yes," Myles says, without missing a beat.

"I do want to leave here." I gaze around the store. "I want to get away from Mark."

His brow knits. "Of course. It must suck that he's your landlord. Besides, you said it yourself: this isn't how you pictured your business. So do something different, stop settling. Let's make this the best it can be."

"Rousing speech," I say wryly.

He closes the lid on his laptop with a chuckle. "Look, it's up to you. But I think it could be cool."

I feel an odd sensation roll through my chest, and it takes me a moment to recognize it as hope. Hope for saving my business—for building something even better, on my own terms.

"Okay." I grin at Myles. "You're right. Let's do it."

10

I take a seat and place my purse under the table, smiling at Shane. This restaurant is *to die for*.

After Myles and I decided to go ahead with creating my online business, I felt empowered. And I figured, why not take control of my love life too?

So I texted Shane. He replied straight away, explaining he'd been swamped with work, had been meaning to get in touch, and could he take me out for dinner soon? I tried not to appear too eager when I replied, but I've got a good feeling about him.

And, fuck—he is even hotter than I remembered. Tonight, he's in navy chinos and a crisp dress shirt, sleeves rolled to the elbows and the top button undone. His blond hair is styled, his jaw clean-shaven, and he's wearing the same fancy cologne he had on at Bounce. In other words: yummy.

He's taken me to a restaurant called La Bouffe. I haven't even tried the food yet and I'm impressed. We're on the sixtieth floor of a building in the Financial District, and the views uptown are like something out of a magazine on this gorgeous spring evening. The Empire State Building sits tall and proud in the center of our view, nestled amongst the familiar cluster of midtown skyscrapers. Not far behind, on the border of the park, I can see the colossal Central Park Tower, taller than anything else from this viewpoint. As the sun sinks toward the horizon, it hits the building at just the right angle, sending golden light scattering across midtown.

God, I always forget how stunning this city is. I spend so much time with my head down, running between the West and East Village, I forget that there's a whole city teeming with life and beauty around me.

"I hope you like it here." Shane's eyes flash as they explore my dress. I went to a bit of extra trouble tonight, knowing he'd take me somewhere classy. I haven't been on a date this nice in ages, and I'm doing everything I can to make sure it goes smoothly.

I smile at Shane from under my lashes. "It's great. I've never been here before. The views are amazing."

He nods, picking up the drink menu and perusing the contents, ignoring the view. He must come here so often that it's boring for him.

The waiter appears beside us with a bottle of sparkling water, setting it down on the table. "What can I get you to drink this evening?"

Shane lowers the menu. "We'll take a bottle of the Krug." He pauses, looking at me for confirmation.

I blink. "Uh…"

"It's champagne."

I bite back a smirk. I know it's champagne, for God's sake. But I was thinking I might get a vodka cocktail, or something. Not to mention, isn't Krug hugely expensive?

Surely he'll be expecting me to put out after he buys a—I grab the drink menu and glance over the list—*three hundred dollar bottle of champagne*. Holy shit. I can't drink that. My body won't know what it is and will probably reject it.

I glance back at Shane's expectant face. He seems to think I'm worth a three hundred dollar bottle of champagne. And I never go on fancy dates like this. In all our years of marriage, Mark never once took me somewhere this nice. Maybe it's time I raise the bar for myself.

I grin, setting the menu down. "Perfect."

The waiter nods and turns back to the kitchen.

"So the food here is French-inspired," Shane says, clasping his hands on the table. "Have you ever been to France?"

"No, but it's on my list." I give a light laugh, as if I've been meaning to book a trip to France for ages now, and gosh darn it, if it weren't for the tiny issues of my failing business and difficult ex-husband I would have popped over already.

"You should go. It's beautiful." He tilts his head as he gazes at me. "Like you."

I feel an overwhelming urge to snort—which, thankfully, I manage to suppress. That might be the cheesiest thing I've ever heard, but he can get away with it. He's handsome, charming, and *really* knows how to choose a restaurant.

The waiter presents the Krug with a flourish, popping the cork and pouring us each a small glass, then hovering by the table. It's then that I realize we are supposed to taste it and give our approval. As if I'd ever send back a three hundred dollar bottle of champagne.

Raising the glass to my lips, I take a sip of the cool liquid and let the bubbles fizz on my tongue. I wait to be blown-

away by how extravagant and decadent it tastes but—
honestly?—I couldn't tell this from a bottle of the Costco
sparkling cider my mom likes to drink. But when I look up
the waiter is watching me with anticipation, so I give him a
meaningful nod.

I glance at Shane and he does the same. "That's great,
thanks."

Phew. Got that right.

"Fantastic," the waiter says, straightening up. "Your first
course will be out shortly." He pivots on his heel and
heads off.

"Our first course?" I look at Shane, puzzled. "But we
haven't ordered."

He winks. "I took care of it. The menu is a prix fixe with
only a few options, and I chose the best. You'll love it." He
says the words "prix fixe" with a flawless French accent and I
would be impressed, if it weren't for the words that followed.
Because a guy choosing my food for me? That pisses me off,
big time.

I begin to protest, but his lips tip into a warm, sexy smile
and I clamp my mouth shut. He's trying to be thoughtful,
isn't he? Besides, it's kind of nice having someone else take
care of things for a change. And he *is* paying for everything,
so I shouldn't complain.

"That sounds great." I brush my hand against his arm as
I reach for my glass of champagne. "Thank you."

The waiter arrives with two plates, setting them down
between our cutlery, without saying anything more than,
"Enjoy." On the plate is a cast-iron dish with small holes in
it, like a small muffin tray, each hole filled with something
green.

When I glance over at Shane, he's tucking into his green
stuff eagerly, so I pick up my fork. I've never been into

eating unusual food, and I don't know what this is. Some kind of spinach? That's probably okay; spinach I can handle.

I take a deep breath and raise a fork-load of it to my mouth. The taste is... interesting. But it's definitely not spinach; the texture is wrong. It's kind of slimy, a little chewy, a bit salty. I'm sure it's nothing strange, but the fact that I don't know what I'm eating is making me a little uneasy.

I give Shane an enthusiastic smile, making sure to keep my lips together because my teeth are undoubtedly green. A swig of the champagne washes it down nicely. "Um, are you enjoying your..." I leave the sentence hanging, hoping he'll fill the rest in. I don't want to ask outright, in case he thinks I'm some kind of destitute loser who doesn't eat at French-inspired restaurants very often.

"Scotch snails?" Shane supplies. "Yes. So good."

I freeze in horror, feeling the smile vanish from my face. Snails? He ordered me *snails*? On our first date? Is this some kind of joke?

Whoops. I'm not doing a very good job of keeping it together, because he pauses, fork halfway to his mouth, a little frown gathering between his brows. "Have you not had scotch sea snails before?"

Sea snails?! Holy fuck. They're not even your garden-variety snails—they're from the freaking sea. Who wants to eat these? *Why*?

I contort my face into a joyless smile—it's the best I can manage under the circumstances—and stab my fork into another snail, lifting it to my mouth.

I know I have a choice here; he's hardly forcing them down my throat. But I'm going to take the high road and *not* ruin this date, in this spectacular restaurant with this gorgeous man, simply because I'm feeling squeamish over what is, apparently, a normal thing for someone to eat.

"Oh, I have," I say breezily. "It's just... been a while." I pop another snail in my mouth and chew, forcing myself to stay calm, wishing my taste buds would shut down. *It's just a snail*, I tell myself. It's not like I'm eating an eyeball or, say, the fetus of a small mammal. But who knows? They could be next.

Each mouthful is followed by a healthy slug of champagne, and somehow—God knows how—I manage to get the snails down. Then I push my plate away, delicately dabbing at the corners of my mouth with my napkin. That was horrendous.

When I glance up, Shane is giving me another sexy smile, and guilt swirls through me. So I had to eat a few snails on our first date? Big deal. This can just be a funny story we tell one day.

Our second course arrives, and I'm overcome with relief when I see it's steak—just normal, run-of-the-mill, old-fashioned beef. No frogs' legs, no tentacles—not a sea creature in sight. And it's good.

After dinner, we wander out onto the terrace to overlook the city. It's beautiful; the Empire State Building glittering in the blush of dusk, the distant hum of traffic a familiar soundtrack, the warm evening air reminding us we're on the cusp of summer. Shane turns to me, pulling me close, and before I have a chance to take a breath or grab a mint, his lips land on mine in a warm kiss.

And it's... nice. I don't know if it's the snails, or the fact that I've had a few glasses of champagne or what, but it's more of a slow-burning kiss than a fireworks-exploding kiss. But that's okay, because—assuming he wants to see me again—we have plenty of time to get there.

When he pulls away, his eyes are dark and his cheeks are a little flushed. God, he is one good-looking guy, I'll give him that.

"You want to come back to my place?" he murmurs, sliding his hands down to my waist.

I inhale, drawing on my reserves of self-control. It's been a good year since I last had sex, and I *do* want to go back to his place. I'd be quite happy to enjoy that gorgeous body of his for a few hours.

But I've got my eye on a prize here. I've got the endgame in mind. And I know that sleeping with a guy on the first date is a sure-fire way to mess things up. That's why it's one of my rules.

I make myself take a step back, tilting my face up to his and pulling out my well-rehearsed speech. "I like you, Shane. I've had a nice time tonight. But I don't go home with guys on the first date. I'm looking for something more, and I hope you are, too."

He folds his arms, considering this. It's at this point that a guy does one of three things: throws his hands up in exasperation and takes off; pretends he's okay with it but totally ghosts me later; or genuinely understands and respects it. The latter is hard to come by.

But Shane nods, giving me a sincere smile. "Okay. You're going to make me work for it. I can respect that."

I stand up on my toes to give him a quick kiss. "Thanks. I appreciate it."

He eyes me for a moment longer, then places his hand on the small of my back, gently steering me inside toward the elevator.

"Thanks for this evening," I say, once we're out on the street. "It was great."

"It was." He pulls me close for another kiss, and his

breath smells like the banana mousse he had for dessert. "I'll text you soon."

As we part ways and I head toward the Fulton Street subway, I can't help but grin. Shane is basically the embodiment of everything I want in a man—and he doesn't break rule number three. I'm excited to do this again.

You know, without the snails.

11

"Any more disaster dates?" Alex asks over her glass of wine.

I pry my eyes away from the bar, where Cory, Eddy and Josie have been slammed all evening, and lean back against the booth. "No. Actually, I had a great date last night."

"Ooh!" Geoff leans forward. "Tell!"

"His name is Shane. He's tall, hot—"

"Picture!" Geoff cries, reaching for my purse.

I laugh and pull my phone out, bringing up Shane's picture. Geoff and Alex lean over the screen in stunned silence.

"Holy shit," Geoff whispers. "He *is* hot."

Alex nods vigorously. "Good work."

I can't help my big grin. "He took me to La Bouffe—you know that restaurant downtown that's on the sixtieth floor?"

"Wow." Alex's eyes widen. "I've heard about that place. Was it amazing?"

"Uh... yeah. It was great."

Geoff gives me an odd look. "What was that?"

"What?"

"It doesn't sound like it was great."

I flap a hand. "Oh, it was. It was just a bit fancy. Like, they serve snails and stuff."

"Snails?" Alex's face turns green. "You didn't order them, though, right?"

"Er..."

"You did?!" Geoff gapes at me. "You never eat strange food. What possessed you to do that?"

I glance between my friends, gnawing on my lip. I wasn't planning to tell them that Shane ordered for me, because I know how that will go down. But they weren't there—they won't understand that it made sense with the set menu and everything. "I just... wanted to try something different. Oh, and you should have *seen* the champagne he ordered."

"Expensive?" Geoff guesses.

"Like, unnecessarily so."

"Well, he was obviously trying to impress you."

"Yeah." I feel my mouth pull into a smile as I stir my drink. It's been a long time since a guy went out of his way to impress me, and it was nice.

"So, he's rich," Alex says.

I shrug, as if it hadn't occurred to me. He is pretty well-off, that's obvious. But I'm not going to get together with a guy just because of that.

"Wow." Geoff straightens his glasses, looking impressed. "So when's the wedding?"

"Ha ha. We've had one date, Geoff. I'm not Alex." I throw her a good-natured grin and she smirks.

"Did you sleep with him?"

"No!"

Alex gestures at something over my shoulder, but I'm thinking back to last night, to the amazing self-control I demonstrated.

"It was tough," I continue. "It's been ages—at *least* a year —since I had sex. Seriously—"

"Cat—"

"—I'm *dying* over here. The sooner I can have sex with Shane the better. But—"

I hear a throat clear beside me and I turn, my eyes landing on Myles.

Oh, oh shit.

Mortification washes over me in hot waves, and I grimace, looking down at the table. I don't know why I'm so embarrassed—it's just Myles. Who cares what he thinks?

I do, apparently. And now I could just *die*.

"Hi," I mumble, trying to ignore the heat I can feel spreading across my neck. "I didn't know you were there." I wait for him to offer some funny quip, or for his cheeks to push into his usual self-assured grin, but when I look up he's staring at the table and the tips of his ears are pink.

"Sorry, didn't mean to interrupt." He rubs the back of his neck, not meeting my gaze. "Just wanted to see if you needed more drinks."

"We do," Geoff says, leaning across the table toward Myles. "We'll take another round, please."

Myles gives a quick nod and spins on his heel, heading back to the bar. He can't get away fast enough.

The air rushes out of my lungs as I drop my head into my hands. *Why* did he have to overhear me rant about my sex life? That was hideous.

When I glance up, Alex and Geoff are gazing at me. "What?" I ask, pressing my cool glass to my hot cheek.

A smile tugs at Geoff's lips. "Who was that?"

"That's Myles, the new bartender." I let my eyes wander to where he is behind the bar, mixing me a vodka soda. His gaze collides with mine and he quickly looks away. I shift on the vinyl seat of the booth, uncomfortable.

"What just happened?" Alex cocks her head. "You got super awkward."

"What? No I didn't." I utter a strained laugh and they stare at me dubiously. "Well, you know..." I scratch my arm. "That was kind of embarrassing. He heard me say I haven't had sex in a year and I'm dying to sleep with Shane."

"So?" Geoff leans over to get another look at Myles. "Do you have a thing for him? Because I can totally see that."

"No, Geoff." I roll my eyes. "I'm dating Shane, remember? Besides, Myles is *way* too similar to Mark. You know I don't date guys like that anymore."

"Right," he says, watching me over his glass of merlot. "How is he similar to Mark, exactly? Okay, they both have tattoos, but otherwise—"

"It's more than that. He's a bartender, like Mark was. He flirts with anything that walks. Honestly, watching him work is like being back at the bar with Mark. Even their *names* are similar."

Geoff opens his mouth to respond when Cory appears at the booth with our tray of drinks.

Oh, God. I embarrassed poor Myles so much that he couldn't even face coming back over. This isn't good.

Cory unloads our drinks then slides into the booth beside me. "Have you been avoiding me? I sent you a bunch of texts."

I reach for my vodka and take a long sip. "Yes."

"Why?"

"Because you told Myles I was having trouble with my business and asked him to help, and it made me feel pathetic."

Cory crosses his arms over his broad chest, his forehead scrunching. "No. He asked me what was wrong and I just told him the landlord raised your rent. That's all I said." He pauses, looking at the others then back to me. "He's helping you?"

Alex leans forward, placing a hand on my arm. "You're having trouble with the store? Why didn't you say something?"

I lift a shoulder. "Mark raised the rent and I thought I was going to have to close, but Myles had a cool idea to rebrand and open a store online, selling my own designs." I smile, thinking of him in the store the other day, convincing me to dream bigger with my business. "He's going to help me build something new."

Geoff grins. "That's fantastic! See? I said you need to do more with your designs."

"Yeah. I'm really excited about it, actually."

I glance at Cory. There's a deep V between his brows and his gaze is trained on Myles. Eventually it swings back to me and he puffs out a breath. "There's nothing going on with you guys, right?"

I chuckle at the way Cory has slipped into protective big brother mode. "No, Cors, I swear. He's just helping me out. And it couldn't have come a moment sooner." I scan Cory's concerned face, then add, "I'm actually seeing someone—a guy named Shane."

"He took her to La Bouffe," Geoff chips in helpfully.

"Really?" Cory's eyebrows spring up. "Woah."

I grin, sipping my drink, feeling fancy.

"Well, that's great. Just... don't get involved with Myles."

Déjà vu sends a shiver over my skin. I remember all too clearly the bar downtown all those years ago, where Cory worked with Mark and told me he was bad news—and I got together with him anyway.

"What's wrong with Myles?" Geoff asks.

Cory's eyes narrow. "I've just heard some things about him. Plus he hits on women left, right and center."

I snort with amusement. "So do you."

"Well, yeah," he admits, giving a guilty laugh. "But... I'm not dating you. You don't want a guy like that, trust me." Cory's gaze locks with mine and I swallow hard. We were sitting in this exact booth when Cory told me he'd seen Mark out in the East Village with another woman. I try to stop the memory but it floods onto the screen inside my brain, forcing me to watch it play out again.

"I'm so sorry," Cory had said. He took my hand, squeezing it hard. "I wish I didn't have to tell you this, but you need to know."

My heart took a nosedive as I tried to ignore the panic weaving through me. "Maybe it wasn't what you think," I'd said. It was pathetic, the way I so desperately clung to a tiny thread of hope. But even before Cory responded, I knew the answer.

"It was. I know what I saw."

Cory's tone made my blood run cold. I'd always had my suspicions about Mark, especially after I'd caught him at the bar all those years before, but I'd just told myself I was being paranoid.

But as Cory took me home and sat with me while I confronted Mark, everything unraveled. Apparently it wasn't his first affair, though I don't know how many there were. I didn't dare ask; I just sat on the sofa, numb with shock, while Cory yelled at Mark to get the fuck out before he broke every bone in his body.

And the next day when Mark came home to collect his things and begged me to reconsider, I dug deep inside and found a reserve of inner strength I didn't know I had. I told him I was divorcing him and I was keeping the apartment, then I swore to myself that I would *never* let this happen to me again.

My gaze drifts to Myles now, where he's chatting up a woman sitting alone at the bar—a scene so familiar I shudder. I know better than to get involved with a guy like him. You don't make that mistake twice.

"I wouldn't, Cors. After Mark... I wouldn't." I push all images of Mark from my brain. "Besides, I'm excited about Shane. I have a good feeling about him."

Cory puts an arm around my shoulder. "I'm glad, sis," he says, squeezing. Then he heads back to the bar.

We sip our drinks, watching the crowd slowly gather on the dance floor as the DJ turns the music up. After a while, Alex and Geoff go and dance, but I stay in the booth, enjoying my—fourth?—drink. Ah, it doesn't matter. Things are turning around for me. I've met a cute guy who takes me out to nice dinners, and I've got a friend who's helping me regain control of my business and escape my ex-husband.

Actually, do I still have that? I hope I didn't weird Myles out with all that talk about how much sex I'm not having. He seemed strangely disturbed by that information.

I watch him work, serving customers without much chatter, just getting through the crowd. Finally, there's a lull and I wave my arm, trying to catch his attention. But it's like he's avoiding me or something; no matter what I do, he won't look my way. Why can't he see me flailing my arms over here?

I pull out my phone and scroll through my contacts. We exchanged numbers to set up a time to work on the site, but we haven't been in contact yet. Now is as good a time as any. I press his name and watch as he pulls his phone out, glances at the screen with a frown, then raises his eyes to mine. I smile, gesturing for him to join me. With a glance up and down the bar, he reluctantly wanders over. He motions to the empty glasses scattered on the table, saying something I can't hear over the music.

"What?" I bellow.

He leans closer. "You want me to clear these?"

"You think that's why I called you over?"

He shrugs, still leaning close, gaze averted.

"Myles, sit down."

He hesitates, then slides into the booth beside me. Placing his elbows on the table, he stares straight ahead, not saying anything.

What is going on with him? I've never seen him like this.

"Is everything okay?" I ask.

He gestures to his ear to indicate that he can't hear me. The music is pumping, the dance floor is heaving, and I'm going to have to yell to be heard.

I grab his arm, pulling him closer so my mouth is right by his ear. "I'm sorry about before. That was embarrassing."

He gives a tiny nod, eyes fixed out on the dance floor somewhere. I follow his gaze and the room swims a little. His bicep flexes under my hand as he shifts his weight. He's still being weird and I don't like it.

I lean in toward his ear again. "I didn't mean for you to overhear me. I don't make a habit of telling people I haven't had sex in forever."

He turns to me now, his face inches from mine. For the

first time I notice he has a tiny freckle on his left cheek and my fingertips tingle with the urge to reach up and touch it.

"That's not... I mean, I didn't—" he breaks off, turning away again. His jaw is set, his brow is furrowed. I realize I haven't seen him smile all evening.

I sag back against the booth, raking a hand through my hair. I don't know what I've done to annoy him, but really, this is none of his business. What does he care?

He turns to me again, his steel-blue eyes sharp in the dim light. "So you'll be sleeping with Shane soon, then?"

I'm taken aback by the bluntness of his question, my head already clouded and fuzzy. "Well, yeah, but not for a while. Can't give it all away too soon," I say, chortling at my own joke and hoping to see a smile crack his flinty facade.

But Myles simply nods once, his eyes darting over my face. "That guy..." He shakes his head then leans a lot closer. "Just make sure he deserves you." As he speaks, his lips brush over my ear and goosebumps erupt across my skin. A pleasant feeling rolls through me, settling over my thighs.

Shit, I must have drunk a *lot* more than I realized. It's the only explanation I can give for the way I feel light-headed and breathless all of a sudden.

I pull back, trying to shake off the sensation. Dragging my eyes up to his, I expect to see that self-satisfied smile on his mouth, but it's not there. His dark, piercing gaze is unsettling.

An uneasy laugh rushes up my throat as I reach for a glass of water. "I will," I say, gulping the water down. Ah, that's better. All that vodka was making me woozy.

Cory walks past the booth and Myles glances at him, pulling away from me. "I'll come by the shop tomorrow and we'll work on the site?" he yells over the music.

"Sounds good." I smile, relieved to finally see his lips lift into a smile too.

He stands and clears the table, then heads back to the bar without looking at me again. I gulp down another glass of water, trying to get my head on straight. Because I didn't like that odd sensation I just felt one bit.

12

I can't believe it—Hayley's fliers worked. I've had loads of customers already, so much so that I've hardly had time to sit at my sewing machine. But I don't mind; I've sold more this morning than I have any morning these past few months.

I'm so rushed off my feet that I almost forget Myles is coming to work on the site before he goes to Bounce later. When he pushes into the store, his eyebrows shoot up. He has to actually squeeze between customers to get up to the counter.

"Hey!" He slides onto a stool, pulling his messenger bag off his shoulder. "It's packed in here."

"I know!" I'm practically beaming as I wrap some pants for a customer.

Myles leans toward the woman, wearing his trademark grin. "We're going to be opening an online store soon."

She smiles. "Oh, that's cool."

He pulls a sheet of paper and pen from his bag, sliding it over. "If you're interested, put your email address down here and we'll let you know when it launches."

She adds her email, then reaches for the bag from my outstretched hand. "Thanks."

"Have a great day!" I turn to Myles with a chuckle as the woman walks away. "We'd better get to work if you're going to start telling people about us already."

"We are." He gestures to the sheet of paper. "Get people to put their email addresses down there, and we'll create a mailing list. That's the best place to start." He pulls his laptop from his bag and sets it down across his knees. "That way when it's time to launch, you've already got a whole bunch of people waiting to buy from you."

"Huh," I say, running my eyes over him. Today he's in his usual faded jeans and a fitted crimson T-shirt, his black cap perched high on his head, tilted up so a few curls peek out the front. I'm still finding it jarring to hear him say stuff like that. He looks like a skateboarder, or something—not like someone with an MBA.

He glances up at me and his mouth slants into a smile. "Also, I had a thought." Placing his laptop onto the counter, he stands, gesturing to the rack of my designs. "May I?"

I nod, curious.

He takes a moment to look around, waiting for a break in the flow of customers. Then he wheels the rack up the store toward the front, shuffling a bunch of shoes and a hat stand out the way, positioning my rack of clothes front and center. He steps away to inspect his handiwork, then wanders back to the counter. "I want you to stop hiding those all the way down the back."

I raise my hands to my hips. "I wasn't—"

"Yeah, you were." He takes his cap off and places it onto the counter, raking a hand through his hair. "But we're building your new brand around your work, so let's make it the focus of your store. If you keep being this busy you'll run out of vintage stuff soon enough anyway. Keep building up your designs and we'll work with those."

I glance over at my rack of clothes and feel an uneasy pang in my gut. They're the first thing a customer will see when they enter the store now, and for some reason that makes me a little nervous. Look, I know they're good—I know I'm a good designer and seamstress. But it's hard to put your creations in someone's face and hope they'll love them as much as you.

Still, Myles is right. This is the future of my business and it's time to embrace it.

"Fine," I relent.

A pair of young women enter the store and I hold my breath. They flick through the rack of my designs, and one of them pulls a dress out to show the other. They both ooh and ahh over it.

Myles looks at me, triumphant. "See?"

I offer him a tiny smile. "I see."

One of the women approaches the counter, holding out the dress of mine. "Do you have fitting rooms?"

"Yeah, they're downstairs. I'll show you." I lead her down to the basement and into one of the cramped, dank stalls. God, the sooner I can get out of here, the better. I never noticed before how awful it is down here. It's amazing what you put up with when you think you have no other choice.

I head back upstairs to find the other woman writing her email address down for Myles. As she wanders off to find her friend, I chuckle. "You know, I think it helps having *you* here asking for their emails. You'll get twice as many as I would without you."

"Oh yeah?" He gives me his cocky bartender smile. "Why's that?"

"You know why."

"No," he says, eyes dancing. "What do you mean?"

I shake my head. He knows damn well what I mean, he just wants to hear me say it.

"I'm really confused, Cat." He continues to gaze at me, lips twitching. "I have no idea what you're talking about."

I fight a smile, reaching for a crumpled shirt on the counter and sliding it onto a hanger.

"Ohhh, I get it. It's because I'm so cute." He puffs out his chest, grinning from ear to ear, and I can't help but laugh.

"*So* cute," I say, my voice heavy with sarcasm.

"I knew you thought so." He looks back down at his laptop and, despite knowing better, I let my eyes track over him—over the muscular curve of his shoulders, the scruff lining his jaw, the concentration on his face as he works. My gaze lingers on his curls, messy in the kind of way that makes me want to push my fingers into them and tug.

His gaze flies up to mine again, catching me mid-stare. I feel like I've been caught doing something I shouldn't, and my cheeks warm as little creases form around his eyes.

"I don't hear you denying it..." he teases.

"This is gorgeous, I'll take it."

I pull my gaze away from Myles, to the customer standing at the counter. She's holding up a fifties pin-up dress, fitted through the body down to the knee, thick halter straps, black polka dots. She's right: it is gorgeous.

I take the dress from her to wrap it. "I'm so glad you like it. It's one of my designs."

"Oh, wow," she says, handing me cash. "I wish you had more of them."

I hazard a glance at Myles. As expected, his mouth is curved in a smug smile. Then he pushes the paper across the counter toward the girl.

"I've already got your friend's email address. I'd love

yours too." He gives her a flirtatious grin, handing her a pen. "It's for the launch of our online store," he adds, almost as an afterthought.

I stifle a snort as she giggles, blushes, and writes her email down. Then I hand her the dress with a smile. "I'll have more designs online soon."

"Great, thanks." Her eyes flit to Myles, who has now fixed his attention back on his laptop. Poor girl, she doesn't seem to realize what a menace men like him can be.

When they've left and I turn back to Myles with a smirk —only to find him deeply engrossed in his work—I feel a ripple of guilt. He might be infuriating around women, but it's not fair to call him a menace. The truth is, if he wasn't here helping me, I'd be royally fucked. I'm hit by a sudden wave of gratitude for his kindness and generosity, and I smile to myself as I tidy and straighten up the store, surprised to find I'm in a great mood.

The cherry on top comes when my phone buzzes with a text from Shane.

Shane: Hey babe, hope you're having a good day. Can't wait to take you out again soon.

There's a little thrill through me as I read his words. Granted, I don't love him calling me "babe," especially after only one date. But I can't believe how lucky I am to have met someone like him—and on Tinder, no less. Talk about a needle in a haystack.

Still, I deserve this. I've waited for ages, refusing to settle, and now I've met a fantastic guy. This is my reward for sticking to my rules.

I grin as I wander back toward the counter, reaching absently for the duster. I have a good feeling about Shane and where this could go.

"What are you so happy about?" Myles asks without

looking up from his laptop. Sometimes it feels like he's got a sixth sense.

"Oh, I just got a text from Shane." I dust along the counter, humming to myself. When Myles doesn't say anything, I glance back at him, noticing his jaw is tense.

He looks up at me and his expression softens. "That's... great."

I fiddle with the duster, remembering our conversation in Bounce last night. It stirs an odd feeling in my chest. "You really don't like him, do you?"

Myles frowns. "What? I don't even know him."

"Exactly. So I'm not sure why this is a problem."

"It's not."

I eye him, wondering whether or not to remind him of last night. Probably best to leave it, I decide, and return to my dusting.

Over the next hour we get another rush of customers, and Myles works in the corner on his stool, occasionally asking people to sign up to our mailing list. I sell a couple more of my designs and I can't help but feel thrilled each time. Myles was right; they do sell better when I put them somewhere people can easily see them. It makes me more excited for my online store.

When the rush finally dies down, I make some coffee and take a seat at the counter beside Myles, happy to be off my feet for five minutes. It's good to be busy, but it's exhausting. It also means that I don't get to use any time during the day to work on creating new pieces. I'll have to work tonight to get some more of my own designs out on the rack for tomorrow.

"Can we talk about stuff for the site now?" Myles asks.

"Sure."

"Okay, let's start with values. What are your business values?"

I scratch my head. "Um... money?"

He chuckles. "Sure. But that's the same for all businesses. What is important to your business? What makes your business unique?" When I don't answer, he tries again. "Okay, how about this. What matters to you?"

"What *matters* to me?"

"Yeah. This is your business, we're building it based on your values. What matters to you more than anything?"

"Honesty," I blurt.

He nods, noting that down.

Before I can stop myself, more words tumble out. "Integrity, trustworthiness, loyalty, reliability—" I pause. I'm not sure if this is what he means, but these are the first things that come to mind.

"I'm sensing a theme here."

A bitter laugh slips out my mouth. "Yeah, well, when your dad walks out on your family, then your husband cheats on you, then your best friend stabs you in the back... you start to develop trust issues."

He stops typing, looking up at me. "Shit." His mouth opens, as if to say more, but he closes it again and fastens his gaze back on the screen.

It's quiet for a moment. A car horn sounds outside and I stare across the empty store, feeling exposed. Why the hell did I say all that?

"Maybe," Myles says, clearly trying to be delicate, "something a little more upbeat?"

I give him a wry smile. "What, tales of my abandonment and betrayal aren't upbeat enough?"

He laughs gently. "Well, let's think about what sort of feeling we are trying to create with the brand."

I reach for my mug of coffee. "Okay. I want it to feel fun and playful. You know, like it's not taking itself too seriously. And sort of nostalgic." I take a long sip, thinking some more. "Flirty, sexy, feminine."

"Great, this is good. And what's your mission? What are you trying to achieve?"

"Um..." I gaze down into my coffee. "I'm trying to get women to buy clothes?"

His eyes flick up to mine again, shimmering with mirth, and I know he wants me to be more specific.

"Okay," I say, straightening up as I think. "I guess I want my clothes to make people feel good—to make them feel cute. But it's more than that. I want them to feel like they stand out, like they're wearing something different from what every other damn store sells. Like, I don't care about fashion trends or whatever. I care about self-expression—about using your clothes to show the world who you are and how you feel."

The bell on the door trills as it opens and Stevie's little body squeezes through the gap. I feel a rush of joy at the sight of her, tempered with dread as the familiar figure steps in behind.

"Mark," I say warily as he approaches the counter.

"Hey." He nods, then looks at Myles. "Niles, wasn't it?"

Myles spits out a laugh, glancing up from his laptop. "Myles. But I like Niles, actually."

I smother a smile, impressed by the way he took Mark's attempt at a jab and immediately diffused it.

Mark grunts a sardonic laugh toward Myles, then hands Stevie's leash to me. "Did you get Claudia's email?"

"No," I say, pulling my phone out. Claudia Cooper is a friend of ours. Well, she and her husband were friends with me and Mark—and a wider group—when we were

married. I really liked Claudia, though her husband Andy
was kind of a dick. Even though they were mutual friends,
it felt like Mark got to "keep" them in the divorce and I've
always been annoyed by it. Claudia and I have been in
touch, but it's not quite the same. I don't have a lot in
common with her, if I'm honest. But it's about the
principle.

Scanning through my inbox, I spot an invitation to a
dinner party at her place in a few weeks. I glance up at
Mark. "So?"

"Are you going to go?"

"Probably not." She's invited us both to dinner parties in
the past, asking us to bring dates, insisting we could all be
adults and enjoy each other's company. It's like she's
forgotten what happened between me and Mark, or
something.

Mark deflates with relief. "Okay, cool. Because Mel
thought it might be awkward if we both went."

Irritation prickles across my skin. "Oh, did she?" Maybe
if she wasn't fucking my ex-husband things wouldn't be so
awkward. Did she ever think of that?

Mark jams his hands into his jeans pockets. "Well, yeah.
And she'd like to go."

"Oh, *would she*?" I say through gritted teeth. Now I wish I
had a partner I could take, just to make them feel uncomfortable. Because it's not fair that Mel gets to go and take my
place—gets to be friends with people who used to be my
friends.

And then it dawns on me. Of course! I have Shane. Well,
I don't *have* him, exactly, but I'm quite certain I will soon if
that "babe" is anything to go by. And, boy, he's a catch. He'd
be great to show off, with his nice watch and expensive
haircut and sexy smile. He'd fit in well with that crowd, in

Claudia's Upper East Side townhouse. It could show them all that I've moved on—and moved on in style.

I twirl my phone in my hand, thinking. Is it worth the awkwardness of seeing Mel for an evening to make her feel jealous? Is it worth going just to piss Mark off?

Yes. Yes it is.

"You know what," I say, bringing the email up on my phone again, "I think I will go."

Mark's brow furrows. "Really?"

I type out a quick reply and send it off, then slide my phone back into my pocket. "Yes. I'll bring my new boyfriend, Shane. I'm sure he'd love to come." Beside me I see Myles's eyebrows go up, but I ignore him.

Mark cocks his head. "You have a new boyfriend?"

"Mm," I say noncommittally, reaching for my coffee on the counter.

"Right. Well... we are still going to go."

"Of course." I give him a bland smile, raising my cup to my lips. "I'm sure we can all be adults about it."

He regards me skeptically.

"Is that it? I have work to do, Mark." I'm itching to tell him that we've been swamped all day, that Myles and I are building something that's going to be bigger than this tiny little space in the East Village, that their plan to put me out of business isn't going to work. But I don't. He'll find out in due time.

"Yeah, okay. Catch you later."

Once he's gone, I let out a long sigh, realizing it's the first time I've actually felt *better* after seeing him. Most of the time I feel a little more worn down—and a lot angrier. But not today.

I turn toward the counter to pick up Stevie for a cuddle, and when I see where she is, a laugh bubbles up in my chest. Myles is cradling Stevie in his arms, on her back, like a baby. I think back to what he told me the last time he was in here; that he has a *daughter*. He once held a tiny baby in his arms, just like that. I try to picture it but the image won't form properly in my mind.

I remember, suddenly, his suggestion to create a children's line. That unicorn print *would* look great on a little girl's dress, as well as some of the other prints I have. There's mountains of fabric in the basement—there might be something in there I could use to create a dress for his daughter. And since I can't afford to pay him right now, maybe that could be my way of showing my appreciation for everything he's doing for me. Not to mention it would be fun to create a range of dresses for kids. Why didn't I think of that before?

Myles lifts his eyes to mine. "So Shane's your boyfriend now?"

I clear my throat. "Not really, no." I'm about to explain that he *will* be, but for some reason I feel compelled to stop there.

Myles turns his attention back to Stevie, scratching under her chin while she turns to jelly in his hands. I watch him, trying to make sense of the way the atmosphere has shifted between us all of a sudden. I'm relieved when he sets Stevie down and slides his laptop into his bag.

"I'd better get ready for work. Will I see you at the bar later?"

"No. Once Hayley gets here, I'm going to head home and work on some more pieces."

He nods, resting his gaze on me. "Okay. Then maybe... do you want to come to my place tomorrow night?"

I blink. "Uh..."

"To work on the site," he clarifies, an amused smile nudging his mouth. "I hardly had a chance to talk to you, and we have a lot to figure out. It might be better to do it somewhere quiet."

"Oh, right." My cheeks heat and I turn so he can't see, pretending to busy myself with a scarf. For one stupid second, I thought he was asking me to come over to...

Anyway.

"Yeah," I say. "That's a good idea. I want to get the website up and running as soon as possible."

The bell at the door rings and I glance up to see Hayley enter. Today her long hair is wound up into two buns on top of her head, like Mickey Mouse ears. She drops her purse onto a stool, turning to Myles with a bright smile. "Hi. I'm Hayley."

"Myles." He slings his messenger bag over his shoulder and extends his hand.

"Oh *you're* Myles. Cat mentioned you."

His lips quirk into a smile, his playful gaze sliding to me. "Did she now?"

"Yes." I resist the urge to roll my eyes at what he's implying. "I told her you're going to help me save the store."

"Well, of course." He grins as he saunters past. "What else would you have told her?"

Hayley snickers beside me and I cut her a look.

"See you tomorrow night," Myles says with a chuckle.

"So, I have an idea." Hayley turns to me eagerly as the door closes behind Myles. "I want you to come and look at the East Village Market Collective with me."

"What? Why?"

"Well, I was thinking. Since you're going to be getting most of your customers from online soon, you're not going to need a big shop space. Maybe a permanent booth in the market would do."

"Huh," I say, turning this over. The EVMC is a seven-day

market that runs in an old industrial building a few blocks away. It's filled with all kinds of funky booths, selling art, crafts, beauty products, organic food—you name it. She's right, actually; a booth there could work. I'd never considered that.

"The only problem is the booths aren't huge," Hayley continues. "So you'd want to use all the space for your dresses. There's nowhere for your sewing machine and stuff."

"I could keep it at home," I hear myself say. "I could do my sewing and store the other things at home. I have space in my living room." I pause, thinking. "Do you want to keep working with me—with my designs?"

"Definitely. I know things are probably going to change once we're out of here, but your stuff is gorgeous, Cat. I'm so inspired every time you bring something new out."

Pride glows in my chest at her words. "I need to focus on sewing, not running a booth. And when I'm not sewing, I'll have my hands full managing the online store." I take a deep breath. "If we can get this booth—if it's right for us—how would you like to run it, full-time? I know you have a lot going on, and you like your freedom, but—"

"Yes," she says, a smile breaking over her face. "I'd love to run it. Would you really trust me to do that?"

"Of course, if I can make it work financially. And we have to make sure we can even *get* a booth; there's probably a bit of competition. But we do need to start making plans to move out of here, and I think the booth is a great idea."

She bounces on the spot, beaming. "I knew it! This could totally work."

I grin, feeling an odd sense of relief. I haven't wanted to think about the next move, instead focusing on clearing our vintage stock and making new stuff. But this is the perfect solution.

"So..." Hayley turns to straighten up the display table in front of the counter. "Myles is cute. Seems like your type, too."

I give a huff of amusement. "Uh, why?"

"You know. The tattoos, the clothes, the hair. Like Mark." She lifts a shoulder, as if it's obvious.

"Yes, well. That might have been my type in the past," I say. I ignore the unusual twinge in my stomach as I add, "But it's definitely not anymore."

13

———

Myles lives in a basement apartment out on Avenue D, Alphabet City. It's—well, I'm not going to lie—it's a bit of a dump, at least from the outside. There's graffiti all down the side of the building and a collection of trash cans right on his doorstep. As I climb down the steps and knock on the door, I can't help but wonder if I should have suggested we meet at my place. But he's doing all this work for me, for free, so it's only fair that I come out here. I owe him, big time.

I glance down at where I'm clutching my hands together, empty. Should I have brought something? A bottle of wine, maybe?

No, that would be stupid. It's not like this is a party, or anything. This is... something else. This is a work thing.

The door swings open and Myles gives me an easy grin. "Hey."

"Hi," I say, stepping past him into the apartment. I'm hit by the smell of a fresh, zesty cologne, like he's just spritzed himself. My eyes sweep around the space, taking it all in. And by "all" I mean, well, not a whole lot.

It's a studio, and it's pretty small—though it's not as bad inside as I thought it would be. With eggshell-white walls and hardwood flooring, it's surprisingly bright and clean. But it's so sparse: down the back there's a bed sitting on a bunch of wooden pallets tucked behind a partition wall, opposite a beat-up dresser. On the wall beside the bed he's pinned a map of the USA, and underneath it is a yoga mat and a meditation cushion. In the living space to my right, there's a single thread-bare sofa and an ottoman with a couple of books sitting on top. To my left is a small kitchen that looks like it hasn't been touched. Afternoon light spills in from the windows behind us, giving the whole place a sort of ethereal glow. He doesn't even have curtains.

"Do you want a drink?" he asks, wandering into the kitchen.

"Sure." I turn back to him, frowning. "Are you moving, or something?"

"What?" He emits a bewildered laugh, taking two bottles of water from the fridge. "No."

"Where's all your stuff?"

He glances around the room. "This is my stuff. I don't own much."

"Oh." I feel a pang of sympathy. It hadn't occurred to me that he might not make much working at Bounce. No wonder he flirts his ass off for extra tips. Guilt gnaws at me as I think about the fact that he's doing all this work for me for free, when he could probably use the money.

He tilts his head, examining my expression. "What?"

"Uh—" I blush, hoping my thoughts aren't evident on my face. "Nothing." That's it, I decide; as soon as I can afford it, I'm going to start paying him for his work. No one should have to live without decent furniture and curtains. This isn't a home.

I take my bottled water and wander around, casting my eyes over his few belongings. When I get to the yoga mat and cushion, I glance back with a smile. "You're really into the meditation and yoga thing, huh?"

"Yep." He hauls himself up onto the kitchen island, dangling his legs. "Have you gone to any more classes?"

I shake my head.

"You should," he urges. "It's tough at first but it's so powerful. It helps to clear your mind, so you can hear yourself."

"I hear myself just fine," I mutter, sipping my water. I hear myself too much—my mind won't shut up.

He chuckles. "Sure, but when you meditate, you hear your *true* self. And when your true self speaks, it cuts through the bullshit. You know it's speaking the truth."

"Mm," I say, giving him a faint smile. What new-age malarkey is this?

I continue around the space, Myles watching me with interest from his perch on the counter. On the wall map I can see a bunch of marks and lines, charting some kind of journey. Turning to my left, I spot an old piano tucked behind the bedroom partition, out of sight of the door. There's a stack of large framed photographs leaning against it, as if waiting to be hung. I set my bottle down and run a finger along the closed lid of the piano. Dust gathers under my fingertip.

"That was here when I moved in," Myles says, raising his tumbler to his lips.

A sad little smile lifts my mouth as I push the lid up and plunk on a couple of the out-of-tune keys.

"You play?" He hops down off the counter and wanders over.

"My dad used to play." I'm hit with a flashback of us

sitting around the piano at Christmas, singing along to Dad's drunken mish-mash of Christmas carols. So long ago.

"Used to?" Myles asks gently, leaning on the partition wall beside me.

"Yeah." I tap another piano key. "Before he left us."

Myles is quiet, creases of compassion around his eyes.

"Well, he's dead now." I slam the piano lid shut and Myles jumps. "Heart attack. But he was pretty much dead to me the day he left." Because when you're eight and you watch your father walk out on his family knowing he's not coming back, what's the point in keeping any love for him alive?

I inhale a deep breath, forcing the memories from my brain. I don't go there often, and I'm not going to go there now.

My gaze falls to the framed photographs. They're not your usual shots of families or dogs or whatever; they're shots of the city. But it's not the city tourists see. It's details that most people miss or even try to overlook: graffiti on a brick wall, the crumbling facade around a window, a fire-escape zig-zagging down the front of a building with shattered windows.

"These are cool," I say, flicking through the frames. In the bottom corner of each is a signature: *M. Ellis.*

"Thanks." A smile peeks around the edge of his mouth. "They're mine."

"*You* took these?"

He nods, twisting the lid open on his bottled water.

"Wow." I'm both amazed by his work and stuck on this new piece of him—*Ellis. Myles Ellis.* I wordlessly roll the name around on my tongue as I crouch to look over the images again more closely. Each one has something unexpected about it that draws your focus and makes you look twice. He has a real eye for spotting beauty in the most broken, overlooked places. "You should hang these."

He shrugs. "Maybe."

I straighten up, considering giving him the same speech he gave me about hiding my dresses, but decide against it. Silence settles around us, but it's not uncomfortable. In fact, it's not nearly as bad as I thought it would be in here. It might be a bit Spartan, but it's not awful at all.

"So..." Myles gestures to his bed. "Shall we?"

I glance at the bed, then back at him, narrowing my eyes.

He laughs, pushing away from the wall and reaching to retrieve his laptop from where it is half-tucked under the comforter.

"Oh," I say on a nervous titter. "You pointed to the bed and I thought..." I gulp the rest of my words down with my water.

Shit. What the hell was that?

His eyebrows climb his forehead. "We could, if you like. I know it's been—what was it? A year?" He chuckles, wandering over to the sofa.

Heat streaks across my cheeks as I stare at him in disbelief. He's teasing me about *that*? I knew it was only a matter of time until that came up. "Fucking hell," I mutter, setting my bottle down.

He's still laughing as he opens his laptop, but when his gaze shifts back to me, he sees my embarrassment and cringes. "Sorry, I was just kidding."

I thrust my hands up into my hair, groaning in frustration. I *really* wish he hadn't heard me say that. It's like he now knows a secret weakness he can use against me.

I'm about to make some smart quip about Shane when Myles turns his laptop around to show me the screen. "Come see what I've been working on."

I stomp over and lower myself onto the sofa, making sure to keep a healthy distance between us as he hands me the laptop.

"So these are the colors I'm thinking. Fun, with a bit of a retro vibe." He leans across to scroll down. "And fonts like this."

Immediately, I forget his teasing. The colors—hot pink, turquoise and canary yellow—jump out at me from the screen. They feel like me, like my designs. And the font is retro cool, with a modern hand-lettered twist.

"I love it."

"Great." He takes the laptop back with a grin.

"How did you know?" I ask. Somehow, he's taken the feeling of my work and translated it into something tangible.

"I've gotten a feeling for who you are. But there's a lot I still need to know, like how you want the site to function and what services you're going to offer."

I rub my temples, overwhelmed. I reach absently for my water and realize I left it on the piano. Myles notices and sets his laptop down, crossing the room to get the bottle and hand it back to me. I smile gratefully and feel myself relax as he settles back beside me.

We spend the next hour talking about the site, sharing ideas and clarifying the vision for it. Every time Myles notes something down, I feel a frisson of excitement.

"So, the name of your business; Loved Again." He stops typing, tapping his chin. "Does that still make sense, now that you're not doing vintage clothes?"

"Yeah, I guess if we're moving in a different direction from the store, I should change it. I just don't know what to change it to."

"I don't need to know right now; I can build the site with a placeholder. But you'll need to think of something soon."

"Okay." I rest my head back on the sofa. It might be threadbare but it's comfortable, and I kick my feet up on the ottoman in front of us, accidentally knocking a book to the floor. I pick it up and inspect the cover: *The Power of Now* by someone called Eckhart Tolle. The blurb is all about living in the present to find inner peace, or some hippie crap like that. He's really into this stuff, isn't he?

The typing beside me stops and I turn to find Myles watching me curiously. I hold up the book with a little chuckle. "This looks... interesting."

"It is. It's about being present and escaping the ego. Most of us spend our whole lives controlled by our egos, which stops us from being content."

I nod sagely, as if he's imparting some great wisdom. But his use of the word "ego" is interesting, given he seems to have, well, a huge one. I muffle a laugh, turning the book over in my hand.

"What?"

"Well, you know." I glance at him, biting my lip to hide my smirk. "You talk about how we need to escape our egos, then you go to the bar and strut around like you're God's gift to women."

He wiggles his eyebrows playfully. "Of course I do. That's how I get the ladies to hand over their cash." He flashes me a grin and it's pure Myles, all gleaming teeth and self-confidence.

With an eye-roll I go to place the book back. *Point proven.*

"But you know," he continues, and I pause, "that doesn't mean I have a big ego. It's not like I actually think I'm hot shit. I just know how to play to the crowds."

"So you're telling me you don't believe those women think you're hot? You don't think they want you?"

A smile slowly widens his mouth. "Yeah, I mean, they do —that's why it works. But only because of the way I'm acting. I'm giving them what they want. It's all a game; there's nothing real there."

Well. That's surprisingly profound for the bartender who, just a few days ago, told three different women they were each the most beautiful ladies in Manhattan for a few extra bucks.

"You know what I mean, right?" Myles says, setting his laptop to one side. "Things like looks or status or money mean nothing, if there's no real connection—if you don't make each other laugh, care about the same things, really *understand* each other." He rakes a hand through his hair, his gaze drifting off somewhere else.

I'm not sure how the conversation has ended up here, but there's something in his eyes that makes me want to ask him more. I'm about to open my mouth when he speaks again.

"That's why all that stuff at work doesn't matter. It's just a transaction. I give the girls a little extra attention and they pay me a bit more." He lets his eyes come back to me. They roam my face for a moment, and a peculiar sensation sweeps down my spine.

"Like a prostitute," I murmur, and he barks a loud laugh.

"I guess. But I don't have to fuck random strangers."

I give him a funny look. "Wouldn't that be the best part? From what I can gather, that's what most men want."

"What?" His brows draw together. "You don't actually believe that?"

I look down, running my hands over the smooth book cover in my lap. Logically, I know it's not what all men want, of course. But it's what my dad wanted, what Mark wanted. And Cory was pretty clear about Myles being the same type of guy.

"I'm hungry," I say, desperate to change the subject. "Are we done? I might head off and get something to eat."

He reaches over to close his laptop with a heavy exhalation. "Yeah. But..." He rubs the back of his neck, frowning again. "Why don't we grab something and hang out? Or do you have another date?"

"No. That's tomorrow."

He reaches for his water, draining the bottle. "Right. So Shane gets lucky tomorrow?"

"No! God no. It's only our second date."

"How many dates till sex, then? What's the rule?"

"Um... I'm not sure. I'll play it by ear." I fiddle with the book, avoiding his gaze. Silence descends upon us and when I glance up, Myles is studying me. The intensity of his gaze makes my blood rush, and I look away again. "Do we have to talk about this?"

He gives a light laugh. "No. Sorry. So... dinner? Is Chinese okay?"

I nod, relieved.

He stands to grab a menu and I set his book down on the ottoman again. It's so threadbare that the foam stuffing underneath is spilling out. If only I had my staple gun and a piece of fabric here, I could tidy that up in five seconds flat.

Actually, I think, letting my eyes meander around the room, I could make this whole place a little nicer without much work. A throw over the couch and some cushions, curtains on the windows, a cover for his comforter. And he should hang up those pictures of his, they're stunning. It wouldn't take much to get this place feeling more like a home, and less like somewhere a destitute bartender crashes in between shifts. Not to mention it would make a much nicer pad for him when he brings women home.

Myles orders us some food while I look around, thinking. He's doing so much to help me out. I can't pay him right now, but maybe I could do this place up a bit, as another way to pay him back for his help. Well, that and the dresses I want to make for his daughter.

Dinner arrives a few minutes later and Myles pads to the door. When he reaches for his wallet, I spring to my feet.

"I've got it."

"It's okay," he says kindly. "I'm happy to pay. I know things are tight with the store."

That's true, but I'm worried that *his* financial situation might be worse. "Oh, it's fine. You're..." I gesture around his apartment and cringe at my tactlessness. "You're helping me out so much, it's the least I can do."

"No, really—"

"Myles," I say, exasperation creeping into my tone as the delivery guy knocks again.

He gives me a lop-sided grin. "Okay. Let's split it, yeah?"

I hesitate, then sigh. "Fine." His poor male ego is probably taking a bit of a hit with me trying to pay.

He rummages in his wallet, pulling out a fistful of bills. "You sure you don't want me to—"

"*Myles*," I repeat, handing him a twenty.

He laughs, taking the bill. "God, you're stubborn."

"Yeah, yeah," I mutter as he opens the front door. I don't want him to waste his money buying me dinner. If that makes me stubborn, then so be it.

We settle on the sofa with the cartons of food, eating in comfortable silence.

"I've been thinking about what you said yesterday, about

clothes," Myles says after a while. "You said they're a way to express who you are and how you feel."

I nod.

"So what are you expressing?" He gestures to me and I choke on a laugh.

"What?"

"You always wear black. The same thing, every day. What's up with that?"

"Oh." I look down at my clothes. He's right: black jeans, black tank top, combat boots. Every day, unless I've got a date, and then it's usually a little black dress of some kind. "Nothing."

"I don't know. Black is one of those colors that blends in, especially in the city. I think you don't really want to be seen."

"Thanks, Freud."

"It's funny, though." He chuckles. "You make these beautiful, vibrant dresses with all these bright colors and patterns. And then you dress like that."

"Hey," I begin, feeling defensive.

He shakes his head, eyes smiling. "I'm not saying you don't look hot. You always do—"

Wait. *What?*

"—but it's interesting. You say you don't use clothes for self-expression."

"Or maybe my soul is black, did you ever think of that?" I pop a spring roll in my mouth with a smirk, waiting for him to laugh. But he doesn't.

"Why don't you wear your own designs?"

I look down at the box of takeout in my hands. "I used to. A long time ago."

"What changed?"

"Mark didn't—" I pause, wondering how much to share.

I don't want to give him more ammunition to mock me. But his gaze is gentle, and I feel my defenses lower, ever so slightly. "Mark didn't get why I loved all the colors and the whole fifties thing. And when he talked me out of opening a store with my own designs, I guess... over time I just stopped wearing them altogether."

"That's really sad." Myles's brow folds. "He made you feel shitty about the thing you love."

I shrug, stuffing noodles into my mouth. He's going to pick this apart now, like everything else. He really does like to talk, doesn't he?

"You should wear them again. Make yourself a dress you love and wear it. Fuck Mark."

A smile touches my lips.

"You talk this big game about integrity and honesty," Myles says, setting his food down. "But then you dress to hide your true self. You're at odds with yourself."

I give an indignant huff. "I don't hide—"

"Yeah, you do. It's like when you're on dates and you don't show your true self." His eyebrows settle into a knowing look. He's back in smug mode and it riles me.

"Well, what are you saying with your clothes?" I gesture at him with my chopsticks. "That you're some sort of over-grown-adolescent skater-boy?"

"You think I look like a man-child?" he says, mouth tilting up at the corner, not at all bothered by my attempt at a dig. "Why, because I wear a cap sometimes? Because I have tattoos?"

I sigh, out of ammo. "I don't know."

Something shifts in his expression and his eyes glint at me. "Would you prefer I dress in a suit, like a pompous prick?" He doesn't mention Shane's name, but we both know that's who he's referring to.

"Maybe you should," I say, meeting his challenge.

He juts his chin out. "I'd never change the way I dress for a woman. I won't change who I am for anyone. Not even you."

I scrunch up my nose, bewildered. Not even me? What does *that* mean? I survey his stony face, wondering what on earth we are even talking about now.

"Ugh, I'm sorry." His eyes soften. "I'm not trying to argue with you."

"Yeah. Sorry for calling you a skater-boy."

He chuckles. "It's okay. I've never skated in my life, but I guess wearing a cap makes me one." He turns his hands up helplessly and I laugh. "It's just... I don't know why you won't just be yourself. With your clothes, with guys—whatever. What are you afraid of?"

"I'm not afraid," I mumble.

"I think you're great." He tucks his bottom lip between his teeth, dropping his gaze to my mouth. "Really great."

Well, shit. If I didn't know any better, I'd think he was full-on hitting on me, right here on his sofa.

Despite myself, there's a flutter in my stomach, a zing through my body. This is the problem with men like him: they know how to make a woman melt, what buttons to press.

I clear my throat, setting my food down. "Thanks, Myles. That's... thanks."

He can hit on me if he wants, it doesn't matter. I've got a hot date tomorrow night with someone else; a guy who doesn't flirt with half of Manhattan for a living, who doesn't resemble all the worst parts of my ex-husband.

Just as I'm about to remind Myles of this fact, an odd laugh rushes out of him. His cheeks are stained a dark pink, but he fixes his eyes on mine, stretching his lips into that cocky grin again. "So that worked, huh?"

"What?"

"It's a new move I'm going to try with the ladies at work." He reaches for the food again.

I open and close my mouth, stunned. What was that? One minute it feels like he's genuinely hitting on me, and the next... Was he really just rehearsing a line? God, it's just as well I didn't fall for it. How humiliating would that have been? "You are the worst," I mutter.

"Oh, no. Did you think—" His eyes widen with exaggerated worry. "Did you think I was coming onto you? Fuck, sorry." He raises his hands in surrender. "It's a curse; women can't resist my charm."

I roll my eyes, standing. "Somehow, I think I'll manage." I wander to the kitchen and grab my purse. "I'd better go. Are you good to keep working on the site?"

"Uh-huh," he says, pushing to his feet.

"Cool." I check my phone and there's a new text from Shane, saying he's looking forward to our date tomorrow. An uneasy sensation shivers across my skin as I stand there, reading his words. I can't put my finger on what it is, but getting a text from Shane while I'm here with Myles makes me feel a little... funny. Almost as if I'm doing something wrong.

Which I'm not, I quickly tell myself, shaking the feeling away.

"I was thinking," Myles says, "I need to get some pictures of the items you're going to sell so I can list them. They're at the store, right? I might stop by and take some photos after you close up?"

I nod, typing out a reply to Shane, only half-listening.

Dropping my phone into my purse, I turn to Myles with a smile.

"What are you so happy about?"

"Oh." An uncomfortable laugh slides from my mouth. Why do I feel like I've been caught doing something I shouldn't? "I, um, I'm just excited about the site."

"Me too. It's going to be great." He gives me a sincere smile, opening the front door for me. This is the nice Myles —the one I can relate to, the one I actually like. But I know smug Myles is always in there, waiting to pop out.

"Well, I'll see you later." I grin as I turn to go, calling over my shoulder, "Try not to woo half of Manhattan with your irresistible charm in the meantime."

He rumbles out a laugh behind me, and I smile all the way home.

14

"**D**o you like jazz?"

Shane slips an arm around me as we step out of the restaurant after dinner. Since he chose La Bouffe for our last date, he suggested I pick somewhere I like this time. I was going to choose somewhere fancy and upmarket, but I've been thinking about what Myles said last night, about how I don't show who I really am on dates.

So, I decided I'd try and be a bit more myself tonight. I picked a place I love called Piscitelli's—a tiny, rustic Italian cafe on St. Mark's Place in the East Village. And even though I still dressed in my usual black dress, on the walk over here I plucked a flower and tucked it into my hair. It's a bright, vibrant pink blossom—a little homage to the color I used to wear.

"There's a great place nearby that has experimental jazz," Shane says. "Want to go?"

"Okay." I'm not entirely sure what "experimental jazz" is, but I love Ella and Etta and Louis—all the usual suspects.

We walk for a few blocks until we come to a Chinese takeout place. Shane leads me inside, lifting up the counter partition as he pulls me after him. I trail along, glancing around in confusion, until we turn a corner and come face-to-face with a surly bouncer. Shane leans forward, mumbling something, and a huge wooden door is opened. It's then that I realize we are at some kind of speakeasy. I've heard about these places but never actually been in one. They always seemed so... preposterous.

We step through the door, down a metal staircase that opens up into a dark, cavernous space. But I can't process where we are, exactly, because I'm too overwhelmed by noise. And I say "noise," because I'm honestly not sure how else to describe the bizarre jumble of notes spewing forth from the ensemble of musicians buried in the depths of this place. Is this experimental jazz? If so, count me out. No wonder we had to come to some random, hidden basement to hear this crap. No one else wants to hear it.

Shane turns to me with a broad grin. "What do you think?"

I pause, listening some more. I can't pin down any sort of melody or pattern to the music. It's a mess. "Well, it's..." I struggle to smile as I inch toward the bar. I don't want to lie; I'm trying to be more myself. But... shit. This is awful. "It's interesting," I say at last. There, that wasn't a lie. Not totally.

Shane nods, his handsome face looking thoughtful. "Isn't it? It's so avant-garde, so sophisticated, most people don't get it."

I try not to snort at how pretentious that sounds.

"I find it fascinating," Shane continues. "So intellectually challenging."

It's definitely challenging, I'll give him that. But is music supposed to be intellectual? He makes it sound like a physics lecture. When I like music, it's because the lyrics mean something to me, or the melody hits me at an emotional level, or because I feel the beat in my body.

Suddenly I miss Bounce, with its dirty hip-hop on Thursdays, its eighties pop nights and the live bands that sometimes play. I haven't danced there in ages—most of the time I'm in for a date and out pretty quickly when it tanks—and I miss it. How did things get so complicated that I wound up here, standing in a dark basement, pretending to like something that sounds like a cat being mangled in a garbage truck?

Shane hands me my drink and we sip for a while, listening to the music. I try—trust me, I *really* try—to like it, to find some redeeming quality about it, but I can't. And I know I'm supposed to be honest, but when Shane looks at me, I give him an enthusiastic thumbs-up. Whoops. It's a reflex.

He sets his drink down, his hungry gaze pinning me to the spot. Before I know what's happening, he leans down, pressing his mouth to mine. It's so sudden and unexpected that I stumble backwards. He thrusts his tongue into my mouth, then draws back with a grin.

I blink, trying to make sense of what just happened. Between the racket violating my ears and Shane's tongue in my throat, I'm feeling strangely disoriented.

"You want to go?" he asks.

I give a swift nod. Anything to get away from this place.

Out on the street, I pull in a lungful of the warm evening air, delighting in the glorious relief my ears are feeling. It's like they've been assaulted. They'll be ringing all night.

Shane turns to me. "Let's get out of the East Village." A scowl pulls his eyebrows together. "I hate it around here."

I flinch. "Seriously?" I might have chosen the restaurant, but *he* was the one who chose that awful bar.

"Yeah," he mutters, looking up the street for a cab, and annoyance settles over me. This isn't the first time he's complained about a place I like; he didn't like Bounce, either. Besides, if I can put up with his ridiculous experimental jazz without complaining, why does he have to tell me he hates the East Village?

Shane catches my expression and tries to backtrack. "It's okay. I can come here if you like it." He leans in to kiss me then stops, cocking his head, and reaches into my hair. "You know, you've got something stuck... here. You must have brushed past a tree." He hands the pink flower to me with a chuckle.

I take the blossom, staring down at it in disbelief. Does he really think I stumbled backwards through a bush, inadvertently snagging a flower in my hair? How stupid is he? I toss it into the gutter with an exasperated sigh.

A cab turns down the street and Shane lunges forward, flagging it down. I step up to the curb, then hesitate. This evening has been a bit frustrating, if I'm honest. Perhaps I should just head home.

But when Shane opens the car door and turns to me with a hopeful smile, I feel myself relent. Maybe we're just having an off night.

I slide into the backseat with him. He gives the driver an address, then shuffles closer to me as the cab pulls away from the curb.

"Where are we going?" I ask warily.

"I figured you'd come back to my place."

Right. Well, getting into this cab was clearly a mistake.

"You did?"

A dirty grin crawls across his face. "I was getting a vibe."

"You *were*?"

But he doesn't answer. Instead, he leans forward and

kisses me suddenly, fiercely. Despite how sexy Shane is, I feel myself tense up. I try to pull away, but he drags me back so my lips are hard against his. There's a bolt of anxiety through me at the aggressiveness of his kiss, at the way he's holding my head and pinning me against the seat. And when he slides a hand up my thigh, my whole body recoils. Panic seizes me as I get a flashback to that awful night a year ago, in the back corner of a Brooklyn nightclub, pushing a hand away and searching desperately for someone to help me. It's like I'm back there again, my lungs tight as I struggle for the air to scream for help—

We stop at a red light and relief floods through me as Shane draws away.

It's okay, I tell myself. *You're just in a cab, everything is fine.* I gulp in a breath, trying to calm my racing pulse as the light turns green and we pull away.

"Stop!" The word slices through the cab and it takes me a second to realize it came from me.

The cabbie swerves to a stop and Shane turns to me, heaving out a long-suffering breath.

"Come on, Cat. It's been long enough."

"What?" My heart is still thumping as I try to make sense of what's happening. "Are you serious?"

"I've been pretty patient. I've done all the right things: bought you an expensive meal, sent you nice texts, came all the way out here"—he gestures out the window with a grimace—"so, you know, now—"

"What, I *owe* you?" I gape at him. This is what happened last time—the guy bought me a couple of drinks and seemed to think I "owed him." How did I not see this coming?

"No, no. Of course not." Shane laughs uneasily, raking a

hand through his blond hair. "But, you know, at some point I have to wonder what's going on."

"Some point?"

He shrugs helplessly. "I'm a guy."

I stare at him, slack-jawed. He says it like it's some kind of get-out-of-jail-free card. You know, boys will be boys, they're going to expect sex—so you have to give it to them.

"Fuck this." I snatch my purse up off the seat and reach for the door handle. "I don't put out on demand, or because some guy thinks I owe him." And with that, I yank open the door and step out of the cab.

Shane leans across the backseat, saying something I can't hear, but I slam the door in his face and whirl on my heel. I fully expect him to get out of the cab and follow me, to apologize and plead with me. But a second later the cab just pulls off into the night, and I stare after it in shock.

Fucking hell. I can't even... What an asshole.

I root around in my purse with shaking hands, surprised to find that, more than anything, I feel relieved.

And that's when I realize my phone is missing.

15

This is *just* what I need.

I raise a hand to my forehead, blowing out a breath. All I want is to call an Uber home and climb into my bathtub, but I'm not going anywhere without my phone. Where did I last have it? I don't remember checking it since I was at work...

Oh, right. I left it charging in the store.

With a grumble of resignation, I turn and trudge back through the East Village. I finished work at seven, leaving Hayley to lock up, and wasn't planning on returning until tomorrow—hopefully with a huge grin after my hot date. Boy has this evening gone pear-shaped.

But as I turn down our street, I'm surprised to find the light on. It must be after ten now, why are the lights still on? Hayley wouldn't leave them on. Unless she's still here, doing something? But—no, she told me she was meeting friends tonight.

I creep along the sidewalk and peek in the front window, feeling my gut clench with anxiety. I can't see anyone inside, but a bunch of my clothes have been pulled off the rack, some tossed over the front table. Hayley would never leave the store like this.

Shit. We've been robbed.

I tentatively push the front door open, being careful not to knock the bell. I can't see anyone inside so they've probably just broken in, realized there wasn't anything worth stealing, and taken off.

With a weary sigh, I close the door behind me. This is the *worst* night. First the whole Shane fiasco and now this.

I'm just about to straighten up the front table, when a sound from the basement makes me freeze.

Oh my God. There's still someone here.

My heart catapults into my throat and I glance at the door. I should back out of the shop and make a run for it; grab my phone off the charger and call the police. That would be the sensible thing to do.

But out of nowhere, anger surges through me: hot, forceful, visceral. I'd put good money on the fact that it's a *guy* down there, looking for something to steal. Fucking men—they just take whatever they want, without stopping to think about who they might hurt in the process. Like Shane, expecting me to sleep with him tonight. I was too shocked to be angry—I just let him leave. I should have punched him in the throat.

I shake my head, practically vibrating with rage at the thought, my teeth grinding hard. Shane might have gotten away unscathed tonight, but I'll be damned if I let this guy go without inflicting some kind of bodily harm. He's picked the wrong store on the wrong night. Because suddenly, I'm feeling crazy.

I glance around me in search of a weapon, but there's nothing. Oh well, guess I'll have to do this the old-fashioned way.

Reaching down, I whip off my shoes. At least if I have to run, I'll be able to do it easily. Not only that; these stilettos have a killer heel on them. One thunk to the forehead and he'll get the message. I might even be able to take out an eye.

There's another noise from the basement and my rage ratchets up a notch.

Okay. It's die time.

I creep across the store, raising a shoe. My heart jack-hammers against my ribs. *Thud, thud, thud.*

I hear footsteps across the concrete floor of the base-ment. Then, footsteps on the stairs. *Thud, thud, thud.*

The footsteps climb higher. With each step, my heart beats harder, faster. *Thud-thud-thud-thud-thud.*

I keep myself back behind the railing, crouching out of view. Surprise is crucial. And then—I can't fucking believe it —I hear whistling. This asshole is not only in my store, he's relaxed enough that he's whistling merrily as he goes about ripping me off.

That. Is. *It.*

I leap up from my crouching position just as he reaches the top of the stairs. "Arrrghhhh!" I scream, lunging toward him. I've never felt such a rush of fury and it's intoxicating— it's working through me so that I'm no longer in control. I can't see straight, I'm not thinking, I just hurl myself at the figure, bringing the shoe down onto his head.

But before I can make contact, he grabs my wrists, spins me around and pins me face-first against the wall, and I realize much too late that I've made a terrible mistake. Of course I can't take on an intruder with a stiletto. What was I thinking?

I shrivel against the wall with my heart thrashing in my chest, pressing my eyes shut, waiting for a hand to strike me. But nothing happens. And as I just stand there cowering, my senses come back online and I inhale a lungful of familiar cologne.

My eyes fly open and I twist around to see Myles, inches from the back of me, holding me against the wall. His nostrils are flared, his brow pulled low, his breathing heavy.

"Holy shit, woman. What the *hell* are you doing?"

Relief crashes through me so violently that I sag back against him, catching my breath, clutching my stomach. He turns me around, gaping at me. Never in my life have I been so happy to see someone.

Before I know it, I'm laughing. I'm laughing so hard my shoulders are shaking and I'm struggling to stand. Myles pulls a stool up behind me and nudges me back onto it, peering into my face with concern.

I wipe my eyes, trying to pull it together, waiting for my pulse to slow. He disappears down the stairs then reappears, handing me a glass of water. I down it gratefully, then set it on the counter with an embarrassed look.

"I thought you were an intruder," I say at last.

He stares at me incredulously, hands on his hips. "And you were going to kill me with a shoe?"

"Not kill," I say, lifting my chin. "Just... maim."

"Jesus, Cat. That's crazy. If you thought I was an intruder you should have called the police, not confronted me."

"I know," I mumble. "I was just so angry I couldn't see straight."

"Why are you here, anyway?"

"I could ask you the same question."

"I told you I was going to come in to photograph some of your dresses for the site." He gestures to the front table where there's a fancy camera sitting.

Oh. I didn't see that through my rage-induced haze.

Come to think of it, he did mention something the other day about all that.

"Hayley left me a key to lock up," he adds.

I put my elbows on the counter and lower my head into my hands. "I'm sorry, I forgot. I've just had the worst night." I glance up at Myles, giving him a weak smile. "Still, at least I didn't get almost beaten to death with a stiletto."

"Yeah, I don't think that's what would have happened." He pulls a stool up beside me. "Why was your night so bad? I mean, before this."

"Ugh, just... Shane stuff. I don't want to bore you with it." Silence falls over us and I shift uncomfortably, wishing we were at the bar. "I could use a drink, actually."

"You want to go for a drink then?"

I smile. "Nah. I don't want to interrupt your work." I pick at a loose thread on the hem of my dress, then remember something. "I think Hayley has some herbal tea in the basement. I might just—"

"I'll get it," he says, standing. "You relax." He heads down the stairs and I kick my bare feet up onto the counter, leaning back on the stool against the wall behind me. A few minutes later he returns with two steaming mugs of chamomile tea. A smile plays on his mouth as he hands me one. "This should help you chill out a bit."

"Thanks." I chuckle as I take the cup from him. This is far from the night I had planned, and yet I'm feeling almost... well, happy.

Weird.

"Want to tell me what happened?" he asks gently.

I eye him over my tea, feeling that same odd sensation I felt the other day, when I was at his place and Shane texted me. "It was nothing. But... it's safe to say there will be no more Shane."

"Oh." He looks down at his cup. "Shit, that sucks. Sorry."

I snort. "Yeah, right. You never liked him."

Myles releases a quiet laugh. "I didn't really know him. But, I don't know. He didn't seem good enough for you."

I blow on my tea, mulling over his words. It's funny—before tonight, I almost thought Shane was *too* good for me, with his fancy clothes and expensive taste. That's why I was planning to take him to—

"Oh God," I mutter, rubbing my nose. "I just remembered I agreed to that stupid dinner party at my friend Claudia's house. I was going to take Shane and now I'll have to cancel."

"Why?" Myles cocks his head. "Go alone. Show them you're fine as you are."

"No way. You don't know Mel. She'll make me feel like crap, and then her and Mark win."

He's quiet for a moment. "I could go with you if you like. Pretend to be your boyfriend for the evening."

I trail my eyes over him. Tonight he's in his usual ripped jeans, with a gray Henley, his chestnut hair ruffled. I think of Claudia's friends from the Upper East Side and how snobby they are. I don't think Myles would enjoy having dinner with that crowd. "Thanks, but... I'm not sure you'll fit in with them."

"Why not? I can tidy myself up. If it helps, I won't wear a cap—then no one will know I'm a skater."

I can't help but giggle. There's something so disarming about the way he doesn't take himself too seriously. Somehow, I can't see Myles making me eat snails at La Bouffe or listen to whatever that was back at that speakeasy, and that makes me smile.

"Besides," he adds, "Mark sure doesn't seem to like me. If you want to piss him off, taking me should do it."

"Huh." He might have a point there. "Would you really come?"

"Sure."

"It would take a lot of work," I say teasingly. "You'd have to dress up a little, pretend to have good manners, attempt intelligent conversation—that sort of thing."

"Oh, then no." He rolls his eyes. "I'm not a caveman. I know how a dinner party works."

"If you're really serious—if you wouldn't mind—then yeah, maybe."

He gives me his cocky, self-satisfied grin. "You'd have me as your boyfriend for the evening?"

"Pretend boyfriend. And yes, if you don't mind pretending to be into me for a night."

"Who says I'd be pretending?"

I laugh. "Don't waste your lines on me, Myles. I'm not tipping you tonight."

He pretends to look hurt, then for one awful second I think he actually *is* hurt. He can't have been serious, surely?

I tear my gaze from his. "Do you like experimental jazz?" I ask, reaching across the counter for my phone. I unplug it from the wall and flick the stereo on, connecting the cable.

"What?"

"Listen to this." I search for the band we saw earlier and put the music on. Well, "music" is a bit of a stretch.

Myles listens, screwing up his face at the clashing notes. "What the fuck is this?"

"Right?!"

He raises his hands to his ears. "Please make it stop."

I turn the cacophony off and we both sit for a moment, enjoying the sweet silence.

"Were you trying to punish me, or something?"

"No." I lean back against the wall and place my feet up on the counter again. "Shane likes it."

"Jesus Christ. That guy's a nutjob."

I take a long sip of my tea, setting the mug down with a sigh. I'm feeling much more relaxed, and now, I find myself wanting to talk about tonight, to get it off my chest. Maybe that will help me shake off this odd feeling. "You want to know what happened?"

Myles nods, kicking his feet up on the counter beside mine. His gaze rests on my bare legs before shifting to my face. "Sure, if you want to tell me."

"He was annoyed that I wouldn't sleep with him. He basically said that I owe him and he'd waited long enough, so I left." I draw breath to tell him about the kiss, the one that made me panic in the backseat of the cab, then decide against it. It will only invite more questions—questions I don't want to answer. I'll have to explain that some guy tried to force himself on me in the back of a nightclub last year, and I don't make a habit of telling people that because they freak out. I told Cory and now he watches me like a hawk. I told Geoff and he tried to get me to see a shrink. So I decided it was best to keep that little tidbit to myself.

Myles grimaces. "What an asshole. I'm sorry."

I tilt my head, regarding him curiously. How funny that after everything, Myles is the one apologizing when it should be Shane.

"Yeah," I murmur, smoothing my hands over my dress, running my finger along the hemline where it sits mid-thigh.

I glance up to find Myles watching my hands, then he lifts his gaze to mine, swallowing audibly. "You didn't want to sleep with him?"

"I was probably going to, eventually. But I was trying to

wait, see if it could be more than that—you know, not rush
that stuff. But he couldn't understand." I sag, looking down
at my lap. I seem to be having this conversation with a few
people lately. It's starting to feel like I've developed a
complex about sex or something. "Maybe I should have just
done it and gotten it over with," I mumble.

"You're kidding."

"Well, you know, it's been a while for me. It feels like it's
becoming this big thing. I kind of just want to do it now." I
give an awkward laugh, reaching for my tea again. "Look, it's
not like I don't... I mean, I own battery-operated devices
that, you know, make me—" I break off, cringing. God, what
am I saying?

I sneak a glance at Myles and he's staring down into his
mug, eyebrows raised, cheeks pink.

"Sorry." I feel my own face warm. "You don't want to
hear this."

"Maybe I do," he says, his voice a low rumble beside me.
His eyes meet mine and I notice they're darker than usual,
his pupils dilated until they're almost black.

We stare at each other. My pulse quickens, and for the
briefest second I imagine what Myles might be like in bed.
That feeling from earlier is stronger than ever now, telling
me I shouldn't have been out with Shane at all tonight.

Then a siren screeches past outside and I come to my
senses, wrenching my gaze from his.

What the hell am I doing? He might be nice to look at,
and very sweet for listening to me bleat on about my atro-
cious sex life, but the absolute *last* person I should be fanta-
sizing about is Myles. Cory made it pretty clear what a
mistake that would be—a mistake I'm *not* going to make
again.

I drain my tea and set the mug down, pulling my legs off

the counter. Beside me, Myles clears his throat and stands, reaching for his camera.

"I should get back to this."

"Sure," I say, relieved to feel the electricity between us dissipate. I watch as he grabs a dress and hangs it on a hook against one of the walls, snapping a few photos. "Do you need any help?"

"Not right now, but..." He pauses, his eyes traveling over me. "I think these would look a lot better on a model."

I glance at the dress, nodding. "Yeah, but I can't afford a model. And—"

"I know someone."

"Oh yeah?" I ask, pushing away the uncomfortable feeling I get when I picture him hanging out with models.

"Cat." His eyes glimmer with amusement. "I'm talking about *you*."

"What? I'm not a model. I'm too short, too fat, and not even—"

"Okay, for a start, you're none of those things. But what I mean is these are your designs and they suit your personality. It would be cool to see you model them, for your own business."

I shake my head firmly. "No way. I would never—I mean, I'd feel stupid. I'd look—"

"Great," he finishes for me, the side of his mouth kicking up in a grin. "You'd look great. Just think about it, okay?"

I turn back to the dress, trying to imagine myself modeling it for my website. He's right about them looking better on a model, but me? I'm not so sure. "Maybe," I mumble, reaching for my purse. "Do you mind if I head home, then?"

"Of course." He hangs a new dress on the wall. "I wasn't even expecting to see you this evening. It was a nice surprise." His brow furrows into a frown. "Except for the whole Shane thing. Sorry about that."

"Stop apologizing for something another guy did."

He lifts his shoulder. "I guess I'm just apologizing for men everywhere. They're awful."

"That they are."

"You know," he murmurs beside me, "if you ever need help with... any of that stuff, you just have to let me know."

"*That stuff*?" I glance up at him, puzzled.

He chuffs a laugh, holding his camera to his eye again. "Yeah. If it's been that long, and you want someone who is going to treat you with respect and make you feel good..." he trails off, leaving me to fill in the blanks as he clicks a photo.

"Are you suggesting we have sex?" As I say the words, I'm surprised to feel heat uncurl and spread through my belly. Apparently my body likes the idea, and for a fleeting moment, I consider it.

He shrugs, lowering the camera and turning to me. "I'm pretty good." Then he shoots me his trademark self-assured grin and I snap out of it.

"Sure you are." I force a laugh, squeezing my thighs together. I'm quite sure he *would* be good in bed, actually. I expect he has a lot of experience. Pulling my purse onto my shoulder, I turn for the door. "Thanks for the offer, Myles, but I think for now I'll just stick with your business services."

He chuckles, raising his camera again. "Suit yourself."

16

I t's been three days since my Shane date, and every time I think back to it, I smile. Not because of Shane, obviously, but because of Myles. After everything that happened, I still went home with a smile on my face.

I mean, okay, he offered me sex. And that was weird. And I definitely haven't thought about it multiple times since.

Anyway, I'm not stupid enough to sleep with him, no matter how desperate I might be. I may as well just sleep with Mark again if I'm going to do that. And I certainly won't be doing *that*.

But—before the offer of intercourse—Myles was sweet, listening to me blather on. So I thought I'd finally do the things I've been meaning to do, to pay him back for all his help. I made two dresses for his daughter, and a couple of things for his apartment. I had to take an Uber over here just to bring everything.

Setting down several carrier bags on his doorstep, I raise a hand to knock. Over one arm is a garment bag with the dresses. I hope he likes them—or rather, his daughter likes them. I had to guess the sizing, but it will be easy enough to adjust once she's tried them on. It was fun making them, actually; I'm definitely going to create a child's line on my new site.

I shift the garment bag to the other arm, knocking again. Where is he? I'm sure he told me to come at two o'clock.

The door swings open and Myles stands there, grinning. He's wearing nothing but a towel, his bare torso gleaming with water.

I almost drop the garment bag.

"Sorry, was just in the shower," he says, stepping aside for me to enter.

But I'm frozen to the spot, my eyes betraying me as they roam shamelessly over his form. He's lean, with the slightest definition in all the right places. On his chest is a little patch of hair, tapering down to his navel, trailing down below the towel. And his tattoo isn't just his arm; it stretches up over his shoulder and across half of his chest. It's intricate and detailed and for one hideous second I almost step closer to inspect it, to trace it with my fingertip.

His lips twist humorously. "Enjoying the view?"

God.

Heat sears across my cheeks and I clear my throat roughly. What am I *doing*?

"Sorry," I mutter, reaching for one of the bags. "I was just... surprised." I push past him into the apartment, willing myself to stop blushing. Has it been so long since I've seen a man shirtless that I just lose it?

Apparently, yes. It has.

I stride back to the doorstep, avoiding his gaze as I collect the rest of the bags. I set everything down on the kitchen counter, and once I'm feeling a little more normal, I turn back to him, forcing a neutral expression.

But he's just standing there, still in his towel, still wet, gazing at me with his smug grin.

Is this part of his plan, or something? First he suggests we sleep together, next he opens the front door practically naked, then...

Because that is *not* going to work.

Water is dripping from his hair down onto his shoulder, and I'm shocked to feel an intense urge to lean forward and lick it.

Fucking hell. *Get it together!*

"Will you please put a shirt on?" I say, exasperated.

His grin widens. "Just a shirt?"

"For God's sake," I mutter, turning back to the counter and unpacking some of my things. "Just get dressed."

He chuckles, and I hear him wander over to the dresser. It takes all my willpower not to turn around and watch him towel off. Because if the rest of him is anything like what I just saw—

I shove the thought away and concentrate on unloading the bags. A few minutes later Myles appears in front of me, fully clothed, and relief washes through me.

Right. Good. Now we can just focus.

"What's all this?" He gestures to the counter.

"I had an idea—a way that I can pay you back for helping me. I will eventually pay you back—with money, of course—but for now, I thought I could do this."

He scrubs a hand over his jaw. "Okay. And... what is this?"

"I thought I might do up your apartment for you."

His eyebrows jump. "Really? Why?"

"Well..." I stall, wondering how to phrase this without offending him. "You've been so busy helping me with the store, plus you're always working. And, you know, guys aren't naturally good at this stuff. So I thought, if you're okay with it, I might do a few little things to help your place feel a bit more cozy."

"Okay..."

"You said you don't own much," I add, trying to be delicate. "But you don't need a lot of stuff to have a nice home."

"Yeah, I've only been back in the city for a couple of months. And before that I was living in a van, so—"

"A van?" I echo, shocked. Wow, he's so broke he was living in his *car*. This is worse than I thought. "Oh, Myles. I'm sorry. No one should have to live in their car." My heart squeezes at the thought. "You've been so generous with me, and you deserve a nice home. I know you could use the money, and I swear I'll pay you as soon as I can, but until then—"

"Wait." He holds up a hand, mirth dancing in his eyes. "You think I'm broke?"

"Uh..." Whoops. I didn't mean for it to come out like that. "No! Well, you know, if you were living in your car..."

He cocks his head, studying me. His lips tremble with repressed laughter and for a moment I wonder what's going on. "I'm not broke, Cat." He shakes his head, finally chuckling. "I wasn't living in my *car*, I was living in a van—a proper van, converted for living in—while I was on the road. And I haven't done anything with this place because I'm never home and, well, I guess I just don't put much emphasis on material possessions. I've got what I need."

Oh my God.

"I'm sorry. I just assumed..."

He's shaking with laughter now, one hand clutching his stomach. "You thought I was so broke I was living in my *car*?"

"I..." I rub my face, horrified. "I'm so sorry."

He folds his arms across his chest as his laughter subsides, then leans against the kitchen island, observing me with amusement. I grab my things and start stuffing them back into the bags, burning up with mortification. After everything he's done for me, all I've managed to do is insult him.

"Wait." Myles puts a hand on my arm. "It's okay, I get it. This place doesn't exactly reek of money." He leans over to peek into the bag. "What were you going to do, anyway?"

"Nothing," I mumble, leaning back beside him, unable to meet his gaze. "I'm sorry."

"Hey." He turns to face me. "Don't be sorry. It's sweet. I'd like to see it, if that's okay. It might still be nice to do this place up. And you're right—I'm terrible at this stuff."

I risk a glance at him. He's smiling at me kindly, and I sigh. "Fine." I reach into the bag and pull the curtains and sofa throw back out. "I made these. Nothing fancy, just some curtains and a throw to go over the sofa."

Myles takes the navy fabric from me. "You made curtains? For both my windows?"

"Yep." I hand him the throw I made. It's also blue, but lighter than the curtains, with a faint plaid pattern over it. "And this is for the sofa."

His forehead crinkles in confusion, so I take it from him and wander across the living room.

"Here. Like this." I unfold the throw completely, pleased to see I got the measurements more or less right, and drape it over the threadbare sofa. Then I tuck it in along the back and down under the front. I turn back and Myles is grinning.

"That looks way better." He strides over and sits down. "It's softer too. I love it. Can I keep it?"

I laugh. "Well, yeah. That's why I made it."

"Can we put the curtains up too?"

I smile, delight blossoming in my chest. "You really like them?"

He nods, rising to his feet and grabbing the curtains. "With the sofa and the curtains, the place will definitely look nicer." He glances up at the curtain rods and frowns. "Shit, how does this work?"

"Here." I take the curtain from him and drag a chair over from the counter, then grab my little packet of hooks and set about hanging the curtains. When I step down to examine them, Myles is beaming.

"They're great! You were right—this place was looking kind of bare. I hadn't really noticed, but this is way better." He turns to me and, before I can register what's happening, he pulls me into a hug. "Thank you," he murmurs into the top of my head.

But I can't respond, because my whole body is suddenly buzzing, hyper-aware of all the places his body is pressing into mine. My head rests against the firm chest I was ogling a few moments ago, and all my nerve endings spring to life, tingling with—what is that? Lust? And that smell—that same zesty cologne I smelled when I first came here, that I smelled at the shop—mixing with the smell of his soap... it's making my thighs quiver.

"You're welcome," I mumble as he releases me.

He's just gazing down at me with a gentle smile on his mouth, apparently unaware of the effect that innocent hug had on me. "Cat... you're so generous. I know you've been super busy with the shop but you still made time to do this. It's really thoughtful."

I swallow, wishing he'd take a step back, or crack one of his cocky lines to ease the tension snaking through me. But he doesn't, so I wrestle my gaze away and turn back to the bags. "I did some other things too, if that's okay?"

He chuckles, lifting a tattooed arm to rake it through his damp curls. "You can do whatever you like."

I ignore the suggestion in his words as I hand him the cover for the comforter and the pillow cases. "You can put these on," I mutter. Right now I don't trust myself to go anywhere near his bed.

He saunters over and collapses back on the mattress, denim-clad legs splayed as he pulls the pillowcases over the pillows. His smoldering gaze is riveted to mine, and my heart stumbles against my ribs. My mind replays his words from a few days ago—*I'm pretty good*—and I have to force myself to look away.

I turn my back and focus studiously on fixing up the ottoman. I brought some of the fabric that I used to make the throw, and my staple-gun from the shop. I used to up-cycle furniture ages ago, back before Mark and I moved in together.

I kneel in front of the ottoman, pulling the fabric over one corner and stapling it under the top, out of sight. The staple-gun jams and I hold it up, firing a few times until it's working again, then line up the fabric and staple some more.

Myles appears in front of me, watching with interest, but I ignore him as I work. Things feel different between us today. Maybe it's because the last time I saw him I talked about my vibrator and he offered me sex. I don't know. But I'm feeling all hot and bothered.

I flip the ottoman over, continuing to staple the fabric around the edges. The stapler jams again and I curse under my breath. I hold it up, firing a couple of times. Myles bends to pick up a book from the floor and against my better judgment, my eyes stray to his ass, noticing for the first time that it's quite nice, and—

"Ow!" He leaps up, one hand grasping his butt cheek as he whirls around to glare at me. "What the fuck was that?"

Oh... shit.

"I'm so sorry!" I drop the staple-gun, raising a hand to my mouth in horror. I feel my lips twitch and I clamp my hand over them. I cannot laugh at this. This is *not* funny. "It was the gun. It jammed, and I accidentally—"

"You *shot* me?!" He looks down at the weapon in disbelief. "In the ass?"

I jump to my feet. A laugh squeaks out of my mouth and I press my lips flat, trying to contain it.

"Are you *laughing*?"

"No! Of course not." I attempt a serious expression, but it's no use. My lips tug into a grin and another laugh breaks free.

Myles stares at me incredulously.

"I'm sorry," I say, full-on chortling now. "But it's pretty funny, if you think about it—"

"It's not funny!" He gives me a hurt look. "It really stings." He twists around to look but the staple is too low, under his back left pocket.

I stare at the tiny piece of metal lodged in his backside, my shoulders shaking. Who knew something so small could bring a guy like Myles down so easily? I should have shot him ages ago.

"Stop laughing!" He shoves me. "You have to help. You have to get it out."

"What?!" I roar with laughter. "I'm not taking a staple out of your ass!"

"Please?" He twists around again, patting his backside tentatively. "It really hurts."

I slow my giggles, sucking in a breath as I wipe my eyes. "Okay, fine. Let me take a look." I crouch down behind him, but I won't be able to reach it properly with the way he's standing; it's tucked under his butt cheek.

I push to my feet, trying to keep a straight face. "You're going to have to bend over."

"I'm not bending over, Cat."

"Then I can't help you."

He groans. "Fine. Fuck." He kneels on the sofa and bends forward, his cheeks coloring. My lips twitch again and he sends me a look. "Don't you *dare* laugh."

I raise my hands. "Okay, okay." I step behind him, kneeling down behind his butt, leaning in to inspect the staple. I reach out to touch it and he squeaks. "It's in pretty deep. Give me a second."

His eyes follow me as I walk to the kitchen, rooting in the drawer before pulling out a fork. He blanches as I saunter toward him, brandishing the fork with an evil grin.

"You know," I say casually, "it's quite strange seeing you like this. Wounded and desperate for my help. Usually you're so damn smug, but here you are on your knees, begging for mercy."

He manages a half-grin. "If you wanted me on my knees you could have just asked. You didn't have to shoot me."

I snort a laugh. Typical Myles.

I kneel behind him again, placing a hand on his right butt cheek to keep him still. Despite the situation, he lets out a growl—and *not* a growl of pain.

"Stop it," I warn, holding up the fork, "or I'll stab you, too."

He chuckles, then grips the back of the sofa. "Okay, just get it out."

I press down on the denim and slide one tine of the fork under the staple. "Ready?"

He nods meekly. I suppress another laugh at his response. *Not such a big man after all, Myles.*

But this *is* going to hurt. So, to distract him, I give his right butt cheek a good squeeze at the same time that I pull the fork, wrenching the staple from him.

There's a little howl then he turns to see me holding the staple up proudly. A patch of red spreads across the denim on his butt.

"Shit, you're bleeding." I glance around for tissues or something, then dash to his bathroom, grabbing a roll of toilet paper. I hand the paper to him and avert my gaze as he unzips his fly and slides his jeans down, pressing the toilet paper to the wound.

The tiny, *tiny* wound. Talk about melodramatic.

"I've got antiseptic cream in the bathroom, can you grab it?"

"Oh no, do you think we'll need to operate?" I say, eyes wide.

"Shut up."

I chuckle and pop back into the bathroom, grabbing some antiseptic cream and a Band-Aid. Myles is still pressing the toilet paper to his butt when I'm back, and he gives me a sheepish look.

"Will you... Can you..."

"No way."

"Please? I can't reach properly. And let me remind you, this is *your* fault. I'm the innocent victim here."

I cringe, feeling a dart of guilt. Ugh, he's right.

"Fine," I mutter, unscrewing the cream.

He's practically triumphant as he lowers his boxers over one ass cheek and turns around. I kneel down behind where he stands, but just as I'm about to put the cream on, the cocky bastard drops his boxers over both cheeks so that his butt is level with my face. I chew my lip, trying not to notice how smooth it is as I rub antiseptic cream into the olive skin. And I definitely don't think about the fact that if he were to turn around at this moment, I would be facing a *lot* more than just his butt.

"There." I place the Band-Aid on, resisting the urge to reach both hands up and squeeze his firm ass.

"Should I turn around while you're down there?"

"Don't even think about it, or I'll staple your dick to the wall."

He flinches visibly, pulling his boxers up. I stand, rubbing the rest of the cream into my hands as he goes and changes into a fresh pair of jeans.

"I'm really sorry, by the way. I didn't mean to shoot you."

"Whatever." He strolls toward me with that confident grin back on his face. "You just wanted to touch my butt. I totally felt you give it a good squeeze."

"That was to distract you from the pain. For a guy with such a massive tattoo, you don't have a very good pain tolerance."

"Or maybe I just wanted you to play nurse." He winks as he grabs the fork and takes it back to the kitchen.

A giggle slides from my lips and I turn back to the ottoman, trying to deny the charge I feel in the air between us. I don't know how, but everything has shifted, has turned sexual. It feels like every line is laced with innuendo, every look filled with meaning. And now that I've massaged cream into his butt, I'm not sure how to come back from that.

I finish off the ottoman while Myles hovers, scared, in the kitchen. When I'm done, he crosses the room and runs a hand over the smooth surface.

"It looks great, thank you. I love it." He lowers himself onto the sofa, then kicks his feet up on the ottoman, resting his head back with a contented sigh. "Home sweet home."

I smile, putting the staple-gun away. "So why did you live in a van, then? You said you were on the road?"

"I went through a bit of a phase where I didn't want to be settled, didn't want to stay put for too long, and being in a van was pretty sweet. It meant I could live wherever I wanted, pack up and go anytime—and I wasn't paying rent. But I got sick of living like that, decided it was time to grow up. So I came back to the city, got this place." He gestures around us with a smile. "Then your brother hired me and the rest is history."

"And you like it at Bounce?"

"Yeah, it's not bad. Easy money."

"Plus you get to hit on women as much as you like."

He laughs. "Yeah, that's really fulfilling. Much better than a real relationship."

I roll my eyes. Typical guy.

"Cat, I'm kidding." He contemplates me for a second, screwing up his face. "You have some pretty fucked-up ideas about men, you know that?"

I cut him a look. "I'm not doing this again with you, Freud. You love to psychoanalyze me. I've never met a guy who did that as much as you."

"So it's bad to think about things, to talk about things?"

"No. It's just exhausting."

"Fine, I'll stop. I'll stop trying to get to know you. I'll just drink beer and watch football and grunt in response to everything."

I smirk. But the truth is, it's kind of hard to picture him being that guy, with his philosophy books and his meditation and his thoughtful observations.

He releases a long breath, reaching for his laptop. "We should probably do some work before I have to head off to the bar."

"Oh, yeah." I laugh. Somehow, I'd forgotten the whole reason we're working together in the first place. "But, um, I want to show you something first." I grab the garment bag and take it over to the sofa, unzipping down one side. Then I reach in and pull out the two dresses I made for his daughter. One is the unicorn print he pointed out in the store, with a gold band around the waist; the other a mermaid print on a teal background with yellow details around the neckline. "I hope the prints are okay." I hold them up, one in each hand, and look at Myles for approval.

He stares at the dresses for a moment, saying nothing. Then he blinks and his gaze swivels to me. "What are these?"

"They're for your daughter, like you mentioned a while back."

He sets his laptop to one side and stands, reaching out to inspect the unicorn fabric. His eyes sweep over the dress, but he doesn't say anything.

Shit, I hope I've done this right. It was the unicorns he liked, wasn't it? I'm sure it was.

"It's just a little something to say thanks for the work you're doing. I've had to guess her measurements, but we can adjust them once she's tried them on. And if they're no good, I can always—"

"They're great," he says, avoiding my gaze. But I can see his eyes are shining as he looks at the other dress, and my head clouds with confusion.

"I thought you wanted me to make her a dress? I mean, if you think she won't like them—"

"Sorry." He huffs self-consciously, wiping a hand down

his face. "She'll love them. But—no. It's not... I can't..." His gaze turns steely and he shakes his head, turning away.

I frown, puzzled by his response. This is not how I thought this would go at all. He's been such a vocal supporter of my designs, but maybe he had something completely different in mind when he suggested I create a children's line. Whatever it is, I've obviously missed the mark.

He lowers himself back onto the couch without saying anything more, and reaches for his laptop.

"I'll just put these over here," I mumble, hanging the dresses over the back of a chair. I wish he would just be honest with me. He's hardly held back on anything else, why is he being weird about this now?

"So, the site," Myles says without looking up from the screen. He gestures for me to sit beside him. "Come see what I've done."

I flop down onto the sofa with a half-hearted smile. He's working hard for me with this website and I want so much to pay him back. I'm going to have another go at making a dress for his daughter, I decide. I want to create something beautiful—I want to show him how much his help means to me.

17

"**H**ey, Cat."

"Hi, Jimmy." I smile at the tall, fifty-something guy who's manned the entrance at Bounce for years. He opens the door for me with a welcoming smile. He looks like a puppy-dog, but I've seen him pick up drunk guys almost twice his size and hurl them out. Another reason I always feel safe having a date here: they'd never survive Jimmy.

I scan the crowd, spotting Alex and Geoff in a booth near the back. Myles waves from the bar, gesturing that he'll bring me a drink, so I thread my way over and drop into the booth, pleased to finally be sitting down to relax.

It's been a hectic few days, but that's good. The store is busy as Hayley has continued to spread the word. And we went to the East Village Market Collective to check it out, and she's right—a booth there would be perfect. We put in an application for one when an opening becomes available. I'm pretty excited about it.

Myles has been working hard on the site, emailing me updates. And I've made some more of my dresses, doodling ideas for new designs in my notebook when I get a second. I haven't felt so on fire and inspired in my work in ages, and it's fantastic. I'd forgotten how thrilling this feeling is.

The only bummer is the whole sex thing. God, I know it's stupid, but ever since Myles suggested we have sex it's like my whole body has woken up from hibernation. I'm suddenly ravenous, ready to gorge myself at the first opportunity. I had to take myself off to a yoga class after work tonight just to work out some of the tension in my body.

Seeing Myles shirtless the other day certainly didn't help. It was much easier when I didn't have the image of his treasure trail burned into my brain. And don't even get me started on his perfectly-formed ass. I'm only human. Human and... horny as fuck.

Anyway, the more I think about it, the more I realize he was probably kidding when he offered me sex. He's flirted with me so much since we met that I don't even think he's aware he does it anymore. It's just who he is.

I place my purse on the vinyl seat beside me, smiling at Alex and Geoff.

"Oh, that's what you look like," Geoff deadpans. "I remember now."

"Shut up." I pinch his arm affectionately. "Sorry. I've been crazy busy with work and getting things ready for the new business."

"It's okay, we get it." Alex smiles over her wineglass. "I just hope Shane is as understanding as us."

Warmth creeps across my neck. I was kind of dreading this, because I'd talked him up so much, but I'm going to have to come clean. I draw in a breath, facing them squarely. "Yeah, that's not happening anymore."

Geoff's brow knits and he sets down his glass of merlot. "What happened?"

"He just annoyed me, and"—I shrug, trying to be nonchalant—"it didn't work out."

"Aw, really?"

Alex scrunches her nose. "You let the guy who took you to La Bouffe get *away*?"

I open my mouth to reply but Myles appears at our table with my drink. I give him an appreciative smile, pleased for the distraction, but apparently my friends aren't about to let this go.

"Myles—it *is* Myles, right?" Geoff places a hand on his tattooed arm, gazing up at him. Jesus, is he fluttering his damn eyelashes?

I stifle a laugh at his misdirected flirting. He knows as well as I do that Myles is straight, but Myles, bless him, just nods at Geoff with a sincere smile.

"Geoff." He extends a hand and Myles shakes it. "Now, what do you think about Cat letting the gorgeous Shane get away? Apparently he 'annoyed her,'" he says, raising his hands to do air quotes around the words.

I take a long sip of my drink, glancing between Geoff and Myles. A shadow crosses Myles's face, and he lowers himself onto the seat beside me.

"Is that what she said?" He leans back, folding his arms across his chest. "She told you he *annoyed* her?"

"Yes," Alex says, chuckling. "She's so picky."

Myles barks a sardonic laugh. His gaze swings to me and he stops, reading something on my face I didn't know was there. "Well, that's... her call."

"It's okay." I place a hand on his arm. "I was going to tell them."

"Good," he murmurs. He's wearing a black T-shirt tonight, fitting snugly in just the right places, and I can't help but notice how his bicep curves nicely into his sleeve with his arms folded like this. There's an electric crackle in my fingertips where they rest against his skin, and when our eyes meet, that electricity sparks, forming a current down through my center.

Fuck.

I withdraw my hand, laughing unsteadily. A tiny part of me wishes he hadn't been kidding the other day because, well, would it *really* be so terrible to have sex with Myles?

Yes, I quickly remind myself. He's helping me build my business, for Christ's sake. And I've seen him flirt with every woman that's walked in here. I know he said that was just for tips, but that's exactly what Mark used to say.

Myles rakes a hand through his messy hair, letting his gaze slide from mine. "I'd better get back."

I nod, using all my strength to keep my eyes glued to the table, when what they really want to do is watch his tight little ass while he walks away.

"What's going on?" Geoff asks, bringing my attention back to them.

"What? Nothing." An awkward laugh escapes me. "Myles is just a friend."

"I meant with Shane," Geoff says. "But how *interesting* that you thought I was talking about Myles." He raises his glass to his lips with a knowing look.

Heat hits my cheeks and I take a big gulp of vodka. "Oh, right, Shane. Um... he wanted sex and I didn't."

"Wait." Alex squints, puzzled. "I thought you *did* want to sleep with him?"

"Well, yeah, eventually. But you know I'm looking for more than just sex. I've had enough one night stands that go nowhere and I'm over it. I thought we had something, but he couldn't wait. He got annoyed when I refused to go home with him on our last date, so I walked out."

Geoff screws up his face. "What a dick."

"Yeah, that sucks," Alex says, nodding in sympathy. "What a shame. He was sexy *and* rich."

"You're welcome to him."

"Oh, no thanks. I've got Michael, and he's better than any other guy out there. He's it, for me."

"How do you know that?" I ask. Geoff directs a warning look at me, but I wave him away. I'm not going to get all cynical on her—I'm genuinely interested to hear her explain it.

"Because the feeling is different. Being with him feels unlike any other guy I've been with."

"But... how?" People always say this—that they *knew* this person was "the one" because things were different—but they never say how.

Her lips curl dreamily. "I don't know. I can't describe it. There's just this quality that my other relationships never had. A kind of knowing, deep inside. Things just *feel* different, you know?"

I suppress the urge to roll my eyes. Typical Alex and her romantic nonsense.

"Yeah," Geoff chimes in. "It's like that with Daniel. Things—"

"Who's Daniel?" I ask, bewildered. I glance at Alex and she hikes up a shoulder, then turns back to Geoff.

"Well?"

But instead of answering us, he just sits there with a Cheshire grin.

Alex emits an impatient huff. "Geoffrey Howard, if you don't tell us who this *Daniel* is, I swear to God..."

"Alright!" He laughs. "I met him at a class in the Village a while ago."

Alex squeals in delight. "I can't believe you didn't tell me!"

Fantastic. Even Geoff, my stalwart single friend, is jumping on the love train.

"Yeah, I didn't want to jinx it," Geoff says. "But he's great. And you're right, Alex; things just *feel* different when you meet the right person."

I release a long, frustrated breath, furrowing my brow. How am I the only one who hasn't felt this "different" feeling? The last time I felt something close to that was with Mark, and look how that turned out. I thought I'd felt that spark with Shane—thought things had felt different with him—and that wasn't right either. Fuck, that wasn't even *close*. My internal compass is completely off. Maybe I don't even have one.

I look at my two friends, chatting excitedly about their partners, and feel a trickle of despair. What's so broken in me that I can't figure this out?

"And the sex is different, too," Geoff says, his eyes twinkling behind his glasses. "Like, things just feel better than with anyone else."

"Yes!" Alex clasps her hands together. "It's way different. Sex with Michael is easily the best sex I've ever had."

A wicked grin splits Geoff's face. "I bet it is," he says, bouncing his eyebrows.

I chuckle. Even in love with someone else, Geoff can still appreciate the thought of Michael in bed. I know Alex certainly does—she's filled an entire romance novel with the things they've done. And let me just tell you, as a friend... it was way too much information.

Alex swats Geoff on the arm. "You've got Daniel now. You have to stop crushing on Michael."

"Yeah, you're right. And anyway, Daniel is better."

"Ugh, you two," I mutter. "Let's get another round." I catch Cory's eye from the bar and wave, gesturing for more drinks.

"There's just something about having sex with the right person that makes all the sex you've had in the past pale in comparison," Geoff says.

I drain my glass, setting it down with a thud. Are we still on this? I'll need a lot more to drink if we're going to sit here and dissect Alex and Geoff's sex lives. I wave to Cory again, gesturing that I want a shot, too. He laughs and holds up a finger, mouthing, "One minute."

When I turn my attention back to my friends, they're still talking about sex. I feel like I'm on some kind of reality show where these two have been sent to test me, to see how long it takes for me to crack.

"Michael is really attentive in bed," Alex says. "Like, he'll always make sure I'm satisfied. And I *always* am."

I swirl the ice in the bottom of my glass, feeling myself deflate. I can't remember the last time anyone made sure I was satisfied. Most of the time it's about them getting what they want before passing out.

"He *sure* knows what he's doing," she adds smugly.

I raise my eyes to the ceiling in a silent prayer. I'm not religious but, *God*, I could really use some help right now.

Myles saunters past the table with a tray of drinks and I twirl a strand of hair, letting my eyes follow him. I don't know if it's because I've seen his ass up close now, or what, but his jeans are fitting him differently tonight. There's a little ache low in my abdomen as I watch him.

"Yeah, Daniel is the best sex I've ever had," Geoff agrees.

Alex tilts her head, giving an embarrassed laugh. "I've always wondered how two men, er, you know—"

"How?" Geoff chuckles. "You really don't know how two gay men have sex?"

Color blooms in her cheeks. "Well, yes, I know the logistics of it. But how do you decide who, um—"

"Oh." Geoff drains his wine, grinning. "It's different for everyone, of course, but with us—"

"Stop." I hold up my hands. Shit, even this is turning me on. "You guys need to stop this conversation right now." They turn to me in surprise and I groan. "Seriously? I just dumped a guy who wanted me to put out when I haven't had sex in *forever*. Meanwhile, you guys are sitting here telling me you're having the best sex of your lives? Way to rub my nose in it."

They exchange looks, cringing.

"Sorry," Alex mumbles. "You're right. That was insensitive."

Cory sets a tray of drinks down on the table, sliding into the booth beside me. "Hey, sis." He nudges me, smiling. "How are you?"

"Horny," Geoff says, smirking as he reaches for his drink.

I cover my face, shriveling with mortification. *Jesus, Geoff.*

"Right." Cory shifts his weight. "I was meaning, like, with work or whatever."

Alex and Geoff chortle beside me.

"Good." I lower my hands, but I still can't meet Cory's gaze. I'm going to kill Geoff. "Things with work are good." I reach for the shot and throw it back. It burns like acid; just what I need.

"You sure?" Cory looks concerned as I set the shot glass down and reach for my vodka soda.

"I think the shot was to help with the *other* issue," Geoff explains to Cory. "Things ended with Shane."

"The La Bouffe guy?"

I nod. "It was for the best. Turns out he was a dick."

Cory's face darkens. "Did he *do* something?"

"No, no," I quickly reassure him. "I just... wasn't feeling it."

Cory's jaw remains set. "Right. Well, let me know if you need me to—"

"Cors," I say, mildly exasperated. "I don't. Thanks, though."

He considers me for a moment, then relents, putting one arm around my shoulder and pulling me into a half-hug. "Okay, if you're sure. I just worry about you."

"I'm fine, really. Even better now," I say, gesturing to the empty shot glass.

"That's what a big brother is for." He pushes to his feet with a chuckle and heads back to the bar.

"You're so lucky," Alex says, watching him go.

I narrow my eyes. If she gives me the whole "you're so lucky to have such a hot brother speech" I've gotten my whole life—and, naturally, have never understood—I'm going to thump her.

"I wish my sister and I were as close as you guys," she adds.

"Oh." I glance over at Cory with a little smile. "Yeah, well, Cory and I didn't always get on so well. He used to make my life hell when we were little."

"Harriet and I have never been that close, but now I wish we were. Of course, that's never going to happen with her on the other side of the planet."

"Well, yeah," Geoff says. "Have you invited her to visit?"

"Of course. But she always makes excuses. She hasn't traveled outside of New Zealand, so I think maybe she's intimidated."

Geoff nods in understanding. "New York is a lot if you're not used to it."

Alex's shoulders slump as she gazes down into her wine, and sympathy swoops through me. I don't know what I'd do without Cory. I wish I could help her be closer with Harriet.

My gaze floats across the bar to where Myles and Cory are working side-by-side, pouring drinks. I notice how the longer curls on the top of Myles's hair fall across his forehead, and he pushes them back with his tattooed arm. Cory's warning to stay away from him comes back to me, and I frown. Even if I wanted to sleep with Myles, Cory would have a fit.

"It's not all good, though," I mumble. "Cory can be way too overprotective." My eyes linger on Myles, on the way he's twirling the bottle for a girl in front of him, laughing at something she's said. He glances up to find me watching and falters, nearly dropping the bottle. He pours her drink without any further fanfare, and once she's gone he sends me a grin. But it's not his smug one, which is kind of jarring with him behind the bar, where I always see him as the cocky bartender. I smile back, chewing my straw distractedly, my mind replaying that thing he said to me at the store the other day.

Ah, it's probably a good thing it was a joke. With the way I'm feeling tonight, I might be tempted to take him up on the offer. In fact, I should probably stop drinking right now, just to make sure I don't do anything stupid.

I sigh, turning back to my friends. They're both peering at me with amusement.

"Jesus, Cat." Geoff snickers. "Could you be any more obvious?"

"What?" I push my vodka aside and reach for a glass of water from the table, gulping it back.

"Cory doesn't want you to hook up with Myles," Alex says. "Is that what you mean?"

I blink, focusing my attention properly on them. "What are you talking about?"

"Come on." Geoff elbows me. "You *obviously* have a thing for him."

"No, I don't," I say, and they share a laugh.

"I think you should go for it." Alex leans past me to look at Myles. "He's hot and he's totally your type."

Why does everyone keep saying that?

"I shouldn't," I mumble. Whoops—I meant to say, *I'm not interested.* I reach for another glass of water and take a long pull.

"I knew it!" Geoff grins, triumphant. "And yeah, you should. He's definitely into you."

"But—" I fiddle with my glass. Is Geoff right?

"Is it the Mark thing?" Alex guesses.

"What?"

"You said he reminded you of Mark, and that put you off him."

"Right, yes. That's one of my rules; I don't date guys who share the same traits as my ex."

Geoff rolls his eyes. "Who cares? You don't have to *marry* him. Just have some fun! It's been ages—you should just do it."

Should I?

"Yeah. I think you should too." Alex pulls her phone out. "Shit, I'd better go. I have plans with Michael tonight."

"I have to go too," Geoff adds. "I'm meeting Daniel after this."

"You're both abandoning me for guys?"

Geoff drains his wine glass. "Yes. But it's okay, because

you'll have a guy too." He waves at Myles across the bar and I grab his arm, pulling it down.

"Stop it!" I hiss, blushing. "He's going to think something is up."

"Something *is* up," Alex says, setting down her empty wine glass. "If you have any sense, you'll have hot sex with Myles tonight. Because Geoff and I will be."

I give her an odd look and she laughs.

"I mean, we'll be having hot sex. *Not* with Myles," she clarifies, rising to her feet. "Enough wine for me."

Geoff grabs his jacket and stands too. "Come on, Cat. You don't have to take *every* guy so seriously. Just have a little fun, then you can get back to following your rules."

"A little fun?" I echo, my gaze wandering traitorously to Myles.

Could I?

"And you never know," Alex says, slinging her purse onto her shoulder, "Myles could end up being more than fun—"

"Yeah, right." I twirl my glass with a snort.

"Well, whatever." Geoff reaches down to give me a hug. "Just think about it, at least. You clearly want to, and so does he."

"I'm not going to—"

"Bye!" Geoff and Alex wave and turn, pushing through the crowd.

I drain my water, watching them go. Those two are crazy. As if I'd ever have sex with Myles. And besides, he was kidding when he suggested it.

Wasn't he?

My gaze meanders back to him at the bar, serving a line of people. I stand and stretch, feeling more clear-headed after a few glasses of water. I should go home, maybe get an early night, but for some reason I find myself drifting up to the bar and hovering impatiently, waiting for Myles to be free.

Finally, he's reaching for the Absolut bottle with a smile. "Another vodka?"

"Water, please."

He lifts his eyebrows but doesn't say anything as he fills the glass. Then he leans across the bar to a guy sitting on a barstool, chatting with his friend. "Let the lady have a seat, yeah?"

The guy looks at me, sighs, then rises to stand beside his friend. I smile my thanks and slide onto the stool, turning back to Myles.

"That was a paying customer," I say with a giggle. "I'm not even paying."

Myles shrugs. "It won't kill him to learn some manners." He turns to serve another woman nearby, and disappointment washes cold over me. I was expecting him to stay and chat, maybe flirt a little, but I guess he's working. And he needs his tips.

I sip my water as I watch him take the woman's order, waiting for him to toss up the bottle and tell her she's gorgeous and none of the guys here are good enough for her —or whatever bullshit he's spinning lately—but he just pours her drink and hands it over.

I'm guessing she's a regular, because she waits, as if expecting something more from him. I feel a tiny swell of triumph when she slinks away, and I turn back to my drink.

Ugh, water is boring. I want another vodka, even though I know that's a bad idea. I should stay sober. I'm supposed to be sensible, in control...

Just have a little fun.

Geoff's words echo through my brain and I straighten up

in my seat. He's right—why do I always have to be sensible? What if I *want* to make a bad decision for once? I'm a grown woman, for God's sake. If I want something, I should damn well go for it.

Another woman appears to order a drink from Myles, placing a hand on his tattooed arm, and there's a sharp, involuntary twist in my stomach. I don't know why, but that one action ignites a feeling in me that I have to act on. Now.

I lean forward on my barstool just as Myles hands the woman her glass of bubbly. "Hey," I say, reaching out to brush his hand.

He smiles, grabbing my glass. "Another drink?"

"No. Um..." How do I phrase this? What am I asking, exactly?

I gesture for him to come closer and he wipes a dish-cloth across the bar, then lowers his elbows onto the surface, so we are eye-to-eye. It reminds me of the first night I met him here—when he asked me for a drink, so sure of himself.

Is this a good idea?

"What's up?" The corner of his mouth tilts into a smile. My gaze rests on his lips and I notice my own mouth feels suddenly dry.

Fuck it. I don't care if this is a good idea or not.

I lean in, so I'm right by his ear. "Do you remember what you said to me at the store the other night?" I draw back just enough to see his expression.

He scratches his scruffy chin, frowning. "Uh... no?"

Oh, shit. What if he really was kidding? Or maybe he doesn't remember? Or maybe, like the cocky bastard he is, he wants me to actually say the words—to *ask* for it.

I place a meaningful hand on his arm. He glances down at it, then back at me, and realization breaks across his face.

"Oh." He huffs a laugh. "*That.*"

"Yeah." I suck on my bottom lip. "Were you kidding?"

His gaze drops to my mouth and he swallows visibly, dragging his eyes back up to mine. He shakes his head.

I trail my finger over his skin, feeling a frisson up my spine. So he *wasn't* kidding. Do I really want to do this?

A tingle between my legs answers for me.

"So if I were to head back to your place tonight," I say as casually as possible, "you'd be okay with that?"

He nods, speechless, and his eyes flash with heat. A woman beside us is asking for a drink, but he can't seem to hear. Satisfaction rushes through me at having his rapt attention.

He clears his throat roughly. "Are you serious?"

I glance around the bar, checking for Cory. He's over at a booth chatting to a couple of women, and I exhale in relief, turning back to Myles. "Yes. I'm serious if you are."

He brings his mouth to my ear. "I'm dead serious." His voice is like gravel and his breath tickles my earlobe, making my pulse rush with anticipation.

I draw back, giving him a shy smile. His mouth curves into a sexy grin, but he's not smug at all and I'm glad.

"You want to go right now?" He says it almost as a challenge.

"What about work?"

He stops, as if only just remembering where we are, and gives me a pained look. I watch the struggle on his face, before he finally says, "Fuck it. I'll tell Cory there's an emergency or something. If I make you wait, you might change your mind."

I laugh, leaning back and pulling a mint from my purse, popping it into my mouth. Part of me thinks he might be right, and I don't want that to happen either.

I drop a mint into my palm and hold it out to him. But

instead of grabbing it with his hand, he leans down and takes it with his mouth. His teeth graze my skin, his lips press hot against my palm, then he straightens up and locks his dark gaze on mine. Heat races up my body and settles in an ache between my thighs.

I lean over the bar, pressing my mouth to his ear. "Let's go. Now."

———

18

The door to Myles's apartment clicks shut behind us and he flicks the lights on.

I stand rooted to the spot, clutching my purse to my chest. We took a cab here, which I was hoping would be quick, but even the five minute drive was enough to break the spell from the bar. Now here, in the quiet, well-lit space of his tiny basement apartment, everything feels strange. What on earth was I thinking?

Myles turns to me, grinning as he steps closer. He reaches out to touch me and I take a step back, colliding with the closed door.

His forehead creases. "You okay?"

"Yeah, sorry." A nervous laugh sneaks out of me. "It's just hitting me what we are about to do."

"Yeah." He laughs too, scrubbing a hand down his face. "Look, we don't have to do anything. I'm surprised you even mentioned it again. I never thought you'd take me up on it."

"I wasn't sure if you were kidding or not." Another awkward squeak from me. "You're always joking about that sort of thing."

He gives a slow shake of his head. "I wasn't. And for the record, any time I've suggested that I want to have sex with you, I wasn't kidding." His eyes track over my face, dark and intense. It makes my blood heat and I flush all over.

"Well…" I lift my chin. "If you still want to, then I do too."

He bites his lip, taking another step toward me.

"Wait," I say, holding up a hand. "I just, um, need a moment to get ready."

"Oh, yeah." He steps back with a self-conscious laugh. "Totally. Me too."

I lower my gaze to the unmistakable bulge in his pants and smile teasingly. "You appear to be ready."

He reaches a hand down to adjust himself, color painting his cheeks. "Shut up," he mumbles, turning away. I'm not used to seeing him embarrassed like this, but strangely, it makes me more attracted to him.

"No," I say in a low voice, a satisfied smile pushing at my lips. "I like it."

He turns back to me, breathing hard. I expect him to step toward me again but he just stands there, arms hanging by his sides, waiting for me to make the first move.

I stare back at him, wide-eyed. I can't make the first move. This is *Myles*, for crying out loud. He's the guy who works for my brother, who's helping me build my new business. He's my friend.

"Should we have a drink?" he asks.

"*Yes.*" I pounce on the suggestion. Anything to break this tension.

He heads into the kitchen then hesitates, turning back to me. "How drunk are you?"

"I'm not drunk; I switched to water a while ago. But… it might help us to relax a little?"

"Yeah. Okay." He pulls out a bottle of whiskey and pours two glasses, handing one to me before clinking his glass against mine.

We drink in silence, refusing to glance at each other. A car alarm sounds on the street while we both stand there woodenly, sipping whiskey and pretending we aren't about to have sex.

"Maybe some music?" Myles suggests after a while.

"Sure."

He pulls a Bluetooth speaker out and grabs his phone. A moment later I hear an awful, strangled screeching sound from the speaker and I glance at him in confusion.

"What do you think?" He raises a hand to cover his smile. "It's a new genre I've just discovered; experimental jazz."

I throw my head back as a laugh rushes up my body and bursts out.

He grimaces at the music, reaching for his phone. "Fucking awful," he mutters, changing the song. The soft voice of Etta James comes on and he smiles at me hopefully. "Is this okay?"

I nod, biting back a grin. *Good choice, Myles.*

With a sigh, he sets his glass down and takes a step toward me. "Can I touch you now?"

I hold my glass tight, eying him over the top of it. "In a minute," I say, thinking. "If we are going to do this, we need to have some ground rules."

"Okay." He regards me warily. "What are your ground rules?"

I drain my glass and set it down. "We don't tell Cory."

"Of course."

"No joking about it afterward—making me feel weird

when we're trying to do business stuff or when I see you at the bar."

His eyes glitter and I shoot him a look. "Alright, alright," he says, holding up his hands.

"And no kissing."

His mouth opens in surprise. "What?"

I shrug, looking at his lips. They look soft and delicious and—I'd never noticed before—*very* kissable. But kissing is too intimate, and the very fact that I *want* to kiss them is enough to tell me I shouldn't. There's no point pretending this is something it isn't.

"It's just... it's too intimate. This is about sex, nothing else."

Myles sags, staring at my mouth. "But I want—"

"*No.*"

He rubs the back of his neck and I watch the way his shirt lifts up, exposing his firm, taut abdomen. A shiver runs through me at the sight, and for a brief second I waver. I *really* want to kiss him. I'm sure he'd be a fucking fantastic kisser. Would it be the worst thing to—

"Fine," he says at last, and relief and disappointment battle in my chest. A grin peeks at the edge of his lips. "I won't kiss your mouth. But I can kiss you other places, right?"

My pulse accelerates at the promise in his words, and I nod.

"Good." He takes my hand and leads me to the bed.

I stop at the edge, turning back to him. "Do *you* have any conditions?"

He pauses, thinking, his hand still in mine. Then he gives me his cocky grin, squeezing my hand. "Yes. That you have a good time."

"We'll see," I say wryly, relieved to see the old Myles again. Things were beginning to feel a little too serious.

We kick off our shoes and socks, then stand there facing one another, trapped in each other's gaze. Then slowly— like, intentionally slowly—he pulls his shirt up over his head and tosses it onto the floor. His hair is all rumpled now, and as I let my eyes rove across his bare chest, his mouth hooks into a smile.

I run my tongue over my lips, moistening them. *God*, he's hot. Has he always been this hot?

His eyes spark as he steps toward me, taking my hands and placing them on his chest. I slide them down over the warm skin, trailing my fingers through the patch of hair. My whole body hums from touching him, and even though I was the one who said no kissing, I can't help but lean forward and press my lips to the hot, salty skin of his shoulder.

His head tips back and he lets out a little sigh, before nudging me onto my back on the bed. When he climbs over me, my hands go to his shoulders, smoothing down the curve of his biceps. I study his tattoo, admiring the detail in the map and compass as it wraps around his wrist, then lean in to drag my teeth over the indelible lines, biting gently. I haven't touched a man in so long and I'm famished. I could swallow him whole.

"Fuck, Cat." His voice is thick as he watches my mouth graze his skin. "I never thought I'd get you here."

I glance up into his eyes. "You've really thought about this?"

"Uh, yeah." He gives me a strange look. "Surely you know that." He lowers his head, burying his face in my neck. "You smell amazing."

He smells good too—a combination of his cologne and sweat, in just the right way. He's so close, pressing his lips to the sensitive skin of my neck, and I inhale a lungful of his scent, realizing how familiar it is to me now.

With each brush of his lips, I feel a flutter between my legs, an ache building. I find myself opening my legs and wrapping them around his. Then I slide my hands onto his butt, pulling him down until I feel his arousal pressing into me, right where I want it. "Fuck," I mutter, loving the firm feeling of him through his jeans.

"You're telling me," he says, a laugh in his voice as he presses against me. "See what you do to me?"

I giggle, woozy with desire. I know this is the sort of crap he probably says to all women, but I have to hand it to him—it's working.

He pulls back to stare longingly at my mouth. "This is the part where I'd kiss you."

I shake my head, reminding myself why I won't—why I *can't*. I'm not doing this to be coy—I really don't want to cross that line. Sex with our bodies is one thing, but gentle, tender kisses... that's something else. I kissed Shane because I thought we were heading in that direction and it's a natural part of it. But Myles and I are *not* heading there. I don't want to know what his lips taste like.

"I'm like a prostitute with this no-kissing rule."

I give him a playful grin. "Are you feeling used? Do you want to stop?"

"No." He chuckles, pushing up to a sitting position, and smooths a palm over my belly through my shirt. I suck it in and he frowns. "You don't have to do that. Not for me."

"It's a reflex."

"It shouldn't be. You're perfectly sexy as you are."

I let out my breath, releasing my stomach muscles. "There you go. Still think so?"

"Yes. Fuck yes." He grasps the hem of my tank top, and I sit up enough for him to pull it over my head. His eyes move over my exposed skin, mapping every contour and curve. "You're beautiful, Cat."

I look down at myself with a snort. I'm wearing an old, beige cotton bra that I'm quite certain has a hole in the back, and my usual black jeans. Not exactly sexy clothes to seduce a guy—*definitely* not something I'd wear on a date.

"I mean it," Myles says, lowering his lips to press them to my skin. They land on my tattooed shoulder, which he stops to trace with a finger, then they work their way along my collarbone, down my chest, reaching the edge of my bra. "Take that off." His voice is rough as he lifts himself off me so I have room to wriggle out of it. I toss it onto the floor beside us, then lie back, one arm across my chest, covering myself.

A laugh rumbles from him as he reaches for my arm. "Come on. Don't tell me this is another rule? I'm not allowed to touch them, or something?"

I can't help but laugh too, reluctantly letting him take my arm away. "No. It's just... you know, it's *you*. This is going to take some getting used to."

He nods, tracing a circle around the outside of my bare breast. "What are you worried about?"

"I guess..." I breathe a self-conscious laugh, thinking of the many women he's bedded and the fact that I haven't done this in a long time. "I don't know. Maybe you'll look at me differently if you don't enjoy it, or something."

His brows rise. "You're worried about disappointing me?"

"I—" I glance away, cringing. I hadn't meant to be so

honest; that just slipped out. See, this is the problem, doing this with Myles. We're in this gray area now where I feel like I should be following rule number one—*always be my best self*—like I do with all guys I'm attracted to. But then, he's also my friend, and I'm used to not worrying about what he thinks of me. I don't know how to behave and that makes me feel... nervous. "Never mind." I force myself to look at him. "Let's do this."

He sighs, lowering himself on top of me. His bare skin feels amazing against mine and I shiver involuntarily, my eyes fluttering closed as I delight in the warm, soft sensation of being skin-to-skin with him.

"Cat, you couldn't possibly disappoint me. All I want is to be with you. I'm already so unbelievably *not* disappointed, you have no idea."

"Yeah, yeah." I give a little laugh. "I know you want to kiss me. That's disappointing you."

He presses his lips to my neck, nuzzling against me. "I do want to kiss you. But I also know you're not comfortable with that, and I can respect your boundaries."

Well, fuck. That's possibly the hottest thing anyone has ever said to me.

"Thank you," I murmur, finally feeling the last of the tension drain from my body.

"Now—" He pulls back to look at me. "Tell me what you want."

"What?"

A grin lifts one side of his mouth. "You heard me. Tell me what you like."

"Oh." I wrinkle my nose. "I don't know. The usual. I don't do dirty talk."

"That's not what I mean. I just want to know what you want from tonight. I want to *give* you what you want."

I run my eyes over his sincere face, watching him brush my hair out of my eyes, and suddenly it's not hard to answer at all. It's the one thing I've been refusing to acknowledge for weeks now, the one thing I want more than I'm willing to admit.

"You."

19

A hard breath shudders out of him at my words. "Cat..." he begins, and he looks like he wants to say more. But he doesn't, and I find myself feeling relieved.

Instead, he lowers his mouth, trailing feather-soft kisses from my neck, along my collarbone and down to my breast. I watch him, entranced by his patience and gentleness. Then just as things are feeling too sweet, he slides his tongue over my nipple and sucks it into his mouth.

Holy *hell*.

Need streaks through me, all the way down to my toes as they curl into the mattress. And just like that, I forget about the fact that this is my friend, Myles. Now, I can only see a gorgeous, sexy man with his mouth on me, and my body turns to liquid heat.

I moan, threading my hands up into his curls, tugging as he works his tongue over my nipple. I feel him smile against my skin, then he lifts his mouth off me, raising his eyes to meet mine. My heart pounds at his wild gaze, his heavy breathing, the pulse I can see ticking in his neck. I haven't even touched him yet and he's so turned on. It only makes me want him more.

He sits back, grabbing my jeans and sliding them down my legs with my panties, throwing them onto the floor. Then he repositions himself between my legs. His fingers brush over my sensitive inner thighs before landing where I want them. "Oh, fuck," he mutters as he strokes a finger over me, feeling how ready I am for him.

I grin at his slack-jawed expression. "It's not just you who wants this, you know."

He growls—a low, broken sound from his throat—and he crawls back, dropping to his elbows. "I have to taste you," he says, pausing to look up at me. "Is that okay?"

I nod, breathless, and he slides his hands up my inner thighs, urging them open and lowering his mouth.

Oh, shit. I'm not going to last two seconds, I realize, as his warm, slick tongue slides over me—tentative at first, then urgent and greedy. I drop my hands to his head, groaning, pleasure shooting out through my whole body as I inch closer to the edge. His gaze flicks up to mine as he devours me, and when I see his hooded, smoky eyes, that does it.

But just as I'm about to tip over into bliss, he pulls his mouth off me.

"What?" I cry in protest. "Why did you stop?!"

"Not yet," he says, his lips twitching with satisfaction.

I blush, glancing away. "Sorry. I couldn't help it."

"Don't be sorry. It's awesome. But I want to take my time."

"You know I can have more than one, right?"

"Yes." He chuckles, climbing onto his hands and knees above me again. "And you will, don't worry."

"Big promises. I hope you can deliver."

"Oh, I've got the goods," he replies, his self-assured grin back.

My eyes travel down to the bulge still straining against his zipper and I have to swallow back the saliva pooling in my mouth. I'm pretty sure he *does* have the goods—a fact which is confirmed as I mold my hand to the outline of him through his jeans. I stroke over his rigid length, smiling to myself at the way his breath breaks, the way he presses himself into my palm. He growls again, then pulls back.

"You might be able to go multiple times, but I can't."

I laugh. "I've barely touched you."

"I know." A sly smile slants his lips. "But you've done that a hundred times in my head already."

"You've really imagined me touching you?"

"You have no *idea* the things I've pictured you doing to me."

His words make fire spread down through my middle, burning up everything until I'm little more than a hot, writhing mess under his gaze. He's probably just talking shit to get me horny, but it feels like he's actually talking about *me* in this moment. And—God—I really, *really* like the thought of that.

"But not as much as I've imagined doing things to *you*," he adds.

He braces himself above me with his left hand and uses his right to reach down, sliding his fingers over the wet, throbbing heat between my legs. I gasp as his sudden touch sends pleasure rocketing through me.

"Right there?" he asks roughly, moving his fingers in practiced, purposeful strokes.

"Fuck—yes," I rasp.

His eyes burn with lust as he watches me slowly come

undone at his touch, and while I want to look away, or make a joke, or just run for my damn life—I can't. I feel myself unraveling as the ecstasy builds inside me, his attention capturing every breath, every movement, every moan I make. The sight of that sexy tattooed arm down between my legs is making me crazy, pushing me closer to the edge. And when he slides two fingers inside me, working his thumb up over me in slow circles, I can't hold back anymore. Sensation crashes through me and sweeps me away, so that I'm clutching at his sheets, panting and arching up against his hand in surrender.

When the room finally stops spinning, when I've caught my breath and remembered who I am, Myles sits back, grinning the smuggest fucking grin I've ever seen.

Holy, *holy* shit. That was... I have no words. I'm certainly not going to be telling him, anyway. Look at that face. He knows he's done good.

"You seem very happy with yourself."

He blurts a laugh of disbelief. "Is that all I get? After *that*?"

I force myself to sit up even though my whole body feels like jelly. He's resting back on his knees between my parted legs, and I lean forward to press a kiss to his hot, firm chest.

He releases a gentle sigh, bringing both arms around my back, holding me against him. It's an oddly tender gesture, but I'm too weak to protest. I nuzzle into his skin, breathing in a lungful of him, heady from the scent. Has he always smelled this good?

"That was amazing," I admit.

His self-satisfied grin stretches so wide I think his face is going to break. The ego on this one, honestly.

"Right." I pretend to feel around for my clothes. "Thanks

for that. I'd better go." His lips part in disappointment and I laugh, winking. "Gotcha."

He huffs a relieved laugh, then gives me a serious look. "But... you know, you can go, if you want to. I would understand."

"Oh, really?" As if I'm that selfish. Besides, I want to see if I can do that to him—if I can make him come undone like that. Maybe take his ego down a notch.

"It's okay, Cat." There's a little fold on his brow, and I can see he's having a mental battle between being a good guy who's selfless and the horndog that he is.

"It's not okay. No way." I pause, thinking about what I want. And as I look at the tangle of sheets around us, I can't help but wonder how many girls he's had here. An unpleasant sensation swirls through me and I force the thought from my mind as I turn back to him, pointing up the bed. "Sit there."

He obeys, pulling himself up so he's sitting with his back against the wall.

Right. It's time for me to reclaim a little of the power.

I crawl over on my knees, lowering my hands to his belt buckle, keeping my eyes locked on his. As I slide his zipper down, I watch his slate-blue eyes darken. I drag a finger up over the soft cotton of his boxer-briefs, tracing the hard line of him. He groans, shifting his weight so I can wriggle his pants down a little. When I slowly release him from his underwear, there's a new shock of heat between my legs. Now I understand why he's so damn smug. He is *magnificent*.

But when I glance up at his face, he's not wearing his cocky grin. His eyes are glazed with desire, desperate for what I'm going to give him, and I revel in the knowledge that I have him at my mercy. I might be the one on my hands and knees here, but we both know who's in control.

"This is to make up for shooting you in the ass," I say.

He begins to chuckle, but as soon as my hand slides around him, the smile drops from his face and his eyes roll back. "Fuuuck. You should have shot me the day we met."

I laugh, stroking him gently, loving the velvety-hard feeling of him in my hands. "Maybe I should have," I murmur, thinking back to that first night at Bounce when he asked me out and I immediately said no. Why did I do that? Right now I'm struggling to remember.

I lick my lips, leaning down, then caution stops me. "Have you... you know, are you..." I scratch my head, looking up at him awkwardly. I don't mean to break the mood, but I've seen the way he is with women and I need to be safe.

"Am I clean?"

I nod, still stroking him.

"Of course. I had a check when I got back to the city."

I lift my hand away. "That was a couple of months ago, Myles—"

"I haven't been with anyone since."

"You're kidding."

Amusement creases his eyes. "No."

"You haven't had sex for two months?"

"Longer, actually."

"But..." I take a second to process this. "Really?"

"Look, it hasn't been a *whole year*," he says, a smile dancing on his mouth, "but yeah, it's been a while."

"Huh." I reach out to take hold of him again, trying to make sense of this as I slowly stroke my hand up and down. I mean, he flirts *constantly*. I trust what he's saying about being clean, but the rest of it? Hmm.

But as I see the need grow in his eyes, I don't care. Unable to wait anymore, I lean forward and lower my mouth over his thick length. His breath hisses out between his teeth, followed by a low roar in the back of his throat. I wait for him to put his hands on my head and push me down onto him, like most guys do. But when I glance up and see his arms draped down on the pillows beside him, I'm surprised. He's watching me still, his eyes darker than ever, but he's not trying to control me, and this makes me want to please him even more.

I slide my free hand up over his stomach, loving the feeling of hard muscle under smooth skin. All that yoga has done amazing things for his abs.

But actually, I need both hands for this.

I take my time, listening to his breathing become ragged, waiting to feel him let go. I can tell he's holding back, I can tell he doesn't want to give in, and I hope he doesn't, not now. Because the longer I have him in my mouth, the stronger the desire building inside me.

"Cat," he says, his voice a hoarse whisper, "I want you."

I stop, drawing away from him. There's something about the plea in his tone, about the longing on his face, that makes my heart beat erratically. It's such a powerful, unfamiliar feeling that I quickly shake it off, pushing to my feet to grab a condom from my purse. When I turn back, he's stripped his pants off and is just standing there, totally naked, gazing at me.

Christ, he's beautiful. I make no attempt to hide the fact that I'm enjoying the view as my eyes feast on the muscular contours in his torso and arms, the detailed pattern of ink over his skin, the proud jut of his erection. He grins and puffs his chest out, full of confidence, and I come to, handing over the condom with a laugh as I flop onto the bed. I watch him roll it on, then he settles himself beside me on the mattress.

"Come here," he murmurs, reaching out to hold me

close. I shake my head, even though I'd like nothing more than to climb onto his lap and lose myself in his mouth. Instead, I nudge him onto his back and straddle him, positioning him between my thighs. I meet his expectant gaze, loving the little flush on his cheeks, the way he's holding his breath, waiting for me. Slowly, I ease him inside me, breathing out as I adjust to the thickness of him.

Oh, *wow*. I'd forgotten how good sex feels. I let out a blissful sigh at the way he fills me so completely.

His head drops back onto the mattress, his hands sliding up my thighs. "Oh my God," he groans, pressing himself up deeper into me. "Cat."

I grin, gently rocking my hips over him, letting a little whimper escape me. Pleasure ripples out from my center, hitting every cell in my body, and—oh, *God*. I don't remember sex being *this* good. There's something about the feeling of him, the way he fits me just right. There's no way I can hold back. I want all of him. Hard. Now.

I lean forward on my hands, bracing myself above him, rocking faster. It's not long before I feel the build-up again, gathering low and deep as I grind my hips against him.

"Fuck, fuck, fuck," he's saying, his hands on my waist, his eyes watching me with raw hunger. "You need to slow down, now."

I lower my mouth to his ear. "No way. I'm not stopping for anything." My tongue slides out and dips along his earlobe, then I push right back until I'm sitting up straight, feeling his whole length fill me.

I roll my hips, watching his face, aching to feel his release. He raises his hands, threading his fingers through mine, and something about that nudges me over the edge. But it's not just me; I watch his face contort with ecstasy, and a loud moan tears from his mouth right as my own body slips into oblivion.

A moment later, I find myself lying forward on him, trying to catch my breath. His chest heaves under me, his fingers still laced with mine. He turns his head and kisses my cheek, my neck, my shoulder.

"Jesus, Cat. I wanted to last longer than that."

I chuckle, lifting myself up and collapsing onto the sheets beside him. I still can't quite breathe right, I'm still getting my bearings.

"I wanted to give you—"

"You did," I assure him. "I'm sorry. I couldn't hold back. I wanted—" I stop myself. I'm not going to say how much I wanted him. Because I did—I *do*—and...

Shit.

I'm lying in bed with Myles—with his sweat all over me, with the imprint of his hands on my skin—and unease creeps up my spine. Not because of him, or what we did, but because of how much I wanted it. Because of how much I want to do it again.

I force a laugh, turning away and reaching for my clothes. I need to get the hell out of here, right now.

"Hey." He sits up beside me. "Where are you going?"

"Well, you know." I shrug like it's no big deal, doing up my bra.

"You could stay. I'd like you to."

I turn around, letting myself look at him. He's not smug. He's not his usual arrogant self. He's sincere and open and sweet—and I can't stand it.

"Sorry." I yank my panties and jeans up my legs. "I have a ton of work to do with the store, so I need to get up early." I pull my tank top on over my head, glancing around for my boots.

"Seriously?" His tone makes me turn around again. He almost looks hurt, and I soften.

"Seriously. Come on, Myles. Snuggling and sleepovers weren't part of the deal."

His face falls a little. "Yeah, I know. I didn't think you'd run out of here immediately, though."

I ponder his disappointed expression, feeling a tug in my chest as I waver. He reaches for me, taking my hand, letting his thumb trace a little circle on my palm. For a moment I imagine crawling back into bed with him, snuggling into his warmth, falling asleep beside him. That would be... fuck, that would be really nice.

But then what? I wake up and go to work and... what? It's been a long time since I slept beside a guy, and I'm not going to start doing that unless it's part of something bigger—something *real*. And I know I can't have that with Myles. I know better than to want that with someone like him. Cory's warning comes back to me and I feel my resolve harden.

"Thanks for tonight. It was fun. I didn't realize how much I needed it."

His eyes dart over my face and he exhales heavily. "Yeah. It was fun." He pulls his hand away, dragging his gaze from mine.

"Hey." I give him a gentle shove. "It's not supposed to be awkward, remember? We agreed."

He looks at me again, squaring his shoulders and giving me a grin that doesn't quite reach his eyes. "Yeah. It won't be. I've got lots to do on the site anyway, so it's probably best if you go."

"Great." I pull my boots on and push to my feet, grabbing my purse off the bench.

Myles props himself up on the bed, still buck naked. "Let me call you a cab, or—"

"It's okay." I hold up my phone. "I'll get an Uber." I take a moment to mentally record the sight of his bare, beautiful body, then turn for the door. "Bye, Myles," I say, stepping outside.

And as much as I really don't want to, I make myself close the door and head home.

20

R oses.

Today, I was sent roses—from Shane, of all people. It's like he sensed I was out there having sex with someone else and felt the need to get in touch, to tell me that he "hated how we left things in the cab."

I mean, honestly. Too little, too late, buddy.

I've never been sent flowers at work before, and for one stupid moment—I'm embarrassed to admit—I thought maybe they were from Myles. I tried to ignore the disappointment that seeped into me when I saw Shane's name on the card instead.

And when Myles emailed me with an update about the site—and made no mention of last night—I should have been relieved. But I'd be kidding myself if I said I didn't feel a little sting at the way he acted as though nothing had happened between us. I know I was the one who wanted that, but the truth is I haven't been able to stop thinking about him. The feeling of his hands on my skin, that sound he made as I took him into my mouth, the way he looked at me when he asked me to stay...

Anyway. Maybe it's a good thing the roses weren't from Myles. The last thing I want to do is develop some sort of crush on him after sleeping with him. Besides, I don't think sending a girl flowers would be his style, somehow. It certainly wasn't Mark's.

I set the flowers down on the kitchen counter and toe off my combat boots. It's been a long, busy day at work and I should be happy to be home, but after last night with Myles, it's feeling a little lonely coming back to my quiet apartment. I can't help but imagine what it might be like if he were here, sharing a drink with me, maybe climbing into bed—

Ugh. Enough.

There's a knock on the door just as I'm taking a bottle of wine from the fridge, and I sigh. There go my plans to flop down in front of Netflix and try to forget everything.

I swing the door open and Alex is on the other side, beaming. "Finally, you're home!" She's effervescent with excitement as I let her in.

"Hey." I survey her expression. "What's up?"

"I have to tell you something."

"Okay," I say warily, turning back to the kitchen. "You want a glass of wine?"

She shakes her head, glancing at the door then back to me. "Can we wait for Geoff?"

"Geoff?" I lift a brow. She's invited Geoff over to announce something? This can't be good. Well, she's always been a bit dramatic, so really, it could be anything. "Fine," I mutter, wandering into the living room and collapsing onto the sofa.

A moment later there's a knock at the door and Geoff pokes his head in, breathless. "Hey!" He lets himself in, closing the door and turning to us. "I got a text from Alex saying to come over and bring champagne. What's going on?"

I kick my feet up onto the coffee table with a shrug, watching as Alex drags Geoff into the living room and pushes him down onto the sofa beside me. Then she stands in front of us proudly, both hands on her hips. And out of the corner of my eye, I see a sparkle of light from her left hand.

"No way!" I exclaim.

She nods, radiant with happiness. "Michael proposed."

"Oh my God!" Geoff leaps up, pulling her into a hug. "Oh my God, oh my God," he repeats and I laugh at his theatrics as I stand to hug her too.

"That's awesome, hon. Congratulations."

Her eyes are shining with tears as I release her. I turn straight for the kitchen and grab some wine glasses—the closest thing I have to champagne flutes—and set them down on the coffee table, gesturing for Geoff to uncork the bottle. While he does, I take Alex's hand and inspect the ring. It's a beautiful marquise cut diamond set in a gold band—and it's breathtaking.

She gazes down at it. "This was his grandmother's ring."

"Huh," I say. "He didn't give that to his nightmare ex-wife?"

Alex takes the glass of champagne from Geoff's outstretched hand. "No. Isn't that funny? It's like he knew, on some level, she wasn't really the one. But with *me*, he drove to Vermont to ask his Nana for the ring." She lets out a long, dreamy sigh.

I look at Geoff and we share a grin. That is just the right amount of romantic gesture to satisfy Alex. She'll be telling that story for years.

Geoff hands me a glass of champagne, then raises his

own in a toast. "To Alex and Michael, and a lifetime of hot sex."

We all laugh as we clink our glasses.

"So how did he do it?" Geoff asks, settling back on the sofa.

I sit too, folding my legs under me, but Alex stays standing, apparently too full of energy to sit still.

"Oh, it was so romantic." She clasps her glass to her chest. "Last night after I got home from seeing you guys, Michael and I were sitting on the sofa just reading—you know, not doing anything special. He asked me to hand him this book—"

"What book?" Geoff interrupts, eyes like saucers.

"*The White Company*, by Arthur Conan Doyle?"

"What?" Geoff looks mystified and she holds up a hand, grinning.

"Wait for it. So, he asked me to hand it to him and I was like, 'stop being so lazy, get it yourself.'" She pauses to giggle. "And then he asked again like five minutes later and I was getting a bit annoyed at this point, because I was up to this really good part in my novel. But he turned to me, gave me a pointed look, and said, 'Alex, just get the damn book.'"

"And?" Geoff leans forward eagerly.

"So I got it and sat back down, holding it out to him. But he told me to turn to a page, and he'd underlined this phrase: *You are my heart, my life, my one and only thought.*" She stops, closing her eyes and smiling to herself.

Envy snakes through me. I can't imagine a guy ever doing anything romantic like that for me. When Mark and I got married he didn't even propose; we just decided one night at the bar after we'd both had too many shots. We did it the next day at City Hall.

"And underneath," Alex continues, "he'd cut this tiny

hole in the pages—like one of those book safes—and sitting inside it was this ring."

"Awww!" Geoff swoons against me. "That is *so* romantic. And so perfect for you two bookworms."

"I know," Alex says, her eyes gleaming. "It was perfect. I couldn't believe it—I sat there staring at the ring. I just couldn't process that he was actually proposing to me, now, like this. Then he got down on one knee in front of the sofa, and said all this amazing stuff. And I was crying my eyes out."

I snort into my wine glass. Typical Alex.

"Wow," Geoff breathes. "You're going to be Mrs. Alexis Hawkins. I can't believe you're marrying Sexy—I mean, Michael. I'm so happy for you."

"Yeah," I murmur, staring at my champagne.

"I was so excited I came down to tell you last night, Cat, but you were still out."

"Wait." Geoff puts a hand on my arm, and immediately I feel heat spreading up my neck, because I know what's coming. "You were out *late* last night?"

I clear my throat, avoiding his gaze. "Mm-hm."

"*Wait*." Alex drops onto the sofa on my other side. "Were you...?"

I examine my nails. "Was I what?"

"Did you sleep with Myles?" Geoff practically squeals.

"Is this *really* the thing to be focusing on right now? Alex just got engaged, for Christ's sake."

"That's a yes," Alex says, trading a look with Geoff.

"I can't believe it!" He adjusts his glasses, struggling to contain his grin. "I can't believe you actually did it. How was it?"

I force out a frustrated breath. "It was..." *Fantastic. Mind-blowing. Possibly the best sex I've ever had, and something I'm desperately trying to forget, but can't seem to stop obsessing about.* "It was okay." I pick at a piece of lint on my jeans, the weight of their collective gaze bearing down on me. "Okay, fine!" I throw my hand in the air. "It was amazing."

Geoff gasps, and when I glance at him he's pink with elation. "I *knew* it. You two—"

"*No.*" This is exactly why I didn't want to tell them. "There is no 'us two.'"

Alex's brows draw together. "Why not?"

"Because—" I push down the odd feeling stirring inside me. "Come on, you know that's not what I want. I'm looking for more than just a quick fuck with the local bartender. The one who—let me remind you—is very similar to my ex-husband."

Geoff rolls his eyes. "Do you seriously believe that? Why, because he's a bartender with tattoos? That doesn't mean he's the same person Mark was."

"You don't even know him, Geoff."

"No, I don't. But, you know"—he shrugs—"you do this sometimes."

I narrow my eyes. "Do what?"

"You form judgments about people based on the wrong things. Take Shane; you thought he was great, just because he was hot and loaded. Then he turned out to be a total dick."

I clench my jaw, irritated. Because that observation is correct. Obviously.

"Besides," Geoff adds, "I don't think you would have slept with Myles if you truly believed he was like Mark. Not to mention how much you're letting him help you with the business. I know you see it as a sign of weakness, Cat, but I think you trust him."

My gaze flits to Alex and she nods in agreement.

I look down at my champagne, watching the bubbles float to the surface. Shit, they're right. I *do* trust Myles—and not just with the business stuff. No wonder I felt comfortable enough to sleep with him.

And as for the similarities to Mark, is it possible they're just superficial? Admittedly, his personality isn't all that similar to Mark's. He's kind and generous and surprisingly deep, sometimes.

But... I get a flashback to him twirling the bottle behind the bar, flirting with a group of women, and something in my stomach sours. It doesn't matter how much he tells me that he only flirts for tips, that it doesn't mean anything. Because this whole situation is too damn familiar for me to simply dismiss it.

And that's not the only thing that feels familiar, I realize. I'm trusting Myles to help me with my business, just like I trusted Mark to do the same. The last time I mixed business and pleasure it was a fiasco and nearly cost me everything. Myles is supposed to be my ticket *away* from that—to help me save my livelihood, my passion. I need to keep my head on straight here.

Besides, if I get involved with him and it blows up, I wouldn't only lose my new business, I'd also lose a *friend*— one I've recently come to understand I really value. It's all just... too messy.

Still, after last night I can't deny how much I want something real. The feeling of Myles touching me doesn't even compare to the shitty meet-ups I've been having with guys from Tinder. I'm so over all that.

My eyes land on Alex's engagement ring and determination grips me. Before I can talk myself out of it, I grab my phone and delete all my dating apps, one by one. It's time to take a step in the right direction.

"I'm not going to pursue something with Myles, but—" I take a deep breath. "Maybe you could set me up with someone. Do you guys know anyone?"

They exchange a long look. This is the problem with these two: they work together at the bookstore and they've developed this secret little language I'm not part of.

Eventually, Alex sighs. "Fine. I think I know someone."

Geoff frowns at her. "You do?"

She nods. "Stefan, from work."

"Stefan?" Geoff looks doubtful. "Really?"

"Yep."

Geoff's frown deepens. "Are you sure? Because—"

"*Yes*," Alex says, giving him a meaningful look. They glance back at each other and there's another moment where they seem to be communicating telepathically. I raise my eyes to the ceiling with impatience.

"Yeah, actually." Geoff turns to me, grinning broadly. "Stefan. He's... nice."

"Stefan," I repeat, trying the name on for size. "Okay, yes. Set me up with Stefan."

That should take my mind off Myles. Right?

21

So far, the plan to forget about Myles is *not* going well.

In fact, over the three days since we had sex, I haven't been able to get him out of my mind. It's driving me crazy—and not in a good way. Because I don't *want* to be thinking about him. This is the complete *opposite* of what I wanted.

So, when Alex and Geoff told me Stefan could meet me tonight, I leapt at the chance. Maybe he'll help me reset, help me erase my mind of Myles. Like a sort of... palate cleanser.

I glance nervously around Bounce, smoothing my hair. I didn't really want to do this here, but Josie told me Myles wasn't working tonight. Just as well. I don't love the idea of going on a date right in front of him. That would be unbelievably awkward.

I could have done this somewhere else, I suppose. But after that whole thing a year ago, Cory made me promise not to meet new guys anywhere else. And really, this is the only place I feel safe enough to do this.

Besides, this was my bar first, right? My brother owns it;

I was meeting guys here before Myles was even in the city. And why am I even feeling weird about this? It's not like Myles and I are dating. In fact, in all his emails over the past few days, he hasn't mentioned anything about the other night. I need to stop making a big deal out of nothing.

Anyway. At least I won't have to see him until—

"Hey." I look up to find Myles leaning against the bar and my heart jolts.

Fuck. What? *Why* is he here?

His gaze dips to my dress, lingers, then comes back to my face, and a line forms between his brows.

"Hi," I say as casually as I can. For some reason there's a corkscrew suddenly twisting through my middle. "I, uh, thought you weren't working tonight."

He shrugs, wiping the bar. "Cory called me in at the last minute."

"Right." I roll my lips to the side, trying to be normal. This definitely feels weird. *Why* did I think meeting Stefan here would be a good idea? "Um, this might be a bit awkward, but I have a date coming. I'm sorry, if I'd known you were going to be here, I wouldn't have... you know."

He looks down at the bar and scrubs hard at an invisible stain, before glancing back at me with his trademark grin. "Sure. No worries. Business as usual."

Oh. Okay then. He clearly isn't bothered. And that's good—that's what I wanted.

Right?

"Well... vodka soda, please."

He nods, reaching for the Absolut bottle, and I force myself not to watch his hands as he works. He slides the drink across to me with a lackluster smile, then turns to a woman at the end of the bar.

I take a sip of my drink, looking around, but there's no

sign of anyone who could be Stefan. When I turn back to the bar, Myles is leaning forward, talking to the woman— young, blond—as she runs a hand over his tattoo. My stomach pitches at the sight, but I ignore it. I mean, he can talk to whoever he wants, right? He can let whoever touch him.

I swallow hard at that last thought. *Shit.*

It's just stupid hormones, I know that. I had sex with him a few days ago and now my body is going into overdrive, wanting me to mate for life or whatever. I just need to wait for it to pass—for these stupid feelings to go back to wherever they came from and for things to get back to normal. At least Stefan will distract me.

And as a tall, slim guy slides onto the stool next to me, I smile in relief.

"Hi. Are you... Cat?"

"Yes!" I extend a hand. "Cat Porter. Hi."

He gives my hand a half-hearted shake. "Stefan." Then before he can say anything more, Myles appears in front of him.

"Hi there. What can I get you?"

"Budweiser, thanks."

Myles busies himself with the drink. I watch him without realizing that I am, until he places the bottle down and his gaze collides with mine.

Jesus. Get it together.

I tear my eyes away from Myles, turning to Stefan with a smile. "It's nice to meet you, Stefan. So... what do you do?"

"I repair photocopiers."

"And you know Geoff and Alex from the bookstore?"

He nods. "I maintain their machine."

"Oh, right." I wait for him to ask me something about

myself, but he doesn't. Shifting my weight on the stool, I say, "Tell me about your job."

He eyes me dubiously. "You want to hear about my days fixing photocopiers?"

Not especially, if I'm honest, but I don't want to sit here in silence. "Sure."

"Well, it's not much fun." His features warp into a scowl. "People are fucking stupid when it comes to technology. I mean, how hard is it to put the right paper in the right tray? You can't put letter size in the A4 tray and expect a smooth print run. And the number of people who never check their toner levels—then wonder why it's not working. Just check your fucking toner levels!"

He jerks his beer up to his mouth and I silently gesture to Myles for another drink. We exchange a look as he slides me a vodka. Who gets this angry about *toner levels*?

Stefan, apparently, because he's not done. In fact, it takes him a full fifteen minutes to say everything he needs to say, and by the time he finally takes a breath, I've had two more vodka sodas and the bar around me has a nice fuzzy edge to it. I'm just starting on another when Stefan sets his beer down, turning on his stool. I straighten up, pleased that he's finally showing some interest in me.

"Do you know where the bathroom is?"

Maybe not.

With a gusty sigh, I gesture toward the back of the bar, then watch him slump off to the bathroom.

"How's it going?" Myles appears in front of me out of nowhere. "He seems interesting. Very invested in photo-copiers."

I take a long pull from my drink, stalling in my reply. I don't want to tell Myles that Stefan is boring me to tears, because I'm certain he'll find that amusing. In the end I just shrug, as if I haven't really figured Stefan out yet. "And how's your evening going? Making lots of tips?"

He crosses his arms over his chest. "What do you care?"

"I don't." It comes out harsher than I intend, and he rolls his eyes, going to serve a group at the end. More flirting, I notice, more arm-touching, more tips. Then another crowd, and there's some bottle twirling, some compliments, the usual crap.

Ugh. I don't know why, but watching him work tonight is irritating the shit out of me. It makes me want to crawl out of my skin. Still, it's a good reminder of why I'm better off staying away—and right now, I need that reminder more than ever.

I can't say Stefan is winning me over, though. I feel a pang of disappointment as he returns to his seat, and I lean back on my stool, looking across the crowded bar at the dance floor. Maybe if I could get him to come and dance with me, he'd loosen up, shake off some stress. He just needs to have a little fun.

I turn to him with a grin, the alcohol making me giggly. "Want to dance?"

He observes the dance floor, frowning. I wiggle on my seat, watching the crowd as they move to the beat. Tonight it's hip-hop and I love it, but I'm sensing it's not his jam.

"Never mind," I mumble.

I turn back to see Myles, wiping the bar in front of us, and I can tell he's listening. So damn nosy. He leans down onto his elbows. Stefan is right beside me but Myles doesn't seem to care.

"I'll dance with you."

"Don't you have tips to earn?" I know I sound like a petulant child but I can't seem to help myself.

The side of his mouth pulls into a smirk. "I could take a

break." He throws Stefan a megawatt smile. "You don't mind, do you? If a lady wants to dance, someone should dance with her."

Honestly, the nerve of this one.

"Sure." Stefan gives a disinterested shrug. "I've got a drink to finish anyway."

What the—

"Great." Myles drops the dishcloth and steps out from behind the bar. "Come on. I'm a good dancer."

Ah, what the hell.

Setting my drink down, I hop off the barstool. I know this is a bad idea, but the heavy beat of the song is pulsing around me, throbbing through the bar, and I'm itching to dance.

Myles slides his hand into mine, taking me by surprise, and pulls me through the crowd to the dance floor. I glance back to see if Stefan's watching, but the crowd is thick—I can hardly see the bar from back here.

My attention flicks back to Myles as he places his hands on my waist and draws me into him. He swings his hips, keeping his touch light, but he's so close—his face is so close—I can't relax. His eyes are penetrating, watching my every move. The last time he was watching me like this I came undone.

God. I am *not* drunk enough for this.

I throw my arms up above my head, swaying, turning around so he's behind me, so I don't have to see his face. But as soon as I've turned around, I want to look at him again. I sneak a glance back over my shoulder. His gaze is pure heat and his fingertips curl into my hips. He draws me back so I'm tucked close to his body and I let myself settle against his firm, lean form. I drop my head back onto his shoulder, delirious from his contact. He's so close behind me that I can smell his cologne, and it's doing something crazy to me.

His mouth is by my ear as we rock together to the music. "You're a good dancer," he says, his warm breath fanning over my skin. It sends a thrill up my spine and before I can think too much about it, I push my ass back into him, wanting to feel him again—wanting him like I did the last time we were this close.

He lets out a little groan into my ear. His hands tighten on my hips, holding me against him as he presses himself into my ass. There's a distinctive hardness grinding against me, and my thighs squeeze together with need. This—*this* is what I've been thinking about since the other night. Him, hard, pressed against me. And now that he's touching me again, I'm losing it.

But instead of stepping away like I know I should, I turn my head so my face is tucked into his neck, and huff in his delicious smell. He knows what I'm doing, too, because he rubs his bristly cheek against my lips. Lust shoots down through my center and burns white hot between my legs, making me quiver all over.

This is *not* good. I hate that he's got this power over me —that one minute I'm fine, then the next he's got me salivating with desire. I lose all control and I can't stand it.

I move away from him, swinging my hips to the beat, attempting to put some distance between us. When I spin around, daring to glance at his face, my heart throws itself against my ribs. Because he's not smiling and cocky anymore—he's staring at me with serious, fiery eyes. And I hate to think what my own expression must look like, but I can feel my cheeks are hot and I'm breathing hard.

You don't want him, I try to tell myself. *This is a bad idea*.

I need to break this tension, fast.

I try to send him a goofy smile, but it doesn't work. He just shakes his head, catching my hand in his and hauling me back against him.

"Cat, what are you doing to me?" he rumbles into my ear. There's a quickening below my navel at his words, because I've spent the past three days wondering the exact same thing about him.

The music slows and he lowers his hands to my waist again, holding me close. My arms, apparently with a mind of their own, circle around his neck. When I let my gaze return to his, he's looking at me desperately.

"Why are you on a date?"

I give a nervous titter. "What?"

He drops his head beside mine. "Why are you here with some other guy?"

"It was a set-up. Alex and Geoff know him."

"Really?" He draws back to meet my gaze. "It's got nothing to do with the fact that you're freaking out about us having sex?"

"I'm not freaking out," I hiss.

"Yes, you are. I know you felt something when we were together, and that's freaking you out. Why else would you be here with him?"

I squirm, unwilling to admit that he might be right. I let him pull me closer, and when his gaze fastens on my mouth, I find my own eyes straying to his. He had that mouth all over my body—everywhere but on mine. And as the bar spins around us, I find myself unable to remember why I wouldn't let myself kiss him. Right now, that mouth looks like heaven. It's like he's reading my mind, because he dips his head, lowering his lips to mine.

But my body has some kind of in-built mechanism, and I duck away from him before he can make contact. The haze of booze in my system clears, and I find myself suddenly feeling very sober.

Holy shit, that was close. What is wrong with me? I'm here on a date with someone else, for Christ's sake—I can't go kissing Myles. And that's besides the point. I know better —I'm here with *Stefan* for a reason.

My heart is thundering but I try to be breezy. "I should probably get back to my date," I say with an unsteady laugh. It sounds hollow to my own ears, and Myles isn't smiling. In fact, he looks almost stunned.

"Are you serious?"

My mouth opens and closes as I waver, and he reaches for my hands.

"Don't push me away. Why won't you just give this a chance?"

I bite hard into my lower lip. *God* how I want to give in to him, to drag him into the alleyway out back and do everything I've imagined us doing on repeat for the past three days. But just as I'm about to tell him that I don't want to be here with Stefan—that I'd rather go home with *him*—I catch something from the corner of my eye. It's the blond from the bar earlier, trying to get Myles's attention. Bitterness rises in my throat and I step back.

"Cat—"

"I have to go."

Myles heaves out a sigh. "Why are you doing this?"

"What?"

He leans in close. "Do you think I like seeing you on a date with someone else?"

"Do you think I like watching you flirt all evening?" I spit back.

Shit, where did that come from?

"It's just a job. It's meaningless."

I pull away, wrapping my arms around myself. I've had this conversation so many times in the past that I've lost count. "It's never meaningless, Myles."

"Of course it is—I've told you that before. But you know what's *not* meaningless? You going on a date right in front of me, three days after we slept together. Either you're trying to make a point, or you're freaking out."

"I am *not* freaking out," I say through gritted teeth.

He folds his arms across his chest, leveling his gaze in a knowing look. He's so damn sure of himself, so self-righteous, and it makes me furious. He doesn't get to flirt with women all night and then be irritated that I'm on a date. And he *definitely* doesn't get to tell me how I'm feeling.

"Fuck this," I mutter. "I'm leaving."

His eyes move over my face, his expression hardening. "Fine. But you know, I'm not just here to entertain you. I'm not just someone you can fuck in between dating other guys."

My breath catches. "What?"

"You know what I mean. So if you walk away now, then... I'm done."

My stomach drops and anger sweeps hot through me. Then I turn and stomp off the dance floor, away from him— away from another stupid mistake.

———

22

I blame myself.

I never seem to learn, do I? I have my dating rules for a reason—because I have no inner guidance system, because I can't trust my own judgment. Then Myles comes along and I just throw them out the window.

And now everything has fallen apart.

It's been six days since Myles told me he was done with me. Six days since the end of our friendship, and whatever else had been quietly blossoming between us, pushing up between the cracks toward the sunlight, sprouting hopefully. And even though I was the one tearing it up by the roots at every chance I got, now that I haven't seen him for a week I'm feeling all... I don't know. But I don't like it.

"I love your hair," a customer says as I pause at the top of the stairs.

I raise a hand absently to my cotton-candy-pink bob. That's right; I dyed my hair pink. After that fight with Myles I just felt the intense need to do something different, to make some drastic change. It was either that, or a tattoo I'd probably end up regretting. Maybe I'll do that next.

"Thanks," I mumble in response. I turn to Hayley. "I'll be downstairs if you need me." Then I step down into the basement, where I've been all day, stress-sewing.

It's a lot emptier down here now. It used to be both storage and an extension of the shop, but now it's a quiet place for me to put my EarPods in and sew when Hayley is working upstairs. I get a lot done when I do that. I've got two whole racks of new items down here now.

We haven't heard about the East Village Market Collective yet and I'm a little anxious. And as for the website, well. I guess a tiny, naive part of me had hoped that maybe Myles would stay good on his word and finish that. But I haven't heard anything from him all week—when before our fight he was sending me updates every day. So obviously, when he said he was done with me, he meant *all* of it.

I've tried not to think about what he said to me on the dance floor—that I was freaking out because we slept together. Mainly because... ugh, he was right. The only reason I went on the date with Stefan was because I was feeling so wrecked after sleeping with Myles. But I couldn't bring myself to admit that, so I lied to him. And myself.

I do that a lot, I've noticed—I lie to myself. Myles was always calling me out for lying on dates, but it turns out I lie to *myself* just as often. I couldn't admit that I was freaking out about Myles—about how amazing the sex was. Because it was; it was raw and satisfying and hot. But if I'm daring to get *really* honest with myself, it was less about the sex, and more about the way it felt when we were in bed together. It felt real and vulnerable—and I didn't like it. Or rather, I did like it, a lot. But I didn't like that it was with *him*. If you're going to let yourself get vulnerable with a guy, well... I don't know. A guy like him just doesn't seem like a good bet.

And he's helped to make that pretty clear, now. Because if he can be "done" with me that easily, if he can give up on all the promises he made me just like that... that's all the proof I need.

With a heavy sigh, I stand, pulling the dress from the sewing machine. It's been a long day, but—

"Ahh!" I leap back, my heart lurching in my chest. Myles is standing right in front of the sewing machine, looking at me.

Jesus Christ. I didn't hear him come down, and he's—

Wait, what is he wearing?

I pull my EarPods out. "Hey." Taking a deep breath, I try to calm my stammering heart as I trail my eyes over his outfit. He's in black jeans and a white button-down shirt, sleeves rolled to the elbows with—get this—a skinny black tie. His hair is styled messy, his jaw is still scruffy, but it's his version of dressed-up.

And, well. He looks *good*.

"Hey." He gives me a tentative smile. "I love your hair."

I frown, saying nothing. What is he doing here?

He brings his hand out from behind his back, holding a bunch of wildflowers in all kinds of gorgeous colors, wrapped in pink cellophane.

Oh.

My stomach clenches into a fist as I realize he must be going on a date. And he's taking flowers, which surprises me. He didn't seem the type. But I don't know why he's stopped in here first—unless he's doing this to get back at me for my Stefan date. Perhaps he's come to rub my nose in it, or—

"These are for you." He steps forward, holding out the flowers.

Oh.

I take the flowers from his outstretched hand. In spite of myself, my pulse ticks up hopefully.

"So," Myles says, shifting his weight, "are you ready to go?"

"What?"

"The dinner party."

I raise a hand to my forehead. "That's tonight?" With everything else that's been going on, I'd totally forgotten about Claudia's dinner party. "You're actually here to take me to that thing?"

"Well, yeah. I said I would."

"Yes, but you also said you were done with me, and since you've stopped working on the website, I assumed—"

"I haven't stopped working on the website. It's almost done, actually."

"Oh," I murmur, taken aback. "I just thought, after Bounce..."

"What?" His brow wrinkles, then smooths with realization. "No, Cat... I'd never ditch the site because of something like that. Whatever happens"—he gestures toward me vaguely—"the site will get done. You don't have to worry about that."

I blink, absorbing this information. Over the six days since I walked away from him at Bounce—and felt like complete and utter shit—I told myself I'd done the right thing, clinging to the fact that he'd ditched the website to console myself. But now as he's standing here, dressed up and ready to take me to a dinner party I'd forgotten about, telling me he's been hard at work all week even though we had a fight...

Emotion constricts my chest and I look down at the flowers. This is the problem with having such a faulty inner compass. I end up all over the map, lost.

"I'm sorry," he says, and I glance up in surprise. "I should have been in touch."

"I'm sorry too." I think about our argument on the dance floor, and regret chews through me. I need to fix this. "Myles... what you said, at Bounce—you were right. I was freaking out, I just didn't want to admit it."

"Why?"

I swallow. "You know how I said I don't date bartenders?"

"Yeah?"

"I never told you this, but... Mark was a bartender. He used to cheat on me with women from the bar." I look away, feeling pathetic. When I finally let myself glance back at Myles, his jaw is like granite.

"Are you serious?"

I nod.

His eyes flare. "What an asshole."

"Sometimes when I see you flirting at work, it reminds me..."

"Oh." Understanding breaks over Myles's face. "Right," he says slowly. "That... explains a lot."

"And I want you to know, I truly didn't think you were going to be working that night, or I never would have had a date there. I didn't mean to do it right in front of you, but... I go to Bounce for a reason. It's the only place I feel safe, because a year ago..." I trail off, feeling the usual sense of unease I do when I think about this. Despite the fact that I never share this with anyone, there's a tiny voice in my head saying, *you can tell him.* But I can't coax the words up my throat, and when I see worry etch into his forehead, I have to glance away.

"A year ago...?" he prompts, taking a step closer.

"It's... um..." Oof. This is harder than I thought.

Awkwardness settles over us while I fiddle with the flowers. The cellophane crinkles in my hands, filling the silence.

"Cat," Myles says, gently taking the flowers from my hand and setting them aside. "What happened a year ago?"

I sigh, sinking back down into my chair. "It wasn't a big deal. Just... some guy at a bar who got super handsy in a dark corner." I shudder as the images rush back to me. "He shoved his hand up my dress, saying I owed him because he bought me a couple of drinks. I was trying to fight him off but he was big and we were down this corridor, alone. The only reason I got away is because some chick stumbled down the wrong corridor trying to find the bathroom and maced him in the face." I realize my hands are trembling and I quickly sit on them, forcing myself to take a calming breath. I don't replay this memory very often, because it just reminds me that there are really, really bad guys out there. "Anyway. That's why I meet all my dates at Bounce now. I feel safe there."

"Oh my God." Myles sinks down to crouch in front of me. "Have you told anyone?"

"I told Cory and Geoff. Cory lost it and Geoff thought I needed therapy." I attempt a laugh. "So, yeah... I don't make a habit of telling people."

"Did you tell the cops?"

"Yeah, I tried to file a report. But I didn't even know the guy's real name, and there was no security footage or anything, so..." I shrug.

"Shit, I don't know what to say. I'm so sorry that happened to you." He rubs his chin, concern written across his face as he gazes up at me. "You deserve to feel safe, wherever you go. You get that, right? You should be able to go into any bar, without some creep—" he breaks off, wiping a hand down his face as he straightens up. "Oh, fuck," he mutters to himself.

"What?"

He gives me a pained look. "I had no idea, Cat. I would never have, well, you know."

"Never have what?"

"The night we met. I totally hit on you."

I stand, placing my hand on his arm. "It's okay. You didn't know."

"But it's the one place you go to feel safe, and I—"

"I *do* feel safe there."

"But then..." He growls to himself, frustrated. "Then I propositioned you, didn't I? I basically talked you into having sex, and—"

"Hey. That's got nothing to do with this."

He wrings his hands, his brow pulled low as he surveys my face.

"Seriously. You didn't talk me into anything. I made that decision for myself."

"Really?" He looks unconvinced. "If I've ever done anything to make you feel uncomfortable, I'm sorry. I never—"

"Well, yeah. You make me feel uncomfortable all the time."

His eyes widen in alarm and I laugh.

"Only because you call me out on my bullshit, Myles. But with the other stuff, no. I've never felt uncomfortable like *that* around you." It's true, I realize. I've been alone with Myles in his apartment, with his pants down, with his shirt off, with his sly, cocky smile—all of this well before we had sex—and I've never once felt like he could do something to hurt me.

Well, not physically, at least.

He lets out a long, uncertain breath. "Okay," he says at last. "But if I do, please tell me. I don't ever want to make you feel—"

"Myles," I say, chuckling. "Stop it. You don't have to worry."

He gives me a weak smile, his thoughts elsewhere. I can tell he's mentally scanning his mind for anything he's done or said to me in the past, and it makes me want to hug him.

"I'm aware that probably wasn't the best way to respond to that—making it all about me." He grimaces. "But I'm sorry, I don't know what to say. I've never had a woman tell me something like that before and it just makes me want to punch something."

"Me too." I think of how angry I was after the taxi incident with Shane and how Myles nearly took a stiletto to the head because of it.

"Do you want to talk about it?"

"It's okay, really. Mostly I'm fine and I never think about it. I'm just more cautious now. I actually thought maybe I was getting over it, but after what happened with Shane—"

Fuck. I didn't mean to bring *that* up.

"What?" Myles stares at me, his features slowly hardening with realization. "Is there something you haven't told me? Did he hurt you?"

"No," I say hastily. "I mean, not really. He just kissed me in the cab, and it made me panic, but—"

"I'm going to fucking *kill* him."

"Nothing happened," I assure him, watching his fists clench at his side. "I got out of the cab before anything could happen and sent him home alone."

Myles cracks his knuckles. "And where does he live?"

"Nice try. Seriously, it's okay. Let's just forget it."

"I—" He contemplates me for a second, then nods reluctantly. "Fine. If you want me to forget it, I will. Although, as your stand-in boyfriend, I have to say—"

A laugh tickles my throat. "What?"

"For the dinner party. I'm your stand-in boyfriend, remember?"

"Oh, yeah." I wrinkle my nose. "I don't think I'm going to go."

His face falls. "Really?"

"I wasn't planning on going after what happened at Bounce. You said you were done with me."

"I know. I was just…" His eyes search my face as he struggles to find the right words. "It wasn't fun for me to see you on a date with someone else. I was jealous as hell." He pauses, then adds, "And I don't think I was the only one who was jealous that night."

I open my mouth, ready to spit a sarcastic retort, but I bite it back. Even though I don't like hearing him say that, I think he's right.

We stare at each other, the air between us thickening, pulsing with a palpable current of chemistry and emotion and words unsaid. I'm afraid to move in case I get electrocuted.

Eventually, Myles looks away. "I'm not asking you for anything, Cat. I didn't know… the things you've just told me… fuck." His eyes meet mine again and his face softens. "But I'm not done with you. I shouldn't have said that."

My heartbeat skips at the tenderness in his gaze, at the way it looks like he's fighting the urge to reach for me. For a second, I think he's lost the battle—that he's going to hug me, or kiss me—and I'm almost breathless with anticipation.

But his face splits into his usual grin, shattering the tension. "Anyway, I can't leave you to face your ex-husband at a dinner party alone. What kind of friend would that make me?"

Friend.

I shouldn't feel the sting I do at that word, but it's there, mixed with a faint sense of relief. He's giving me an out and I should take it. I should grab it like a lifeline and hold on tight. That's the sensible thing to do.

"Well…" I give an uneven laugh. "I would have fixed my hair if I was going to go."

"What's wrong with your hair?"

"It's pink."

His cheek twitches playfully. "Shit, did you not mean to do that?"

"Of course." I smile, inspecting a strand. "But I'd never wear it like that to dinner."

"Why not?"

"You don't know these people, Myles. It's a pre-war townhouse on the Upper East Side. I can't go with pink hair."

He rests his hands on his hips. "Tell me how the world is going to end if you do."

I open my mouth but nothing comes out.

"Exactly. You're being ridiculous."

"Well, I don't have anything to wear. It's already"—I glance at my phone—"six. By the time I get home and change, it will be too—"

"You don't have *anything* to wear," he repeats, his forehead crinkling humorously as he gestures around us with sweeping arms.

"What? No, I mean my own clothes. I don't have—"

"These *are* your clothes, Cat." He cocks his head, a playful gleam in his eye. "You know what? I *dare* you to wear one of your own dresses. I dare you to go with pink hair, in one of your own dresses."

"No way."

"Why not? Because you're worried they'll think you're not classy? You're taking me; your cover's already blown."

A laugh slips from my lips. I study him for a moment, trying to discern exactly what that feeling is, flickering in my chest. He's so persistent, so patient, so…

"Ooh, this one's really sexy." He holds up a polka-dot mini dress and wiggles his eyebrows suggestively.

Annoying. That's what he is.

I snort, taking the dress and stuffing it back on the rack. "I'm *not* wearing that."

"Okay, okay. You choose one, just for fun. If you *were* going to wear one, which one would it be?"

I heave an exasperated sigh. I know what he's doing and I don't want to play along. But when my gaze comes back to him, he's looking at me beseechingly and I give in. "Fine. Okay."

I flick through the rack to buy myself some time, but the truth is, I know which dress I'd love to wear. I made it last week, and I've kept it down here because I couldn't quite see myself parting with it. It's my usual style: a fifties pin-up dress, with a fitted waist, halter straps, and an A-line flare from the waist out to sit just on the knee. The fabric is like nothing else, though—navy blue with the tiniest, most delicate little flowers on the hemline and the sweetheart neckline.

"Yes, that." Myles is grinning as I pull it off the rack. "That's really pretty." He pushes me toward the fitting rooms. "Come on, put it on."

"No," I protest, but now that I've got it in my hands again

I'm itching to try it. I won't wear it, of course, but I could just try it, couldn't I?

I close the curtain to the fitting room, wriggling out of my clothes. Then I check the curtain to make sure Myles hasn't stuck his head in. I can absolutely see him doing something like that. Although maybe not now, after what I told him.

But the curtain is closed. And when I poke my head out, he's standing with his arms folded, staring off into the distance, his brow creased in thought. I know he's worrying about me, trying to recall the ways he's behaved around me, and I feel a little tug in my heart.

I duck back into the fitting room, taking the dress off the hanger. For whatever reason, he really wants me to go out with him in one of my designs with my silly dyed hair. I don't quite get why, but if it will make him smile, I know I'm going to do it.

I pull the dress on and glance over my reflection. Wow, it really is gorgeous. It fits perfectly through my waist, displaying my modest cleavage nicely. And with my pink hair, the navy and the flowers really pop.

"Right," I say, placing a hand on the curtain. "Just turn around until I organize some shoes, okay?"

"Okay."

I peek out and he's got his back turned, so I tiptoe up the stairs. Hayley's at the counter, helping a customer. Her face lights up when she sees me in the dress.

"Woah! That looks great." She hands the parcel to the customer and turns to me. "I hope it's okay that I let Myles downstairs. He had flowers and was all dressed up, so I figured..." She shrugs, a grin slowly creeping across her lips. "I didn't know you two were—"

"We're not," I say with a laugh. I scan the row of shoes

we have left, picking out a pair of strappy wedge heels. They're a size too big, but they'll look great with the dress. I slip my feet into them, turning to Hayley. "Look okay?"

"Uh, no. You look *awesome*. You should dress like that more often."

I smile, about to tell her that I did, once, but I stop myself. Another time.

"Wait," she says, digging into her purse. She pulls out a lipstick and hands it over. "Wear this. It will go with the pink in the flowers on the dress."

"Thanks." I take the lipstick, then turn and clomp down the stairs, pausing near the bottom. "Myles? Keep your back turned, okay? I just need a minute."

"Okay," he says again. "But with every minute, my expectations are only growing."

I laugh, grabbing my purse and slipping into the fitting room. I take out my makeup bag, touching up my face, dragging a brush through my pink hair and pinning it back on one side. A coat of Hayley's dark pink lipstick and I step back to admire my reflection in the dim light.

I smile at the girl in the mirror staring back at me. I haven't seen her in so long—I thought she was gone, actually—but there she is. She was always there, buried under piles of black clothes. If it wasn't for Myles, I wouldn't have put this dress on tonight. But here I am, wearing it.

There's a sudden burst of gratitude behind my breastbone—for Myles, for all the things he's brought into my life. He just elbowed his way in and made me better, made me see what wasn't working, and now I can't imagine my life without him.

Shit. I can't imagine my life without him.

My gut churns as that realization is quickly chased by unease. I don't want to think that. I *can't* think that, because it's crazy. I push the thought away and bring my attention back to the mirror, fixing a smile on my face. And as I gaze at my reflection, it turns into a real, genuine smile.

"Right, I'm ready." I draw back the curtain and step out. Myles still has his back turned dutifully, and I laugh. "You can look now."

He spins around with a chuckle, but it dies away when his gaze reaches my dress. "Fuck," he mutters, gaping at me.

I smooth my hands self-consciously over the navy fabric. "Something a *little* more encouraging might be nice."

"No—" He takes a step closer. "I mean: Fuck, you look amazing."

Delight spreads like warm honey through my veins. "Oh."

"Seriously." His gaze tracks over me; slow, thorough, ravenous. "Jesus, Cat. You look, uh..." He wipes a hand down his face, letting his dark eyes meet mine as he breathes out hard.

I tilt my lips into a teasing smile. "What's wrong with you? You've seen me dressed up before."

"Yeah, but not like this. I've never seen you wearing something so colorful, so beautiful, so"—he gestures at me vaguely—"*you*."

I nod, because he's right; I *do* feel more me in this. More me than I have in ages. "Expectations met, then?"

"Exceeded," he says roughly. He continues to drink me in with greedy eyes, then groans, wrenching his gaze away.

I laugh. "What *now*?"

"I shouldn't stare at you like that, I'm sorry. After what you told me—"

"Myles." I place a hand on his arm, turning him back to me. "Please stop. You have nothing to worry about, and I don't want you to change anything, okay?" I resist the urge to add, *and you have no idea how much I like it when you look at me like that.*

He's silent and I square my shoulders.

"Look, what happened to me was shit, but I haven't let it stop me. And I don't want anyone walking on eggshells around me, thinking I'm some delicate, fragile thing that needs to be handled with care."

He shakes his head. "You're not weak, Cat. I'd never think that. But... that's not going to stop me from wanting to look out for you."

He glances at the wildflowers sitting on the table and I follow his gaze, smiling. They're nothing like the impersonal roses Shane sent. They're just like the flowers in my tattoo, which I'm quite sure is not a coincidence. And here I was thinking that Myles wasn't the type to give a girl flowers at all.

"Here." He plucks some kind of blue flower from the bunch and his lips curve into an affectionate smile as he reaches up to tuck it into my hair.

I remember how Shane thought the flower I wore on our date was there by accident, as if I'd fallen head-first into a garden on the way to meet him. The moron. How on earth did I convince myself that something real could happen there?

As Myles places the flower into my hair, I'm struck by the realization that he really does get me. The real me, under all my bullshit. How does he do that?

"Thanks," I murmur, giving him a shy smile.

He hesitates, his hand lingering beside me, and my heart flips as I think he's going to lean closer—to touch me, to kiss me... But he lets his hand drop, hooking his mouth into a grin. "Okay, let's go make Mark's night miserable."

23

My stomach seesaws with nerves as I knock on Claudia's heavy oak door. I haven't seen her in years and I never really felt like I fitted in with this crowd, in this place—a four-story pre-war brownstone, just off Park Avenue. And now, here I am on her doorstep, in a frilly dress with pink hair. What have I let Myles talk me into?

He slides his hand into mine, as if he can sense my anxiety. I wait for him to give it a quick squeeze and release it, but he doesn't. He just keeps it tucked inside his own warm palm.

I glance at him with a funny smile. "What are you doing?"

"I'm your stand-in boyfriend. We're supposed to be in love, aren't we?"

"Right. Yes."

"So there's going to be lots of hand holding, lots of kissing..." His gaze drops to my lips and they tingle, as if they can feel it. "Not your mouth, I know. But if we're boyfriend and girlfriend, we need to act like we're in love." He allows himself a cocky little grin. "I wouldn't be surprised if by the end of the night you actually *do* fall in love with me."

I roll my eyes, chuckling as I turn back to the door. It's a relief to see the old Myles still in there. After everything that's happened between us recently, it's nice to feel like things could maybe get back to normal.

The door swings open and Claudia greets me with a huge smile. Her dark, glossy hair is still chin-length, her figure still tall and slim, her clothing still stylish. She looks exactly as she did when I last saw her years ago, except for a few more lines around her eyes.

"Cat!" She reaches out, yanking me into a hug. "I can't believe you're finally here. It's been way too long." When she releases me, her gaze snags on my pink locks. "Your hair! What an... interesting color."

I shoot Myles an *I told you so* look, but he ignores me, thrusting his hand toward Claudia. "Hi there, I'm Myles. Cat's boyfriend."

"Yes, hello. Claudia. Welcome."

I take a breath, bracing myself as we step inside. Everything is just as I remember it, as if we're stepping back in time: rich, heavy fabrics, parquet floors, designer wallpaper, ornate and intricate details, antique furniture—the works.

Claudia met Mark through her work in real estate. Years ago she sold properties downtown and, after marrying, moved to work on the Upper East Side. I think she and her husband Andy inherited this house from his parents, but I'm not totally sure on the details. Suffice it to say, Claudia lives in a *very* different world to us now. Still, she's always been friendly, and out of the whole group we used to hang out with, she was the one I liked the most. Andy, on the other hand, was a philandering jerk.

Huh. I wonder if that's why he and Mark get on so well.

I suppress a smile as I watch Myles beside me, hands in his pockets and eyes wide, taking in the lush interior. Seems this is pretty far from his world, too.

"Everyone is up here," Claudia says, gesturing up a staircase. "But Bill and Stacey had to cancel. They had some babysitter issue at the last minute and couldn't get away." She turns to us with an apologetic smile. "So it's just going to be the six of us, I hope that's okay."

I let this information sink in. I was hoping for a dinner party with several other couples to provide a buffer between us and you-know-who. Still, nothing I can do about that now.

"Of course."

"Oh, good." Relief breaks over her face. "Mark has brought his girlfriend, Mel. You have to come meet her, she's lovely."

I resist the urge to laugh hysterically as we follow Claudia up the stairs and down a hall, trying not to let my too-big shoes clomp on the parquet floor. Before I know it, we are in the living room—well, one of them, anyway—and Claudia is introducing everyone.

There's an awkward pause, until I say, "We all know each other already."

"Oh." Claudia glances between us in confusion.

I inhale, ready to explain the situation, but decide against it. "It's a long story," is all I say, giving a strained laugh.

She smiles, not quite in on the joke, then gestures to a Chesterfield sofa. "Take a seat. Andy must be getting drinks. What can I get you two?"

"Vodka soda for me, please." I look at Myles.

"Whiskey, thanks."

Claudia nods, then hurries out of the room. Perhaps she

can sense the tension vibrating around the four of us, ready to implode at any second.

Mark frowns at Myles, then his gaze slides to me. "I thought you were bringing some guy called Shane?"

I send him a syrupy smile. "No."

Mel doesn't miss a beat, her eyes focused on me like lasers. "What are you even doing here?"

"I wanted to see Claudia. I was invited, you know."

"You could have at least made an effort. What are you *wearing*?"

Myles takes my hand, and from the corner of my eye I see his jaw tighten.

"It's one of my designs," I say.

Mel emits a derisive snort. "Oh, how *cute*. And your hair is—"

"Fucking sexy," Myles interrupts, tightening his grip on my hand. "She looks gorgeous. Stop being so passive-aggressive."

Mel's lips purse and I see her shrivel slightly. I turn to Myles, fighting a smile. I forgot how little tolerance he has for bullshit, and suddenly I feel so very grateful to have him here, on my team.

"Thanks, babe." I lean over to plant a kiss on his cheek.

"Wait." Mark is looking between the two of us, the cogs in his brain turning visibly. "Are you two a *thing*?"

I glance at Myles. He's doing me a favor, so I'll let him take the lead. I mean, just having him here holding my hand is apparently enough to give Mark a hernia. And Mel is on the verge of exploding after only five minutes. It was almost too easy.

But Myles surprises me when he slides his arm around my waist, pulling me close. It's just for show, of course, but goosebumps shiver over me as he nuzzles into my neck, his scruff brushing the sensitive skin.

Jesus. I forgot how much my body enjoyed his touch.

"Yep. We're a thing," Myles says when he finally pulls away. His mouth is stretched in a giddy grin as he turns to the others. "I couldn't resist her." It sounds so corny I have to laugh.

Claudia enters the room with a tray of drinks, Andy in tow. He comes over to shake my hand, his eyebrows inching up his forehead as he takes in my appearance.

"Good to see you, Cat. It's been a while."

"It has," I say, giving him a once-over. He's average height and stocky, with almost-black hair, thinning on top. There's more gray there now. And there's a gleam in his eyes that's always been there—like he thinks he knows something you don't, and he finds the whole thing so amusing. I'm pretty sure the only thing a guy like him knows is the location of the nearest strip joint.

He turns to Myles, extending his hand. "Andrew Cooper."

Myles shakes his hand firmly. "Myles Ellis."

Claudia hands me my vodka and I take a big gulp, feeling myself begin to loosen up. Beside me, Myles raises the glass of expensive whiskey to his lips and takes a measured sip. I watch the column of his throat as he swallows, noticing the contrast between his rugged tattoo and the crystal low-ball glass. He might be very out of place in this townhouse, but he sure looks good with a nice glass of whiskey like that. And that shirt and tie...

Anyway.

He catches me watching him and leans in close to my ear, speaking in a low voice, just for me. "I meant it, by the way. You do look fucking sexy."

There's a fizzle through my abdomen at his words, his closeness. I tuck my nose into his neck, unable to stop myself from breathing in his scent. It does something funny to my brain, because next I hear myself whisper, "So do you."

Whoops. I probably shouldn't have said *that*. I might be thinking it, but saying it is a different thing altogether. Just as it was beginning to feel like things between us could be okay, I go and blur the lines again.

I pull back slowly, reluctant to look at him. I know he'll be wearing his self-satisfied grin and I don't want to see it.

But when I meet his gaze, there's no sign of his smug self. Just dark eyes, boring into mine. His tongue slides out to moisten his lips and, fuck, I have to look away at this point.

This whole situation is so strange, pretending to be together—especially since we've already been together in bed. And after the things he said to me at Bounce, the things he said earlier this evening... I don't know where the acting stops and reality begins, and it's messing with my head.

When I look at the others they're all watching us, and an embarrassed laugh trickles out of me. Somehow, I'd almost forgotten where we are.

"So, how's the career, Cat?" Andy asks over his glass of rum. "Are you still working at that dinky little shop in the East Village?"

"I own the shop. And yes, still there."

I make the mistake of catching Mel's eye, and she smirks. "But it's been a bit tough lately, hasn't it? Financially?"

Wow, she's really going for the jugular tonight. Usually she's a bit more clever in her attacks—more underhanded and less openly hostile. I must be really getting to her.

"Actually, business has been thriving," Myles says beside

me. "Cat's decided to focus on her own designs, and it's about time."

Mark's nostrils flare and he narrows his eyes at Myles. "Let me guess, that was *your* idea? Are you sure you should be giving her business advice?"

Myles takes a slow sip of whiskey, refusing to get sucked into Mark's little game. And as I glance between the two of them—Mark with his hackles raised, Myles calm and level-headed—realization nearly blinds me.

Holy shit, Geoff was right. Myles isn't like Mark at *all*. Mark is petty and immature, thinking only of himself, always wanting to tear others down. Myles is the polar opposite—he has been since the moment I met him. How did I not see this before?

Myles sets his glass down, ignoring Mark as he turns to Claudia and Andy. "People have been snatching up Cat's designs. She even has a waiting list of clients who want her to create something for them."

I stifle a chuckle. A bunch of random emails for our website is hardly a "waiting list of clients," but I appreciate his support nonetheless.

"Wow," Claudia says. "I might have to get you to design something for me, Cat. I want to redo my wardrobe and I'm so sick of the same old designers."

"I'd love to," I reply, with a genuine smile. I'm not sure she'll like the style of my designs, but it's nice to have her interest. Who knows, maybe I'll start some kind of retro-inspired fashion trend on the Upper East Side.

Myles nudges me, grinning, and there's something about this tiny gesture that makes my heart swell. Almost instinctively, I lean into him. He slips his arm around my waist, pulling me against his side and pressing a kiss to my temple.

And I find myself wondering if this is part of the act—or something else entirely.

"You two are so sweet." Claudia's eyes sparkle as she watches us. "How long have you been dating?"

I glance at Myles for him to take the lead, and he smiles. "Only a month. But you know what they say: when you know, you know."

I poke him in the ribs. "Mister romantic over here," I tease. I give him a look that says, *where do you come up with this crap?* but he just gazes at me, little creases around his warm eyes.

"And what do you do, Myles?" Andy asks.

Myles glances at me uncertainly, and I nod. "I'm a bartender in the East Village, and I'm in the process of building a web-design business." He reaches again for his whiskey, and there's a twinkle of mischief in his eye. "But my true passion is experimental jazz."

A laugh bursts out of me. I almost choke on my vodka, quickly trying to disguise it with a cough. What the hell is he doing now?

"Oh... uh, wow," Andy says.

"Do you know the genre?" There's a smile in Myles's voice, and I can't even look at him or I'm going to explode.

"Well, of course." Andy nods hastily. "Big fan."

"Great!" Myles pushes to his feet. "Let's put some on."

"That's okay, honey." I grab his arm and yank him back down onto the sofa beside me. "Maybe another time." I try to send him a *cut it out* look, but when I see the laughter dancing in his eyes, I almost lose it. I look away from him, flattening my lips, but they're trembling and I know I can't keep this up. "Bathroom, Claudia?" I manage, one hand covering my smile.

"Of course." She gestures toward the hall. "You remember where it is?"

I rush to my feet, fleeing the room. Once down the hallway, I take a left and step into the spacious powder room, collapsing in a paroxysm of giggles behind the door. *For God's sake, Myles.*

He's such an idiot. He's an adorable idiot, and I don't know what I'd do without him.

Shit.

I gaze at my reflection, feeling unease crawl across my skin. What am I thinking?

Look, okay, I can no longer deny how much I like him. He's always been cute, and he's looking extra fine tonight. I remember what's under that shirt, those jeans—I know the shape and the taste of him now, and that's driving me crazy. Tonight he's being so sweet and affectionate, and while I know he's putting on an act for the others, part of me also senses it's not just that. Now that I can see how much he's *not* like Mark, it's like a veil has been lifted. I can see parts of him I couldn't—or didn't want to—see before.

But... I also can't deny the urge I feel to stay away from him. Because if he's not like Mark, then it's something else —something making me want to keep him at arm's length. Maybe I'm just worried about Cory's words after making the mistake of not listening to him last time. Or maybe it's my inner compass, giving me a warning. I have no idea, but it's scaring the shit out of me.

I shake my head at myself in the mirror. *Don't make another mistake, Cat.*

With a sigh, I open the bathroom door, stepping out into the corridor. Myles is waiting outside, leaning against the wall. He straightens up when he sees me.

"You okay?"

"Yeah. But I couldn't keep it together when you started talking about experimental jazz."

"I just wanted to see you smile." He chuckles and his expression softens. "They're assholes. You know that, right?"

"Well, Claudia's okay," I say and he nods. "But otherwise... yeah."

We stare at each other for a minute, then he lets his gaze sink down the length of my body and slowly climb back up. Somehow, I can *feel* it. All my nerve endings spark, and when his gaze meets mine again and his pupils dilate, swallowing up the blue in his eyes, heat blooms low in my belly.

He steps closer, reaching out to trail a fingertip along the flower details on the strap of my dress. There's a gruff edge to his voice as he says, "You have to let me photograph you in that dress."

It takes all my strength to stop myself from saying, *you can do whatever you want to me in this dress.* Instead, I clear my throat and give him a neutral expression. "Sure. If you think it will be good for the site, we can do that."

The light dims in his eyes and he slips his hands into his pockets, turning to leave. I can feel the shift in his energy, and it makes my chest tense up. What is wrong with me? So he's being flirty and fun—wasn't that the deal for the evening? He doesn't deserve me being a bitch.

"Hey." I grab his arm and he turns back to me, eyebrows raised. I slide my hand down, slipping it into his. "Thanks for coming tonight. I really appreciate it."

A small smile lifts his lips. "Sure. I can see why you didn't want to come alone."

"I probably shouldn't have come at all," I mumble, looking back down the hall.

"You want to go? We could leave." He gives my hand a squeeze.

"What would we say?"

He shrugs. "We don't owe them an explanation."

I smile. I guess he's right.

"Up to you," he says. "We'll do whatever you want."

I gaze at him, feeling warmth unfold inside me and spread out along my limbs. Even after I went on a date with someone else, after I pushed him away... he still got dressed up, bought me flowers, and came to take me to this stupid thing tonight. He's happy to be here and support me, even though it's no fun for him, and he's happy to go, even though I dragged him all the way uptown and wasted his night off. This definitely isn't part of the act—this is *him*. He couldn't be any sweeter if he tried.

Why is he so good to me? And why am I so awful to him?

I can't keep doing this. I need to tell him, to show him...

I take a step closer, sliding a hand around the back of his neck. Then I stand up on my toes and press my lips to his in the briefest, gentlest kiss.

Well, it was supposed to be brief. But as soon as his lips touch mine, electricity surges through me and I lose all sense of reason. I melt against him, circling both arms around his neck and crushing my mouth against his.

Holy, *holy* shit.

A tiny moan escapes him and his fingers curl into my waist, tugging me closer. But it's not enough; I'm hungry to taste him. I tilt my head, nudging his mouth open, and when I feel the soft lick of his tongue against mine, heat blazes down to my core.

Oh my *God*. Why didn't I kiss him before tonight?

I thrust a hand up into his curls and his hips press forward. I can feel how much he wants this—wants *me*—and it's making me lose it. There's another moan from him, this time echoing right through me, and I can't help but let out a whimper in response. I've never been kissed like this—both sweet and dirty at the same time. His hands are so soft on my waist, but he's claiming me with his mouth, his tongue making my legs shake with need.

Jesus Christ. This is, *wow*, this is—

"Cat?" Claudia's voice approaches the hallway and I draw back from Myles, breathless, as if we're doing something we shouldn't.

Well, we are. But Claudia doesn't know that.

"Oh, there you are." She laughs uncomfortably. "Sorry, didn't mean to interrupt. The lobster's ready."

"Okay," I say overly-brightly. I try to look away from Myles, but I can't—I'm captivated by his glassy, unfocused gaze. His hands are still on my waist and my body is pulsing toward him, desperate to jump back into that kiss.

After what feels like an eternity I hear Claudia leave, and Myles drops his hands, breathing hard.

"What was that?"

I yank my gaze away with a grimace. Shit, I don't know what that was. *Why* did I kiss him? Wasn't that the most important rule I had—to *not* kiss him? I'll never come back from this now. I'll never be able to un-feel his lips, un-hear that moan he made. And I was right—it was different from sex. It was more intimate.

Way too intimate.

"Cat?"

"Not now, Freud," I mutter, rubbing my forehead.

A deep V appears between his brows. Dammit, I've gone into bitch mode again.

"Sorry." I take his hand, just to reassure him. But I can't help myself. I raise it to my mouth, brushing my lips over the tattoo on the inside of his wrist.

Fuck, fuck, fuck. I'm in trouble.

"You want to go?" His voice is a rough scrape up his throat, and he squeezes my hand, attempting to pull me closer.

But I'm panicking. I can't leave with him—not now. Because I know exactly what I'll do—what we'll do—and I can't do that again. I've kissed him now and it will be different. I don't think I'll be able to handle it.

"Lobster," I blurt.

Amusement skims across his features. "Lobster?"

"Yes. We can't leave yet. Don't you want some lobster?"

He scrubs a hand over his face with a chuckle. "Okay, let's eat some lobster. But that's not going to make me forget what just happened."

"I know." I give him a wry smile. "You never let anything go."

"No, I mean—"

"I know what you mean, Myles. We can analyze it later."

He sighs, relenting. "Fine. Let's eat lobster."

24

We manage to make it through dinner in one piece. And by one piece, I mean that we don't fall into another life-altering kiss or accidentally have sex on the table.

So that's something.

But the whole time, Myles is making eyes at me over his lobster. I know what he's thinking, what he wants. And I want it too—he has no idea how much. I'm doing a pretty good job of acting aloof, but underneath I'm just a horndog like him. I want it. I want *him*.

Still, we're in polite company right now—well, company, at least—so we need to keep it together. And I'm relieved, because I'm not sure about sleeping with Myles again. I'm really not.

After dinner we retire to a different room, with a bar cart and an upright piano against the far wall. The first thing Myles does is wander over to the piano with a smile.

"This is nice. I've always wanted a Steinway."

I look at him oddly. What the fuck is he talking about now?

"You play?" Andy asks, handing him a whiskey.

Myles runs a finger along the lid. "Yeah."

I snort a laugh as I take my vodka from Andy, and Myles glances at me.

"What? I do."

Ah, this must be part of his experimental jazz bit. Though it's a bit risky to pretend to play the piano—what if they actually *ask* him to play?

"No you don't," I say with a light laugh, attempting to breeze past this.

He lifts an eyebrow. "Want me to prove it?"

Oh, a challenge. "Go on, then."

"Alright." He sets his whiskey down, one side of his mouth kicking up into a confident grin, then he links his fingers together and stretches his arms out, clicking his knuckles. He sits on the stool, raising the lid of the piano, letting out a low whistle. "Beautiful," he says, and I resist the urge to snicker.

I lean against the side of the piano, glancing over at Mel and Mark. They both look bored but I couldn't care less. At least Andy and Claudia are interested, poised and ready to hear Myles, though I hate to think of how disappointed they're about to be.

I glance down at him and he gives me a wink. Well, if he wants to humiliate himself, fine.

"I'm a bit rusty." He rests his fingers on the keys. "Haven't played in a while. But I'll do my best."

"Okay," I say sardonically. I'll be lucky to get *Chopsticks* from him.

There's a beat of silence, then he begins to play. And to my astonishment, he's playing—properly playing. It only takes me a second to recognize the song—Pachelbel's *Canon in D*—and as soon as I do, something inside my chest squeezes hard.

Immediately, I'm transported back to my childhood home, to the shaggy orange rug in our living room. Dad is at the piano playing this song, and I'm on the rug, on my stomach with my chin resting on my hands, watching him play, thinking he's the best thing in the world. He could make the most beautiful music seem so effortless and I thought it was magic. The memory is so vivid, I can smell the smoke from his cigarette, feel the wool of the rug on my skin, hear Mom humming along in the kitchen.

Myles looks up at me, grinning proudly and playing seamlessly, and I swallow against the sudden stinging in my throat. I know he can sense it, because he hesitates and a little line forms along his brow, but I nod at him and he turns back to the keys.

I put my drink down, resting my chin on my hands on the top of the piano. And as I watch him play, I can't help but think that he is not who I thought he was at all. He glances at me again, checking if I'm okay, and I gaze back at him in awe. Myles is playing my favorite song to me on the piano, and he doesn't even know what it means. But somehow, he does. Because he knows me—because he sees me.

There's a fierce ache inside my ribcage as his eyes meet mine again. He has the most tender expression on his face, and now he's playing just for me. I can *feel* it, in my heart. I don't know how he does this, but he does—he gets through to me. It's equal parts exhilarating and terrifying.

When the song comes to an end, I want to sob. Myles lifts his fingers off the keys, looking up at me with a soft smile. But I feel as if I've been torn apart and stitched back together, a patchwork quilt of sad memories and new, intense feelings I'm too afraid to acknowledge.

He steps out from the piano and pauses in front of me. His eyes map my face, charting every emotion I can't hide. Cupping my jaw in his hands, he draws my mouth up to his and kisses me, feather-soft. Then he gathers me into his arms and holds me tight against him, and I can't even breathe because it feels so good.

"Well. I should learn to play like that," Andy says with a chortle, and that's when I remember we aren't alone.

"Sorry," I say, my voice croaky as I draw away from Myles. "I just... I've never heard him play that before." I glance up and his gaze is trained on mine, like he's only got eyes for me, an affectionate smile tugging at his mouth.

That mouth.

I wrestle my gaze away and reach for my drink, taking a long sip. Because if I keep staring at that mouth of his, I'll kiss him again—and this time I won't be able to stop. I suddenly find myself longing for cocky Myles—the one who struts around like he's God's gift to women, the one who irritates the shit out of me. I don't know who this sweet guy is and it's rattling me.

"So, Myles," Mark says over his glass of rum, "how's your real estate game? Got much in the way of investments?"

I raise my eyes to the ceiling. I know what Mark's doing. He's trying to show Myles up, show him he's a bigger man, and I feel a stab of defensiveness for Myles. Because he might not have much in the way of property, but he has a lot more than Mark—things you can't put a price on.

God, I don't know how I ever convinced myself that these two were the same. I couldn't have been more blind.

I glance at Myles apologetically, but he gives Mark a nod, sipping from his glass. "I'm doing okay."

"Really?" Mark asks in surprise. "Because—well, no

offense—but I can't imagine you're earning enough as a bartender to buy much in the way of Manhattan real estate."

I turn back to Mark with a scathing look. "You'd know, right? You were a bartender for years."

"Yeah. But then I grew up."

My fist balls at my side, and I decide enough is enough. It's one thing for these assholes to have a go at me, but I'm not going to sit here and let them attack Myles. He's done nothing to deserve this.

"You didn't grow up, Mark," I mutter. I drain my glass and set it down, turning to Myles. But of course, he's not mad. He's his usual calm self, regarding Mark with quiet amusement.

"I didn't have a lot of spare cash for a while, no. But once I'd paid off my MBA, that freed up some money. And then I sold my app and made a pretty decent sum."

I smother a smile. That was a good one, with the app. Where does he come up with this stuff?

"You sold an app?" Mel asks, perking up with sudden interest, clearly sensing a gold-digging opportunity.

I shoot her an icy glare, sliding my hand into Myles's and squeezing protectively. If she thinks she's getting her claws into him, too, she is mistaken. I'll punch her in the throat.

Okay, it's not like he's mine, or anything. But it's the principle. That's all.

Myles squeezes back. I see he's noticed her sudden interest too, because the amusement is glimmering in his eyes again. He looks at me and we share a secret eye-roll. A warm, comforting sensation blossoms in my chest, and it takes me a second to realize what it is. It's the feeling that I'm not alone. Because right now, I have never felt more supported—never felt more like I have someone in my corner, looking out for me.

And now it's time for me to look out for him, and get him the hell away from this lot.

I lean into his ear and whisper, "Want to go?"

He glances at me, trying to read my expression, then nods.

"Thank you so much for having us, Claudia," I say with a smile. "Dinner was lovely and it was really nice to see you again. But we need to get going."

She rises to her feet. "Sure. I'll be in touch about you designing some clothes for me," she says, pulling me into a hug. "I have a friend who owns a boutique around here who might be interested, too."

"Great." I turn to the others, forcing a civil tone. "Nice to see you. Good night."

Mel gives a scornful snort and I grit my teeth, taking a step toward her, but Myles tugs me back by my hand.

"Come on, baby," he says soothingly, "let's get you home."

I grumble, letting him lead me out. When we're finally alone on Claudia's doorstep, I blow out an aggravated breath. "They're the worst. I'm so sorry I dragged you all the way here."

A smile brushes his lips. "I'm not."

"You're not?"

"No. If you hadn't dragged me here, you never would've kissed me."

I turn away from him with a shaky laugh. "I don't know," I mumble. Would I have kissed him anyway, at some point?

"Hey," he says gently, touching my shoulder so I turn back to him. "I'm not expecting anything, okay?"

"What?"

He shrugs. "Nothing has to happen between us. I know

you're worrying that because we kissed, I expect something. But I don't."

Relief rolls through me. Not at his words, exactly, but at how he's letting me put some space between us. Except, he's being so damn sweet and sincere about it that my heart squeezes again. It's this kind of shit that makes me *want* to kiss him.

"Oh yeah? Then what was with all that 'let's get you home baby' stuff?"

He chuckles, gesturing for me to head down onto the street. "You looked like you were about to punch Mel. Anyway, we need to get you home before midnight, because once that clock strikes twelve—"

"What, I'll turn into a pumpkin?"

"I think you'll find that was the carriage. She just turned back into a spinster."

"I hate to break it to you, buddy. I'm a spinster twenty-four seven—not just after midnight."

He laughs as we turn down Park Avenue, the balmy evening air warming us through. The traffic hums along beside us and the pleasant chirrup of birds drifts from the park as they settle down in the fading copper light.

"I'll order an Uber," Myles says, taking his phone out. I nod, pulling out my own phone, but he gestures for me to put it away. "Let's share one. I'll drop you home like the Prince Charming I am."

"I guess a stand-in boyfriend should drop me home."

"Exactly. I need to see out my duties for the evening." Our ride pulls up a moment later and he opens the door with a grand flourish, turning to me. "M'lady. Your carriage."

I climb inside with a giggle, trying to make sense of the light, pleasant feeling coursing through me, despite the fact that I spent the evening with Mel and Mark.

I think it might be happiness.

25

O n the ride home, Myles is unusually quiet. I'm just about to ask him if he's okay, when he turns to me with a thoughtful look.

"Tell me about your dad."

"What? Why?"

"The piano," is all he says.

"Oh." I release my breath in a long stream, fiddling with the strap on my purse. "Well, what do you want to know?"

"What was he like? What happened?"

I lift a shoulder. "He was... he was great. He was the best cook—my mom's hopeless. He used to take us to basketball games when we were kids. He was convinced Cory would be in the NBA because he was so tall at such a young age."

Myles makes a face. "I can't picture Cory in the NBA."

"I know, right?"

"What else?"

I pause, thinking about Dad again. "He loved the piano. I thought it was amazing, the way he could play. It was like magic, making that music with just his fingers. That song you were playing—that's one of my favorites. It totally took me back to one afternoon at home when I was lying on the floor, watching him play." I think again of Myles playing the piano just like Dad tonight, and sigh. Dad might have been a brilliant pianist, but he was also the first man to break my heart. "He was gone a few weeks later," I add quietly, letting my gaze float over Myles's shoulder and out to Seventh Avenue.

"Gone?"

"Yep. I didn't know why at the time, but later Mom explained that he left because he wasn't happy."

He doesn't want us anymore, Catherine.

I hear Mom's words in my ear, clear as day, and they make me shudder. "I'll never understand. It was like he just stopped loving us—like he cared about himself more than us. What kind of man just walks out on his family like that?"

Myles glances down at his hands, saying nothing for a moment. When he finally looks at me, his eyes are sad. "That's... shit, that's awful."

I nod slowly, twisting the strap of my purse in my hands.

"Between Mark and your dad... I can understand why you don't trust men."

"Thanks, Freud." I cut him a look. "And it's not like I don't trust all men, I'm just... careful." But when I think about my broken inner compass, I realize I don't even know *how* to be careful anymore. I don't know which way is up.

I turn in my seat to face Myles, and when I see the pensive expression on his face, I nudge him playfully, trying to lighten the mood. "Hey. I trust you, don't I?"

"Do you?"

"How else could you have gotten me to go out in this crazy outfit?"

A grin plays on his mouth. "You call it crazy. I call it something else."

Fucking sexy, he called it. I remember, and I'm hot all over just thinking about it. It must be showing on my face, because he sinks his teeth into his lip as he stares at me, lust smoldering in his eyes.

God.

I make myself look away before I lunge at him across the backseat, forcing myself to watch the scenery. By the time we pull up outside my building I'm feeling more relaxed, and I pause as I reach for the door handle. After everything Myles has done for me tonight, I want to give him something to say thank you. Something I've been working on.

"Would you come in for a minute? I want to show you something."

His eyebrows shoot up. He makes no attempt to hide the suggestive smile on his lips and I shove him.

"*Not* that."

He follows me out of the car with a chuckle, stopping on the sidewalk to look up at my building. "Nice place."

"Thanks." I tilt my head to look at the redbrick building too. "Mark and I lived here, then I got it in the divorce. But sometimes I think I'd like to move. I prefer it over in the East Village." I lead him up the front steps and inside, dropping my purse and kicking off my too-big shoes.

He smiles to himself as he stands in my living room, looking around. "I never thought I'd get to see your place."

"What?"

"I figured you'd be sick of me before I ever got here."

"Oh, I am. And yet here you are." I laugh as I wander into the kitchen. "Do you want a drink?"

"Sure. What do you have?"

I open the cabinets. "Hmm. I have some whiskey." I reach for a bottle I've had for ages, opening the lid and sniffing. "Whiskey doesn't go bad, does it?"

"It does, actually." He slides onto a stool at the breakfast bar, taking the bottle and sniffing. "It's probably fine."

I grab two glasses and watch as Myles pours them both. Even at my house, he's serving me a drink.

He takes a swig and nods. "It's fine."

"Sorry I don't have anything else." I take a sip, savoring the malty burn on the way down.

"Well, I didn't come in for the whiskey."

"Right!" I place my glass down and wander across the living room to the corner behind the partition. I've set up my old sewing machine and there's a rack of dresses I've been working on for his daughter. For some reason, not hearing from Myles for the past week didn't stop me from working on them—it only made me more determined to create a beautiful dress. Maybe there was a tiny part of me that hoped he hadn't given up on me, I don't know. Whatever it was, every night after work I'd come home eager to create a new piece, imagining what it might look like on his daughter, if she'd like it. If *he'd* like it.

I wheel the rack over to him, feeling a nervous twinge in my gut. "I made some more dresses for your daughter."

"Really?" He sets his glass down, frowning.

"Yeah," I say with a hopeful smile. "Just because, well, if the other ones weren't right, then—"

"Wait. Is that what you thought? That I didn't like them?"

"Well, yeah." I shift my weight. "You seemed totally bummed when I gave them to you."

He steps past me, looking at the rack of new dresses. There's another mermaid one, one with hearts and stars, one with tons of sparkly sequins and tulle and another one with multicolored flowers.

"Oh my God, Cat." Myles turns to me, slack-jawed. "I can't believe you made all these. They're stunning."

Yes! I worked my butt off all week, and it was *so* worth it to see that look on his face. I want to punch the air, I'm so happy, but I settle on a beaming smile instead.

He gazes at me, opening and closing his mouth. "Come here," he says at last, pulling me into a hug before I can protest.

Because I would have protested, believe me. I would have said, *I can't, Myles. I can't stand to have your hands on me again, in case I lose my mind.*

But I don't say any of that, of course, and now I'm pressed against his chest, breathing in a lungful of him, feeling my knees go weak. I can hear his heart beating hard and it makes me want to unbutton his shirt and snuggle inside.

Fuck.

"I can't believe you did this," he murmurs into my hair. "The other dresses you made are perfect. I love them, that's not..." He pauses as his voice breaks, and I find myself squeezing him tighter. "I guess... I never really told you much about my daughter."

"It's alright. You don't have to if you don't want to."

"No, I do."

He releases me, and I take in the somber expression on his face as I perch on a stool. He sits too, exhaling wearily as he rakes a hand through his hair. I watch the way his tattoos peek out from the sleeve of his button-down shirt, trying not to be insanely attracted to him, sitting here in my kitchen. Or maybe it's the fact that he's looking so vulnerable.

Jesus. What is wrong with me?

"Her name is Amber," he says, staring down at his lap. "I don't get to see her at all. I *want* to see her, but my ex—Nikki

—won't let me. I—" He pauses, his gaze flitting up to mine and down again. "Things with Nikki didn't end on good terms. And whenever I try to speak with her, she just verbally abuses me and tells me I'll never see Amber again."

"Shit," I mumble, noticing the way his shoulders sag as he talks, wanting to hold him. I have to sit on my hands in case I do something stupid.

"Yeah. The dresses are amazing. I think Amber will love them—at least I hope she will—and if I'm lucky, they might also convince Nikki that I'm not all bad."

Jealousy floods my bloodstream. *That's* what this is about? Trying to win his ex back?

"Right, okay," I manage, reaching for my whiskey and taking a large gulp. "I didn't realize you were trying to get back together with—"

"No." His gaze flies to mine and he shakes his head firmly. "No, I do *not* want to get back together with her. I just want her to let me see my daughter."

"Oh." The intensity of my relief surprises me. "But... couldn't you take her to court? You have rights, as the father."

His face crumples and he looks down at his hands. "I couldn't do that to Amber, not after everything, not after I —" He cuts himself off. "I couldn't put her in the middle. She doesn't deserve that."

I nod slowly, understanding. He's feeling selfish, wanting to see Amber—like he doesn't have a right, like it wouldn't be good for her, too.

"Anyway." He sniffs, forcing himself to sit straighter. "I can only hope that one day Nikki will come around, I guess." He shrugs, like it's no big deal, and when his eyes meet mine and he gives me a watery smile, I feel like I've been punched in the heart.

This time, I don't hesitate. I push to my feet and stand in front of his stool, reaching over his shoulders to pull him close to me. His body relaxes as he circles his arms around my waist, resting his head against my chest.

"I'm so sorry, I had no idea. That sucks." I hold him lightly, keeping my head up, just wanting to offer a little comfort. I can tell he's hurting. This is about him.

But really, I'm kidding myself. I let my head drop, so that my nose is in his messy hair. I can smell the product he uses, I can smell *him*, and as he parts his legs on the stool, drawing me into his body, I let him. I let him tighten his arms around me, let him hold me close.

"Yeah, it does suck," he says on a sigh.

I sigh too, pressing my lips to his hair, aching to kiss him properly.

But I shouldn't. I shouldn't kiss him again, because if I do, I won't stop.

"Can I ask you something?" Myles murmurs, his head still against my chest.

"Sure."

"Why did you kiss me tonight?"

I swear, he's got a sixth sense. But he's right—why *did* I kiss him tonight, when I'd sworn I wouldn't kiss him at all? I cast my mind back to Claudia's hallway, to the way he was being so sweet and understanding, the way he had my back when the others were being shit, the way his shirt fit him just right.

"I just... couldn't not," I say at last.

"Like, you felt as though you had to."

"Yeah."

He draws back, lifting his eyes to mine. "And what if I feel that way?" He's tracing tiny circles on my back with his fingertip, his touch so light I can barely feel it. But it's enough to make me dizzy.

"Are you feeling that way?"

His gaze falls to my mouth and he nods.

"Me too," I whisper. I slide my hands up the back of his neck, over the short prickles of his closely-shaved hair, tilting his head back. I watch as his eyes soften with longing, as he parts his lips for me. My whole body is humming with anticipation as I finally lower my mouth to his.

Somehow, even though the thirst has been building in me all evening, I kiss him tentatively. My lips graze his, just testing the waters, seeing if it feels as good as last time.

And it does. Fuck, it does.

He sucks on my bottom lip, sliding his hands up and around my waist until his palms are flat against my back. I feel his tongue dip out, searching for mine, and with a moan I sink deeper into his mouth, finally giving in. The whole world tilts around us as we kiss, our bodies inching closer until we're pressed against each other, our tongues merging, frantic with need. Heat builds between my legs, throbbing and urgent. I don't care about all the reasons I have to stay away from him—I just want him naked, his skin pressed against mine, his arms tight around me.

I break the kiss, trying to catch my breath enough to tell him what I want.

"Holy shit," he mutters, pressing his fingertips into my back as if he's afraid I'm going to slip from his grasp. I love the little grin he's trying to contain. I feel the same.

"You, um... do you have to go?"

His grin widens and he glances away. It's like he's trying to stop himself from being too excited and it's adorable. He's adorable.

I lean down, kissing into his neck, inhaling the smell of

his skin, feeling his moan vibrate against my lips. Every tiny indication that he likes what I'm doing is gasoline on a flame, until I'm ablaze with lust. This place is going to go up in smoke.

"I can stay," he manages, his voice thick.

"Good." I give him a slow, seductive smile and turn for the bedroom. "Come with me."

26

I close the bedroom door behind Myles, then cross the room to flick on the bedside lamp. A warm, yellow glow falls over the room, and I cringe when I spot a pile of laundry in one corner. I was hardly planning on bringing him back here.

But he can't see any of that, because he won't take his eyes off me. "Come here," he murmurs. He reaches for me but I shake my head.

Instead, I slowly unzip my dress and let it pool around my ankles. I'm wearing awful underwear again—I had no idea he'd be showing up to take me out this evening—but I don't care, and neither does he.

He adjusts the impressive bulge in his jeans, giving me a sheepish smile. Somehow, he's both sexy and cute at the same time. I stare at him, trying to soak this moment in. How did I ever convince myself I couldn't want him?

I close the distance between us and slide my hands up the front of his shirt. His fingers brush over the bare skin on my back, sending little fireworks scattering across my body.

"Cat..." His eyes dart over my face. "Are you sure you want to do this?"

"Yes," I reply without hesitating. I might have all kinds of feelings whipping through me that I don't want to acknowledge, but he needs to know there's not a doubt in my mind over what we are about to do. Because tonight, everything feels different. "Myles, you're not..." I pause, swallowing hard. "You're not who I thought you were. At all." I raise a hand to his face, dragging my thumb over his smooth skin and rough jaw, and he lets out the softest sigh. "I really do trust you, you know."

"I know," he says quietly. "And I don't know if it means anything to you, but I trust you, too."

"Why wouldn't that mean anything to me?"

"I don't know. I guess... you're not the only one who's scared of getting hurt."

I laugh uneasily, stepping back. "What? I'm not—"

"Hey." He pulls me back against him, wrapping his arms around me. "Let's just be honest tonight, yeah?" His eyes pierce mine and I realize I couldn't hide even if I wanted to. But for the first time in forever, I don't.

"Okay," I whisper, letting myself sink into his gaze. I want to ask him what he meant—how he could possibly be afraid of getting hurt—but I can't find the right words. I want to know if he's serious, or if it's just another one of the things he's saying to get me in the mood, like last time.

But the more I turn that idea over—the more I think back to his words on the dance floor at Bounce, the way he's been with me all night—the more I begin to think he *didn't* just say things to get me in the mood. He meant what he said. He always means what he says.

"Tell me what you're thinking," he murmurs.

Oh, no. I'm not sharing any of that with him. He'll go all

Freud and we'll have to talk for hours and that's *not* what I want.

I rest a hand on his chest with a playful smile. "I was just thinking about the best way to thank you for coming out with me this evening."

His eyebrows rise. "Well, it was a *huge* inconvenience..." A warm, sexy laugh reverberates against my fingertips. "Seriously, though. You don't have to thank me."

"No?" I ask, trailing my hand down the front of his shirt, tugging teasingly at his belt buckle, sliding my palm over the thickness behind his zipper.

He presses his hips forward with a groan. His hands skate down to grip my butt and he walks me backwards to the bed. I climb on, pulling him down beside me. When he removes his tie and reaches for his buttons, I push his hands away, wanting to undress him myself. He chuckles and sets his hands down, letting me take control.

"I love this shirt on you," I say, slowly working my way down the buttons, each one exposing more of his chest, the start of his tattoo, the patch of hair.

"Oh yeah?"

I nod, pausing my unbuttoning to lean forward and kiss his chest, unable to wait until his shirt is off. I breathe him in deep. His masculine smell is like a drug and I can't get enough. I want to huff it in until I see stars.

"Why's that?" he asks roughly.

"It's sexy as hell," I say against his skin. I finish the buttons and slide my hands inside, over his firm chest. "But then"—I shrug—"you always look sexy."

He reaches behind himself to pull his shirt off, keeping his eyes locked on mine. "Do you actually mean that?"

I give him a funny look. He's the most self-assured person I know; is he really asking if I think he's hot?

"Uh, yeah," I say with amusement, waiting for his cocky grin to slide into place. But it doesn't.

"You've never told me that before."

"Of course I haven't." I lean in to kiss his tattooed shoulder. "The last thing I want to do is further inflate your ego."

"You know, you have this really crazy idea of who I am."

"What?" I murmur, pressing my lips into the soft skin of his neck, only half-listening.

"That's not the first time you've said something to me about having a big ego. Do you honestly think that's who I am?"

I draw back to find his brow furrowed into a deep frown.

"You've formed this opinion of me based on what? How I behave at the bar?"

I sigh. Looks like I've woken Freud anyway. "Do we have to talk about this now?"

He gazes at me for another second, then gives a low chuckle. "You're right, sorry. I just kind of lost my mind when you said I was sexy."

"Whatever," I mutter, leaning in to kiss him again, nipping at his bottom lip. "I've seen the women all over you at work. You must get told that all the time."

"Well, yeah, I have been told that before." He glances away with an uncharacteristically bashful look on his face. "But I guess I never really cared."

"And how is this different?"

He takes my hand, bringing his gaze back to mine with a shy smile. "Because it's *you*."

Oh.

My heart stutters. I examine his face; the way his eyes are searching mine hopefully, the way he's biting his lip, the slight flush in his cheeks. He looks so vulnerable—so *open* —that emotion claws its way up my throat, tightening my chest, and all I know is that if I don't kiss him right now, the world will stop turning.

This time, his kiss is different. It sends a shower of sparks down through my center, across my skin, until my body feels nothing beyond the ferocious ache to have him. It must be an ache he's feeling too, because suddenly we're yanking off the rest of our clothes and he's rolling on a condom, unable to wait a second longer to be together.

I lie back on the bed, parting my legs as he climbs on top of me and takes my mouth in a scorching kiss. When he pushes inside me, my body opens in surrender. In this moment, nothing exists beyond his skin on mine, his heart drumming against me, the stroke of our tongues desperate to taste every drop of the other. It's like we've forgotten that we've been together before, because that feels like another lifetime and this feels like the first time all over again.

"Fuck, Cat," he rasps against my ear, his hot, hard body pressing me into the mattress. "I can't get enough of you." He's an inferno, every inch of his skin setting fire to me in the best way. I have the fleeting thought that he could burn me away to nothing and I wouldn't care. I want him to use me up.

He lifts himself onto his arms, changing the angle, watching as I gasp at the new sensation. But there's no self-satisfied grin this time, just raw need in his eyes as he drives into me, wanting to see me lose control.

And I am—I feel myself unraveling again, unspooling, coming apart at the seams. I can't make sense of the feeling in my ribcage and the way it expands when he looks at me like that, the way I want this moment to never end. I can't remember ever feeling like this.

Shit, I don't want to think about what that means.

He pushes back onto his knees and lifts my hips, slowing

to deep, rolling thrusts. I raise a shaky hand to brush a curl off his forehead, and he turns his head, kissing my wrist. It's the tiniest thing, but it makes my breath catch in my throat.

Suddenly, he feels too far away. I reach for his shoulders, pulling him back down until he's lying on me, skin to skin. "I want you close," I murmur, threading my hands into his hair, bringing his mouth down onto mine again. In between kisses I say, "I can't get enough of you, either." I feel him smile against my lips and this makes me giddy, until the whole room is spinning around me and I can't remember where I am. What is he doing to me?

He rolls us onto our side and wraps me in his arms, hands tightening, claiming my skin, possessing me. His mouth tracks over my collarbone, onto my shoulder, sucking and biting, like he's trying to leave a mark. I imagine his bite tattooed on my skin and my pulse rushes dangerously.

"Myles," I breathe, sliding my tongue out to lick the salty skin of his neck. "You taste so good." I can't help myself—I bite him back. Maybe I can leave a mark, too.

He gives a guttural growl and his hand fists in my hair, tilting my head back to kiss me hard. He hooks my leg around him, holding me there as he grinds against me, so deep.

Fucking *hell*. I love how he's not being gentle—how he's taking control with me. This isn't like the last time we had sex, where he followed my lead. Now he's wild, desperate, insatiable. He's taking what he wants, and I'm going to give him everything.

I can feel the release growing inside me, hot and heavy and urgent. I can feel it from him too, because his kiss becomes more forceful, more demanding. I don't know how I had sex with him without kissing him; I must have been out of my mind. His mouth is the best thing I've ever tasted. I'll never be satisfied with any other lips again.

Then I'm on the edge—so close—when he pulls his mouth off mine to meet my gaze, his eyes fierce and passionate. He can see right into me—I know he can—and he brings his lips to my ear to whisper, "I don't ever want to let you go."

Those words wreck me. My body takes over, splintering into a thousand pieces, until I don't remember who I am, until I'm nothing more than energy and heat and waves of ecstasy. Just as I hit the peak, I feel him finally give in. His arms tighten around me, his hot skin slick with sweat, his mouth ravaging mine. He lets out a raw, primal groan against my lips, giving himself over to me.

After, we lie together for a long time, trying to slow our breathing. I keep my legs and arms wrapped around him, holding him close, holding him inside me. He's very still but I know he hasn't fallen asleep, because he's looking at me.

Right at me.

His gaze is pinning me helplessly to the spot, and just as I'm about to look away, or push him off, or make an inappropriate joke to shatter the mood, his lips touch mine in a tender kiss. And I melt for him, wanting him all over again.

Oh, shit. I'm in so much trouble.

AFTER SOME TIME, he rolls off and heads to the bathroom. And I lie on my back, staring at the ceiling, my heart galloping. But it's not from the sex. It's from what he said.

I don't ever want to let you go.

And that, well... I don't know. I should be thinking that's too much, too intense—just plain crazy.

But I'm not. The truth is, I love hearing those words from him. I want to believe them—hell, I want to say them back. And I haven't wanted to say anything like that in a long time.

A tidal wave of thoughts and questions and fears crashes over me, pulling me under. I'm so busy fighting the current, trying to find my way to the surface, that I don't even notice when Myles climbs back into bed, pulling me close. But as he tucks me into his arms, the waters calm and the thoughts ebb away. I close my eyes, pressing my nose to his warm, soft skin. There's something about the smell of him—of his cologne and just *him*—that soothes me, and I burrow into his chest. His hand strokes gently over my hair as I listen to his heart beating a slow, steady rhythm. And for the first time in a long time, I completely relax, feeling safe.

Wow. I never realized how much that was missing from my life, but now that I'm here in his arms, tracing my finger over the compass tattoo on his wrist, the feeling of safety is palpable. I can't remember the last time I felt something even close to this.

I'm barely aware that I'm on the cusp of drifting off to sleep when Myles speaks.

"Do you want me to go?"

I blink, drawing back to look at him. I should say yes; it would make this so much less complicated, but—

"I really want to stay, but only if that's what you want."

I nestle back against his chest, knowing there's only one thing I want to say, and that I'll deal with the consequences later.

"Stay."

27

I shouldn't have let Myles stay.

I'm awake at least an hour before him, my mind spinning as the early morning light sneaks in under the curtains. I feel like a madwoman, trying to make sense of my tangled thoughts. One minute I want to roll over and curl up in his arms, the next I want to throw on some sneakers and run for my life.

I can't deny that last night was amazing. But I also can't shake this reluctance I feel, this undercurrent of... something. What *is* that sensation gnawing at me? Is it regret?

No. I can answer that immediately. There's no doubt in my mind about how much I wanted him—how much I *still* want him.

But there's more to this than that. Being certain about the fact that I *want* him doesn't mean I'm certain about whether or not it's a good idea. And that's what they all say, isn't it? When you know, you *know*.

And now, in the cold light of morning, I suddenly realize I don't know shit.

I slip out of bed before he wakes, showering and

dressing in the bathroom, trying to get my head on straight. It doesn't work, of course, and by the time I'm curled up in the chair in the corner of my bedroom watching him sleep, I'm more confused than ever. He's gorgeous, his olive skin a shade darker against the white of my sheets, that tattooed arm slung across my side of the bed, as if he was reaching for me. I like the thought of that.

But... I don't know if that's enough.

My phone buzzes in my hand and I look down.

Geoff: Hey, you awake?

Cat: Yep. What's up?

A throat is cleared across the room and I glance up to see Myles, sitting back against my pillows. "Morning."

"Morning," I murmur, trying to ignore the little spark of pleasure I feel.

"Why are you up?"

I shrug. "I woke early."

"Well, why are you lurking all the way over there?" He sends me an amused look, but I can sense he's feeling apprehensive. He's not the only one.

"Oh, you know." I try to laugh but it comes out kind of strangled. "I'm just... doing my thing."

"What thing?"

"That thing where I freak out after we have sex."

"Right." The amusement in his eyes flickers out. "And is that all last night was to you? Sex?"

I fiddle with my phone, saying nothing. I need more time to figure this out. I don't want to talk about it now—to pick it apart—because I'm not sure how to hold myself together at the same time.

I glance down as my phone vibrates with Geoff's reply.

Geoff: I think things are over with Daniel :(

Oh. Poor Geoff, I hate to think of him hurt. Sometimes he's too trusting for his own good.

Cat: That sucks. What happened?

As I send off my reply, I feel a cold trickle down my spine. Even Geoff, who was so sure that things were "different" with Daniel, is getting hurt. What chance does someone like me—with no sense of anything—have of getting out of this unscathed?

I look at Myles with a grimace. "Maybe you should go." I stand and reach for his shirt, throwing it across the room to him. But when he doesn't move and his forehead wrinkles with hurt, there's a pang in my heart.

I drop onto the bed beside him, taking his hand. "I'm sorry. I just... don't know how to handle this. But I want you to know, last night was the best night I've had in a really long time."

"Yeah?"

I nod.

A smile quirks the corner of his mouth and he leans in to kiss me. But I turn my head, so his kiss lands by my ear. When he leans back, his brow is knitted in question.

"I..." I suck in a shaky breath. "I don't know."

He sighs. "Please don't do this again."

"Do what again?"

"You're pushing me away. You did this last time we had sex."

I'm quiet, mulling this over. He's right, I did—I ran out of his place as fast as my legs could carry me, then went on a date with someone else. I cringe at the memory.

"Why are you doing this?"

"I don't know," I say again. I pick at some lint on the comforter. "I can't explain it."

"Try. We should talk about this."

An exasperated groan rushes from me as I push to my feet. "You and *talking*." I pick up his jeans and toss them at him.

"Come *on*, Cat. You know last night things were different. The kiss—"

"See! This is why I didn't want to kiss you!"

His eyebrows go up. "So you admit things were different. It was more than just sex."

"Okay, fine, it was more than just sex. But that doesn't mean—"

"Do you remember what you said? You said I'm not who you thought I was."

"I know, and I meant that. I just..." I hesitate, unable to even put my finger on it—this vague sense that I shouldn't jump into this. I want to shake it off; to leap back into bed and spend all day curled up there with him, but... "I don't know," I say helplessly.

He stares at me hard, his jaw tightening. "Fine," he mutters, swinging his legs out of bed and pulling his underwear on. "Then I'll go." He reaches for his jeans, avoiding my gaze as he steps into them. I watch him yank his shirt on and button it with fumbling, agitated fingers. My mind skips back to the last time we had sex and I pushed him away, and —as unreasonable as it is—a faint sense of panic weaves through me.

"So I guess you're really done with me this time, huh?"

His flinty eyes meet mine. "You honestly think I'd ditch the website over this?"

"No! I meant..." I look down at my hands. "*Me*."

He forces the air from his lungs, softening. "No. I'm not done with you, Cat. I'm just..." He drags the heel of his hand across his forehead. "Frustrated."

I nod. I'm fucking frustrated with myself.

My phone buzzes in my hand and I glance down.

Geoff: Can we meet for a coffee at Beanie in twenty?

"I have to meet Geoff," I mumble. "He's going through something and he needs me. But... why don't you come by the store later, if you're free?"

Myles rubs his chin, considering this.

"I'd like you to," I add.

"Okay. I need to photograph you in some dresses for the site anyway, so... yeah, okay."

I breathe out in relief and follow him out to the front door. "Cool. Then I'll see you later."

He hesitates, then pushes his mouth into a grin. It's one of his self-assured ones—one I haven't seen that much lately —and I notice that these smiles never reach his eyes like the other ones.

"Yep, see you," he says, and he saunters out the door in his usual way, leaving me to my jumbled thoughts.

GEOFF IS ALREADY SITTING at a table, chewing his nails down to stumps, when I arrive late at Beanie—a tiny coffee shop just down the street from my apartment.

"Hi," I say breathlessly, flopping down into a chair. "I'm so sorry, I was... caught up."

"Thanks for coming." He wrings his hands. "I just didn't know what else to do."

"Of course. You know I'm always here." I gesture to the guy behind the counter for a coffee and he nods, then I turn back to Geoff. "What happened?"

"I saw Daniel with someone else last night."

"Oh, no." I reach over to squeeze Geoff's arm. "I'm so sorry."

"Yeah. I can't believe it. I really thought this was it, you know?"

"What made you think that?"

Geoff shrugs, nudging his glasses up his nose. "Just a feeling. A feeling here"—he taps his chest—"that's hard to describe."

I stare at Geoff's chest, thinking about the way my own chest fills with that warm, tingly feeling around Myles. Meeting Geoff's sad gaze again, I push the thought away. I can't let myself think about that right now.

"He made me laugh, and it just felt like he *got* me." Geoff sets his cup down with a humorless laugh. "Still, it seems like he's also *getting* half of Manhattan, too."

A coffee is placed in front of me and I direct a grateful smile to the barista, before fixing my attention back on Geoff. "What did he say when you confronted him?"

"Oh, I haven't spoken to him yet. I'm going to go do that after this. I just wanted to see a friendly face first, find my strength." He gives me a weak smile and I squeeze his arm again.

"Are you sure he was with this other guy romantically? Because if you haven't actually spoken to him—"

"Yeah, I think so. He had his arm around him."

"Is that all?" I ask, surprised by the doubt in my voice. Okay, if I saw a guy I was dating with his arm around another woman, I'd be livid. But somehow, talking to Geoff about this objectively, I can't help but wonder if maybe he misread things.

Wow. When did I become such an optimist?

"I'm sure, Cat. I saw them and I know in my gut."

I survey Geoff's face. More of that certainty, that knowing that everyone seems to have—everyone but me. But then, Geoff was just saying he *knew* that this guy was the one, and now he's saying he *knows* what he saw... How reliable is this knowing, anyway? What does anyone really know?

Despite everything, I feel a smile on my lips as I think of Myles. I'm sure this is a philosophical question he'd love to pick apart.

"What are you smiling about?" Geoff asks, glaring at me through his misery.

Whoops.

"Nothing, sorry. Just thinking about... something else."

"More than anything," Geoff says, "I'm just starting to feel like I can't even trust my own feelings."

I stop, setting my coffee down. "What?"

"Well, I thought he was this great guy—like, I felt really certain. Now I don't know what to think."

I nod vigorously. "*Yes*, I know what you mean. With Myles—" Shit, shit, shit. *Stop.* "Sorry," I backtrack. "This is about you. Keep going."

But Geoff's interest is piqued. "Myles?"

"Nothing."

He gives me a pointed look. "Come on, I'm suffering here. Give me something else to think about."

"Fine," I mumble. "I... slept with him again. Last night."

Geoff slaps a hand down on the table and I jump. "Again!? Is that what you were 'caught up' with this morning?" He can't resist a devilish smile.

"Yes. I was *caught up* with trying to get him out of my house. He wanted to stay and talk, blah, blah, blah. He's all about talking."

"How awful," Geoff says sardonically. "And yet Mark hated to talk."

I grind my jaw. *Well played, Geoff.* "Yeah, okay, you were right. He's nothing like Mark. At the dinner party last night—"

"Wait. You actually went to that?"

"I did," I say with a chuckle. "Myles came as my date, and he was really sweet and affectionate, pretending to be my boyfriend." I smile to myself as I raise my cup for a sip of coffee. Geoff arches a knowing eyebrow and I drop the smile, rolling my eyes. "*Anyway*, at the dinner party I realized that they aren't alike at all. You were totally right. The similarities between them are superficial."

"Hmm," Geoff says, ripping open a packet of sugar and dumping it into his cup with a smirk.

"Hmm what?"

"Well, you're out of reasons now."

"Reasons?"

He gives me a sly little grin. "Reasons to stay away from him. If he's really sweet, if he's nothing like Mark... Why won't you just admit you like him?"

"Because..." I hesitate, rubbing my arm. *Because...?* I've got nothing. Shit, this isn't good.

Geoff reaches across the table for my hand, taking me by surprise. "Cat," he says gently. "It's not going to kill you to admit you like him."

I glance down, feeling all my snarky, sarcastic retorts vanish. "It might," I say unsteadily. "I just... I don't *know*, Geoff. I don't want to make another mistake."

Geoff sighs. "I know this doesn't look exactly how you thought it would, but that doesn't mean it's not good—that *he's* not good. Do you think he's a good guy?"

I nod before I've even had a chance to think it through. Because he is, I know that much. All I have to do is think about the way he reacted when I confided in him yesterday, or all the work he's done for me, or just... him.

"Well—" Geoff shrugs, picking up his coffee again.

"That's all you need to know right now. If he's a good guy, and you like him... just be open to seeing what happens."

Just be open. He makes it sound so simple.

"You could try meditating on it," he suggests, chuckling to himself.

I give him a withering look. "No. Thank you." But as I raise my cup to my lips, I wonder if maybe he's right about the other thing—if maybe I could try being more open.

28

I can't believe it—Hayley and I got the booth!

We officially got offered a booth at the EVMC via email this morning, which means we can begin selling there in two weeks. We celebrated with an impromptu in-store party, putting up some balloons and pumping up the music. It's been so much fun.

And by the early afternoon I've thought about Geoff's words a lot. After getting the good news with the booth, I'm feeling more optimistic. I want to try being open; I want to see if something could develop between me and Myles. It's not like we have to jump into a relationship, or anything—but maybe we can spend some more time together, like we did last night, and just... see. He enjoyed last night as much as me, that was obvious, so hopefully he'll be open to this idea, too.

But when Myles arrives at the store and throws me his usual self-assured grin, I know everything has shifted; we've veered right back into friendship territory. I guess I did kick him out of bed this morning, so it's not surprising he's pulled away.

It's probably for the best, anyway. We need to focus on getting the site up and running so I can leave here and stop worrying about money—and Mark. Still, I can't deny the disappointment that wraps around my ribcage when he doesn't try to kiss me.

"Hey," he says, lugging a huge bag over one shoulder, his camera bag over the other.

"Hi." I try not to gawk at the white T-shirt he's wearing with his faded jeans—the one I've seen at least a dozen times but has never before looked *quite* so gorgeous. He's got his black, flat-peaked cap on again with a few curls escaping out the front. I know I made fun of him for looking like a skater, but right now he just looks *hot*.

He sets the heavy bag down on the front table, glancing around. "What's with the balloons?"

I smile. "We got the booth, so we're celebrating."

"Oh, that's awesome!" A grin tears across his face and he holds up his hand to high-five me. I smack it with a laugh. There's a moment between us where we stare at each other, grinning like idiots, and I feel like I did at dinner last night: there's someone in my corner, cheering me on, and I'm not alone.

Gazing at him, I get the sudden, desperate urge to kiss him, to thank him for everything he's done, for making this possible by believing in my business—by believing in *me*. I think he sees it on my face, because there's a flash of something in his eyes before he pulls his gaze away, clearing his throat.

"I, uh, was thinking we should shoot downstairs." He gestures to his camera bag. "That way I can control the lighting better. Plus there's that wall with the peeling paint that would look really cool in the background."

I nod, reaching over to pat Stevie on her cushion. Mark

dropped her off a few hours ago and—I couldn't believe it—had very little to say to me. Maybe Myles really did put him in his place last night.

Hayley arrives at the top of the stairs with a cup of coffee. "Oh, hey," she greets Myles as she wanders to the counter. Her gaze swivels to me and I see her attempt to suppress a smile.

I turn toward the basement. "We're going downstairs to shoot some pictures for the site."

Myles hauls the huge bag up onto his shoulder and follows me down the steps. Stevie trots along with us, curious. She sniffs around then snuggles onto her cushion, watching as Myles pulls some lights from the bag and sets them up.

I stand there watching him too, arms hanging limply at my sides. I'm afraid if I step any closer, I might slide my hand over the smooth muscle of his bicep and press a kiss to it.

Fuck.

"The website is pretty much ready to go," he says, snapping a light stand together. "It should be up in a couple of days. I just wanted these pictures to convey more of the feel of the brand, of you."

"Awesome," I say, grinning. I watch him adjust a light. "Do you want some help?"

"No, I've got this stuff. Why don't you pick out some dresses and get changed?"

"Right." I glance at the rack of dresses beside us. I brought the navy dress back in for this because he said he wanted to shoot me in it. But now the thought of putting it on feels strange.

He finishes fiddling with the light and turns back to me. "Everything okay?"

"Um..." *Pull it together. God.* "Yep. All good." Yanking the dress off the rack, I duck into the fitting room. I tidy my hair, check my makeup, and when I can't delay it anymore I finally put the dress on again, slipping my feet into the shoes. I look exactly the same as I did last night, when he...

Anyway. I can be professional.

Myles is concentrating on his camera when I step out of the fitting room. "Go stand by that wall," he says brusquely, and I try not to be offended. The last time I put this dress on down here he couldn't even form a coherent sentence—and now, apparently, he couldn't care less.

Still. That's not what this is about, is it?

I stand in front of the wall, trying to make myself relax. He adjusts one of the lights then turns back to me.

"Okay, smile."

I lift my mouth, waiting for him to take the picture, but he doesn't.

His brows slant together. "Is that the best you can do?"

"Hey, this was your idea. I told you I'd look stupid."

"You're not even trying."

"What?!" I huff. "I'm not a model. I don't know what to do."

"I know," he mumbles. He sets his camera down, coming over.

My body goes rigid. Is he going to kiss me? Because I wish—

He doesn't, of course. He just takes my hand and places it on my hip, posing me like a Barbie doll. Then he steps back, assessing me for another second, frowning. He turns to look around us for inspiration and his gaze lands on Stevie. "Here," he says, picking her up.

I take Stevie's tiny body, still feeling uncomfortable as I watch Myles pick up his camera again.

"Just play with her and forget I'm here."

Easier said than done, but okay.

I gaze down at Stevie. Her tiny brown eyes stare up at me and I tuck her against me with one arm, stroking a hand over her fur. I feel like I haven't seen her much recently and I miss her.

Myles clicks a bunch of pictures and I glance up, surprised.

"Don't look at me," he snaps.

I shrivel at his tone, focusing back on Stevie. When I hold her up to my face, she licks my nose, which makes me smile. Myles takes some more pictures, then he lowers the camera, watching me nuzzle my nose against Stevie. I let my gaze flick to him and he quickly glances away.

"Maybe... another outfit."

I set Stevie down with a sigh. "I'm sorry if this isn't what you thought it would be, Myles. I'm doing the best I can. I'm not *trying* to fuck this up."

He turns back to me. "You're not fucking it up. I got a few good pictures. It's just, that dress..." He shakes his head, muttering, "Let's try something else."

"Oh." I drag my gaze away from his, trying to ignore the plunge of disappointment I feel at his tone. "Right."

I change into another dress—one that's totally different —and step back in front of the wall. He tells me to pick up Stevie again, and I cuddle and play with her, pretending I'm not prancing about like an idiot in front of the guy I had in my bed last night—and want so badly to have there again.

I mean—dammit. *Stop thinking that.*

"Maybe I should put some music on?" Myles suggests, pulling his Bluetooth speaker out of his bag. "I have a great eighties playlist."

I nod, feeling a smile form on my lips. "I love stuff from

the eighties." The opening notes of *Thriller* echo through the basement and I can't help but laugh, immediately loosening up.

"Right, arms up," he says and I giggle again.

And strangely, I do feel better. While he stands there with the camera, I find myself singing along and dancing a little—because really, who can listen to *Thriller* and not dance? He's happier too—grinning as he bops his head to the beat. And when our gazes meet and we share a smile, that sensation blooms in my chest again—the one where I feel like he knows how to make me relax, how to make me laugh—like he just *gets* me.

We fall into a routine where I change into a dress then dance and play with Stevie while he snaps pictures, the soundtrack switching between Bowie, Whitney, Prince and a whole bunch of others I just adore. By the time I'm reaching for the last dress, I'm actually in a fantastic mood.

I pull on the polka-dot mini dress, smiling to myself. Even though Myles and I had super intense sex last night, we're still able to hang out and laugh and be okay, and that's great. Things aren't weird and I'm so pleased.

Well, I'm mostly pleased.

It's just... I don't know. Last night he looked at me like he could hardly breathe, and today I could be his sister with the way he's acting. It's my fault, I know that. I've sent him so many mixed signals. But while I like that things don't feel awkward, I'm surprised to find that—more than anything— I want things to feel like they did between us last night.

I open the curtain and step out, running my hands over the dress, admiring the fit. It's the one Myles pulled off the rack yesterday, commenting on how sexy it is—and he's right. It hugs my figure snugly, cutting across mid-thigh, scooping low at the neck. I wait for him to notice I'm wearing it, but he's concentrating on adjusting the camera lens. I feel desperate, all of a sudden—I just want him to see me, to give me some sign that he wants what I want.

I step in front of him and he nearly drops the camera. "Oh—shit," he mutters, his mouth falling open as he drinks me in. "Cat—" His breath hitches on my name. "That dress... I can't photograph you in that dress."

Satisfaction surges through me. "Why not?" I ask, playing innocent. When he looks at me like that, I lose all sense of reason. I can't keep being hot and cold—not when I'm burning up with how badly I want him.

He groans, turning away. When he glances back at me his eyes are almost black. "You know why."

"I do," I murmur, taking a step closer to him. "Look, I'm sorry about this morning. I shouldn't have kicked you out. Because last night was... amazing."

He swallows visibly. "It was."

There's a beat of silence.

"Maybe..." I shift my weight, feeling uncomfortably vulnerable, asking for this. "Do you want to come to my place again tonight?"

He lets out a growl. "Of course I do. You know I do. But —" His brow creases. "That's not enough for me, Cat. Casual sex... that's not enough. Not with you."

I can't say I'm entirely surprised by this, but I don't know how to respond. And the longer we stare at each other, the thicker the tension gathers between us again, until it feels like I'm suffocating.

"Well," I joke, in an attempt to lighten the mood, "you could be my stand-in boyfriend—"

He growls again, this time in irritation. "Can we stop saying that, please?"

I flinch, surprised at his change in tone. "Okay... Why?"

"Because I *hate* it. I don't want to be your fucking stand-in boyfriend."

"Why not?"

"Why do you think?!" He throws his hands up. "I want to be your *real* boyfriend."

My heart jumps. Shit, this whole conversation is getting away from me. "What?"

His slate-blue eyes study me for a moment. "Surely you can tell that I'm in love with you."

I freeze, uncertain, then a nervous laugh creeps out of me. "Okay, Myles."

"I'm not kidding."

Confusion crowds my head as I run my eyes over his earnest face. Surely not. He can't... "Are you serious?"

He nods.

"How... how long have you been feeling this way?"

He rubs the back of his neck. "I sort of realized after we had sex."

"Which—"

"The first time."

"But... I didn't hear from you for a whole week after that."

"Yeah, I know." He glances down at the floor. "When I saw you on a date with someone else I just kind of lost it."

I stare at him in a daze. I can't make sense of this, can't process this revelation. He's in *love* with me? "Myles, we've only known each other for a month."

"So?"

"So..." I scratch my arm. "That's... quick."

He shrugs. "Well, it's how I feel." He meets my gaze again, calm and collected, as if he hasn't just confessed his undying love. "And I think you feel the same way."

I jolt with shock. "What?"

"I said, I think you feel the same way." He's just standing there, telling me what I feel, so damn sure of himself—like that time on the dance floor at Bounce—and irritation rips clean through me.

"How the hell do you know that?"

"Jesus, Cat—"

"Just stop it!" I snap. I'm suddenly feeling all hot and shaky and my pulse is slamming in my ears. I don't know what's happening to me.

"Why are you so angry? I'm telling you I love you. How is that such a terrible thing?"

There's a sharp twist in my heart and I turn away, my throat burning. "Because the last guy that told me he loved me fucking broke me, okay? I just... I don't trust it."

"Trust what?"

"Love."

There's silence. I've never said that out loud before but now that I have, I know it's true. It's everything. Hell—*there's* my inner compass.

But how could it not be? Dad said he loved us and he left. Mark said he loved me and he cheated. Even Mel, one of my best friends and someone I never expected to betray me, did. It doesn't matter if someone says they love me. It doesn't mean anything.

Myles's eyes soften. "But you trust *me*. You told me you trust me."

"I know," I mutter, digging my nails into my palm. "But—"

"But what? I know you meant it."

I glance up at him, feeling my heart trip over itself. But I don't say anything. I can't say anything more.

"Please, Cat." He shoves a hand through his hair. He looks so despondent that I can't stand it. I want to turn and run out of here so I don't have to look at his face, don't have to hear what he's saying. Because with every word, that feeling in my chest is intensifying and it's too much. It feels like it could engulf me.

"I just want you to be honest, that's all I'm asking for." His eyes search mine. "Just tell me what you're feeling."

Something inside me breaks and I let out a frustrated groan, feeling all my defenses crumble down around me. "Of course I have feelings for you, Myles!" My words ring through the basement and I realize, in the silence, that the music has stopped.

There's the tiniest, hopeful twitch on one side of his mouth. "Really?"

I raise my eyes to the ceiling in exasperation. "What do you think?"

"Why do you keep pushing me away then?"

"I don't know. I'm just..." I give a humorless laugh. I'm sure he's seen this coming a mile away. "It's freaking me out. I have a terrible sense for these things and I've made so many mistakes. It's like I can't trust my feelings." I glance up at him, asking quietly, "How are you so sure?"

"What?"

"How are you so sure that you... love me?"

He lifts a shoulder, offering a tentative smile. "Because I've never felt this intensely for someone before. I've liked you from the moment we met, and it's only grown since then. Now, I guess... I can't really imagine my life without you in it."

I feel a smile nudge my lips. I had the exact same thought yesterday. It's like he knew that, too. "And how are you so sure that I feel the same way?"

"Because I know how to trust my instincts. I feel like I'm pretty in touch with what's going on here. My intuition tells me that deep down you feel the same, and I can trust that."

Intuition. That's what I'm missing—that's what I *think* I'm listening to, but it's always something else, pushing me in the wrong direction.

"I don't have that," I mumble. "I don't have any intuition."

Myles tilts his head. "Everyone does. You just have to know how to hear it."

"How do you do that?"

Amusement touches his mouth. "Meditation helps."

"Fucking meditation. Everyone is obsessed with meditation."

"For good reason." He chuckles, gazing at me gently. "Look, all you have to do is stop listening to what others are saying—what you *think* you should feel. If you listen closely, you'll know what matters to you. What does your head tell you?"

"Run," I answer honestly, cringing.

He nods, as if he expected that answer. "But what does your *heart* tell you?"

I meet his gaze again. "I think you know what it's telling me."

"Yeah." Little crinkles form around his eyes. "You just have to decide which one you want to listen to."

I ponder his kind, patient face, letting his words sink in. I've been so stuck in my head, overwhelmed by relentless, fearful thoughts that insisted I need to keep my distance from him. Every time I felt like taking a step closer to Myles, those thoughts pulled me back, convinced me nothing real could happen between us, made me certain he's wrong for me. But then I remember what Geoff said earlier—how he was certain about one thing, then he realized he was wrong.

What if all this certainty I've had about Myles is wrong? What if I've been thinking one thing, but the opposite is true?

And then it occurs to me: maybe my inner compass is just pointing in the wrong direction. Instead of leading me toward things, it's directing me *away* from them—not only in my love life, but in everything. It took Myles showing up for me to trust my own designs again, to believe I could get away from Mark, to take a new risk with my business. It took Myles showing up for me to question the way I've been dressing, the way I've been hiding myself from others. And it took him showing up for me to risk letting another man into my bed—and possibly into my heart.

Maybe I don't trust love right now, but I *do* trust Myles. That means I could learn to trust love again. And while I'm not there yet, I think it's possible I could maybe, one day, love *him* too.

Holy hell.

I gulp in a breath as this realization hits me. This is the problem with being honest with yourself—it's terrifying.

Myles lets out a little sigh, picking up his camera and flicking back through the photos. I gaze at him, marveling at how he's gotten through to me, once again. How does he do this? How does he cut through everything I put up to keep the world out? How does he really, truly, *know* me?

I step closer and press my lips to his cheek. He sets the camera down and turns to me, eyes roaming my face. Emotion rushes under my skin, too close to the surface. It feels like he can see everything and I want to turn away, to hide. But then, that's never worked, has it? He's always seen me anyway.

"My heart," I murmur. "I want to listen to my heart."

"Are you sure?"

"Yeah. I'll have to work at turning the volume down on the other one, but yeah. My heart."

His eyes shimmer with relief. "Can I kiss you now?"

I open my mouth to say *God, yes*, but before I can even get the words out he tugs me into his arms, bringing his lips down onto mine in a warm, tender kiss. My hands ball into fists in the soft cotton of his shirt; his fingers clutch at my back.

When he finally pulls his mouth from mine, he buries his face in my hair and I nuzzle against his chest, breathing in great lungfuls of him. I try not to laugh at how delusional I was, telling myself I just wanted to spend a little time with him and see where things go. Because I don't want just that, I want so much more. I want everything. *All* of him. How could I not?

"Shit," he says, stroking a thumb over my cheek. "I wasn't sure I was going to win that one."

I let out a soft giggle. "It's a good thing you're so patient. I never realized how stubborn I am."

"*Very* stubborn." He leans down to kiss my bare shoulder. "But you're worth the wait."

"So are you," I breathe. And while I can't say the exact words he wants to hear right now, I can say what I've been denying myself for some time. "I'm so crazy about you, Myles."

He tries to curb the disbelieving smile pulling at his mouth. "Are you serious? Is this—I mean, is this really a thing, you and me?"

"I hope so?"

His grin grows wider. "Yes. Fuck yes."

He presses his mouth to mine again, and I tingle all over with wanting. I let out a little moan, angling my head to deepen the kiss. His tongue slides over mine, and I sink my nails into his back as heat rushes up me.

"What time do you have to be at work?" I ask breathlessly.

A low, husky laugh rumbles from him. "Two hours. But if I get into bed with you now, I'll never leave. Besides, if you're going to be my girlfriend, I want to take you on a date. Can you leave Stevie with Hayley? Can I take you to dinner?"

I glance at my phone, checking the time. "It's four o'clock. You want to eat dinner now?"

"Well... this isn't exactly how I imagined it, but right now it's all I can do. Do you mind having a super early dinner with me?"

My heart swoops at the sweet, hopeful expression on his face. "I don't mind at all."

"Good." He gathers me into his arms and holds me against his chest, kissing me on the head. I can hear his heart beating rhythmically through his shirt, and that feeling of safety hums through me again—the one I felt when he held me last night. God, it's amazing.

Why was I fighting him so hard?

29

Myles takes me to a tiny Japanese place a few blocks away. We find a table in the back corner and sit as close as we can, eating takoyaki and talking about his web design business, trying to keep our hands off each other. I changed out of the polka-dot dress—it was far too outrageous for an afternoon dinner date—into another design of mine; knee-length, emerald green, pretty. I keep catching Myles looking at me, smiling this secret smile to himself, and then he stops eating just to kiss me. And my knees go weak, every time.

By the time he has to go to work neither of us wants to part ways, but I promise I'll come see him at the bar later. He walks me back to the store, and as I watch him head off to work with a big, goofy grin on his face, I'm overcome with inspiration to sew. I spend the next four hours making a new dress and thinking about Myles, about how I almost pushed him away again, and how glad I am that he didn't let me this time.

When I finally look up from my sewing machine, I can't believe it's after ten. I'm itching to see him again, to go to

Bounce and kiss him. But before I do that, I do something I've been meaning to do for a long time. Myles pointed out at dinner that I need to stop putting it off, and he's right.

I type out an email to Mark, telling him I'm leaving the store. I never did sign the new lease agreement he gave me and I'm not sure of the legal terms for me to leave, but I figure I'm still under my old lease. I tell him I'll pay the last month of rent as he's expecting, but after that I'm done.

When I finally hit send, I feel a massive, cool wave of relief wash over me. Finally, I'm taking my business into my own hands—into my own control. Soon I'll have my online business, and we'll have the booth, and Mark will have *nothing* to do with it.

And that feels amazing.

With a grin, I change back into the polka-dot minidress, redo my hair and makeup, and slip on a pair of heels. Then I walk the few blocks to Bounce, fighting the urge to skip there the whole way.

I wave to Jimmy on the way in, and once inside I can see it's packed. I suddenly remember who Myles is when he's working here, and there's a pinprick of anxiety in my gut. What if I see him with women draped over him, twirling the bottle and flirting? It irritated the shit out of me before, but now I realize I was probably a bit jealous.

Oh, who am I kidding? I was jealous as fuck.

I spot him through the crowd and my heart does a somersault. *God* he's sexy. But it's more than that; he's sweet, too, and he cares about me—*really* cares about me. I still can't believe that this guy loves *me*.

As I thread through the crowd, watching him work, I notice he's not his usual bartender self. He's smiling as he serves people, but it's not his cocky smile. I don't see him prancing around in front of the ladies, and when a woman leans over the bar to touch his arm—and my whole body tenses with rage—he politely pulls himself away, keeping a professional distance. At every turn, instead of being his old flirty self, he's just a regular bartender—one whose body language says that he's taken.

He's taken. By *me*. A thrill zips through my bloodstream at the thought, and I giggle. He's going to lose a lot of tips because of me.

I push through the crowd until I'm in his eye-line, and he glances up immediately, as if he can sense me, his face breaking into a huge grin. His gaze dips down to my dress and back up, and he bites his lip, giving me a look that's pure lust.

Goddammit. I still have to wait *four hours* to get him into bed.

I inch forward in the line up to the bar, and he leans down onto his elbows, so he's at my eye-level, ignoring everyone around us. It reminds me of the night we first met, and here I am, his *girlfriend*, and I can't help but beam.

"What can I get you, beautiful?"

I chuckle. "There's that bartender charm. I was watching you work and thought you'd lost it."

"I have." He brushes his fingers over my arm, his eyes lit with affection. "For everyone but you."

"Good." I lean over the bar, close to his ear. "It's only for me now."

He rubs the side of his face against mine, so his bristles tickle my cheek. "Fine by me." He draws back with a smile. "Vodka?"

I shake my head. "Kiss."

He gives a grunt, tossing aside the dishcloth from his shoulder. "Josie," he calls down the bar, "I'm taking a break."

Her gaze pings between him and me, and she nods. He

grabs my hand, pulling me down the corridor and out the back door until we're in the dimly-lit alleyway behind the bar, alone. The door slips shut behind him and he turns, pinning me with a gaze so hot I nearly burst into flames.

"That dress," he growls as he steps closer. "You look so sexy."

I sigh as he threads his hands into my hair, tilting my face for a kiss. He captures my lips with his, sweeping his tongue hungrily through my mouth, making me drunk with desire. When we finally come up for air, I glance around, spotting a dark corner behind a Dumpster.

"How long is your break? Do you think we could—"

"I'm not fucking you in the alley behind the bar, you horndog," he says with a teasing smile. "As much as I might want to. But you deserve better than that."

I giggle, half appreciating his sweetness, half wishing he wasn't *quite* so sweet.

"You forced me out of your bed this morning without even kissing me." His fingertips settle chastely on my waist. "You can wait a few hours."

"Is this my punishment?"

"Something like that."

"But the thing is," I say, letting my hands drift down the front of his shirt, "I don't think I *can* wait." I slide my palm over the hard bulge in his jeans, delighting in the rough sound it draws from him.

"Fuck, Cat, you're killing me." His mouth lands on mine again in a blistering kiss. He lifts a hand to cradle my breast, stroking his thumb over my nipple through my dress. Wet, molten heat pools between my thighs and I arch against him, moaning into his mouth.

"Okay, okay." He drags his body away from mine, reaching to adjust the arousal threatening his zipper, breathing hard. "If we don't stop now I *will* have to take you behind the Dumpster and you'll lose all respect for me. Although," he says, grinning as he watches me try to pull myself together, "I'm pretty sure you only want me for my body, anyway."

A smile sneaks onto my lips. Because his body is delicious, yes—but it's more than that. "Also your business knowledge. And the way you play the piano." I pause for a second, thinking. I remember earlier today, when he told me he loved me even after everything I've put him through. "And your heart," I add, quieter.

Emotion glistens in his eyes and he pulls me close, gathering me against his chest. "Cat," he murmurs, kissing my head and burying his face in my hair.

I could just stay here all night, nestled in against him, but I know he has to work. "You should probably get back in there," I say, covering my yawning mouth as I draw away.

He sighs. "Go home and get some sleep. I've still got four hours."

"I want to see you. I've waited all evening..."

"I know." He caresses a tender hand over my hair. "But it's late and you're tired. Don't worry, I'll come straight to your place when I finish up. I mean..." He huffs a self-conscious laugh, rubbing the back of his neck. "If you want me to—"

"*Yes.*" I fumble in my purse, yanking out my keys and sliding my front door key off the ring. Alex has a spare back at the building, and this way he can let himself in. I don't care if this is too forward, if I look desperate—I need him back in my bed tonight. We've wasted enough time.

He takes the key from me with a surprised grin. "Okay. Four hours."

I grin too, glad to know I'm not the only one counting down.

WHEN I GET BACK to the building, Alex opens the door in her dressing gown. And when I explain that I need my key back from her because I gave my one to Myles, she squeals so loud I'm certain she's woken Agnes, the kindly old lady upstairs. But for some reason, I'm not bothered by her theatrics. I just float back down to my apartment and climb into bed with a smile on my face.

It's nearly three in the morning by the time Myles finally crawls into bed with me. There's a moment where I'm still half asleep and I don't know what's going on, but when I feel his warm arms slip around my back and tuck me in against him, bliss sweeps through me. I mumble something incoherent against his skin, fumbling for him through the haze of sleep, and he chuckles.

"Shhh, baby. Go back to sleep. I'll be here in the morning."

And I let out a happy sigh, drifting off with my face snug against his chest, right in that safe spot.

I SPIT my mouthwash into the sink and check my appearance again. I have the fleeting thought that I should put some makeup on—maybe a little concealer and mascara—but I catch myself. If there's one person I don't need to pretend for, it's Myles.

I pad to my bedroom, ready to slip back under the covers and snuggle in beside his warm, sleepy body. But when I nudge the door open, Myles is sitting up in bed with his arms folded and worry carved into his brow.

"Morning," he says uncertainly, and there's a pull in my heart when I realize what's going through his mind. He thinks I'm going to ask him to leave again.

I gaze at him from the doorway, at his bare torso nestled against my pillows, that striking tattoo down his right arm, his chestnut curls ruffled in the golden morning light that spills through my open curtains. Happiness swells behind my breastbone at the sight of this man in my bed. I don't know how I ever made him leave.

"Hey." I cross the room and climb into bed, snuggling into his side. "I'm so glad you're here."

"Good." His breath comes out as an anxious laugh. "I woke up and you were gone, and I thought—"

"I know and I'm sorry. I want..." I fiddle with the comforter, thinking. How can I show him what I'm feeling? "Will you come to a party with me this evening?"

His eyebrows rise.

"It's Alex's engagement party. Nothing fancy, just some drinks at her and Michael's apartment. But I'd like you to come. You know, as my boyfriend."

His eyes sparkle as they move over my face. "I'd love to. I have to work, but I'll see if I can go in a little later."

I smile, and it's reflected back to me on his gorgeous mouth. Then he lowers that mouth to mine in a sweet, soft kiss. Our tongues meet, and I pull him down on top of me impatiently. He threads our fingers together, pinning my hands over my head as he crushes his mouth to mine. His kiss moves to my shoulder, then my neck, and he groans.

"I can't believe I'm in your bed and you're not telling me to leave," he rasps against my collarbone, nudging the strap of my tank top aside.

My chest squeezes. I can't stand that he's thinking that. "Myles..." I stroke a hand over his rough jaw and tilt his face up, holding his gaze. "I'm not going to ask you to leave again. I love having you in my bed."

His eyes darken and he lifts his mouth back to mine, taking it in a hot, dirty kiss. He grinds his hips against me, and when I feel how hard he is, I whimper with need. We tug each other's clothes off in a messy tangle of limbs and he sits back on his heels glancing around.

"I'll just grab—"

"No," I whisper, pulling him down, close. "Don't. I'm on the pill. I want you—all of you."

His lips part in surprise. "Are you sure?"

"Yes. I had a check a while back. So... if you want to?"

"Fuck yes, baby." He lowers his body back down onto mine, positioning himself between my parted legs. He pauses, caressing a hand over my cheek, his eyes exploring my face from under heavy lids. "I can't believe you're mine, Cat."

Then he pushes inside me. And—God—it feels better than *anything*. Every atom in my body is electric, pulsing with pleasure and heat, like it's the dawn of time and everything has just exploded into life.

But it's more than the physical sensation. It's *him*. It's his heart, and the way he makes me feel safe and happy. The way he makes me feel like everything will always be okay, now.

30

"Oh my God," Alex says, staring at me in awe. "I love your dress!"

"Thanks." I smile, handing over the bottle of wine I'm holding. Myles talked me into wearing one of my own designs to Alex and Michael's engagement party, and I'm glad. Every time I put on one of my dresses, I feel part of my heart stitch itself back together. Just like every time he kisses me.

Tonight, it's a yellow polka-dot dress in my usual fifties style, fitted through the waist and flaring out to my knees. Myles hasn't taken his eyes off me since I put it on, but that's okay—he's in his shirt again, sleeves rolled to the elbows and collar open, looking like sex on a stick. We're actually a little *late* to the party, if you know what I mean.

"Hello again, Myles." Alex's lips curve as her gaze swivels between us.

"Hey." He grins, handing her a bunch of flowers he brought. How sweet is that?

"Oh! Thank you." She takes the flowers, stepping aside. I

wander past her and she catches my eye, mouthing, "Keep him."

Delight fills my chest, beaming out of me like sunshine. Maybe I will keep him.

As we enter the living room I spot Geoff, hovering beside our upstairs neighbor, Agnes. Ever since Alex introduced them last year, they've become very close. Geoff says she's like the grandmother he never had, and frequently visits her for tea or to take her books and groceries. It's really sweet, actually.

He spots me across the room and gives me a little wave. A grin streaks across his face when he sees my giddy expression.

God, I've become one of *them*.

"Honey," Alex calls into the kitchen, "Cat and Myles are here."

Michael wanders into the living room with a smile. "Hey, Cat."

"Hey. Congratulations, by the way," I say, taking in his handsome form. He's over six feet and pretty built, with dark hair, a short beard, and deep brown eyes that twinkle when he laughs. He's older than her—she's thirty and he's in his early forties, with a son—but you'd never know it by how smitten they are together. They bonded over their love of writing, but I'm quite sure Alex initially fell for him because, well, *look*.

He turns to Myles, extending a hand. "Michael Hawkins."

"Myles Ellis. Thanks for having me."

"Of course. It's nice to finally meet you. Alex has told me a lot about you."

Myles's eyebrows climb his forehead. He glances at Alex, but she buries her face in the flowers.

"These are gorgeous, thank you. I'll just put them in some water." She disappears into the kitchen, followed by Michael, fetching drinks.

I have to muffle a laugh when I see Geoff weaving across the room with an eager expression. He's loving this. "Hello, you two."

"Hey, Geoff. You remember"—I emphasize the word for Geoff's benefit— "my *boyfriend*, Myles?"

By some holy miracle, Geoff responds with nothing more than a grin and a nod. Alex must have told him.

"Hi, Geoff." Myles takes Geoff's hand in a hearty hand-shake. "Good to see you again."

"It's *very* good to see you." Geoff's eyes glitter as he looks between the two of us. He opens his mouth to say something—something I'm sure will only make me want to smack him—but Michael appears with drinks and he's forced to zip it.

I snicker as I take a sip of wine. I'm going to get the third degree later, that's for sure.

Alex drags Geoff away, and Myles and I stand with our drinks, enjoying the buzz of music and conversation around us. Well, that's what I'm pretending to do—but mostly I'm just gazing at him and counting the minutes until we can be in bed again.

"Thanks for coming with me," I say after a while.

"Are you kidding? I wouldn't have missed this. I love being here with you and your friends. Your *real* friends," he adds, and we share a smile. "I will need to head off to the bar soon, though."

"I know." I pout and he lowers his mouth, pressing it to mine. He tastes like wine and sex, and it takes all my strength not to push him down onto Alex and Michael's sofa and ride him like a stallion.

"I'll come back to your place after? Or"—an apprehensive laugh slips from him—"were you hoping I'd give your key back?"

"Of course not. You're keeping it." I lean close and say in a low voice, "I want you back in my bed as soon as possible. My body is craving your touch. I need you inside me again."

"Fuck, Cat," he murmurs gruffly. "You can't say shit like that to me when we're in company." He draws away with hazy eyes and I grin to myself. "I thought you didn't do dirty talk?"

He's right, that's never been my thing. Whenever a guy has asked me to talk dirty, it's just made me cringe. But with Myles... I want to be filthy.

I shrug. "I guess it's different when you meet the right person."

"The right person, huh?"

My heart skitters. I hadn't quite meant to say that, but maybe... well, maybe he is. "Yeah," I whisper.

He looks at me for a long moment, then his gaze drifts away and he sighs. "It kind of sucks that we live on opposite sides of town."

"Mm," I agree.

"You mentioned you'd thought about moving to the East Village." He sips his wine, eyes fixed across the room. "I love it around there. Did you imagine living there... alone?"

"I did. But that was before..."

Myles finally meets my gaze. "Before us?"

I nod.

"And what about now?"

I shift my weight anxiously. The old me would be panicking at the thought of doing something so monumental as moving in with a guy I've only been dating for five minutes. A move like that has trust and certainty written all over it.

But I don't want to be the old me anymore, and I don't want *him* to think I am either.

"Now..." I touch his arm, stroking a finger over the compass in his tattoo. "I could see myself living there with someone else."

His gaze drops to his glass as he attempts to mask his grin. But I've seen it, and that's all I need to know I have nothing to be scared of.

"So how has the ex from hell taken the news?" I ask, sipping my wine. Alex started mixing cocktails and Myles offered to help, so now I find myself standing with Michael, watching everyone mingle.

"How do you think?" Michael rolls his eyes. "I don't care. All I want is for Alex to be happy."

I glance over at the kitchen, where Myles is trying to show Alex how to toss a bottle of tequila over her shoulder without dropping it. "Make sure you're good to her. She's really sweet, and—don't tell her I said this—a bit naive. She's not hardened to the ways of the world like us."

"I know, that's what I love about her. She's optimistic and romantic. She lifts me up, all the time. And she's great with Henry." He smirks to himself. "Kind of like the mother he never had."

I can't help a snort. And as I watch Myles, I remember the things he told me about Amber the other night. "What's it like, sharing custody with someone?"

Michael's face clouds. "It's not great. Especially when the

other person makes things difficult." He turns to contemplate me. "Why do you ask?"

"Myles..." I pause, wondering how much I should share. "Myles has a daughter."

"Is he close with her?"

"No. He doesn't see her. His ex makes it impossible."

"Yeah, that's tough. There was a time when Henry was being kept from me, last year. We went to court and it dragged on for months. But you know, he's my son. There's no way I was giving up." Michael scrubs a hand over his beard in thought. "It can be hard, but it's never impossible. Myles will fight and find a way to make it work if he wants to see her."

Out of nowhere, Mom's words come back to me: *He doesn't want us anymore, Catherine.* I think of how Dad didn't fight for us, or try to make it work. It wasn't a question of impossible for him, it was simply that he didn't want it—he didn't want *us.*

I examine Michael's kind face. He went to court and fought for Henry because it mattered. There was no doubt about it for him. And when I look over at Myles, a strange, heavy feeling settles into my gut. Why isn't he fighting to see Amber?

Myles gives me a warm grin from across the room, waving me over. *It's not the same,* I tell myself, shaking the uneasy sensation away. I excuse myself from Michael and wander over to Myles.

"I've got to go to work, baby," he says when I reach his side. He tucks an arm around my waist. "I wish I didn't."

"Me too." I look up at him, realizing just how hollow I feel at the thought of going home alone again. "Should I come out to Bounce for a drink later?"

"I'd love that."

He presses his lips to my temple and I slide a hand into his back pocket, squeezing that tight little ass of his. When I glance at Alex she's swooning, watching the two of us, and I giggle.

"Thanks so much for having me, Alex. We'll have to go on a double date with you and Michael." Myles flashes her a grin and she nods.

"Yes! That would be lovely."

I see Myles to the door, promising to pop over to the bar soon, and when I return to the living room, as expected, Alex and Geoff are poised and ready for me.

"Oh my God," Alex gushes. "You two are *so* gorgeous together."

Geoff grins, topping up my wine. "I'm so glad you decided to give him a chance."

"And this dress!" Alex says. "I've never seen you wear anything like this. It's stunning."

I meet Geoff's gentle gaze, and he says, "She used to dress like this all the time."

"Really?" Alex's eyebrows shoot up. "Why did you stop?"

I sigh. "Mark."

"You know, I think Myles is good for you," Geoff says. "I haven't seen you look this happy—this much like *yourself*—in years."

Alex nods in agreement. "You really do seem happy."

My gaze slides away as I try to dial down the huge smile I can feel on my face. I've never been someone who wears their heart on their sleeve, but tonight I'm practically translucent with joy. I can't hide it, and that makes me feel a bit nervous.

"You really let him in," Geoff murmurs, linking his arm through mine and squeezing.

"What do you mean?"

"Come on, hon. You know the way you usually are around men—the way you act, always following your little rules. But with Myles... you're just yourself. You let him see you."

That nervous feeling in my stomach expands, ever so slightly. I *have* let Myles see the real me. I never meant to, it just happened. Somehow he saw through everything, regardless of how I dressed, or what I said, or how many sarcastic comments I made. As I think about it now—and how obvious it apparently is to everyone around me—I feel exposed, like a snail without its shell. It's too dangerous to be out here like this. One misstep and I could be crushed.

"It's a good thing," Alex says softly. "It's the only way real trust is built. You have to see all of each other."

I suck in a fortifying breath. Alex is right. We can't trust each other if we're hiding who we are. If this is going to work, I'm going to have to get used to living without my shell. And I can do that.

At least, I really want to try.

31

A little while later I'm pressing through the crowds at Bounce. Myles spots me immediately and a grin lights his face as I make my way to the bar. He hands me a vodka soda, taking my hand and raising it to his lips for a kiss. Then I find a booth and sit contentedly, watching him work and enjoying my drink. Maybe I'm being too full-on, sitting here while he works, I don't know. All I know is that I missed him ever since he left Alex's place and I just want to be near him.

He doesn't seem to mind, though. He spends the whole time grinning over at me, serving people with a flourish. He's not cocky Myles at all; he's just pure, boyish joy, and my heart is so full to see him like this, to think that I'm the reason he's smiling. Every time he aims one of his sweet smiles my way, anticipation hums through me, knowing that very soon I'll have him back in my bed, in my arms.

And as I sit there, I have the thought that maybe Myles can be my shell now. Because when I'm with him, I feel protected. I feel like I'm safe from the world.

Finally, when the rush has died down and it's not long

until closing, he comes over and slides into the booth beside me. I tuck my hand into his and lean close to kiss him, but he hesitates.

"What?"

"Cory..." He glances around, his gaze hitching on Cory as he leans at the end of the bar, chatting to two women. Josie is further back, cleaning some glasses, and Eddy's clearing tables. But none of them are looking our way.

"Oh." I'd completely forgotten about Cory and the fact that he warned me away from Myles. But he doesn't know Myles like I do—plus he worries about me far too much. "I'll talk to him. He can't fire you for this."

"It's not that. It's just... he was pretty clear with me about not making a move on you."

"I'm a big girl. Besides, I think I actually made a move on *you*, so..." I lean closer, sliding a hand up his denim-clad thigh, feeling him quiver beneath it.

"You did, you bad girl."

"I'm *your* bad girl now. So let's go home and be bad together."

He gives a low groan into my ear, brushing his lips against my skin. I wait for him to say something filthy, but he just gives a soft sigh. "I'm so happy, Cat."

Hearing him say that makes joy glow bright in my chest. I press my mouth to his in a warm, passionate kiss, filled with the promise of what's to come. "Me too," I murmur.

His eyes flit over my shoulder and he cringes. "Shit. Here's Cory."

"Okay, I've got this," I say, steeling myself. "You go finish up."

He nods, slipping out of the booth and dashing away. Cory adjusts his course from the booth to follow Myles, but I reach out and grab his hand, pulling him down beside me.

"What the—"

"Just calm down, Cors, okay?"

Cory stares after Myles, his expression thunderous. "I *told* him; I told him not to even *think* about—"

"*Cory.*" I punch him in the arm and he swivels to face me.

"What are you doing?"

"I'm trying to get you to calm down before you kill someone."

"No—" He balls his hand into a fist on the table. "What are you doing with *him*?"

I place my hands on Cory's shoulders. "Cors, I love you. You're the best big brother a girl could ask for. But I'm big enough to make my own decisions, now. Myles and I are together, and it's okay."

He scrutinizes me with hard eyes. "Did he tell you about Amber?"

"Yes," I say patiently. "I know all about that. There are no secrets, nothing to—"

"So he told you what happened, then?"

"Sure." I give a light shrug. "I mean, not in detail, but I know—"

Cory cuts me off with a disbelieving laugh. He wipes a hand down his face, looking pained, and that same sensation of unease I felt earlier crawls back over me.

"Of course he didn't tell you the details," he mutters, glancing back to the bar. Myles is stacking glasses and he looks up, smiling at me, his gaze quickly shifting away with Cory here.

"Well, it doesn't matter," I say, lifting my chin.

"Oh, really? It doesn't matter that he walked out on his family?"

There's an icy chill down my spine. I swallow, willing myself to stay calm. "He... what?"

"Oh, yeah. He didn't tell you that bit, did he? He left his family to go traveling around the country, to pretend he had no responsibilities. He just *left* them."

My gut lurches and I glance at Myles again. This can't be true. Myles told me what happened, he told me—what did he say, exactly? He said things didn't end well, that's right. But that's...

I look back at Cory wide-eyed, forcing myself to keep breathing.

"I'm sorry, but you need to know. That's who he is. He's the kind of guy who's selfish enough to walk away from people who love him. Just like—" Cory breaks off, grimacing, but he doesn't need to finish, because we both know what he was going to say.

Just like Dad.

Shit.

I glance back at Myles and my vision blurs as I try to make sense of this. This warm, loving, sweet guy walked out on his family? He left his daughter to grow up without a dad, just like our dad? And he kept this from me?

When I turn back to Cory's solemn face, déjà vu hits me like a freight train. Four years ago he sat me down here to tell me the man I trusted had been lying to me, and now... is this really happening again?

No, I try to tell myself. There has to be more to it than that. Cory has to be wrong. I just need to talk to Myles, to hear it from him. He'll tell me that Cory is misinformed— that he didn't do this terrible thing, that he hasn't been hiding it from me this whole time.

I reach numbly for my purse, wriggling out of the booth.

Myles steps out from behind the bar when I approach, his brow scrunching with concern.

"Everything okay?"

I take a deep breath and try to steady my erratic pulse. I trust Myles, I do, but Cory's words are looping through my head: *He didn't tell you that bit, did he? He just left them.*

No. Myles wouldn't have done that. I just need to hear him say it.

"Is it true?"

"Is what true? What happened?" He reaches out for me but I take a step back, shaking my head.

"Cory told me you walked out on your family. Is it true?"

Myles stares at me, unblinking. Time stands still as I wait for him to say something—anything—to prove Cory wrong.

But he doesn't. Instead, his face crumples and he drops his head into his hands.

All the air is sucked out of the room.

I can't believe... Was Cory right?

My voice trembles as I ask, "So it is true?"

Myles can't even look at me—he just gives a tiny, pathetic nod. And as I absorb the shock of this revelation, I feel humiliation and betrayal burn through me. God, I spent so much time worrying that Myles was like Mark, but he's even worse. How could I have been so stupid?

"I have to go," I mutter, turning for the door.

"Cat, wait." Myles reaches for my arm but I push him off. My chest is seizing up, my lungs tight with hurt as I stumble out onto the curb. There's a cab right there and I lurch inside, slamming the door against Myles's anguished face. We peel away and I bury my head in my hands, trying to erase the one image stuck in my mind: Myles at the piano, playing my song.

32

Somehow, don't ask me how, Myles is sitting on the steps of my building when my cab pulls up. He must have left the bar and taken a cab here at lightning speed. I don't even notice he's there until I'm climbing out onto the sidewalk in a daze.

He jumps to his feet when he sees me, wiping his palms on his jeans, and descends until he's on the street. His eyes are shining as they meet mine. "Cat, I'm sorry. I should have told you. It was a long time ago now, and I fought it for years, but yes—"

"Myles, stop." I raise a shaking hand. "Don't try to tell me you had a good reason, because you don't. You can't. You're no better than my dad."

Anger blazes in his eyes as he steps toward me. "Don't you *dare* say that. You don't get to say that to me. You want to know why I left Nikki? Because I was miserable. Amber was —" He winces, glancing away. "Amber was the result of a one-night stand and a broken condom. When Nikki called me up a month after we slept together to tell me she was pregnant... I didn't know what to do. I moved in with her, because it felt like the right thing, to try and make it work as a family. And it was okay for a while, but Nikki and I... we weren't in love—not even close. I tried to tell myself that it didn't matter, that I needed to be there for Amber. And I wanted to stay for her, I really did, but..." He looks down at the sidewalk, his jaw locked, breathing hard. My stomach is in free fall as he keeps speaking.

"One night Nikki and I had a huge fight. We fought a lot but this fight was our worst. And... Amber saw it. She was so shaken by it, and that's when I realized that staying with Nikki just for Amber wasn't the right thing to do, either. It was making us both angry and resentful. I tried to keep things amicable with Nikki after I moved out, because I wanted to be in Amber's life. But Nikki wanted me to move back in and when I refused, everything blew up. She made it impossible to see Amber. And between paying child support and my loans, I didn't have the money to take her to court."

Myles meets my gaze, looking agonized. "I didn't want to leave, but..." His voice breaks and he wrenches his eyes from mine, trying to pull himself together. I'm overcome by the urge to reach for him—to comfort him—but I fight it.

"In the end it seemed like the best thing to do was to leave town for a while. I figured if I gave her space, she'd eventually calm down and see reason. So I left, thinking it would work out. I was wracked with guilt. The longer I was away and the more Nikki told me how selfish I was, how I didn't deserve to see Amber, the more I started to believe her. And then... I couldn't bear the thought of settling down again—of trying to find another home—without Amber. It was easier to just drift, and work, and drink, and not have to think about what a mess I'd made of everything. And that was fine for a few years, until I ended up in the hospital because I'd blacked out drinking."

I inhale sharply. An image of Myles in a hospital bed appears in my head and there's a fierce tug in my heart.

"I met a doctor who told me about meditation and yoga, and I began both, determined to do better. Slowly, I started to heal and I learned that I'm not a bad guy, I just messed up, and I could repair that somehow. And that's what led me back to the city. I finally felt like I'd faced my demons and I could start to build a new life, start to work toward my own dreams with my business. I want to be the best version of myself so that when I eventually get to see Amber, I can be a good dad for her." He raises his steely gaze to mine.

"I never meant to hurt Amber. I've sent every child-support check, I've sent gifts for every birthday, I've tried to visit and been turned away by Nikki more times than I can count. When I sold my app I made nearly a million dollars, did you know that? I put half of that money into a trust fund for Amber. So you can say I'm just like your dad as much as you want, but I'm trying in *every* way to be better."

I stand frozen on the sidewalk trying to process every-thing, but it's an overload of information and I can't make sense of it. He didn't mean to leave Amber—but he did. He's trying to be a good dad—but it's not working. He sold an app—that was *real*?

I rub my forehead as if it might somehow help his words sink in. Despite the scrambled thoughts in my brain, one thing is very clear: he's not like Dad. Dad never did any of that stuff. He just left without looking back, and I'm quite certain it didn't haunt him in the way it seems to be haunting Myles.

I sit with that for a moment, feeling some relief at that realization. And yet... I can't escape this feeling gnawing at me now, that things with Myles aren't right. I went with my heart and let him in, but I had to ignore my head to do that, and that doesn't feel right either. This whole mess just confirms it. And now my head is screaming louder than ever to *run*.

Because it's not the stuff about Dad, I realize. He made this big deal about being honest, about showing your true self to the world and not hiding. He talked about how much he trusted me—made me feel like I could trust *him*—and then he didn't tell me this.

"I was going to tell you," he says after a while. "I was going to explain what happened."

I lift my gaze to his and shrug. "It doesn't matter. The fact is that you didn't. You had plenty of time to tell me, and you didn't."

"You're right, I messed up. I should have told you. But I'm still the same person—I'm still the same guy I was a couple of hours ago. I still feel what I feel for you." He scans my face, eyes filled with pain, and I force myself to ignore the way it sends a crack through my chest. Because this time, I know better.

"I'm sorry. I thought I wanted this, but... there's too much doubt there now—about who you are, about whether or not I can really trust you." I turn and start up the stairs, my heart juddering against my ribs, my eyes stinging.

"Cat—" Myles takes the steps two at a time, until he's in front of me. "Don't do this, not again. You're pushing me away—"

"Yes!" I snap, gripped by irritation. "Of course I'm pushing you away! You kept something important from me, and now you just expect me to forgive you, like it's no big deal." I shake my head, mentally cursing myself. "This is just so typical," I mutter. "I finally decide to put my heart out there—"

"But you didn't really, did you?" Myles interjects, his

tone laced with acid. "Because that lasted all of, what, a few days? And now you're pushing me away again because things are getting too real. This is just your style."

"*Excuse* me? What does *that* mean?"

"You know what it means. And it's getting pretty damn boring, Cat."

My mouth pops open in disbelief. "Are you actually angry right now? Because I don't think you have any right to be."

"Why not?" His eyebrows slash inward. "I put my heart out there too. At least I'm *trying* here. But you won't let me in."

"Is that why you're mad? Because I'm not just forgiving you? You're so used to women falling at your feet that you can't take it when one doesn't?"

"Are you fucking kidding me?" he spits, eyes sharp and dark with fury. "More of this ego bullshit? Do you even know me at *all*?"

"You know what I think the problem is, Myles? I think it's that you don't actually know *me*. Because if you did, you'd understand why I'm upset right now."

He growls, shoving a hand through his hair. "I *do* know you, Cat. That's the problem—that's what you don't like. You can't put on an act around me because I see through it. And that's why you're too scared to be with me, not all this shit about my past."

His words hit me like a slap and I reel back, my breath lodging in my windpipe. "I'm not scared," I say, but even I can hear the wobble in my voice.

He smirks bitterly, turning to watch a passing car before turning back to me. "You are. You won't admit it to yourself, but you are. You want to know what's so ironic? You're always going on about how much you want to meet a decent guy, then when you meet someone who really cares about you—who would do anything for you—you push him away because you're too afraid. It's like you don't even know what you want."

"Well, I know I don't want you." The words rush out before I can stop them, then they hang in the air between us, so heavy and thick that I can't breathe.

The anger in Myles's eyes dissolves into hurt, and he lifts his chin, giving me a sad nod. "Fine. Then I'll leave you alone." He turns and stomps down the steps, the sound of his sneakers echoing along the quiet street.

And I stand there, in my yellow dress, trying to stop the tears stinging my eyes.

33

"Are you shitting me?"

I hear Mark before I actually see him, and as soon as I do, I know this won't be good.

"You're moving? Seriously?"

I throw him a bored look as he barges into the store. "I sent that email over a week ago, Mark. Where have you been?" I just assumed he was giving me the silent treatment because he was pissed. He's childish like that.

"Don't change the subject. Are you really—" He stops abruptly and turns on the spot, noticing for the first time that the walls are lined with nothing but empty shop fixtures.

"I am," I say, forcing a jovial tone. I don't feel jovial in the slightest, but there's no way I'm letting him know that. "On to the next big thing."

Mark's eyes narrow to suspicious slits. "Is this because of Myles?"

There's a shiver of displeasure along my skin at the mention of Myles's name, and I have to fight to keep my expression pleasant. "Yes. And it was a brilliant idea. It's about damn time."

"You do realize you're making a huge mistake, right?"

I perch my hands on my hips. "Really, Mark? Please, tell me how this is a huge mistake."

"Well—" He opens and closes his mouth, glancing around, and I smirk.

"Exactly. You're just pissed because you can't come in here and annoy me anymore. But it's not personal, it's business," I say, parroting his words from a month and a half ago back to him. Then I pause, reconsidering. "Except it *is* personal, too." I glare at him, waiting for more of his usual bullshit, but he gets very quiet, stuffing his hands into his jeans pockets and looking down at his feet.

"Don't do this, Cat."

I falter, surprised by the strange plea in his tone, by the way his posture has slumped. "Do what?"

"I know you're angry with me. But... I don't want to lose you."

"*Lose* me?"

"Yeah." There's something in his eye that makes my stomach turn over.

"Mark," I say uneasily.

"I always imagined we'd end up together again. One day."

I feel my jaw unhinge as disbelief knocks me back. I actually have to grip onto the edge of the counter to steady myself. Is this some kind of joke?

He mistakes my stunned silence as an indication that I'm feeling the same way, because his mouth slants into a sleazy smile. "I always knew this was never really over. And seeing you with *him* the other night, in that dress... Come on. You know this isn't the end."

I absorb his words, each one like a punch in the gut. Fury pulses hot in my veins and I take a step toward him, speaking through gritted teeth. "There are a lot of things in this world that I don't know, but if I'm certain about anything it's that you and I will never, ever be together again."

Mark is unmoved. "You know we were great together."

"Yeah, so great you felt the need to cheat on me repeatedly, then start screwing my friend behind my back."

His lip curls smugly. "What choice did I have? When a woman like Mel wants you, then—"

"Fucking hell," I mutter. "If she's so amazing, why are you in here telling me *we* are meant to be together?"

He peers at me for a second, then gives an indignant huff, straightening up. "You know what? You're right. And you'll never compare to her."

"Ha! Well, thank God. You two deserve each other. Now please..." I rub my eyes and heave out a sigh. "Just go, Mark. It's over."

"Fine. But don't come crying to me when you fuck everything up."

I ball my hands into fists at my side. "I can assure you, I won't be coming to you for anything, ever again. Good bye."

With another huff, he turns and storms out, almost colliding with Hayley on her way in. I stare after him, unable to believe what just happened. He thought we'd *end up together*? How he came to that conclusion, I have no idea. It's as baffling as it is infuriating.

But now I see his odd behavior lately in a whole new light. He lowered the rate when he thought I might leave, because he was scared of losing control over me. He was hostile toward Myles for no reason. Well, not no reason, obviously; he was jealous. And after everything he put me through, he doesn't get to be jealous. He doesn't get anything more from me, ever again. Despite everything, I feel a spasm of triumph. Because *finally*, I've had a chance to put Mark in his place.

Hayley eyes me warily as she approaches the counter. "You okay?"

"Peachy," I say, plastering on a smile. I might have had it up to here with men and their shit, but I don't want to dump that on Hayley. "Ready to take some things over to the market?"

"Sure," she replies, not moving her gaze from me. "Have you heard any more about the website?"

I pause, considering how to answer. It's been a week since Myles walked away from my doorstep. A week since he told me the site was ready to go. A week without a single word from him.

And no website.

I shouldn't be surprised, but I am. Even after everything that happened between us, I never expected he'd bail on the website just to punish me. He even promised as much. But he's let me down and disappointed me in ways I never expected. Turns out so much about Myles was disappointing, I just fooled myself into thinking otherwise.

Anyway, that means I won't have my online business, which was the major part of my plan going forward. And I haven't exactly figured out my next move without that. I've been too busy stewing over Myles leaving me in the lurch.

"Um..." I reach for a box, stalling. I never told Hayley about what happened with Myles—any of it—and while it's great that I don't have to rehash all that with her, it means I don't have a good explanation for our current predicament. "I think it's delayed."

She frowns, pulling her ponytail over her shoulder.

"Really? That's annoying. We need to get it going as soon as possible."

"I know that," I snap, pushing past the counter.

"Okay... Well, have you spoken to Myles? Because if it's going to be much longer—"

"No, I haven't spoken to him. And I don't plan to, okay?" I haul the box onto the front table, immediately cringing. She's quiet behind me and I turn around, taking in her shocked expression.

"Is everything okay?"

"Everything is fine," I say automatically. It's like a reflex.

"Right."

I stand there, grinding my teeth. Ugh, I'm being an irrational bitch and she has no idea why. It's not fair on her. "Look. I'm... not sure we are going to get a website, after all."

"What? Why?"

I draw an unsteady breath, avoiding her gaze. For some reason I feel my throat closing up and the last thing I want to do is lose it in front of her.

"Cat," she says, taking a step toward me. "Did something happen?"

I fight the urge to laugh maniacally. *Did something happen?* Well, yes. Yes it did. I opened myself up to a guy—I took a huge risk in more ways than one—only to have him hurt me.

But while I expect to be mad as hell with Myles, I'm surprised by how angry I am with myself. The whole point of creating the online store was to get away from Mark— away from relying on someone in my business. The irony of expecting help from someone else is not lost on me, especially since he hasn't come through. It's like I learned nothing. I let Myles into my heart and into my business and he did nothing but let me down.

God, I feel stupid. Why on earth didn't I see this coming —I mean, all of it? Now I'm back where I started, just a whole lot angrier. But the anger is manageable, at least. It's energizing, it's spurring me to action. And it's much easier to deal with than the awful, heavy, misery bubbling up underneath it. Sometimes when I'm in bed late at night, and I don't have the energy to be angry anymore, the weight of sadness tugs at me. It's usually at that point that I take a sleeping pill, because—honestly?—I'm not sure I have what it takes to fight that off once it takes hold.

Still. Lesson learned, right? And now, after that confrontation with Mark, I find myself feeling strangely empowered. I'm an idiot for letting Mark—and Myles—hurt me, but I'm not going to do that again. I can make this work without them. Without anyone.

I glance at Hayley and guilt swoops through me. She deserves to know the truth. Well, most of it.

"Yeah, something happened. I'm not going to go into all of it, but I made a stupid mistake by trusting someone to help me with my business again. I was too reliant on Myles and this online business idea, and that wasn't good. So I'm going to sort something out. I don't know what, but I'll come up with something. On my own."

34

By the end of the day I'm exhausted. Hayley and I have taken loads of stuff over to the booth, but we haven't set up yet, because we aren't officially opening until early next week. Clearing out the shop has been therapeutic, though—especially after my visit from Mark today. If I'd had any doubts about whether or not I'm making the right move getting out of there, I don't anymore.

There's still a bunch of stuff to pack, but with each left-over vintage item I box up to list on eBay later, I feel more and more relieved. Things might be scary and uncertain going forward, but that also means that they're open, and anything is possible.

If only I felt the same about my love life. But you can't have everything, can you?

I pull the door to the shop closed with a deep sigh, ready to schlep myself home. But I nearly leap out of my skin when I'm ambushed by Geoff and Alex.

"Okay, so you *are* alive," Geoff says theatrically.

"Yes." I shove my keys in my purse. "I've been busy."

Alex arches a brow. "And that's why you've been avoiding us?"

"What?"

"I knocked on your door last night and you didn't answer. I know you were home."

I press my lips together, glancing up and down the street. "I, well—" I turn back to my friends, both regarding me with suspicion, and annoyance washes over me. "What? I have to check in with you guys twenty-four seven?"

Geoff's forehead creases. "No, hon, but come on. If we don't hear back from you for a week, we start to worry."

"Well don't, because everything is fine. No, more than fine—it's brilliant." I send them a tight-lipped smile and they exchange a look. "*What*?"

"Nothing." Alex links her arm through mine. I stiffen but she gives me a squeeze. "Let's get a drink. Bounce?"

"*Not* Bounce," I mutter. They share another look so I add, "I'm just... sick of it there."

"Okay," Geoff says. "Grim's?"

I give a reluctant nod and we wander toward St. Mark's Place. I'm not sure I'm in the mood for the Spanish Inquisition from these two, but I'm also not in the mood to go home and try and distract myself from thinking about everything until bed. A drink or ten certainly won't hurt.

"I meant to tell you, by the way, you were right about Daniel." Geoff smiles. "It wasn't a romantic thing with that other guy. It was his nephew!"

"Oh," I murmur. I'd completely forgotten about that whole thing with Geoff after everything that happened. And yet here these two are, going out of their way to check in with me. "Sorry, Geoff. I should have been in touch."

"It's okay. I know you've had a lot going on with the shop,

and everything..." He lets the sentence hang, clearly waiting for me to jump. I'm not going to.

"That's great about Daniel."

"Yeah. I think I was just looking for problems, to be honest. It felt like things with him were too good to be true, so as soon as I saw something that confirmed that, I just blew it out of proportion."

"Mm," I say distractedly as we wander into Grim's Bar. Geoff and I used to come here years ago, but lately we've spent most of our time at Bounce. This place isn't nearly as... I don't know, but it's not the same.

We settle at a table and Alex and Geoff turn to me with concerned faces. Right, I'm going to have to nip this in the bud.

"I'll get us a round." I leap to my feet and stride to the bar before they can say anything more. I know they're going to ask me all sorts of questions and I'm not up to it. I'm not up to anything, really.

It's pathetic, I know, but I'm feeling a bit crappy after thinking about Bounce. I know Myles lied to me and let me down, but ever since I let myself believe that something real could happen between us, I feel like I've been ripped open, turned inside out and sewn back together. It feels like the only thing keeping me in one piece is my anger about the whole damn thing, and if I let Geoff and Alex push too hard that could unravel. And then... I don't know what will happen.

Maybe what I should do is get super wasted, drown my sorrows and just forget I ever met Myles. That could work, right?

I eye the bartender as he gets our drinks, feeling unreasonably disappointed that he isn't cute, he isn't flirting with me, and he isn't forcing his way into my life and my heart.

When I get back to the table, Alex is talking wedding planning and I sink down into my seat with relief. Perfect; they've moved on from me.

"So we're not going to have wedding parties," she says, taking her sauvignon blanc from me with an appreciative smile. "You guys are my absolute best friends here, and if we did then you'd be in them. But we're not."

Geoff holds a hand to his chest, aghast, and I shrug absently.

"I'm going to ask my sister to be my maid of honor, but that's it," Alex continues. "My bestie from back home can't make it, and this will mean Harriet *has* to come to New York." Her mouth pulls into a wicked grin. "If she won't come by choice, she'll have to come for this."

Geoff shakes his head, chuckling. "Alex's idea of an evil plan: making someone visit New York."

She laughs too as she takes a sip of her wine. "It's been tough, though. My mother is beside herself that I'm marrying an American man and not moving back home, so I'm fielding hysterical calls from her. *And* I have to convince the government that it's not just a green card wedding because it's so quick."

Geoff nods over his merlot.

"I mean, sure, having the green card is going to help me a lot, obviously. But that's not why I'm marrying Michael— I'm marrying him because I'm crazy in love and want to spend my life with him. Because he's the one."

Ugh, more of this crap. I grunt into my vodka, trying to push down the bitterness rising inside me.

"It's true, Cat." Alex turns to me with a smile. "I know you don't believe in the one, but I do. And I'm certain it's Michael."

"You're *certain*." My tone is heavy with sarcasm and I see

Geoff raise his eyebrows beside me. "Shit, sorry. I'm not trying to be a bitch. Just... having an off night."

She puts a hand on my arm. "It's okay. I know I sound like a romantic fool, but this is just what I believe."

I gaze down into my drink, too agitated to reply. Her words keep replaying in my mind: *I'm crazy in love with him...* She's so bubbly and happy and excited—*this* is what love should be like. Myles told me he loved me but had this big secret from me—then he had the balls to get angry with *me*, to tell me *I'm* scared. He thinks he's some kind of shrink, that's what. He lied to me, then somehow made it out like things were my fault. And it pisses me right off.

"So..." Geoff starts in an elaborately casual tone, and I flinch. "Why are we here tonight then? Why not Bounce?"

"I told you. I'm sick of it."

"Hmm." He sips his wine. "Sick of the bar, or someone who works there?"

I try to give him a pointed look, but he's staring down at his drink in thought.

"Alex and I went for a drink there last night. We figured you'd be in there, but you weren't. Myles was, though."

My whole body goes rigid at the mention of Myles. I've not let myself picture him behind the bar, but now the images flood into my mind uninvited: him tossing up the bottle, flirting with women, saying the same things he said to me. My stomach sours at the thought.

"Well..." I give a hollow laugh, pushing the feeling away. "He does work there, Geoff."

"He didn't look good," Alex murmurs.

I shrug, refusing to get sucked into the conversation.

"He seemed pretty off his game. At one point he dropped a whole tray of glasses."

I roll my eyes. I know Myles and his smooth moves—

he'd never drop a tray of glasses. Now they're just making stuff up to bait me—and I'm not going to bite.

"I spoke to him," Alex says, eying me over her wine.

Anxiety spirals down through me like a corkscrew, but I do my best not to let it show on my face. I just lift a shoulder as if it's the most banal thing I've ever heard, even though I want nothing more than to lean across the table and ask her what he said. If he asked about me. If he told her he missed me.

But what does it matter? I remind myself. *What could he possibly have said that would make up for everything?*

Nothing—that's what.

"That's great," I mumble, itching to change the subject. "Anyway, I was thinking—"

"He said you had a fight," Geoff interrupts, and I feel a dart of irritation. Can't we move on from this already?

"He was surprised that we didn't know," Alex adds.

Well, that's too damn bad isn't it? I don't owe anyone an explanation for what's happened. If anyone should be explaining themselves, it's *him*.

"He was quite concerned that we hadn't heard from you," she continues, "and he wanted us to check if you were okay. He really cares—"

"Oh for fuck's sake!" I set my glass down with a heavy thud, surprised by my own outburst. Then I add more calmly, "He doesn't care about me. He made that very clear."

There's silence for a moment, and I snatch my vodka up again, taking a long sip.

Geoff inhales slowly. "Hon... what happened?"

I drain my glass, waving toward the bartender for another. Then I realize this isn't Bounce—I can't get away with that shit here. I grumble, turning back to the concerned faces of my friends.

"Cat?" Alex prompts, and guilt creeps over me. Myles might have hurt me, but I know these two care. And I'm being such a bitch.

"Fine," I mutter. I don't really want to get into the whole thing, but they seem unusually worried. Maybe getting this out will be good, actually. I've been keeping it bottled up and it's starting to feel toxic. "I found out this huge secret from his past and he basically just told me to get over it. So... that's that."

"What secret?" Alex asks.

I slurp up the melted ice from my drink, unable to look her in the eye. I'm afraid if I do, I might burst into tears or something equally ludicrous. And that's not me—that's more her style. Jesus, what's happening to me?

"He—" My voice catches in my throat, and I take a breath, trying again. "He walked out on his family a few years back."

Geoff's brow dips with compassion. "And that makes you think of your dad."

"Yeah. Or, it did, but he's not like Dad—not really. Dad left and never looked back. Myles is desperate to get back to his daughter. So it's not that. It's more the fact that he lied to me."

Alex gives a little nod, but Geoff looks skeptical.

"Right," he says, adjusting his glasses. "And you think he deliberately tried to keep this from you?"

"Of course. He said he'd meant to tell me, but he didn't. So, you know, he can't really care about me all that much, can he?"

Alex tilts her head. "Er... why?"

"Because if you care about someone, you don't hide stuff from them. You said it yourself—trust can only be built if you see all of each other. Well, I let him see all of me. But he didn't do the same."

Alex sighs. "What happened after you confronted him?"

"He told me everything. Then he got angry at me and said I was pushing him away. Which—hello—of course I was, because he lied. But he kept trying to pin it on me, kept saying I was scared because things were getting too real."

"And then he left?"

"Yeah." The image of Myles's hurt face flashes into my mind, and I feel a pang in my chest I don't want to acknowledge. "He stormed off and told me he wouldn't bother me anymore." The last word sticks in my throat and I reach for my drink, then remember it's empty.

Geoff jumps to his feet, rushing to the bar, and I try to gather myself together. I'm feeling all wobbly and I don't like it one bit.

When Geoff returns, he has another vodka soda and three tequila shots. I'm not sure if they're all for me—but hell, I'll take them.

He sets the shots aside and hands me my vodka with a kind smile.

"I'm sorry." I gaze down into my glass. "I should be over this by now. We were only together for five minutes. I don't know what's wrong with me." When I glance up they're sharing a knowing look again and I frown. "What?"

Alex nibbles her lip, still looking at Geoff. "Do you want to tell her, or should—"

"Yeah, I think—"

"It's probably best coming from—"

"Yeah, okay," Geoff says, turning to me.

More secret communication. I glare at them, drumming my fingers on the table.

"Here." Geoff hands me a tequila shot. "Drink this."

I take it, bemused, and throw it back. It burns all the way down into my empty stomach, then I feel it spread out through my veins, loosening me up. I exhale wearily, watching as they each have a shot. If we need to prep with tequila shots, this can't be good.

Geoff sets his empty glass down and fixes his attention on me. "Whatever Myles said, he's probably right."

I stiffen. "Are you kidding me? He—"

Geoff holds up his hands. "I'm just the messenger, okay?"

"Please hear us out," Alex says.

I survey their faces, so full of apprehension, and feel myself relent. "Fine." I slump back against my seat, folding my arms. This ought to be good.

"We weren't there, so we can't comment on what was said," Geoff begins, choosing his words carefully. "But I'm inclined to think that Myles was right."

I huff. "But you hardly know him—"

"No, I don't," Geoff agrees. "But I know *you*."

I raise my eyes to the ceiling. Here we go. It was bad enough with Myles playing Freud—now I'm going to get psychoanalyzed by these two as well?

"Honey, I love you to bits, you know that." Geoff reaches across the table to take my hand, squeezing it tight. His green eyes gleam with worry behind his glasses, and I feel myself begin to unfurl. "But you're a mess. Well, you're a mess with men."

I glance at Alex and she grimaces, then nods.

"You say you want a real relationship, but you have all these rules. When you go on dates, you behave like some idealized version of yourself—then you wonder why they don't go anywhere."

"They don't go anywhere because the guys in this city suck."

"Sure," Geoff says. "A lot of them do. But I also have to believe you don't let them in, you don't give them a chance. It's easier to find flaws in them to explain why nothing works out, rather than look at yourself."

I glare at Geoff, clenching my jaw. If it were anyone else saying this to me, I'd deck them. But Geoff... I know Geoff, and he knows me. He's clearly uncomfortable having this conversation with me, but the fact that he's here saying this, must mean he really believes it.

"Fine, whatever, I'm a mess. What does this have to do with Myles?"

"I'm not trying to justify what Myles did. But you said he told you everything as soon as you confronted him, right?"

I give a reluctant nod.

"Well, if he did tell you everything right away, then was he really trying to hide it? It seems more that he didn't know *how* to tell you—not that he didn't want you to know."

I look down, stirring my vodka. I'd never thought of it like that.

"And if that's the case," Geoff says, squeezing my hand again, "then that's not really the reason you're walking away from him."

I drag my gaze to Geoff's, swallowing against the thickness in my throat.

"Is it possible that you *are* scared? I know how it feels. When I thought Daniel was with someone else, I panicked. I thought I'd done this stupid thing by letting him get close, and that he was only going to hurt me. I wonder if that's what's happening here with Myles. You've never considered him a real contender, so you've just been yourself around him. He's seen the real you, and there's nowhere for you to hide."

"I don't want to hide," I mumble, but when I think about how I felt at the engagement party—so exposed, so vulnerable—I realize that Geoff is right. Shit.

Geoff sees the realization dawn on my face. "I think maybe you're using this thing about his past as an excuse, because you're scared. No one can blame you, Cat. You've been through so much. But... now you're letting your fear get in the way of something you really want."

I suck in a shaky breath, feeling my heart thud harder against my breastbone. It's uncanny, but Myles said the same thing. Is it possible that they're all right?

But... I stab at an ice cube with my straw. Even if they are, what difference does that make now?

"Either way," I mutter, "that doesn't matter. You know he never delivered on the website? He promised me, no matter what happened between us, he would complete the site. But I haven't seen anything." I utter an ashamed laugh, looking down at the table. "It's my own fault for believing him. Every time I trust someone, they let me down."

Geoff cocks his head. "Every time?"

I glance up quickly. "Well—no. I mean, not you guys. You guys and Cory and Hayley... you're the only people I can really trust. But everyone else... Anyway, it's my fault. I should know not to count on others by now."

Alex's brow pinches. "I'm sure he has a good reason for not doing the website, Cat. He wouldn't just abandon it to spite you. Do you really think that's who he is?"

I let my gaze fall to my glass. Because no, I didn't think that's who he was. And that's what makes this whole thing so much worse.

I think of Mark at the store today, telling me not to come

running to him—and how I told him I'd never come to him for anything again. Because I won't, because I don't need his help—or Myles's help. I don't need anyone's help anymore.

"Oh well," I say, giving a brittle smile. "I don't need him —I never did. I knew better than to let him help, but he talked me into it. I'll do it on my own, as I should have done all along."

Geoff puts a hand on my arm. "You don't have to do things alone, Cat. There's nothing wrong with letting people in, with asking for and accepting help. Like when I needed you when I was upset about Daniel. We've been so worried about you this week. We're here for you, and it's not a sign of weakness to need us sometimes."

My gaze swings to Alex and she's nodding, her eyes shining. "I love you, hon. You've been there for me so much and I'm here for you. Don't push us away."

Don't push us away.

Her words echo around my head, colliding with Myles's words—words he said so often they're permanently lodged in my brain: *you're pushing me away.* I knew I was pushing *him* away, but not them. Is that really what I do—push everyone away? Because I didn't push Dad, or Mark, or Mel —they left all on their own. But as I sit here gazing at my two kind and loving friends, I wonder if I just do it now as a reflex, as a way to protect myself.

"Maybe you should talk to Myles," Geoff says.

I give a slow, sad shake of my head. Because even if I *did* push him away—even if a small part of me wants to talk to him—that doesn't change the fact that he's let me down, right when he knew I needed him the most. And out of everything, that's one thing I don't think I can forgive him for.

35

I wake to the sound of someone pounding on the door, and I lift my groggy, tired body from the bed with a groan and a string of curses. When I yank the door open, Geoff sashays in brightly.

"Morning. Let's go to breakfast."

I push the door shut with a yawn. "Are you kidding? What time is it?"

"Nine," he says, wandering to my room. "Were you still asleep?"

"Yes." I trail after him. "It's my day off." Though I'd never normally sleep this late—I'm usually up at six or seven without an alarm. It's just my body clock. But this past week I've felt more tired than ever.

I enter my room to find Geoff perched on the edge of my bed. "Well, get dressed. I'm taking you to breakfast."

I consider him for a moment. I'm not sure I want a repeat of last night's therapy session, and I'm certain Geoff hasn't magically let things go since.

"My treat," he adds. "To celebrate moving out of the store." There's a mischievous glimmer in his eye I don't like the look of, but the longer he sits there, the harder it is to think of an excuse.

"Fine." I reach for my black jeans off the floor, grab a fresh tank top and underwear, then pad to the bathroom and run the shower. Twenty minutes later, we're heading out the door.

"So, I was thinking we could try this new place a few blocks from here."

"Sure," I mumble, trudging beside Geoff in a fog.

We walk in silence for a while and I drift along, thinking. Usually by this time of the morning my anger has kicked in, giving me a fresh shot of energy to face the day, and I stomp across town to the shop and put on some loud hip-hop to help me pack up the store. But today I'm not feeling that hit of adrenalin. Today, I'm just feeling... empty.

"Oh, I need to duck in here real quick." Geoff grabs my arm, dragging me into a building before I can protest. I trail after him, blindsided and bewildered. His grip on me tightens as he pulls me past some sort of reception area into a hall filled with people sitting on—

Meditation cushions.

I glower at Geoff. "No. Way."

"Shhh!" the instructor hisses from the front of the room. "Take a seat, please."

"Sorry," I say to the instructor. Rows of heads turn my way as I try to pull my arm free from Geoff. "But my friend—"

"Take a seat, *please*," he repeats in a firm tone.

I make the mistake of hesitating, and Geoff yanks me down onto a spare cushion. I cut him a furious look, mouthing, "I'm going to kill you."

But he just shakes his head as if he can't understand me, then gestures to the front of the room.

Ugh. This is the *last* thing I feel like doing right now. I glance back at the door and then—what the fuck?—someone closes it. Am I *locked in* here now? Surely that's illegal?

"Today's meditation is about fear and love," the instructor says warmly.

I turn to Geoff with an exasperated eye-roll. I mean, really? This is a bit on the nose, even for Geoff. But he is studiously avoiding my gaze, so I look back to the front with a sigh. Maybe there will be another beach meditation to help me relax. At least this time I won't crash into Myles—

His face appears in my mind and I mentally scramble to push it away.

I can't.

"We're going to start by taking a few deep, soothing breaths," the instructor continues.

Oh here we go, more of this crap.

"Begin by closing your eyes and breathing in deeply at your own pace."

At least I don't have to keep up with the rest of the class, I guess. That's something.

I begrudgingly close my eyes and force myself to take a slow, deep breath. As soon as I do, I feel at least half the tension drain from my body. Huh, he might be onto something. I take another breath, and another.

"It is often said that the opposite of love is hate," the instructor says. "But it's not. It's fear. And we have the choice between living from love or fear."

This is exactly the sort of new-age bullshit Myles would say, I think, drawing in another long breath. But this one catches on the way down, taking me by surprise. I'm never going to hear him spout new-age bullshit again, I realize with a sting. It drove me crazy, but—

Nope, I quickly remind myself. He let me down. There's no point feeling sad about him.

"And it is often thought that fear is the enemy," the instructor continues. "But it isn't. When we are feeling fear about doing something new, it can be a sign that we are on the right track—pushing ourselves out of our comfort zone."

Despite everything, a small smile touches my lips. That's true when I think of the business.

"It has been said that fear is excitement without the breath. So when you are feeling fearful, try to breathe deeply. By breathing into the fear, you will see that it is not paralyzing, but energizing."

I pull in a deep lungful of air, letting his words sift through my brain.

"Fear is helpful in many ways, because it wants to keep us safe. But it can hold us back from growth, from love, from becoming our truest selves. When our fear interferes with our intuition, then it's hindering us. That's why it's important that you can distinguish between fear and intuition."

My ears perk up at this last part. Myles was talking about intuition, how that guided him. It's the thing everyone but me seems to have.

"We all have fear, and we all have intuition—even if we think we don't. We just have to get past our fear to hear it. Intuition tends to come from the heart, whereas fear comes from the head."

I open my eyes now, gaping at the instructor in disbelief. It's like he's been inside my head, been listening in on my own tangled thoughts.

"When you find yourself torn between fear and intuition, the right way forward is always guided by your intuition. The fear isn't an indicator to stop, it's simply an indicator that you care—that whatever you're looking to do has great meaning to you. And that is exceptionally powerful."

My eyes flutter closed as his words slowly sink in. For the first time since Myles walked away from me, I feel a tiny crack open in my heart, letting the light through. I've spent the past week being angry and suddenly I just feel so, so tired. I can't keep the anger going, can't keep that shield up around my heart.

"When you feel fear, you need to sit with it, to breathe in deep, and know that the intensity of it will pass. Now, we will take a moment to meditate on fear and intuition."

Myles flashes into my mind again. And as I think of him, I think again of my confused, wayward inner compass, my intuition struggling to be heard through my jumbled, mixed-up thoughts about my ex, and my dad, and my business, and myself. No wonder I couldn't hear it, couldn't make sense of anything. What a mess.

But one thing is crystal clear through everything: the fear.

Myles was right—I was scared. Geoff was right, Alex was right. I was steeped in my fear, marinating in it, letting it consume me. Every time I thought Myles might turn out like Mark, or like my dad, or like any number of disappointing experiences from my past, my fear was speaking. It was twisting me up in knots, tugging me away from my intuition. Away from Myles.

But all that fear was just a sign of how much I care.

A wave of sadness crashes over me, so intense my shoulders sag under the weight of it. I care about Myles, of course I do. And I had him—I had the chance for something with him—and I pushed him away again. I let my fear jump in at the first hurdle and push, push, push, until he was gone. It thought it was keeping me safe from hurt, but now, I realize as my chest feels hollow with loss, it wasn't. Now I feel more hurt than ever. Because it doesn't matter if I'm pushing Myles away or not—that doesn't change the way I feel. That doesn't change the fact that I love him.

Wait.

No.

That can't be right. I can't...

I swallow hard against the emotion clogging my throat, my eyes flying open. I want to get up and run from this room, from Geoff and his well-meaning persistence, from this meditation teacher and all his crap about fear, from my own inner turmoil.

And then it hits me—*this* is it. This is the fear in action. And now I have the chance to do something different.

Geoff peeks over at me, his eyes softening as he sees the agony on my face. He reaches out and squeezes my hand. "Just breathe," he whispers and I gulp in a breath.

Just breathe.

And as I do, I feel the tightness in my chest release, feel the fear start to ebb away—so that I'm left, confronted with the truth.

I love Myles.

My brain instantly kicks up a fuss, saying that can't be right—because it hasn't been long enough, because he let me down. But my heart is speaking too, and it's yelling to be heard.

I love Myles.

And suddenly I know, with absolute clarity, that *this* is the only thing that matters.

Wow. I do have a working inner compass buried inside, I just haven't known how to hear it properly. It's been drowned out by fear, by all the stuff from my past, creating a cynical filter that has tinged my whole view of the world gray.

And as soon as I step away from all of that stuff, I can see so clearly how much I love Myles.

I realize now that I don't care that he didn't do the website—or rather, it's not so much that I don't care, as it is that I understand. I know it wasn't to spite me—it was because he was hurt.

"And we're going to slowly bring our awareness back to the room," the instructor says.

I open my eyes again. My whole body is buzzing, my mind is working a mile a minute. I'm itching to get to my feet, to run to Myles, to tell him how I'm feeling. Not just that I love him, but that I *know* it, deep in my bones—that I heard it from myself, that I took a meditation class and it really helped, that I found some truth within myself and he was right about it all.

But as everyone around me stands and stretches, I sit stock-still on my cushion, pressing my eyes shut again.

Because I can't go to him and do any of those things. It doesn't matter that I've come to these profound realizations. I hurt him so badly, and the website is proof of that—that's how I know he won't forgive me. That site meant everything to him; he was working so hard on it and pouring himself into it for me. But he just let it go.

And that's how I know he's let me go, too.

"Hey, you okay?" Geoff scooches over beside me, slinging an arm over my shoulder. "You looked a bit worse for wear there."

I nod, inspecting the carpet. I'm on the brink of bursting into tears and I can't do that. Not here, not with Geoff. If I cry in front of him it will be a whole thing and I can't do that right now. I can't let myself unravel, because I'll never put myself back together again.

Instead, I summon all my inner sass and turn to him with an arched eyebrow. "You tricked me into a meditation class. Of course I'm worse for wear. Can we go now?"

He eyes me for a moment, words clearly dancing on the tip of his tongue, then pushes to his feet with a frustrated sigh. "Sure. But I want you to meet someone first." He grabs my hands and pulls me up, gesturing to the front of the room.

"Really?" I whine as he drags me along. "I don't—"

"Cat, this is Daniel." Geoff gestures to our instructor, beaming.

"Oh," I say, surprised. "Daniel. I've heard so much about you." I pause to properly take him in: tall, hazel eyes, almost-black hair.

He grins. "I should hope so." He slips an arm around Geoff, planting a kiss on his cheek. "Did you enjoy the class?"

"Um... yes." I glance between the two of them, my eyes narrowing. "Geoff, did you set this whole thing up?"

"I might have had something to do with it. Did it work?"

"Work?"

"I saw you figuring out some stuff."

I give a little nod. "Yeah, it—" I cut myself off as a sob works its way up my chest. Taking a careful breath, I fix a smile on my face. "I'm sorry guys, I have to run. It was nice to meet you, Daniel. Thanks for the class."

Then before either of them can say a word, I tear out of the room, past reception and out onto the street. I pound through The Village toward home, trying to keep it together, and I'm just turning down my street when my phone buzzes in my pocket. I know it will be Geoff checking in on me, and once I'm home I'll flick him a quick text to reassure him. I mean, really, I'm fine.

But when I glance across the street, I freeze, feeling my heart leap into my throat. Myles is sitting on the bottom step of my building.

And I'm not fine. I'm not fine at all.

36

M yles gazes at the pavement, head bowed in thought. I notice the way the wind ruffles his curls, how his crimson T-shirt hugs his shoulders, the rips across the knees of his jeans.

God, I am so in love with him it hurts. And now I'm just standing across the street staring at him, gripping my phone with trembling hands, my pulse roaring in my ears.

Just breathe, I tell myself. *Just breathe.*

I should tell him how I feel. I know I hurt him, but maybe there's still hope. Maybe that's why he's here.

A car sails past and he glances up, along the street, his gaze landing on me. My heart hurls itself against my ribs as he pushes to his feet.

Just breathe.

Somehow, I manage to put one foot in front of the other, until I'm standing on the pavement in front of the building with him. I run my eyes over his handsome face. How could I have been so, so blind? I've never been so in love with someone in my life.

"Hey," he says softly, and I nearly fall to my knees. "Did

you get my text?"

I shake my head.

"I got the site done, finally. Sorry it took so long. I was doing everything I could, but I had all these issues with the hosting, and today was the soonest—"

"You did it?" I whisper. "You actually did it?"

Oh my God.

I droop with disbelief. Not with him—with myself. Now that I'm in front of him, looking him in the eye, how could I possibly have thought he'd let me down? I *know* him. I know better.

Realization breaks across his features. "You didn't think I was going to do it?"

I lift a shoulder, glancing away in shame.

"Shit. I'm sorry, I should have been in touch, I just..." He goes quiet, and when I look back at him he's gazing at me sadly. "It was too hard. But I promised you I would do it, Cat. I know you've been let down in the past, but that's not who I am. I'd never do that to you."

"I know," I whisper, wringing my hands. "I know that now. And I also know..." I trail off helplessly. How do I explain this to him? How do I tell him that I've found that knowing in me, and it's changed everything? What could possibly make up for the things I said to him, for how I treated him? Standing here in front of my building, in the exact spot where I told him I didn't want him, I feel lost for words.

No. I have to try.

"I'm sorry about everything," I say, my voice strangled. "About the fight, the things I said."

He gazes at me, unblinking, his jaw hard. After a while he lets out a weighted sigh, and nods. "Yeah, me too. I don't think I handled that very well."

There's a beat of silence, and I try again. "How've you been?"

He shrugs. "Not too bad, I guess. I got a paid web design job, so that's good."

"Oh," I mumble, my heart snagging on his words. *Not too bad*. I've been a wreck—an angry, sad wreck—but he's just business as usual. "That's good about the job."

"Yeah, it is." He tilts his head, eyes traversing my face, and I feel a pinprick of hope.

"Myles... is there any chance, after everything..."

He breathes out hard, his gaze dropping to his shoes. "I can't keep doing this with you, Cat." Then he reaches into his pocket and holds his hand out. Sitting in his palm is my key. "You should take this."

All the hope drains from me and my heart squeezes so hard that I almost choke. How could I have been so stupid to ruin this? How could I have lost the best thing that has ever happened to me?

When I don't reach for the key, he steps forward and presses it into my palm. There's the briefest touch of his fingers against my skin, and my chest collapses in on itself.

"I've got to get ready for work," he mumbles. "I'll... see you around." Then without meeting my gaze, he turns on his heel and strides down the street, out of sight.

I stare after him, holding my breath to stop the tears I can feel gathering. They're burning my eyes, making my throat close, and I can't stand it. I can't stand to think about what I've done.

Instead, I climb the front steps numbly, let myself into the apartment, and crawl back into bed.

I'M AWAKE EARLY the next morning, even though I want nothing more than to sleep. I've had a restless night, tossing and turning, the ache in my chest keeping me up. Misery has wrapped itself around my limbs, and when there's a knock at the door, I can't even bring myself to answer.

But I hear a key, and then I hear the door open and close. It will be Geoff, no doubt, coming to check on me. I don't want to see him. I'm not trying to push him away, I just... don't have the energy to face anyone.

Especially not myself.

But my bedroom door is nudged open, and I'm surprised to see Cory's face appear through the crack.

"Hey, sis," he murmurs into the darkness of my room. I watch the outline of his tall figure as he crosses over to the curtains and opens them a little. Light slices through the space, illuminating Cory's concerned face as he comes around to the bed, sinking down beside me. He smooths a hand over my hair with a deep sigh, and something inside me shatters.

"He's not a bad guy," I choke out.

"What?"

"Myles. He's not a bad guy. He's not like Dad, he's not like Mark. He's nothing like them and... I've lost him." I feel a sob climbing my throat and I try to swallow it. "I love him and I've lost him," I whisper.

There's silence for a while, then Cory finally asks, "You love him?"

Before I can stop it, the sob escapes my mouth into the quiet of my room. I glance at Cory, horrified, but it's too late —the sob is followed by another, and another, until tears are streaming down my face, and Cory pulls me into his shoulder, holding me tight.

"Oh, Cat," he murmurs as I sob against his shirt. "It's okay."

"It's n-not," I stammer between sobs. "I've l-lost him. I was scared and I lost him." I press my face against Cory's shoulder, finally letting myself cry the tears I've been fighting for so long—the tears I held back when I felt powerless with Mark and the store, when Mel betrayed me, when that guy at the bar forced himself on me. The tears I held in when Myles walked away from me.

Cory holds me tightly, rubbing my back, whispering soothing things. I don't know how long we stay like that, but I cry until I've got no tears left, until there's a huge puddle on his shoulder, until my chest heaves its last sob.

When I finally pull away, I feel so empty and tired, I just sag back against my pillow and stare at the comforter, hollow and spent.

"I know he's not a bad guy," Cory says at last. "He told me to come and check on you. He was worried." Cory squeezes my shoulder. "That night after I saw you together, I ripped into him. We ended up talking, and you're right. He's nothing like Dad. I'm so sorry I made you think that." Cory is quiet for a minute, then adds, "Did you tell him you love him?"

"No," I whisper. "It was too late."

"What?"

"It's too late," I repeat in a daze. Even though I've been in bed since yesterday, I'm suddenly so tired that I feel like I could sleep forever. I settle my head back against the pillow as my limbs grow heavy.

"Did you look at the website he made you?" Cory asks, but the fog of sleep is creeping over me and I don't answer. "It's not too late," I hear him say as I drift off. "Just look at the website."

37

Cory's gone when I wake a little while later. I roll over to my nightstand and see he's left a note for me:

Sorry—I had to go into the bar. Call me when you're up.

Then underneath, in huge block letters, he's put:

LOOK AT THE WEBSITE.

My gut roils as I stare at his messy handwriting. I don't want to look at the website, but if Cory is insistent, I know there's a reason. It's just... I'm too nervous. No, *nervous* isn't the right word.

I'm fucking terrified.

Then the words from that meditation teacher—Daniel—come back to me, clear as day: *When you feel fear, you need to breathe deep and know that the intensity of it will pass.*

I wriggle up in the bed. Feeling my pulse tick up a notch, I reach for my phone. On the locked screen, there are several notifications from Geoff, Alex, Cory and Hayley— and then I come to the text from Myles. There's a preview of his message, and all I can see is:

Myles: Hey. Sorry this has taken so long, but—

My heart takes off at a sprint and my vision blurs, the pain in my chest expanding and pressing against my ribcage. I don't think I can do this. I don't think—

Just breathe.

I close my eyes and draw in a faltering breath.

Just breathe.

I draw in another breath. Then another. Slowly, I raise my phone, unlocking it with shaking hands to read his message:

Myles: Hey. Sorry this has taken so long, but I had a whole bunch of issues with the web hosting. Anyway, the site is up and running, and I've emailed you stuff for the social media accounts going forward. I hope it's what you were wanting, any issues just let me know.

Pulling in another deep breath, I click the link he's sent. But when the site opens in my browser, I forget to breathe altogether.

Oh my God.

I sit up in bed, taking in the site, slack-jawed. It's *amazing.* The colors, the photos—the pictures of me with Stevie, laughing and smiling and glowing—I'm *glowing,* because I was so in love with him and didn't even realize it —and the dresses, all of my dresses, listed with prices, and a form to fill in for custom orders, and a page all about me and my style, and links to social media, which I click— there's an Instagram account with—holy shit, *seven thousand followers?* How did he do that?—and a Facebook page and all these gorgeous pictures of me and my dresses and the fabric I love and color, everywhere, color—and everything, *everything* feels so me, so vibrant and alive and me, and it feels like him, too, all of it.

It feels like him and me, all of it.

And he did so much more than the site, because I

open my email to find instructions for managing the social media accounts and huge files with images and captions to keep me going for months—and woah, I already have nine custom order requests and it only went live yesterday.

I clutch my phone tightly, awestruck by what he's created for me and just how perfect it is. The feeling in my heart intensifies as I realize I love him even more now.

And then, for the first time, I see it—the name he's given the site. We never did decide on a name, but it turns out he's come up with one, all on his own, and the words hit me hard in the chest.

Sew in Love.

I blink, reading them over and over. *Sew in love.* So in love. Is it possible, is there any way... Could this be a sign?

Adrenaline spikes inside me and I leap out of bed and pace the room, my mind in overdrive. What if this *is* a sign? I want so badly to believe that it is, because if there's any chance that he still loves me—that I could still be with him —then I'll do whatever it takes to get him back. I know I pushed him away, that he feels like he can't trust me anymore, but—

Oh, God. How did I miss this? All this time I was afraid that I couldn't trust *him*, but *I'm* the one who couldn't be trusted. *I'm* the one who caused the most hurt.

I push my hands into my hair, desperate. If I want to get him back, I need to do something big enough to show him that I'll *never* push him away again.

My fingers type out a text to Cory before I can even register what's happening.

Cat: Thanks for the pep talk. I'm feeling much better. Can I borrow $5000? I'll explain later.

I watch the screen as the little dots appear, then disappear, then appear again. Finally, Cory's message comes through.

Cory: I'm glad. Sure thing. Do you need cash?

Fuck, I love him. Only my brother would have my back like this, no questions asked. And I'll pay him back, of course, when my business starts making some money. Which it will. I know it will. Myles showed me that.

I yank on my jeans and tank, then I'm out the front door and down on the street, holding my phone to my ear as I search for a cab. The call connects and I grin.

"Hi, Claudia. It's Cat. I need your help."

IT's amazing how quickly things can happen when you put your mind to it. Claudia knows a lot of people in real estate, and two hours later I'm in an apartment in the East Village, pacing restlessly.

I asked for two bedrooms and she delivered: a fifth floor walk-up that's dog-friendly, only a few blocks away from the bar. It's got gorgeous hardwood floors, eggshell-white walls, and big, bright windows in the living room. I don't know if this is the kind of place Myles had in mind when we talked about this, but I love it. There's room for all my sewing stuff, for him to have a desk for his web design, and maybe even a spare bed, in case... well, I'm getting ahead of myself, but in case he does reconnect with Amber, she could stay with us sometimes. My heart expands at the thought.

"What do you think?" Claudia leans against the stone countertop. "I love the light in here."

I nod, imagining Myles's framed photographs hanging on the walls, a piano opposite the windows, a little bed for Stevie in the corner. "Yeah," I murmur. "I love it."

Claudia hands me a clipboard with the application form. "I'll need to run a credit check and make sure the deposit clears, but if we can get that done in the next few hours, it's yours." She smiles warmly. "I think you and Myles will be really happy here."

My stomach dips as I take the form from her. I can do this—I can sign this lease and hope and pray that Myles will forgive me, will believe I'm all in. And if he doesn't, well, I can always rent the second bedroom, or—

No. I reach for the pen, determined. This isn't about backup plans and what-ifs. It's about trusting in what my heart is telling me—that Myles and I are meant to be together, that he loves me enough to see past the mistakes I made, as I can for him. It's trusting in *us*.

I fill in the form and hand it back to Claudia with an anxious smile. Then I reach into my purse and produce an envelope of cash for the deposit. "How soon until I can get the keys?"

"I'll process this right away, then have a messenger drop the keys over early this evening. Does that work?"

"Yes." I glance around the apartment again and excitement ripples through me. "Thank you, Claudia. Thank you so much."

"I'm happy to help. It was lovely to see you the other week. We left it way too long."

"We did." I remember how I left the dinner party, ready to tear Mel a new one, and cringe. "I'm sorry if I wasn't as... civil as I could have been, it's just Mel—"

"Yes, wasn't she unpleasant? I won't be inviting her again anytime soon." Claudia wrinkles her nose. "Oh and I meant to say, my friend at the boutique is very interested in stocking some of your designs. I'd love to set up a meeting for the two of you."

My insides tense unexpectedly. I get a flashback to earlier this year, when Mel offered me the same thing, then left me in the lurch. I open my mouth to tell Claudia *no thanks*, but instead I find myself taking a calming breath, letting it fill my lungs.

Claudia isn't Mel. And Geoff's right—I need to let people in. I need to trust again. I've been so hurt in the past, but I can choose to let that go. From now on, I'm going to be open and loving and trusting, no matter how much it might scare me.

I smile. "That would be fantastic."

As I leave the apartment, I feel a weight lift off my shoulders. My whole body is buzzing with the promise of a new beginning, with hope—with love.

And that makes me think of something else I need to do.

I head back across town to the West Village, but instead of turning down our street, I walk the few extra blocks to Between the Lines, the bookstore where Geoff and Alex work. I push into the small shop, relieved to see it's quiet. As the door closes behind me, Geoff glances up from where he's arranging a sales table. His green eyes soften and he sets down the books he's holding.

I stride over and pull him into a hug, squeezing hard. "I'm so sorry, Geoff. I know I've been a shitty friend lately. I'm going to do better, I promise."

"Oh, honey," he says quietly. Tears prick my eyes as his arms tighten around me.

Alex's voice drifts out from an aisle. "Geoff? The photocopier is still doing that thing. Did you call—" She cuts herself off when she sees us hugging. "Cat? What's wrong?"

I reach for her, hugging her tight too. "I'm sorry," I say again.

"For what?"

"You were right. I've been pushing everyone away. Not just Myles—you guys too. But you're always there for me, always looking out for me. I don't know what I'd do without you."

Alex gives me a squeeze before releasing me. "It's okay. I know you've been going through some stuff. But we really care about you." She glances at Geoff, then back to me, before adding, "And I think Myles does, too."

"I know," I murmur, sniffling. "Or at least, I'm really hoping he does, because..." I give a nervous little laugh. "I just put down a huge deposit on an apartment for us."

Geoff's jaw falls open. "You—what?"

"Really?" Alex is beaming.

"Yeah. He said he wanted to get an apartment in the East Village with me, so I figured..." I shrug, as if this is no big deal and I don't feel like an exposed nerve.

"Gah! This is so exciting." Alex is dancing on the spot now and I can't help but laugh. "He's going to be over the moon."

"Yeah, this is huge." Geoff grins. "What made you change your mind?"

"He did the website, and it's..."

Before I can even finish the sentence Alex is behind the counter at the computer, clicking away. "Address?"

"S-E-W in love dot com."

She types the words in, mouthing the name to herself. Then her hands still over the keyboard and her gaze snaps to mine. "Who came up with the name?"

"Myles."

There's a squeal beside me and I turn to Geoff just as he throws his arm around me. "Oh my God, Cat! He's *so* in love!"

"This is amazing," Alex breathes, eyes glued to the computer screen, and Geoff abandons me to go see.

"Wow." He hovers beside Alex, looking over her shoulder. "This is stunning. It's so *you*. This is the Cat I met. I miss her."

The door to the store opens, and I do a double take when I recognize the figure stepping inside. "Hey, Stefan."

He stops when he sees me, adjusting the bag over his shoulder. "Oh. Hi, Cat." He peers past me toward the back of the store. "I'm just here to—"

"Check the toner levels?"

"Something like that," he grumbles, ducking around me. When I turn back to Alex and Geoff, they're watching me with barely restrained mirth.

And that's when I realize.

"Seriously?" I hiss, stepping closer so Stefan can't hear. "You guys set me up with him, *knowing* I wouldn't like him?"

Geoff lifts a shoulder, feigning innocence, but the grin on Alex's face gives the ruse away.

"We knew you should be with Myles," she says, hands clasped.

"Do you know how long he ranted at me about photo-copiers?"

A laugh splutters out of Geoff, and Alex shoves him.

"Please don't be mad, Cat."

I shake my head, surprised to find I'm smiling. "You know what? I'm not."

"When are you going to tell Myles about the apartment?" Geoff asks.

"Tonight." My middle fills with butterflies at the reminder. "I'm going to surprise him at Bounce. But I wanted to see you guys first and apologize for being a dick. Even if you did set me up on a terrible date."

Geoff snickers again. "Call it even?"

"Fine," I mutter wryly. "Right. I'm going to go home and try not to freak out while I get ready for tonight."

Alex steps out from the counter to hug me again. "You've got this. Now go and win back the love of your life."

BY THE TIME I get back to the apartment, I'm fidgety with anticipation. I listen out for the door all afternoon, obsessively checking my phone. After an eternity, a text comes through from Claudia telling me a messenger is on the way with the keys. Then I pace back and forth through the lobby, only exhaling when I'm clutching the keys in my hand.

I shower and get ready for the evening, dressing in the navy dress I wore to Claudia's dinner party. Tonight, I'm going to wear the dress that I love—and from now on, I'm always going to wear my designs. Geoff was right—I miss the old me, too. I'm done with wearing black, with hiding. Myles has shown me what he's seen in me, who he's seen buried under all those black clothes, under all my fear. He's shown me *me*.

When I finally step out the front door, I feel more determined than ever to tell Myles I love him, to thank him—not just for the site, but for everything. He helped me with my business, yes, but more than that, he led me back to myself. And that is worth more than anything.

38

I 'm glad to see the bar isn't too busy when I arrive. Cory spots me hovering by the door, trying to be normal but jittery with nerves.

He lopes over and pulls me into a hug, then stands back to admire my dress. "You look so pretty, Cat. I almost didn't recognize you."

I poke him in the ribs. "Ha ha," I say, glancing past him. "Is Myles working tonight?"

"He's out back. You want me to grab him?"

"No. I'll wait."

Cory nudges me toward the bar. "Come on, have a drink. You look like you need it."

I slide onto a barstool, eyes darting around the place. There's a flash of something familiar—blond hair, suit—in one of the booths down the back, but I'm too skittish to make sense of it. I turn back to the bar to see Josie grinning at me.

"I *love* your dress."

I manage a smile. "Thanks."

"Hot date?"

There's a pinch in my belly as I glance toward the back, checking for Myles. "Maybe… If I'm lucky."

She follows my gaze and her expression turns compassionate. "I think you will be. He's a mess." She gives me a reassuring smile as she slides a vodka soda across the bar, then slinks away.

I guzzle half of it, letting the alcohol take the edge off. I'm almost feeling better, but when Myles comes out with a dishcloth over one shoulder, stacking some glasses absently, my pulse skyrockets again.

He wipes at the bar, lost in thought. He's so gone, it takes him a good few minutes to realize I'm sitting right there. When his gaze finally meets mine, he blinks, swallows, and attempts a smile. "Oh… hey."

"Hi." I chew my straw anxiously. "I, um, looked at the website."

He nods. His eyes stray to my dress, and I watch him physically struggle to get them back to my face. "Is it… okay?"

"No." I try for a playful smile, but my mouth is too twitchy to cooperate. "It's fucking awesome. It's—" Damn, this is harder than I thought. Words aren't enough. "I love it. Thank you."

His shoulders relax and a smile ghosts across his lips. God how I miss his cocky, self-assured grins.

"Myles… the name. Of the site, I mean. Is it—"

"Oh, yeah." He cringes. "Sorry, that was just a placeholder. We can call it whatever you want."

A placeholder.

The word rings in my ears and I look down at my lap, trying to make sense of this. When I glance back up, Myles is serving a couple of guys beside me, laughing with them like I'm not here trying to pour my heart out, and my chest constricts with despair. What am I doing here?

I push away from the bar and stumble to the bathroom. I just need a few minutes alone to collect myself, to figure out exactly what my next move is, to decide if this whole thing has been a mistake.

But as I go to open the bathroom door, a hand closes around my wrist. I spin around, wanting so badly to see Myles's face—but it's not him. It takes me a second to register the blond hair, the nice suit...

"*Shane*?"

"Hey, you." He pulls me away from the bathroom, into the shadowy corridor.

"What are you... How did you..."

"Did you get the roses? I never heard from you."

"I... Yes." I glance past him toward the bar, feeling my stomach knot. If Myles sees me with him down here—God, after Stefan, I don't want him to think—

"You know, I spent a *lot* of money taking you out to dinner."

I turn my attention back to Shane, recoiling at the potent smell of whiskey on his breath. The knot in my stomach tightens and twists, and I realize that Myles isn't the one I need to worry about right now.

"Well, yes, I know," I say, attempting a placating tone. Sweat prickles along my brow as I fumble for my purse. "And I had a lovely time, really, but—"

"Did you?" His hand catches mine, pulling it to his mouth, and panic rushes up my spine. "Maybe you should *show* me how much you enjoyed it."

I try to look for someone to help me, but he steps closer, crowding my vision. "Shane—"

"I think you owe me a little something, Cat," he slurs, his eyes glinting with intent.

My heart slams against my ribcage and I push him away. "Shane, stop." I try to slip past him, but he pins me back against the wall.

Oh *no*. There is no way in hell this is happening again.

Adrenaline surges through my bloodstream and I bring my knee up, hard, right into his balls.

"Argh!" Shane doubles over.

That's right, motherfucker. This is what you deserve.

I raise my knee to strike him again, but he stumbles back and Myles comes into view.

"Get the fuck away from her!"

Gasping in a breath, I sag against the wall and press my eyes shut, trying to calm my stampeding pulse.

"I wasn't doing anything wrong, man. She knows me—"

There's a loud crash and when I dare to open my eyes, Myles is holding Shane against the opposite wall with one hand at his throat.

"Yes," I yell, finding my voice. "I know you're an asshole!"

Shane opens his mouth to protest, trying to duck away. But Myles pins him back in place, cocking his arm to punch him. Despite being nuclear with rage, Myles somehow regains control.

"Don't go near her again," he growls, "or you won't live to talk about it."

Cory appears in the corridor, glancing between the three of us. He takes me by the shoulders, asking, "What happened?" But I can't answer. I'm shaking with shock.

"He was all over Cat," Myles spits, not taking his eyes off Shane. "Get him out of here before I kill him."

Cory's face turns murderous and he lunges at Shane. His

hand tightens into a fist on his collar, then he drags him out through the bar.

Myles turns, face flushed, eyes wide with worry. "Are you okay?" He reaches a hand toward me, then hesitates, and I burst into tears. "Oh, hey." He pulls me into his arms, against his chest, as tears stream silently down my face. "It's okay," he says, rubbing my back. "It's okay."

He steps back and a sob escapes me at the physical loss of him, but he scoops me up into his arms. I press my face into his shoulder as he carries me down the corridor, kicking the back door open, out into the darkness of the alley. He sinks down onto a pile of pallets with me across his lap, and presses a kiss to my forehead. "It's okay, baby," he murmurs.

My whole body surrenders in his arms and I let myself cry harder. I'm not even crying about Shane. All I can think about is Myles; how good it felt to have him protect me, how I want him to hold me like this forever.

He strokes my hair, not saying anything but offering a world of comfort. Because I'm here, even temporarily, in that safe space again. And it feels like home.

Finally, when I've pulled myself together, I draw away just enough to look at him. His face is lined with concern, and he wipes a thumb under my eyes.

"I'm so sorry that happened. Do you want me to call the cops? Or I could pay him a visit—"

"It's okay. Cory will take care of him."

"I hope so. I want to strangle him."

I give Myles a bleak smile. My mouth opens to speak again, but I stop myself, feeling uncertain. I'm still sitting on his lap, and as much as I want to curl up here permanently, I don't want to get comfortable somewhere I might not be able to stay.

I make to stand, but he tucks his arm around me. "Cat
—" His voice is hoarse with emotion and my heart lifts
hopefully. He digs his teeth into his lower lip as his eyes
roam my face. "Don't go," he finally whispers.

Relief unfurls inside me; tentative at first, but as I settle
back down and he grips me tighter, it floods through me in
great torrents. I let myself gaze at him properly for the first
time this evening, trying to record every detail—the rough
bristles on his jaw, the tiny freckle on his cheek, the faint
laugh lines around his eyes as they gaze back at me. His face
is a map to my happiness, to everything I could ever want.

He inhales to say something, but I get there first.

"I went to another meditation class yesterday."

"Oh." His eyebrows rise. "How'd it go?"

"It sucked."

A frown wrinkles his forehead, but I continue,
undeterred.

"It made me realize how much I've been living in fear.
And it helped me to hear my intuition, finally. Everything
you said was right. I've been scared and looking for reasons
to run away. But I don't want to run anymore." I drag in a
tearful breath. "Myles... I'm so sorry. I've been a coward and
you've had to deal with that. You've been nothing but open
and patient and loving and I've given you nothing. But I
can't imagine my life without you. I can't imagine ever
loving another man. I want to be with you more than
anything, if I'm not too late. I want to try to give you the
things you've given me, if you can find a way to forgive me."

He gazes at me for a long moment, calm and collected as
always, saying nothing. And then, I can't quite believe it, his
eyes well with tears and he pulls me close, burying his face
in my hair. "Fuck, baby. I've missed you so much." He
squeezes me tight, and this time it's me rubbing his back,

feeling his chest rise and fall against me. "I can't imagine my life without you either," he murmurs, and with those simple words, my heart begins to stitch itself back together.

"You really missed me? After you came to my place, I thought—"

"I missed you so much it nearly killed me." He sniffs, wiping under his eyes, and a smile hints at the corner of his mouth. "There was no one to tell me I have a huge ego, no one to call me a skater, no one to shoot me in the butt."

A delighted laugh tickles my throat. "You really want that in your life?"

"Hell yes." He drops a kiss on the tip of my nose and I smile.

"I want to be more like you, Myles. You're so open, so fearless."

"I'm not perfect."

"I know. But there's so much I love about you that I want to be."

He aims his cocky grin at me and I laugh, realizing that I even love that side to him. "You should meditate with me," he suggests, and I laugh again.

"I might be open to doing that."

He studies me, quiet. "I'm not fearless, you know. The reason I never told you about what happened with Amber is because I was afraid. I was afraid I would lose you."

My throat prickles at this admission. "I know," I say softly. "And I'm sorry I walked away from you. But after everything I've been through..."

"You have been through a lot." He caresses a thumb over my cheek, then cautiously adds, "I think maybe you should consider seeing a therapist. Just to help you process what happened with your dad, and Mark, and last year."

I lower my gaze, unsure. The thought of telling a

stranger about the things I've been through doesn't thrill me. But I don't want to carry this baggage around forever. And Geoff suggested the same thing, a while back. I was quick to dismiss it at the time, but I've come to see lately that Geoff and Myles are far wiser than I am. Geoff's words come back to me—*there's nothing wrong with asking for and accepting help*—and I nod.

"Okay," I say at last. "I'll try it."

Myles gives me a relieved smile, sliding his fingers into my hair and tilting my face up. When he finally takes my mouth with his, joy sings across my skin and through my bones, making my whole body vibrate. I feel like I'm going to burst with how much I love him.

"I'm never letting you go now," I murmur.

"Good." He kisses me again, and again. "Damn, I missed this mouth."

And I hum in agreement, sinking into his kiss, feeling happier than I have in forever.

WHEN WE EVENTUALLY HEAD BACK INTO the bar, Cory strides over, his brow pulled low. "Are you okay? That dude won't bother you again. Jimmy and I took care of him."

"Did you break a bone?" Myles asks, and Cory gives a harsh laugh.

"Nah. I just broke his nice watch and destroyed his suit."

I smirk. Somehow, I think Shane will have found that more painful than a fist to the face.

"But seriously, Cat," Cory says, scrutinizing me. "Are you okay?"

"Yeah. I'm glad Myles stepped in, though—"

"Are you kidding?" Myles laughs incredulously beside me. "You smashed him, Cat."

"Yeah, you should have seen him," Cory agrees. "I don't know what you did, but he could hardly stand when we got him outside."

Myles nudges my arm. "You didn't even need me. You know how to take care of yourself."

I lift my head high. It's true, I can take care of myself. In fact, I've always prided myself on that—to a fault. But now, I know I don't want to do everything on my own. Because even though I can be strong alone, with Myles, I can be vulnerable. And that's a whole different kind of strength.

"You're right, I don't need you," I say, gazing up at him. "But I'm glad you were there. I always want you there."

His arm comes around my waist, pulling me into his warmth, and he presses a kiss to the top of my head. "Then I'll always be there."

Cory ponders the two of us for a second, standing as close as humanly possible, and a grin splits his face. He turns back to the bar, satisfied that I'm okay.

Myles releases me with a contented sigh. "Let me get my girl a drink." He steps behind the bar and I pull myself up onto a stool. Then he slides a vodka soda across to me, leaning down on his elbows so we're level. And we just stare at each other, grinning like idiots, the rest of the world slipping away.

That is, until a woman leans across the bar asking for a drink. Myles pours her a glass of Prosecco, and as he hands it over, she touches his arm with a flirtatious smile. My whole body goes rigid on the stool. I have to physically hold myself back from tearing her hair out.

"Thank you," she purrs, stroking a hand over his tattoo.

He gives her a polite nod, then carefully lifts her hand

off him, dropping it back onto the bar. "I wouldn't do that. This one here"—he cocks his head in my direction—"is totally in love with me, and she'll throat-punch you."

The woman glances my way and I click my knuckles, definitely in the mood to throat-punch someone. She looks at me like I'm a maniac before scurrying away, and I turn to Myles with a giggle.

"You scared her off before she tipped you."

He shrugs, grinning. "Too bad."

"You know... I never actually told you I'm in love with you."

He contemplates me for a beat, and I watch as his smile evaporates and his whole posture shifts. "Oh, yeah," he says, issuing an embarrassed laugh. "You're right. Sorry." He picks up a dishcloth and wipes the bar, and when I see his cheeks color, I know I can't wait any longer.

I stand and walk around the bar, grabbing the dishcloth and tossing it aside, taking both his hands in mine. "I am, though. I'm crazy in love with you, Myles."

His grin appears again, tugging his mouth wide. "Really?"

I nod, grinning back. "Like, you have no idea how much. When I saw what you named the site, I thought you were giving me a sign, that you were telling me you still loved me."

"I was. I mean, I think it's a cool name anyway. But yeah. Of course it means that."

"But... you said it was a placeholder."

"Yeah, we can change it if you like, if you have a better idea. Because—"

"No." I stand up on my toes and press my mouth to his. "I love it. I love *you*."

"Fuck," he murmurs. He picks me up by the waist and

sets me down on the counter behind the bar. I wrap my legs around him and kiss him hard, sliding a hand under the soft cotton of his T-shirt to drag my nails over his warm skin.

"I wish I could take you right here," he says roughly, and I giggle in response. Because that would be so damn hot, fucking him right here where I met him. You know, if my brother and all these people weren't around.

"Jesus, you two," Cory mutters beside us. "This is a little inappropriate for the workplace."

"Yeah, it is." Myles draws away from me. His eyes track over my face in thought. "You know, you told me you don't date bartenders."

"Well, yeah. But that was just some stupid rule..."

"I'm sorry," Myles says, twisting to face Cory, "but I have to quit."

Cory's eyebrows spring up. "For real?"

"Yeah. It's time for me to do something else."

"Hey," I say, squeezing Myles's shoulder. "What are you doing?"

He glances back at me, smiling calmly. "It's alright, I have a little money set aside."

"Okay, but don't quit because of me."

"I'm not. Honestly? I don't like who I am here—who people think I am. I've been telling you to be your true self and then I come to work and put on a show just to make a few tips..." He shakes his head. "I don't like myself here. Besides"—he nuzzles back against my neck—"I hate going to work at night when I'd rather be in bed with you."

Cory screws up his face, backing away with a laugh. "Alright, I've heard enough. Get out of here."

Myles laughs too, his eyes lighting up as he gazes at me. "You want to get out of here?"

I nod eagerly.

"Your place or mine?"

"Mine?" I go to grab my purse, and that's when I remember. Somehow, in the chaos of everything that happened this evening, I forgot what I did this afternoon. I glance back at Myles, feeling myself waver. It seemed like such a good idea at the time, a grand romantic gesture to win him back, but now—

"It's a long way to your place. But I guess my place isn't that close, either." He sighs. "I wish we'd got that apartment we talked about so I could take you there right now."

My lips open in disbelief. It's like he can read my mind. "Are you serious?"

"Yeah. I'd love to be able to take you back to our own place, to wake up beside you..." He shrugs. "I know it's pretty full-on, given we've only just made up, but—"

"No." A nervous sort of happiness ripples through me as I grab my purse. "Come with me."

39

I open the door to the new apartment with my heart in my mouth. It takes me a moment, fumbling along the inside wall, to find the light switch. The empty space floods with light as we both step inside.

My gaze sweeps over the room and I'm pleased to find I love it as much as I did when I was here this afternoon, a nervous wreck. I'm not much better now, though; apprehension swirls in my stomach as I watch Myles, waiting for his reaction. He slips his hands into his pockets and walks away from me, casting his eyes about the place. When I see a tiny line form on his brow, I'm gripped by the urge to explain, to tell him why I did such a monumental thing without him here, and that we don't have to do it if he doesn't want to, because—shit—it really looks like he doesn't want to, the way he's wandering from the bathroom to the bedroom to the kitchen, taking everything in but saying nothing.

I'm rooted to the spot, my pulse drumming in a mad rhythm as he finally turns back to me. I feel that same sense of vulnerability, like everything I'm thinking and feeling and wanting is so close to the surface and he can see it all.

Just breathe.

I suck in a ragged breath, trying to remind myself that it's okay. It's okay to be seen like this, to let someone know how much you love them and want them. My heart softens as I realize that it really *is* okay, whatever he wants to do. I thought this apartment was a gesture for him—and it is—but it's also a gesture for myself. It's the first time in forever that I've put myself out there, that I've had the courage to openly ask for what I want.

And that's him. It's taken me long enough to recognize it, but now I know... it's always been him.

"Cat—" He shakes his head, taking a step closer. "What is this place?"

I swallow. "Um, I got it... for us."

"When did you do this?"

I scratch my arm, trying not to crawl out of my skin at how exposed I feel. This is definitely going to take some practice. "Today."

"So... before you knew that we would get back together?"

I nod.

"But what if things hadn't worked out?"

"Well, I'm trying to practice trusting things a bit more."

"Things like... me?"

"Yeah. And *us*. And, hopefully, our future together."

He stares at me, dumbstruck, and I'm so close to crying it's ridiculous. Then he steps forward and gathers me into his arms, tucking me right into that safe spot. And I've never felt more like I'm home.

"This is everything, baby," he says into my hair. "This is —" His voice cracks and I squeeze him tighter. "I can't wait to live here with you."

Euphoria rises inside me, bursting like fireworks in my chest; so bright it's almost blinding. *This* is why you do it—

why you keep taking the risk and putting yourself out there. Because when something works out, it's worth every past hurt you've endured.

His eyes are shining when we draw apart, but that's nothing compared to the tears streaming down my face. He wipes them away with a smile.

"Happy tears?"

I nod, sniffling. It's like I've opened some kind of floodgate now and the tears just won't stop coming. But weirdly, I'm okay with that.

He turns to gaze at our new space. "I might sell my place."

"Wait—you *own* that apartment?"

"Uh-huh." His mouth twists with amusement. "Remember when you thought I was broke?"

"Shut up." I thump him on the chest.

He chuckles. "I bought it with the money I made from selling my app."

"Yes!" I say, remembering. "What was that?"

"Just this silly cocktail app I designed. I got a pretty penny for it, which is how I bought my little place, but now... I want to be here with you." He takes my hand, lacing his fingers through mine. "Show me around. Show me what you imagine."

"Okay." I lead him to the living room and show him where I thought we could put a piano, where I want his pictures to hang, where we could put the stereo so we can dance to eighties music together. The whole time I'm talking, he's beaming at me, just pure joy, and my heart feels like it will overflow.

"And what about this room?" He gestures to the bigger bedroom. I explain that that will be our room, then I show him the smaller room, where I thought I could do my sewing. I show him where he could have a desk, too, for his business.

"And..." I take a deep breath, treading carefully. "I'm not pressuring you, or anything. But if things ever change with Amber... there would be room for a bed, too."

He shakes his head, and for a second I think I've over-stepped. But he lifts my hand to his mouth, kissing it softly. "Thank you. Because I've been thinking, and you were right. I have a right to see her and I'm going to fight for that. I'm going to take Nikki to court."

I feel a flash of surprise. "I thought you were worried about how that would affect Amber?"

"Yeah, I am. But not as much as I'm worried about her growing up thinking her dad doesn't love her."

I nod, feeling my eyes well with more damn tears. I quickly blink them away. "Well, I'll be there with you, every step of the way."

"I know. And that's—" He kisses a stray tear away from my cheek. "I wouldn't have the strength to do this without you, Cat. You haven't given me nothing. I don't want you to think that."

More tears. God, I'm a mess—in the best kind of way.

I lead him out to show him the kitchen. It isn't huge, but there's a lovely stone countertop, and I show him the little space where I want to set up a bar to make cocktails.

"I love it. I love all of it." He lowers his hands to my waist, walking me backwards until I'm pressed up against the kitchen island. "I love *you*." His mouth brushes over mine in a soft, spine-tingling kiss. "And what about this?" He smooths a hand over the stone countertop behind me. "What did you see us using this for?"

"Um—" I glance behind me with a baffled laugh.

"Because I have an idea."

I gasp as he picks me up and sets me down on the counter. His eyes focus on mine, and when I see the blue slowly give way to black, desire shivers through me.

"Oh, do you?"

He nods, a sexy grin kicking up one side of his mouth. "I wanted to fuck you on the bar tonight," he murmurs, sliding a hand slowly up my thigh.

I give a huff of arousal, parting my legs for him.

"I wanted to do that the night I met you."

I meet his fiery gaze, knowing he means it. And when I hear myself reply, "Me too," I'm surprised to discover that I mean it as well.

He groans, leaning in to graze my neck with his lips. I feel the scrape of his scruffy jaw against my collarbone and my skin scatters with goosebumps.

"Now, though," he continues, his breath hot against my throat, "I want to fuck you right here, in our new apartment." His fingertips dance in teasing circles just under the hem of my dress. "Would you like that?"

The word "yes" rushes out of me on an exhale. His hand slips between my thighs, and I whimper when it touches my panties. I wore something extra special for him tonight, hoping we'd get to this point. I pull my dress up to my hips, showing him the black lace. Then I reach behind my neck and undo the halter straps, letting them fall, showing him more. I know Myles prefers me in color over black, but he's never seen me wear it like this.

"Jesus, Cat," he says coarsely, dragging his teeth over my shoulder, stroking a thumb over my nipple through the lace.

I can see the hard outline of him through his jeans and I pounce on it, tugging his zipper down and taking him into my greedy hands. His breath is a harsh rasp in my ear and he hooks a finger inside my panties, sliding it into the wet heat.

Holy hell. I know it's only been a week, but it feels like he hasn't touched me in forever. I'm dying for him.

When he draws back, he looks dazed with lust. "I need you. Now."

I nod breathlessly, sliding my ass to the front of the countertop and wrapping my legs around him. He shoves my panties aside and pushes into me, wearing an expression that can only be described as sheer relief. His hips roll forward and I clutch at his shoulders, unraveling for him again. He watches me through heavy-lidded eyes, capturing every quiver, every moan as he slams deeper. I can't take my eyes off him, either—the muscles straining in his neck, the flush in his cheeks, the little grunts he's making. We stare at one another wordlessly, sharing in each other's pleasure, and a moment later we're both swept away in our release.

After, as I'm pulling my dress back into place, Myles chuckles. "I'm going to think of that every time I'm in here, cooking you dinner."

I lift my eyebrows. "You're going to cook *me* dinner?"

"Yep," he says, tucking my hair behind my ear. "I'm a great cook. Just you wait."

I open my mouth to tell him I think he's full of it, but I stop myself. Every time I've doubted him, he's proven me wrong. Based on my track record, he's probably an amazing cook.

"I can't believe I get to live here with you," he murmurs. "I can work on my web design stuff and you can sew and it will be..." he trails off with a shrug, like he isn't describing the most perfect thing I've ever heard.

"Perfect," I breathe, leaning forward to kiss him.

"Perfect," he echoes, his expression tender as he slips his arms around me.

And as we hold each other close, imagining what our life together will be like without all the other bullshit in the way, I know now that I *do* have that knowing. I might not know what's happening tomorrow, or if I'll ever be afraid or hurt again. But I know for certain that I love this man with every fiber of my being, that I don't want to live in fear anymore, that I don't want to live my life without him.

And that is more than enough.

EPILOGUE

Head to www.jenmorrisauthor.com/ykil-epilogue to get access to an exclusive *You Know it's Love* epilogue!

Did you enjoy *You Know it's Love*? Reviews help indie authors get our books noticed!

If you liked this book, please leave a review on Amazon. Or you can leave a review on Goodreads. It doesn't have to be much—even a few sentences helps! Thank you.

ACKNOWLEDGMENTS

It was just over four months ago that I released my first book, *Love in the City*. I've been blown away by how well that was received, and by how supportive the bookstagram community is. So firstly, I want to thank everyone who bought, read, or reviewed *Love in the City*. That gave me the encouragement to believe that, just maybe, I might not be as terrible at this whole thing as I sometimes worry I am.

My partner Carl is the main reason I can do what I do. It turns out that two-time-published indie authors don't make a great deal of money (shocking, I know). Without Carl going to work every day, I wouldn't be able to spend my time writing and slowly building a new career. But it's not just that—it's the fact that he genuinely believes in me, that he knows how to calm me down when I'm stressed or over-whelmed by self-doubt or emotional for no apparent reason, and that he's made his peace with me also being in love with an endless line of fictional men in my head. Thanks for being such a wonderful inspiration for all the book boyfriends I create, Carl.

And to our little boy, Baxter—thank you for letting me

spend so many hours glued to my computer. I hope that one day I can inspire you to go out and chase dreams of your own.

Since publishing *Love in the City* I've made many new friends online, but two in particular have become my unofficial support team and cheering squad. Kira Slaughter and Tammy Eyre, thank you for everything you do. Your unwavering belief in my ability as a writer helps me continue even when I'm feeling lost. Your help with my book launches is invaluable. And the many hours we spend discussing books and sharing pictures of hotties are, quite frankly, essential for my well-being.

Sarah Side is always the first to read my drafts, and the first to tell me my work doesn't suck. Not only is she encouraging, she has a keen eye for things I tend to miss, and she spends hours helping me come up with names for things, fix plot holes, and tweak my writing. Thank you, Sarah, for always making time to read my work, even when you've already read it a hundred times.

This book is actually the fourth novel I've written, because I was so disorganized and wrote my series out of order. But it still needed a lot of work—particularly around Cat's character, who (believe it or not) I initially wrote as much more resistant to Myles. I'm eternally grateful to Jennifer Evelyn Hayes who helped me see that I needed to soften Cat. I also received a great deal of help from my other critique partners: Lauren H. Mae, Mia Heintzelman, Alicia Crofton, and Julie Olivia. Thank you so much for your advice to improve the manuscript.

My wonderful team of beta readers are essential to this process. They read my work with enthusiasm and offer their feedback with honesty and kindness. Thank you Emma Grocott, Caroline Palmer, Michele Voss, Caroline Chalmers,

Laura Harris, Kristen Fairgrieve, Ayla Russell, and Kelly Pensinger. Particular shout-out to Emma Grocott, whose love and support for my work goes above and beyond.

I have to say a huge thank you to my cover designer Elle Maxwell, who always manages to bring my vision to life. She has an amazing eye for detail and works so hard to get my covers exactly how I want them. Working with her is a dream.

Thank you so much to all my advanced readers. There are far too many people to name, but each and every person who has read and reviewed *You Know it's Love* has helped it get off the ground, and for that I'm grateful.

And finally, thank you to you, dear reader, for spending time with Cat and Myles. I know it wasn't an easy journey for these two, but it means the world to me that you went along for the ride.

ABOUT THE AUTHOR

Jen Morris writes sexy romantic comedies with heat, humor and heart. She believes that almost anything can be fixed with a good laugh, a good book, or a plane ticket to New York.

Her books follow women with big dreams as they navigate life and love in the city. Her characters don't just find love—they find themselves, too.

Jen lives with her partner and son, in a tiny house on wheels in New Zealand. She spends her days writing, dreaming about New York, and finding space for her ever-growing book collection.

You Know it's Love is her second novel, and the second book in the *Love in the City* series.

ALSO BY JEN MORRIS

Don't miss the next book in the series, *Outrageously in Love*. See Harriet visit New York and meet a sexy nerd, watch Alex and Michael get married, and catch up with the rest of the gang.

Have you read book one, *Love in the City*? Follow Kiwi girl Alex as she ventures to New York in search of her dreams, and finds a sexy bearded man along the way.

Follow me on Instagram and Facebook: @jenmorrisauthor

See all the book inspiration on Pinterest: www.pinterest.com/jenmorrisauthor/

Or subscribe to my newsletter for updates, release info, and cover reveals:

www.jenmorrisauthor.com

CPSIA information can be obtained
at www.ICGtesting.com
Printed in the USA
BVHW030500131021
618812BV00027B/158